THE BOYFRIEND CANDIDATE

THE BOYFRIEND CANDIDATE

Ashley Winstead

HEAD *of* ZEUS

An Aria Book

First published in Canada in 2023 by Graydon House

This edition first published in the UK in 2023 by Head of Zeus,
part of Bloomsbury Publishing Plc.

9 7 5 3 1 2 4 6 8

A catalogue record for this book is available from
the British Library.

ISBN (PB): 9781035904174
ISBN (E): 9781035904150

Typeset by Siliconchips Services Ltd UK

Printed and bound in Great Britain by
CPI Group (UK) Ltd, Croydon CR0 4YY

Head of Zeus
First Floor East
5–8 Hardwick Street
London EC1R 4RG

WWW.HEADOFZEUS.COM

For my dad, who proudly read each book.
I will love and miss you forever.

I

Alexis Stone Is Not a Mouse

I'll say one nice thing about my ex Chris Tuttle: the man was the entire reason I was here, standing at the entrance to the sultry Fleur de Lis hotel bar, wearing a red dress so plunging I kept it in the back of my closet for fear of scandalizing visitors, on the verge of reinventing myself. The memory of Chris and the still-fresh psychic wounds he'd left me were like a marching drum line urging me forward as I'd left my apartment, Ubered downtown to the Fleur de Lis, and cut a determined path across the lobby to the bar, a place with a reputation as Austin's Grand Central Station of hookups. Unfortunately, now that I was standing at the entrance, the sight of all the laughing, drinking, dazzling people—dressed to the nines like me, but looking much more at ease about it—had me momentarily cowed.

I thought back to what Chris said the day I discovered he was cheating on me (for the second time): "I *do* have needs you can't satisfy. You should really learn to be more adventurous in bed, Lex. You're like a timid little mouse. It can get really boring." Remembering those words, I straightened my shoulders, took a deep breath, and stepped inside. I was *not* a boring mouse—or at least I wouldn't be one anymore. Starting tonight, I was going to be a new version of Alexis Stone: as bold and adventurous as my flaming-red dress.

I tried to soak in the beauty of the bar while beelining through the crowded tables, anxious to leave the peculiar spotlight of being the only person standing among a bunch of cozy, seated people. But then I realized new Alexis wouldn't care if everyone's eyes flitted to her as she walked across a room—in fact, new Alexis would welcome it, because she'd spent nearly an hour straightening and then recurling her hair into movie star ringlets, and maybe that effort should be appreciated. I forced myself to slow and look up at the bar's gorgeous glass ceiling, shaded a twinkly blue thanks to the night sky. Real palm trees lined the circular perimeter, fronds reaching toward the stars. They made the bar look like a very urbane urban jungle, which actually wasn't too far off the mark.

My older sister, Lee, and her friends liked to roll their eyes at the entire downtown bar scene, calling places like the Fleur de Lis "meat markets where you go to spend thirty-five bucks on a martini while beating back horny yuppies" (Lee's words). They preferred the hipster bars on the east side of Austin, where the clientele was cooler yet dirtier (my words). *I* thought the Fleur de Lis was romantic, so it made sense to come here tonight for my critical but one hundred percent private mission: I, Alexis Rosalie Stone, was going to have my first one-night stand. I was going to sleep with a man with no strings attached, no stakes or expectations: just one night to do whatever felt right. Alexis the unadventurous bore? I'd killed her and buried the body.

The gleaming brass bar was crowded, but I managed to slip a

shoulder between two men and catch the bartender's attention. "Vodka martini," I said, feeling a sudden rebellious compulsion to do anything that would raise my sister's eyebrows. By the time my drink came, I'd completed a full three-sixty swivel in my barstool to survey the sea of men for potential candidates. How exactly did one negotiate a one-night stand? Did you lead with it in conversation so all your cards were on the table ("Hi, I'm Alexis; you might be interested to know I'm trolling for a stranger to ravish me"), or did you hold back, let your intention slip out at just the right moment ("I see you're ordering an Uber home; could I interest you in going splitsies back to my place for a wild night of sex")?

I braced a hand on the bar, taking a fortifying sip of my martini. Even if I made a complete fool of myself tonight—even if I was roundly rejected by every man I spoke to—coming here alone at least meant Lee and her crew couldn't witness my flop, then use it to skewer me for all eternity like the jackals they were.

A whistle cut through the bar's ambient noise, followed by a loud, "Now *that's* a dress." Out of nowhere, a man appeared and sidled up beside me. One look at him and my mind blurted *forehead!* Probably because his was shiny as a disco ball, framed by waggling eyebrows, and tilted all the way to the side. The next second, I realized his head was turned that way so he could get a clear view down my dress.

"Thanks." I placed a protective hand over my chest and swiveled in the opposite direction. Hoping my body language would signal my disinterest, I took another sip of my martini and studied the empty corner of the room like it was fascinating.

No such luck. "I'm Carter Randall," the man said, jutting out his hand. "What's your name?"

My deep desire for him to go away warred with my silly lifelong compulsion to be nice. "Um..." I twisted back to shake his oddly moist hand and searched for inspiration. My gaze snagged, as his clearly had, on my dress. "*Ruby...*" The next word came unbidden. "Dangerfield. Ruby Dangerfield." Curse my polite hardwiring that had me sitting here inventing a new name instead of dismissing him with something cool and clipped like, "Not interested."

Carter gave my hand a little squeeze. He was twice my age, probably well into his fifties. Well-dressed, with a massive gold watch on his wrist, and—now that I squinted—a strangely sweaty face, like he'd just done a lap. Was he on party drugs? He used his sleeve to mop his forehead and I pulled my hand away, resisting the urge to wipe it on my dress. Carter's eyes drifted down the length of my body yet again. "Well, Ms. Ruby. Can I buy you a drink? A stiff one?" He grinned.

"Oh," I said. "That's very nice. But—um—no thank you." Inside, I burned with the fire of a thousand suns. Saying no to anyone, even a stranger, stretched the limits of my bravery.

"Aw, come on." Carter leaned in closer and I scooted back so fast I nearly tipped over. "Look at you, sitting there in that dress. Clearly fishing for attention. Well, you caught me. Let's get you drunk and see what happens."

Apparently, I was going to get a lesson in how *not* to proposition someone tonight. But my cheeks were burning, because in a small way Carter was right—I *had* come here to put myself on display and find someone, just very much not him. *Be the new Alexis*, I urged myself. *Stop prioritizing this stranger's feelings and tell him to leave you alone.* But I couldn't—at the slightest provocation, old, sad, doormat Alexis had quickly jumped back in charge.

"I'm not trying to be rude," I said carefully, feeling my heartbeat spike. "I would just like to be by myself tonight." Well, shoot. Now that I'd committed to that, would I have to leave the bar so Carter didn't catch me talking to anyone else later? My palms started sweating.

"One drink—" he started.

"Oh, for *fuck's sake*," came a voice, tinged with an accent I couldn't place—British mixed with Texas panhandle? I nearly knocked over my martini. "She said *no*, mate. Get it through your thick skull and leave the poor woman alone."

Carter spun to get a look at the man who'd interrupted us, and without his body blocking the view, I got a clear line, too. My stomach flipped over and released a conservatory's worth of butterflies. Even wearing a look of contempt, the man on the other side of Carter was stop-in-your-tracks, tongue-tyingly handsome. He was around my age, maybe a little older—he certainly radiated an older person's authority—with a head of dark curls cut close and tight, brown eyes that were currently blazing, and thick eyebrows arched, waiting to see how Carter would respond. He had on a dark suit like most of the other men in the room, but he'd taken off his jacket and hung it on the back of his seat. He was sitting hunched over his drink in a white dress shirt with the sleeves messily rolled back, wearing a dark slim watch that was the antithesis of Carter's flashy gold one. The wrinkles in his suit, creases under his eyes, and day-old stubble gave the impression of a weary business executive after a long, hard day at work. His eyes flitted to mine for the briefest moment before returning to Carter, but the charge that ran down my spine was enough to root me to my chair.

Carter shifted his weight. Apparently, he was going to play the tough guy. "Why don't you mind your business, pal?"

The beautiful, tired man rolled his eyes. "Oh, good. You're one of those." He got to his feet so fast his barstool made a screeching sound as it scraped across the floor. "Then let's go ahead and get this over with, because I've had a shit day and I would like to kick your ass and get back home at a reasonable hour. So come on. You're the one campaigning for Most Punchable Man in the Bar. Let's have your prize." The dark-haired man spoke calmly and quickly in his hard-to-place accent, like he invited people to get their asses kicked at least once a day. He made a little "come on" gesture that conveyed utter boredom.

People around us had stopped talking to watch. The extra attention only made me feel like I was going to melt into the floor at twice the speed. But if I had no idea how to respond to this turn of events—what to say or even where to put my hands—Carter was even more clueless. I could see his eyes dancing, doing quick calculations. On the one hand, Carter was thicker around the middle than the dark-haired man. On the other, the dark-haired man had revealed himself to be tall and well-built when he stood up.

"Nah, man." Carter put his hands up. "We've got no problems. Just making new friends like you're supposed to at a bar, for Christ's sake."

"Great," said the dark-haired man. "Then kindly fuck off as suggested."

Carter didn't wait to be told a third time. As he hightailed away from the bar, a woman nearby muttered, "What a douche." And with that judgment rendered, the room dialed back to a normal volume.

"Thank you," I said to the dark-haired man. He waved me off with a grunt and settled back in his barstool, leaning comfortably over his drink, apparently hoping to resume his night like nothing had happened.

I stared at him. The adrenaline was draining out of my system, which left me feeling hollow. I should have been the one to tell Carter to fuck off. I should have had the guts, but instead I'd tiptoed around and this man had to step in and do it for me. How humiliating. It hit me like a ton of bricks: from the moment Carter arrived, I'd been unequivocally *mousy*. Exactly like Chris said.

As an introverted Virgo, I often had to remind myself to not let speculations and anxieties about other people's thoughts and feelings derail my life. In general, I was used to it taking a long time for my brain to let go of a hurtful comment. But Chris's words had far exceeded what any rational person would consider their rightful expiration date. It had been two years since I first discovered Chris was cheating on me, and a year and a half since the second time, which came with his humiliating accusation. In all that time, I hadn't been able to shake it. On the rare occasions when I went out with someone new, Chris's words hummed in the back of my mind, whispering that no matter how well my date and I hit it off, the moment would come when we got into bed and I revealed what a disappointment I was. It was bigger than sex, though. After more than a year of being haunted by the words *boring* and *timid*, it finally hit me that the reason I couldn't shake Chris's words was because deep down, I believed them.

Little did my ex know that I'd long suspected there was something lacking about me—that when it came down to it, I simply wasn't very interesting, smart, or bold, and this deficiency was the reason I could never quite measure up to my headline-making sister, the second-youngest woman ever elected to the Texas state legislature. Or move forward in my career, or make a solid group of friends, or keep someone romantically interested, no matter how hard I tried. Chris had no clue he was speaking my secret fear into life, that when he suggested there was something wrong with me, I wouldn't argue but agree. Of course there was. It wasn't hard to see when you put me next to Lee, who was brave, ambitious, and take-charge, doing important things to change the world, with a vibrant love life and ride-or-die group of friends to match. People like Lee inspired loyalty: everyone wanted to be around them. I'd known from a young age the differences between us, but I'd never been resentful. Lee might've become a hero to a lot of little girls, but she was my hero first. She was the North Star I'd pointed my life toward since I was young.

So it was almost a mercy Chris had the guts to tell me I was a dud in bed. While surely not the only thing lacking about me, it was at least something I could fix. After months of wallowing, I was finally ready to take the bull by the horns and become someone worldly and exciting. I'd be bold in bed if it killed me—which, quite honestly, judging by how this night was going, it might.

I'd now been staring at the dark-haired man for an embarrassingly long time, but he didn't seem to notice, focused as he was on his drink. So I summoned all my courage and thought WWLD: *What Would Lee Do?*

"Sir," I said. Oh, bad start. Was I twelve? Try again. "Um, you there, in the shirt. With the—sleeves. I'd like to buy you a drink."

8

2

The Gamble

Surprised, the dark-haired man turned to me, and there it was again: the electric reaction, lightning through my body. "Not necessary." His voice was gruff. "Sitting next to that guy was ruining my night, too. It was a self-serving act, trust me. Besides, he wouldn't have fought me. Guys like that fold when challenged."

"Oh, okay," I said. "Great." I was smiling and nodding like he'd just said something terribly agreeable instead of outright rejecting me. Oh, God: he'd *rejected* me. Confident he'd already turned back to his drink, I looked down at the bar and widened my eyes in silent horror at my reflection in the brass.

"Uh," he said. My head snapped up. He was, in fact, still watching me. His velvet-brown eyes tracked from my frozen face to my hunched shoulders. He rubbed contemplatively at the stubble on his jaw. "Okay. Yeah, you know what? I'll take that drink. Thanks."

He would? "Bartender!" I called, a little desperate. The bartender was heading to the other side of the bar, meaning

I'd have to wait in excruciatingly awkward silence next to the dark-haired man if I didn't make this happen now.

Thankfully, the bartender stopped and nodded. "Another martini?"

"Yes. And a—" I glanced at the man.

"Whiskey, neat. Whatever's cheap works." When the bartender shot off, the dark-haired man turned back to me. "I'm Logan, by the way." The way he said it and then watched me, as if waiting for some reaction, threw me a bit, but I smiled anyway. "I'm—"

"Ruby. Yeah, I heard. Kind of impossible not to, sorry."

Oops. Did I correct the lie and look like a weirdo? A thought occurred to me: It might not be too late to make this night what I wanted. Maybe I could still *be* who I wanted—which, to be clear, was anyone other than the old Alexis. "That's right," I said, settling back in my barstool. "Ruby Dangerfield."

Logan's mouth quirked, but at least I hadn't had whatever reaction he'd been bracing for, because his shoulders relaxed. "What brings you out among the goons and buffoons tonight, Ruby?"

"It's the two-year anniversary of the night my ex cheated on me," I said, shocking myself. It turned out Ruby was forthright.

The bartender slid our drinks across the bar. Logan picked up his tumbler and tipped it in my direction. "Well. Cheers, then. It's the one-year anniversary of the night Arsenal crushed Tottenham on their home turf."

"What?"

"Sorry," he said. "Just trying to think of something equally depressing."

Laughter burst from me. "Yes, I'm sure that must've been very hard for you." Okay, the soccer reference told me I'd been right about his accent: the man was clearly British.

"Damn near crushed me. Come on." Logan slipped off his barstool, nodding toward the crowded tables. "A table just opened. If that's the reason you're here, you're clearly looking to tie one on. Been there myself. We can't have any more jerks bothering you while you're on a sacred mission to wipe some fucker from your memory."

He took off without waiting for me, just scooped his jacket and marched in the direction of a small table in the corner, nearly hidden under the fronds of a sweeping palm. I didn't think twice. Given the choice between sitting alone at the bar—technically, what I'd come here to do—or remaining in the cocoon of this strangely acerbic man, I chose the cocoon.

I dropped into the chair across from Logan and he rested his elbows on the table, leaning over to tip his drink at me. "A real toast this time. To fresh starts."

I clinked his glass, feeling the butterflies swoop and dive. I was closer to him now, separated by nothing more than a small circular table, so I could see the tiny details of his face: the soot-dark lashes tipping toward his strong brow, the amber ring around his pupils, the Cupid's bow of his upper lip, topping his wry smile. I shifted underneath the table and my knee slid against his, rubbing the smooth fabric of his pants. I jerked it away and took an overlarge sip of my drink.

"So," I said, once I'd nearly drained the martini. "Do you come here often?" He didn't seem the type, but what if the

Fleur de Lis was his routine hookup spot same as everyone else?

Logan paused midsip and grinned, teeth dazzling. I realized what I'd said and could actually *feel* myself turning red. "That's a pickup line, isn't it?"

"One of the oldest in the book. You know, if you leave now, I think you can catch up with your friend Carter."

I groaned, covering my face. "I was genuinely curious!"

His smile remained wolfish. "No, I come here never. But it's only a few blocks from my office, and I had a long day at work. Needed to drown myself in whiskey somewhere within stumbling distance. Voilà, the Fleur de Lis." He glanced around. "Turns out this place is a scene."

The bar had grown even more crowded since we'd left, and the overflow milled around us, people waiting their turn. One guy in particular seemed oblivious to our presence behind him—he kept edging so close his butt brushed my arm. Logan eyed him disapprovingly.

"Working on a Saturday, huh?" He had to be what, an investment banker? A lawyer like Lee's boyfriend, Ben? Some high-stakes corporate job with no work-life balance. He looked the type.

Logan rubbed tiredly at his eyes. "If it wasn't my dream job, I'd have quit ages ago. Oi," he barked suddenly, just as the hovering guy knocked my arm. "Watch it!" The guy glanced back at us sheepishly and moved away.

I leaned over and braced my elbows on the table. "You really have no fear, do you? You just say whatever you're thinking."

"Sorry. Born this way, as my mum likes to say. Big fan of Lady Gaga, her."

"Your mum...far away in England?"

His mouth quirked. "Here in Texas. My mum's Belarusian and my dad's British. They both emigrated from the UK a year before I was born and set up shop down in Odejo."

"Ah." *That* explained his accent. It was clear, crisp, lilted enunciation one moment and growled twang the next. England meets Texas. Wholly unique and beautiful to listen to.

He sighed. "Yes, I'm one of those classic British Texans you see everywhere. My childhood home was a hobbit hole on a cattle ranch and we ate nothing but fish, chips, and brisket growing up."

"Be careful or I'll believe you."

"Odejo tried its damnedest to make me a cowboy, I'll admit, but I guess some Britishisms stuck. Mostly, my mum's slang and my dad's obsession with the Hotspurs."

"That's another soccer reference, I presume."

He looked affronted by my ignorance.

"For what it's worth, I think your bluntness is kind of amazing."

He drained his drink and dropped it on the table. "Yeah, well, please inform my colleagues. Pretty sure it's shaved years, if not decades, off their lives." He copied me, leaning over and placing his elbows on the table, lacing his fingers together. Our clasped hands were mere inches apart. I could easily lift a finger and stroke the back of his hand. Was his skin soft? He had long, elegant fingers but callused knuckles. The sudden vision of his hands moving roughly up my stomach to cup my breasts sent a stab of electricity through me. I crossed my legs tighter under the table.

"So what, then?" Logan's gaze grew more intense. "You're

not in the habit of speaking your mind? A woman with a name like Ruby Dangerfield, who goes out to celebrate dumping her ex, wearing that dress—I smell bullshit."

I glanced down. "You like the dress?" Technically Carter had liked it, too, but the compliment was different coming from Logan.

Our eyes locked across the table. He cleared his throat and half stood, shoving back his chair. "Yeah, well—you want another drink?"

"I thought you were trying to get home at a reasonable hour?" Companionship aside, I'd feel bad if I ruined Logan's night after he saved mine.

He shrugged. "One more won't kill me."

"Then I'll have what you're having. Whiskey."

His eyes jumped to mine, and he looked like he wanted to say something. But all that came out was, "Right back."

I watched him elbow his way through the crowd and make it to the bar in record speed, laughing to myself as he flagged down the bartender's attention ahead of half a dozen people who turned to him in outrage, which he roundly ignored. It was amazing: I'd managed to find my polar opposite. But our differences weren't aggravating: in fact, simply being around Logan felt like taking a mental vacation. Without anyone nearby to judge, I let myself study him, lingering over the lines of his body, his face in profile. He wasn't bulky, but his white-collared shirt pulled taut across his shoulders, tightest over the swell of his biceps as he leaned against the bar. His shirt was tucked smartly into belted navy pants that were fitted enough to show—oh. His ass was round and firm, the kind you found on baseball or soccer players, men who worked for it.

I bit my lip—who *was* I right now? I never lusted like this. I hadn't even realized I was capable of it. When I met a guy, I certainly noticed whether he was attractive or not, but I'd never had this kind of visceral reaction. Was it Logan's brashness I was responding to, my body soaking it up and reflecting it back like a mirror? Or had I simply morphed into a caricature of a sex-deprived woman? Either way, it felt *good*, like someone had flipped a switch to remagnetize me, the sudden buzzing attraction proof that I was very much alive. Even better that Logan was so wildly out of my league: I could simply sit back and admire him for admiration's sake.

I was still contemplating this when he turned, two whiskeys in hand, wearing an expression of such great annoyance it was like he'd heard my inner monologue. Despite his expression, my chest warmed at the thought that he was making his way back to me, out of all the people in the bar.

"Assholes," he pronounced, sliding my drink to me. "Up there at the bar complaining about having to refurb their company's oil rigs because of environmental rules. Boo-hoo, it's going to cost you a little extra money in exchange for not poisoning the planet. Get over it."

He sounded just like Lee, which I found endearing. I grinned and sipped my drink, prepared to hear all about it, but his eyes followed the drink to my mouth and his annoyed expression dropped, replaced by a guilty smile. It made small wrinkles frame his eyes like commas. His eyes were such a warm, rich brown. It was amazing how much he could convey with them. Now they radiated a sly, amused knowing.

"*Any*-way," he said, drawing it out. "On to more important things. I've told you about me. Now I want to know everything about you, from the day you were born to the moment you walked into this bar. The good, the bad, the ugly, the exes. Unpack yourself, Ruby Dangerfield. I'm prepared to be fascinated."

I laughed to cover the sudden sharp ache. *Alexis Stone, the bore.* I wanted so badly to impress this magnetic stranger. But obviously, my real life wouldn't cut it. A wild hare struck me. "You mean...you want to hear how my parents conceived me on a motorcycle tour around America, and my mom gave birth to me at the mouth of Niagara Falls?"

Logan's eyebrows shot up. "Really?"

My heart raced. Just like that, I was fascinating. Sure, I was lying, but what did lying matter on a night I'd specifically carved out to be a blip in reality, an island of time disconnected from every other day? I would never see Logan or any of these people again. I could do anything. Why not try on another life for a few hours?

"Wait until you hear about my siblings," I said, settling back in my chair. "I'm the oldest of six, and one of them is an honest-to-God international spy. Another knows Oprah."

I proceeded to talk more in one straight shot than I ever had in my life. I told Logan story after story—it turned out it was much easier to talk when I was pretending to be Ruby. During one stretch I ran out of ideas and had to borrow plotlines from the first book that came to mind, a popular children's fantasy novel about dragon hunters (one of the hazards of being a children's librarian), simply praying Logan hadn't read *Charlie Cooper and the Hunt for the Mystical Dragon's Egg.* Mostly, though, I found myself telling him true stories, with the edges blurred—my past actions more heroic, my comebacks wittier, me the star of the shenanigans and my siblings the sidekicks, all the ways I'd wished life had gone. It was exhilarating to be on this side of the storytelling for once.

Unsurprisingly, Logan was not a passive listener—he burst in with questions, forced me to stop when he laughed so hard he shook the table, and made me pause midsentence so he could go fetch another round, then another. Time dilated into a warm fuzzy stretch until before I knew it, the lights in the Fleur de Lis had dimmed and the crowd had thinned to us and a man who'd fallen asleep in his barstool, snoring like a bear.

"Shit." Logan wiped his face and glanced around. "What time is it?" I pointed at his watch to remind him he was wearing one, and he jerked it to his face, then blanched. "Do you want the truth, or—" He grimaced. "A lie that makes you feel better?"

I sighed and leaned back in my chair, feeling the plunging V of my dress pull tight against my chest. Logan cleared his throat, dropping his eyes. "Honestly," I said. "Give me the beautiful lie."

"Come on." He rose to his feet and extended a hand. "I'll walk you out."

I seized his hand and he yanked me with more strength than I'd expected. Instead of stopping upright, I sailed forward so fast I had to grip his shoulders so I didn't end up flush against him. "Whoa there," he murmured, looking down at the small space between us. He dipped his head, his nose brushing mine.

"Sorry." I released him and stepped back. "Lost my balance." I turned to pick up my purse and shivered, a full-body reaction to having been that close to him. When I turned back, Logan was holding up his navy suit jacket.

I shook my head. "I'm okay—"

He shook the jacket so the sleeves danced. "Come on. I can see your goose bumps."

Obviously I couldn't tell him the goose bumps were the result of meeting the mere tip of his nose, so I dipped inside the jacket. Logan draped it carefully over my shoulders, letting it trail like a cape. It was shot through with his scent, which had to be an expensive cologne: subtle but playful, not just woodsy cedar but notes of something sweeter, like berries. Everything about him was a mix of unexpected things. I took a deep breath and wrapped the jacket tighter. Logan tipped his head in the direction of the door, his eyebrows raised in question.

My heels made quiet clipping sounds as we strode across the empty lobby. The inside of the Fleur de Lis was all marble floors and ornate brass-piped ceilings, like a cross between a cathedral and a fancy, old-time bank. I sighed.

"What?" Logan glanced over as we walked.

"I just love this place. It's so romantic."

It was funny, but as we neared the large glass doors that separated the hotel from the street, I realized I was happy. Almost giddy. Even though I hadn't succeeded at the one thing I'd come here to do, there was something about the last few hours spent talking, being the sole focus of someone's attention, that left me feeling the way I'd hoped a one-night stand would: confident, interesting, and liberated. In an unexpected way I was leaving with exactly what I'd come for. Was it possible to have an emotional orgasm?

Logan stopped by the glass doors and shook out his hands—which, if I didn't know he wasn't the type to get nervous, I'd call a nervous tic. "You calling an Uber? Want me to wait?"

I shook my head. I'd already eaten up so much of his night. There was no way I'd continue to impose. "Don't worry about it." I tugged off his jacket and let it hang off the hook of my finger. Logan shrugged it back on and paused, head tilted. He smiled. "It smells like you now. Flowers and lemons." He tapped a finger to his temple. "Strategic thinker."

I cracked a laugh. Flowers and lemons, meet woods and berries. A veritable forest between us. We stood looking at each other for a moment. "Well..." I rocked on my feet, awkward again.

"Right." Logan rubbed his jaw. "So, did it work?"

"Did what work?"

"Did you forget about him? Your ex?"

I smiled. "Yes. Thank you. Quite a charitable service you provided."

"Well, then." He stepped close and cupped a hand to the back of my head. "Good night, Ruby." He pressed a quick kiss to my forehead, his lips there and gone.

Maybe it was the alcohol, or the intoxicant of being stood up for and then listened to, but before my mind could catch up, my body was reaching out for something I had no business hoping for.

"Logan." I took a deep breath and pulled his sleeve, turning him back around. And then everything happened quickly: I brought my hands to cup his face, his eyebrows lifted in surprise, and I kissed him, tasting the warm softness of his mouth, feeling the scratch of his stubble. I pulled away and looked up, heart drumming, waiting for his response. He blinked at me for an excruciatingly drawn-out moment and then bent down, wrapped his arms around me, and pulled me to him with a grunt, canting his mouth over mine in a wordless *yes*. His hand found the back of my head as he chased my mouth, deepening the kiss. *More*, his touch said, and the next thing I knew he'd lifted me off the floor, bracing an arm against my back to keep me close, his other hand tangling in my hair.

His tongue in my mouth shot white-hot electricity through me, all the lust that had been simmering all night boiling over, and I thought, *He* would *kiss like this. Exactly how he talks*. I wrapped a leg around his knee, urging him *closer*, every inch of my skin charged, nearly tortured with sensation. He kissed me back so hungrily I had to break away to gasp for air.

I'd done it: I'd become a different person. Old Alexis, who never would've kissed someone with such abandon in a public place, had burned to ash, giving rise to a new Alexis whose only care was kissing this brash stranger as much as she could before he left.

The clack of approaching footsteps on the marble floors, however, worked like a bucket of ice. I wrenched back from Logan, managing to say, "Public," even in my breathlessness. He nodded, agreeing with my good sense, then immediately tossed it aside, kissing me so fiercely I tipped backward.

His eyes were molten when we righted. "What do you want to do?" he whispered.

Well—I was Ruby Dangerfield tonight. So I answered honestly, pressing the words into the column of his throat. "I don't want to stop."

"Mmm," he hummed, and I felt the vibration against my lips. He wrenched back from me, casting a sweeping gaze around the lobby. I felt a momentary disappointment at the new space between us that ended when his eyes fell back on me, burning with a question. "Then please tell me," he said thickly, "that you want to get a room."

3

Code Red

Here it was. Logan was asking if I wanted to have a one-night stand. The exact thing I'd come for, with the last person I'd thought was an option. A thrill raced up my spine. "*Yes*," I said, putting all the weight I could into the word.

He gripped my hand and tugged me toward the front desk, moving so fast I had to skip a little to keep up. As we walked, he twined his fingers through mine.

"Hi," he said to the small blonde woman behind the desk. She blinked and smiled at us, as if captivated by the possibility of what we might say next.

"Do you have any rooms available?" Logan flipped open his wallet and slid out a card.

"Oh, let me—" I started, but stopped when his protesting scoff actually echoed off the walls.

The woman at the desk smiled wider, clicking her keyboard. "Unfortunately, we're almost fully booked. But we do have the governor's suite available."

Logan tensed. "The what?"

"Governor's suite," she repeated. "Named in honor of Governor Grover Mane. We're big UT football fans around here."

Them and everyone else in Austin. It was no wonder Grover Mane had been able to transition his legendary Longhorn football career into a political position. The governor was a sometimes friend of my sister, who liked him for being a more progressive Republican.

"God has a sense of humor, huh?" Logan looked up at the ceiling, as if expecting an answer. He snorted. "All right. We'll take your ridiculously named suite. Here's my card."

"Great," she chirped, turning the computer screen to face him. "And here's the nightly charge."

"Good God," Logan burst out. "What is it, made of gold?" He looked at me with an incredulous expression, wanting me to share his outrage, and I couldn't help it—I laughed. Thing #958 this man had said tonight that I wouldn't say in a million years, no matter how much I wanted to. His eyes caught on my smile and he turned back to the woman with a resigned sigh. "Okay. Go ahead and fleece me."

"Name on the room?"

"John Smith." I quirked my brows at him, but he only arched his back at me. Apparently we were both playing different people tonight.

My nerves bubbled over waiting for the elevator doors to open. Logan slid an arm around my waist, pinning me to him, and his thumb drew an impatient circle on my ribcage. All I wanted was to ignore the woman watching from the desk and kiss him senseless.

The elevator doors dinged open and we strode inside, casual and slow. Rested our backs against the wall, side by side. "Lovely weather we're having," he said, as we watched the elevator doors inch together. The woman at the front desk waved.

Then the doors closed.

In one fluid movement Logan jammed the button for the eighth floor and lifted me onto the handrail. It was so fast I barely had time to catch my breath, but who needed air? Tonight the only thing I cared about was his mouth, searing kisses down my neck to the plunging dip in my dress. He nudged my legs apart and stepped between them, pressing against me. When I rocked my hips, he gripped them and pulled me closer.

"Bossy," I breathed.

"Driven," he countered.

Too soon, the elevator doors chimed and slid open. We stumbled down the hall, making terrible time, stopping to kiss against the wall, practically falling over each other. Hazily, I thought, *No wonder Lee insisted I do this*. Finally, Logan stopped at our room, swiped the key, and we were inside, lights springing to life of their own fancy volition.

"Whoa," I murmured. This was the biggest hotel room I'd ever seen, nearly as big as my apartment, with a fireplace in the living room, floor-to-ceiling windows overlooking downtown Austin, and a spiral staircase ascending to a second floor.

But—priorities. "Come here," I said, and Logan obeyed, shutting the door and striding to me, dropping his jacket and unbuttoning his shirt as he moved. I slid my hands over his bare chest, curling my fingers in the small dusting of dark hair there, so intoxicated by him, inhibitions swept away in the face of my hunger. He pressed his lips to mine with a small growl in the back of his throat.

"I'm going to—" But Logan's next words were drowned in an ear-splitting noise.

"What is that?" I yelled, pressing my hands over my ears.

"Fire alarm," he shouted. "Fucking A." He wrestled the door open. The hall was flooded with people. "Hey," Logan called. "What's going on?"

Out of nowhere a man came streaking down the hallway in nothing but a white T-shirt and polka-dot boxers, his face bright red and sweaty. "It's not a drill!" he shrieked. "It's a real fire. God save us!" Then he flung himself against the emergency exit door and disappeared. For a moment, the people in the hallway simply stood stunned. Then a young girl clutching a teddy bear burst into tears, and it was like a starting gun at the beginning of a race: everyone started running.

"Shit," Logan said, his expression dark. "We better get out of here. Hurry."

I took his cue and raced behind him down the hall, rezipping my dress as I moved. Logan punched open the emergency exit door and we froze, staring down the barrel of eight long flights of stairs. Curse the governor's suite and its posh elevated address.

"Take off your heels," he said. "You'll never make it down."

"I'll be fine." I shoved him forward. "Now go—we're the last people."

He took off down the stairs like a football player in training, hitting every step with speed and precision. As for me, I'd been lying about the heels. I never wore them and was lucky I hadn't tripped while sitting at the bar. I clutched the railing and tried to shimmy down sideways as best I could. Occasionally I could hear Logan grumble things like, "Of all the nights I've begged for an alarm to save me, you chose this one."

Then, somewhere between flights five and four, I landed too hard on the side of my foot and crumpled to the stairs, sharp pain shooting through my ankle. "Shit!"

Half a staircase below me, Logan whipped around and dashed back up. "What happened?"

"Twisted it," I yelled. The fire alarm was still going, and even in the enclosed staircase, the shrill blast rang in my ears. I fought the sudden urge to cry—not because of the pain, but because I'd committed the mortifying faux paus of becoming a burden. "Go on without me," I called.

"Oh, for the love of God." Logan swooped down, scooping me into his arms. "Hold on."

This was completely unnecessary. Humiliating, even. I clung to him as we bounced down the stairs at a remarkably fast clip, trying not to feel indecent as I pressed my cheek against his chest, still bare thanks to his unbuttoned shirt, and snuck secret hits of his woodsy-berry scent. Finally, we hit the end of the staircase and Logan kicked the door. It didn't budge.

"You picked the wrong night," he yelled, and karate kicked it. The door flung open.

Lights, sirens, and people flooded the street. There were firetrucks and ambulances everywhere, pajama-clad hotel guests and frenzied hotel staff buzzing around, resisting attempts at being herded by firemen. Across the street, a crowd of spectators had gathered, their heads tilted up.

Logan and I turned in the same direction and found the magnificent spired top of the Fleur de Lis ablaze, flames lighting the night sky.

"Oh my God," I murmured. "It really is on fire."

Logan squeezed me tighter. "Hey," he called to someone who looked like a hotel employee. "What happened?"

"They're saying it was a freak lightning strike during the storm." The man shook his head. "What are the odds, right?"

"What storm?" I asked.

The hotel employee frowned at me. "It rained for hours. You didn't hear it?"

Chalk one up to the power of the Logan-and-booze bubble. Speaking of. I tugged his shirt sleeve. "You can put me down now. It's getting embarrassing." I didn't tell him my ankle barely throbbed anymore, for fear he'd think I'd orchestrated the whole thing for a free ride.

"Hold that thought," he said, and took off in the direction of the ambulances.

I pushed at his shoulders like he was some sort of vehicle I could steer. "I said I'm fine!"

Fine or not, the next thing I knew, I was sitting on the edge of an ambulance with my arms crossed while a paramedic turned my ankle from side to side, examining it. "Minimal swelling," she pronounced.

I gave Logan a pointed look, but he rolled his eyes. "Yeah, yeah. I too am an adult who prides myself on shirking my health, but—" His attention caught on something behind me, and he trailed off. I leaned out of the ambulance to get a look, and jumped back when lights flashed in my eyes. The wall of people across the street were taking pictures.

No wonder—the hotel fire was a sight to behold. It would probably make the news.

I turned back to find Logan white as a sheet. He clawed at his shirt, scrambling to rebutton it. "Oh, fuck. Fuck, fuck, fuck."

"What's wrong?"

He ignored me and turned to the paramedic. "She's going to be okay?" He spoke at twice his normal volume and with a rushed franticness, like he was hopped up on speed.

The paramedic nodded, eyeing him quizzically. "Right as rain in a day or two."

"Okay." He gripped my shoulders. "Sorry, I have to go. Right now."

My eyes had to be wide as saucers. "What's happening?" He was going to *leave*?

No, he was currently *leaving*, already twisting away from me. I watched in open-mouthed amazement as the man I'd been about to sleep with turned his back on me and bolted away as fast as his legs could carry him.

As he rounded the block, the paramedic and I turned to stare at each other. "Girl," she said. "What did you *do*?"

4

L'Enfant Terrible

Despite the fact that we'd been downsized a few years ago to make room for the trendier engineering lab, and were now squished into a shoebox-sized hobbit hole that smelled faintly of mothballs and could barely contain our impressive beanbag collection, there was no place on earth I loved more than the Barton Springs Elementary school library. We'd gotten a new shipment of books in this morning, so I'd arrived early to put together a Cool New Reads display splattered with a metric ton of glitter. I'd learned a lot of important lessons in my five years as an assistant librarian, and one of them was that the rate at which my students picked up books was directly proportional to the amount of sparkle I used in advertising said books. Humans developed their shiny-object fetishes at an early age.

I was hot glue gunning to my heart's content—while avoiding any thoughts, whatsoever, about my disastrous attempt at a one-night stand this past weekend—when I heard the telltale sounds of students arriving, aka the trampling of a small herd of elephants. I shifted so I could spy them through a gap in the bookshelf. Not only was it important that I, as their educator, keep an eye on them, but I genuinely loved the sight of students curling up and getting lost in a book. When I was a kid, books were my life—or, as Lee would joke, my entire personality. True, I did once walk home from the library with a pile of books stacked so high I couldn't see and beelined straight into a tree. And I *did* used to request my family call me by the names of my favorite novel heroines (which I still maintain was an adorable quirk, despite my family's insistence otherwise). It's just as far back as I can remember, I've been fascinated by other people, but terrified by how hard they can be to navigate. Books presented the perfect solution: you could follow friends on scores of adventures without having to worry about saying the wrong thing.

The group of students who'd filed into the library slung their backpacks down and flopped onto the beanbag chairs I'd carefully arranged into a circle—a tight circle, since what used to be our Beanbag Corner had turned, post-downsize, into our Beanbag Cranny. I recognized the girls immediately: Sable, Larkyn, Brynlee, and—surprisingly—Mildred. Sable, Larkyn, and Brynlee were popular sixth graders, with Sable as the ringleader, but Mildred was a shy girl who spent an inordinate amount of time in the library alone. A kindred spirit, you might say. My heart warmed to see her taken in by the cool kids.

Sable punched her yellow beanbag chair and frowned. "This one's flat." She looked at Mildred. "Yours is better."

Mildred sprang from her chair. "You can have it."

Okay, I didn't *love* that dynamic, but it was just a little social hierarchy rearing its ugly head. Only normal at this age.

"Why'd your mom name you Mildred, anyway?" Larkyn asked. "Did she, like, hate you or something?" The three girls giggled while Mildred frowned and crouched gingerly in Sable's discarded yellow beanbag.

Now, I *really* didn't love that—

"And what are those books you're always reading?" Sable asked, settling comfortably into Mildred's chair. "The ones with the unicorns?"

The three girls waited with bated breath while Mildred looked down at her shoes. "*The Magical Adventures of Oona the Unicorn,*" she said quietly.

"Oh my God," Sable cackled. "That sounds like it's for *babies.*"

The other girls laughed. Unbidden, a memory came back from my own sixth grade year, sharp as the day it happened. In the Stone household, turning twelve brought an exciting milestone: it meant you were old enough to host a big sleepover for your birthday, as many friends as you wanted to invite, with all the pizza and candy you could eat. Before twelve, our parents allowed Lee and me to have a single friend over at a time, but this was the big leagues, a social *event.* So many girls came to Lee's twelfth birthday party that my parents had to set up a tent in the backyard for overflow. And there'd been shenanigans of epic proportions, clearly, because for weeks after, our high school–aged neighbor had turned red and fled in the opposite direction whenever he saw Lee. Of course, I wasn't privy to those shenanigans, since as Lee's little sister, I'd been shooed out of her bedroom the moment it was time for the real juicy stuff to begin.

But finally, my turn had come: the big 1-2. Like Lee, I was

going to invite every single girl in my class, even the ones I'd never talked to out of shyness. Who didn't love a sleepover? Armed with this cultural capital, twelve was going to be the year I turned it all around. I even talked my mom into buying the fancy invitations with gold foil flowers. They went out in the mail and a whole week went by while I anxiously awaited RSVPs. Eventually it occurred to me that I could just ask my classmates if they'd gotten them, so one day I steeled my nerves and hurried after a group of girls on the way back from the cafeteria, trying to work out the best way to insert myself. Before I could get up the courage to slip into stride with anyone, I heard my name. Kristen Clock, the coolest girl in sixth grade—*of all people*—was talking about me. Of course, because it's just how these things go, she was in the middle of complaining that her mom was forcing her to go to my birthday party even though I was a dork who only liked to read. The comment stopped me in my tracks, leaving me stock-still while the girls continued on ahead. But I still heard Kristen's right-hand girl, Gloria Rodrigo, say, "She'll probably make us, like, work on homework or something. This is going to be the first sleepover we actually want to sleep through." That zinger got a laugh from everyone, which, no surprise, because it was a pretty good one. I'd probably have appreciated it more if it hadn't shot like an arrow through my heart.

Obviously, as any rational person would do, I went home and told my mom in no uncertain terms to cancel my party. Unfortunately, she was an expert at wrestling the truth out of me, and soon I'd spilled the whole story. To my horror, she refused to cancel—instead, she got on the phone with

Kristen's and Gloria's mothers, and before I could say *social pariah*, Kristen, Gloria, and every other girl in my grade had been handed an edict by their mothers to attend my birthday. I'd never wished to contract sudden and incurable consumption more ardently.

But, modern infrastructure being what it is, I caught not even a wisp of the vapors that had felled my favorite Victorian heroines. So the night came, the girls arrived, and it was awkward... I *would* say, if I was employing my gift for understatement. To lean on my talent for painfully accurate description, it was a humiliating living nightmare. There was pizza, ice cream, and a mountain of candy, but I was too nervous to eat. There were brand-new board games stacked on the coffee table, waiting for us to play them, but I was too afraid to suggest one lest someone find my choice boring. I was, in fact, too afraid to do anything but stare anxiously across the room as Kristen and Gloria sat in a corner and whispered. Then, like a miracle, I saw Lee walking down the hall—funny, confident, *sixteen-year-old* Lee, who'd kissed a boy and seen an R-rated movie and owned a cell phone. I'd scrambled after her so fast you would've thought Kristen had lit my butt on fire, and begged Lee to please, *please* drop her plans and come attend a twelve-year-old's birthday party.

I must've looked pretty desperate, because she actually called her best friends, Claire and Simon, and told them their double date was off, then strode into the living room, shook out her long, shiny brown hair, and said, "Who wants to watch *Twilight*?" Everyone, it turned out. Literal pandemonium. (I filed away "Mention *Twilight*," and it turns out, fifteen years later, it still works.) After the movie it was gossip and prank phone calls and Lee dragging out her *People* magazines so the girls could point out their celebrity crushes, none of which were activities I would've thought of on my own.

Lee was older and worldly and they loved her. I watched it all unfold, grateful to be spared the spotlight but also, if I'm completely honest, a little bit sad. That's when it first occurred to me: whatever that magic thing was that made some people magnetic, the je ne sais quoi Lee had—I didn't have it. But chin up, no big deal. Not everyone gets sprinkled with fairy dust. It was simply good to know where you fell on the scale so you could adjust accordingly, perhaps become a more accommodating person to make up for your lack of pizzazz, which I'd been trying to do since roughly the age of twelve.

All that said, it still wasn't the greatest boost to the old ego to finally attempt to seduce a man and have him practically trip over his own two feet trying to flee me. Though I suppose it was good Logan had his abrupt change of heart about me *before* we'd slept together.

But back to the children. I set down my hot glue gun and swept into the Beanbag Cranny, radiating my best Ms. Honey vibes. "Good morning, girls, lovely to see you. Sable, Larkyn, and Brynlee, I heard Ms. Redfield is putting out the sign-up sheet for *The Wizard of Oz*. You'd better run to the cafeteria if you don't want to end up playing a flying monkey." I resisted the urge to say something sarcastically scolding to them about their behavior, even though they probably wouldn't register the full meaning until years later, when it finally clicked and delivered a delayed moral lesson from a source they could no longer remember, thereby making it the perfect crime. No, there was hope for these girls yet. Even Kristen—I mean, Sable. "Mildred, would you stay behind a minute?"

As predicted, the girls rushed off at the flying monkey threat. But Mildred kept still, her gaze locked on her shoes. I crouched in front of her. "Hey. Guess what? I have something for you."

Her head rose, eyes wide behind her pink glasses.

"Come on." I stretched out a hand. "Let me show you."

I led Mildred to my Cool New Reads crafting station, then bent over and reached into the box of books. "I ordered this just for you."

She dropped my hand and seized the book, holding it reverently. "The new one!"

"*Oona Battles the Monsters of the Rainbow Ravine.* And it's all yours—you can be the first to check it out."

Mildred's eyes sparkled as she cracked open the stiff spine. "I'm going to read the entire thing right now." She spun on her heels and started to charge toward the beanbags—then spun back, looking sheepish. "Thank you, Ms. Stone."

"You're welcome. I want to hear all about it when you're done." *I wish I could shield you and keep you this happy*, I thought, then startled at my sudden melancholy turn.

The squishiest beanbag chair had just claimed Mildred as its latest victim, sucking her like quicksand so her little legs were all I could see, when the double door to the library flew open and Gia burst in.

"Jesus!" I put a hand over my thumping heart. "You scared me."

"Good." Gia seized my elbow and tugged me toward the circulation desk, which was tucked in the farthest corner of the library, away from prying student ears. "Then you're in the right mood to hear this."

Gia Russo was one of my two closest friends—not just at Barton Springs, but in general. That was a fact I'd almost let slip one Monday when Gia and Muriel Lopez, my other friend, asked what fun things I'd gotten up to with my "hip young crew" that weekend, and I'd started to scoff at the idea that I had a hip young crew—until I saw the alarm on their faces. Apparently, it was unusual not to have friends outside of work, or friends your own age, as opposed to those roughly two or three times it. But Gia, a fifth grade teacher, and Muriel, the other librarian, were both wonderful and the other founding members of our three-person romance book club, which met every Wednesday during lunch in the teacher's lounge. Gia was fifty-eight and small-boned, with short-cropped black hair, ears lined with silver studs, and a personality she liked to call "aggressively Italian."

"You won't believe what I heard," she hissed, once she'd sat me down at the chair behind the desk. It said a lot about my mental state that my first thought was, *Oh, God, she heard about my epic rejection.*

"My friend at the TEA says the legislature's going to cut the education budget by *twenty percent* in January. An aide for Senator Abington leaked it. Everyone's in a tizzy."

All thoughts of the weekend flew from my mind. "Twenty percent? But we're already on a shoestring budget. They've cut every year. Where else can they pull money from?"

Gia sank onto the desk. "Everyone says they're going to cut jobs. Or pay. Or both."

My heart sank. Since I'd started at Barton Springs five years ago, Texas's dwindling education budget had been a source of endless anxiety, especially for educators like me who worked in the arts and humanities, where the heaviest budget bludgeonings always occurred. When I was hired, Barton Springs's library had been housed in its own sprawling building and there'd been three of us: me, Muriel, and Dawn Kowalski. But budget cuts that first year had gotten us booted to our current tiny cave, and even worse, they'd cost Dawn her job. Each year, as the budget cuts came for more of us—the speech therapist, then the music teacher, then the arts teacher—classroom sizes ballooned and more of the supply budget was pushed onto our shoulders. (I was, for example, paying for all of my own glitter.) Everyone was so scared of being let go that no one dared complain, except to the Texas Educators Association, our advocates to lawmakers. And to each other.

A terrible thought occurred to me: "We're the only school left in the district with two librarians."

Gia's forehead creased in a frown. "At our size, we should have at least three. But you're right. I'm worried for you and Muriel."

And here I'd spent the last year trying to talk myself into asking for the promotion to full librarian Muriel swore I deserved. Forget a promotion; what if I lost my job? If they had to choose between Muriel and me, I'd be toast. Muriel had years of experience and a master of library sciences under her belt, and I was only a lowly BA-educated assistant librarian.

Gia patted my back. "Well," I sighed. "At least you're safe." Gia taught math, the one language we'd all be speaking a thousand years from now when countries ceased to exist and the aliens descended.

"Can you imagine if students only learned STEM subjects?" Gia shivered. "Bring on the robot apocalypse."

As if on cue, the double door burst open once again, and Gia and I jumped. "You'll never believe this," Muriel boomed, arriving in a veritable storm of swirling scarves despite the early September heat. She always dressed like she was about to make a star turn as a Hooverville bag lady in a school production of *Annie*. Despite that, she was sharp as a tack at sixty-eight.

"We already know," Gia said. "I just told Alexis about the budget cuts."

"Budget cuts?" Muriel stood stalwart, hands on her hips. "What budget cuts?"

"You didn't hear?" I sighed. "I'm a goner, I know it. Wait—what are you talking about?"

Muriel's expression changed to one of wonder. "Honey, you're a star! You really haven't seen?"

I squinted. Was Muriel suffering heatstroke from all those layers? "What are you talking about?"

She unlocked her phone and thrust it at me. Gia and I both leaned over. She had some website pulled up, the logo spelling out *The Watcher on the Hill* in big block letters. I frowned at Muriel in confusion.

"It's a Texas politics blog," she said. "A famous one, apparently. Carmen sent it to me. You know she's into all that activism stuff." Carmen was Muriel's oldest daughter, a nurse who cared so passionately about lowering health care costs that she'd started a special interest group called Enfermeras por la Equidad, or Nurses for Equity. I'd introduced her to Lee and they'd both gone starry-eyed. "She says your sister's on the site a lot for such a junior politician." That didn't surprise me. In less than a year as a state senator, Lee was already making waves. "Scroll down," Muriel instructed.

I thumbed down and shrieked.

"I *know*!" Muriel said, at the same time Gia cried, "That's *you*!"

There, in vivid color and crisp resolution, was a picture of me in Logan's arms outside the Fleur de Lis. I'd forgotten until this moment that his shirt had been unbuttoned thanks to our mad dash out of the burning hotel, and—God help me—I was struck anew by how good-looking he was, the commanding way he held his shoulders, his confidence telegraphing clearly through the image. It didn't hurt that he was carrying me cradled to him with ease, or that my arms were wrapped around his neck like he was my personal lord and savior. Whoever took the picture must've caught us right after we'd burst out of the staircase onto the street. Between my plunging red dress—made even more provocative by being hiked up my thighs—Logan's bare chest, our tangled limbs, and the way we were looking at each other, like we'd just rolled out of bed or were maybe on our way back into one, the picture screamed sex. No, worse—*intimacy*.

"You look like the cover of a romance novel," Gia breathed.

Dread filled my stomach like a lead balloon. I was so distracted by the picture that it took me several shocked seconds before I realized there was obviously an accompanying headline.

"'*L'Enfant Terrible* Caught In Flagrante Outside Ritzy Hotel,'" Gia read. "*L'Enfant* what?"

"It means a young person who's so unorthodox they're a pain in the ass," I murmured, forgetting the rule not to curse on school grounds.

Hovering over us, Muriel got impatient with the time it was taking me to process and swiped down. And oh, God. There was an entire article. She read it out loud: "'Upstart Democratic gubernatorial candidate Logan Arthur snapped barely dressed and holding on for dear life to a scantily clad *mystery woman* outside the Fleur de Lis in the wee hours of Sunday morning.'" Muriel paused to grin lasciviously at me, clearly ignorant of the fact that my entire world had just turned upside down.

Logan was a *gubernatorial candidate*? As in, a person running against Grover Mane to become the next governor of Texas? I'd thought he was a run-of-the-mill investment banker or lawyer. How was a man as blunt and hotheaded as him a politician? And how had I not recognized him? As soon as I thought it, I knew the answer. The truth was, besides paying attention whenever Lee called to vent about being surrounded by useless, backstabbing lawmakers, I didn't follow politics all that much...in fact, in a secret I would take to my grave, sometimes when Lee started waxing on about policy change my eyes sort of just...glazed over. I hadn't, in all honesty, been paying much attention to the state elections.

Lee was right: being an uninformed public citizen really had come back to bite me in the ass.

Muriel barreled on: "'Apparently, the powers that be have a rollicking sense of humor—or they're rooting for

Grover Mane—because Arthur and his paramour were caught in a state of undress thanks to a freak lightning strike that started a fire in the upper levels of the hotel. Although rumors of Arthur's playboy past have dogged his candidacy (as they once did, coincidentally, to the now-married Governor Mane), Arthur's team has repeatedly assured high-profile backers the rumors are unfounded.'"

"Playboy past?" I echoed, but nothing could deter Muriel from finishing.

"'These latest snaps,'" she read, "'are going to discredit their claims that the young Arthur, despite his age, is a mature, stable presence Texans can count on. With little more than two months until election day, the stakes couldn't be higher. *Especially* since the latest poll numbers show Arthur's approval ratings rising while Mane's are slipping, evidence the public has been warming to Arthur's new restrained approach. The governor's campaign is sure to pounce on this opportunity to undermine their junior foe, leaving all the politicos in Austin wondering: Just who is this mystery woman, and what kind of sordid tell-all is she about to spill? The hunt for the lady in red is on.'"

One night. One measly, should've-been-*private* night out, to accomplish a *private* goal, and now I was Hester Prynne from *The Scarlet Letter*. What if my students' parents saw this? What if Principal Zimmerman saw it and decided firing me was the easiest way to cut the budget? This was a disaster.

It hit me that Muriel and Gia were both uncharacteristically quiet, so I broke my thousand-yard stare-off with the phone to glance at them. They were both gaping.

"I'm sure you have questions," I said tentatively, and that was it. The floodgates opened.

"How long have you been dating this hunk of *man-meat*?" Muriel's scarves flew as she gesticulated wildly at the word *man-meat*.

Gia hit me on the shoulder. "Why didn't you tell us you had a *boyfriend*?"

"Why didn't tell us he was *famous*?"

"Why didn't you tell us you owned a dress like that? Good God, honey."

"Why didn't you tell us—"

My cell phone buzzed violently, interrupting the barrage. "Oh, thank God," I said, and leaped across the desk to seize the lifeline. Then I looked at the screen. *Blocked Number*. That couldn't be good. But it was either Door Number One—the Muriel and Gia Inquisition Experience—or whatever mystery lay behind Door Number Two. I decided to take my chances.

I waved Muriel and Gia silent. "Hello?"

"Good morning," said just about the crispest, most assured voice I'd ever heard. "This is Nora Igwe, Logan Arthur's chief of staff. Am I speaking with Alexis Stone, alias—" She paused, as if double-checking her notes. "Ruby Dangerfield?"

5

An Indecent Proposal

Someone had scratched out the conference room sign at the Logan Arthur for Governor headquarters and written in "War Room." And, judging by the sea of faces staring back at me from across the table, they were taking the war part seriously. Their tense expressions, plus the fact that someone had hastily erased all the whiteboards—I could still make out bits of campaign strategy—were starting to make me suspect the enemy in this situation was me.

"Thank you for coming on such short notice," said Nora, from her seat at the head of the table. The crisp, assured voice on the phone had turned out to belong to a beautiful Black woman wearing a sharp magenta suit and long, dark locs twisted into an elegant bun. She had a dazzling smile she'd flashed exactly once, when she'd greeted me at the door of the campaign's downtown headquarters (just two blocks from the Fleur de Lis—ugh, there'd been so many clues) and ushered me through an office full of gawking people wearing bright blue Arthur for Governor shirts. Nearly ten of them had filed into the conference room after us, settling into seats around the table. Either I was an all-hands-on-deck sort of problem, or they expected a show. Despite being full, the room was unnervingly quiet. Everyone was waiting for something.

The door to the conference room flew open and Logan barged in. "Sorry I'm late," he said, sounding harried. "Phones are ringing off the hook."

Ah. Right. What we'd been waiting for.

"I can only imagine," said Nora dryly, tapping her manicured fingers on the table.

Logan made his way to the opposite end of the table, nodding at each person as he passed. He looked just like I remembered, like the photograph had captured: tall and darkly handsome, with the intensity of a rushing train, a face I wanted to run from and throw myself in front of in equal measure. The creases under his eyes had only deepened, and his stubble was now the beginnings of a beard. Unfortunately, I found I liked that even better. He looked an order of magnitude more tense than he had on Saturday night. *Well, buddy, welcome to the club.*

He was pointedly not looking at me. I took his cue and tried to pretend he wasn't there, but there was no fooling my body. Even without looking, his presence gnawed at me. Under the table, I bounced my leg.

"Okay." Nora put down the phone in her right hand, then the one in her left (wait—had she been typing on two phones at the same time?). "Let's get down to business." She looked at her gathered colleagues. "For those of you just getting looped in, this morning we woke up to a crisis comms situation. The ever-delightful Daniel Watcher—" She paused to allow for the groans that echoed around the table. "Yeah, that's right, our good buddy Daniel got hold of some pictures of Logan from this weekend, and they're going viral."

Oh, God—they were?

"Other outlets are picking up the story," Nora said. "We're expecting hit pieces from *Texas Monthly* and the *Statesman* at minimum." More groaning.

"Sex sells," lamented a pale young slender staffer. He smoothed a hand over his perfectly coiffed black hair. "Trust me, I would know."

Nora rolled her eyes. "It's earlier in the day than I normally say this, but: can it, Cary."

I couldn't help looking at Logan, but his face was a stony mask. What was he thinking? Is this why he'd run when he saw people taking pictures—because he'd been embarrassed by the idea of them catching us together?

"Though, yes," Nora said. "For those who haven't seen them, the pictures capture Logan and Alexis here—" Finally, she nodded to me. "In a rather undressed state outside the Fleur de Lis hotel."

"Remember? That's the hookup spot where Morgan met that guy who was obsessed with her feet," Cary added, and there were nods of recognition around the table. Everyone's heads turned to me. Great. Now they were either imagining me in a state of undress or trying to guess what weird fetish I was concealing. Dear freak lightning storm from Saturday night, please have mercy and strike me now.

Nora cleared her throat. "Obviously, we're not going to waste time giving our fearless leader hell for his personal choices." She paused. "Because you can rest assured, I've already done that." Snickers from everyone. Logan gave

45

a tight smile that I *think* was supposed to pass for "Look at me, taking this in stride," but instead looked more like "I am currently being tortured and you are witnessing an involuntary pain spasm."

"So, damage control," Nora said. "First thing we did was track down the woman before any reporters could get to her. We were going to run the picture through a reverse image search—"

"Wait." A female staffer near Nora frowned. "Why didn't we know her name if she was with Logan?"

Silence around the table as the pieces lined up: *Caught in a state of undress. Fleur de Lis, the hookup spot. No name.* Logan started coughing, and Cary leaped up and poured him a glass of water from a pitcher in the center of the table. I melted into my chair.

"Luckily," Nora continued, ignoring the question, "Anita recognized Alexis as the younger sister of our very own Senator Lee Stone." This at least earned me some looks of respect. Lee to the rescue again.

An older woman with close-cut white hair leaned over the table and thrust out her hand. "Anita Jones, director of research." Her voice was so gravelly it sounded like she smoked at least a carton a day. I shook her hand and tried not to wince at her firm grip. "Your sister and I go way back. Helped her pass her big green energy bill, you know. I used to work for Mane until *this one* sweet-talked me away." She slid a look at Logan and lowered her voice. "Not bad, eh?"

Logan rolled his eyes. "Keep it in your pants, Anita."

"He's much feistier than Mane," Anita said with a wink. "I like it."

"Uh..." How to respond? This woman was a walking, talking HR violation. I half expected an HR rep to drop from the ceiling and snatch her away.

"*Anyway*," Nora said, shooting Anita a scorching look. "Now that everyone's up to speed." She turned her full and formidable attention on me. "Alexis. You've obviously picked up that this story is bad for us. We've worked hard to quell rumors that Logan is a playboy, all bluster and no substance, someone who's only running for office for the fame and fringe benefits."

Around the table, the staffers snorted or shook their heads, plainly offended on Logan's behalf.

"*We* all know that couldn't be farther from the truth, but unfortunately, the public doesn't."

I darted another glance at Logan, because it was impossible to sit in the same room with him and not look. He was idly tracing a line over his palm as Nora spoke, his face still impassive.

"Logan is young compared to Mane, which could swing either way—it could be a boon for us or an Achilles' heel. Mane's team's doing their best to present it as a flaw, and this playboy reputation plays right into their hands. If word gets out Logan was, uh, acting a little salacious, we're worried it'll sink his credibility. *Especially* with the female politicos we've been courting for endorsements."

"Including your sister," Anita added. And it hit me: of course Lee would catch wind of this. What if I hurt her reputation? What if I humiliated her? It wasn't just my career on the line.

"We need to make this go away," Nora said, as if she'd read my mind. "Take control of the narrative."

"Yes." My voice came out small, so I cleared my throat and tried again. "I mean, I'm all for that. I'm an elementary school librarian—I don't exactly want my one-night stand blasted on the news. And, you know, there's Lee to consider..."

"Perfect." Nora beamed at me, and I winced. Her smile was a tad...predatory, like a cat grinning at a mouse who'd just walked into its waiting paws. I got the distinct impression I was about to get a sales pitch. "Then we're all on the same page. Unfortunately, the pictures are out there and the pundits are clamoring. The truth won't work, so we need a story."

From the other end of the table, Logan crossed his arms tight over his chest. Nora ignored him, keeping her gaze on me. "What we propose—actually, I'll be real—what we're *begging* you to consider is to tell the public that you and Logan are dating. *Seriously* dating. Like, church bells ringing in the distance. We'll say the photos caught Logan with his girlfriend, not his fly-by-night, because everyone knows Logan Arthur is a serious, focused, *mature* man who can commit to things. Like, say, a single woman. Or the entire state of Texas."

"You want us to say we're *dating*?" My head snapped to Logan—and for the first time, he looked back. There was an unexpected vulnerability in his eyes as he searched my face for my reaction. Whatever he saw there made him swallow hard and lean away from the table.

"I told you this was a bad idea."

"Don't mind him," Nora said. "Lying goes against Logan's moral code, which is why we love him. But it's my job to win, and a political campaign is won or lost on public perception. What people think of the kind of person you are is—like it or not—ten times more important than your fiscal policy. That's why we *agreed*—" she looked pointedly at Logan "—that this was our best option."

"I've built my entire career around telling the truth when other politicians wouldn't," he protested, but he sounded resigned.

"And no, Alexis." Nora turned back to me. "We don't just want you to say you're dating. If no one ever sees the two of you together, it'll look fishy. We're proposing you and Logan pretend to be in a relationship from now until election day—upon which time Logan will win and we'll roll out a public breakup plan. Irrevocable differences. Conscious uncoupling. Something vague and mystifying where everyone walks away with their reputations intact."

I felt my jaw drop. "You want us to go on actual dates?"

"More like carefully staged appearances. Mostly attending campaign events together. Speeches, rallies, pancake breakfasts, fundraiser dinners." She waved jazz hands. "It can be quite glamorous. And it's only until November 7th—two measly months. Anyone can do anything for two months."

"I once pretended I was Matt Bomer on Grindr for two months," Cary piped in. He turned so I could witness his profile. "See? The resemblance is uncanny."

Anita snorted, but her words were directed at me. "The truth is, cookie, you're good for business."

"Anita," Nora warned.

"We ran an exploratory poll," Anita explained, "and people responded favorably to the idea of Logan in a relationship. And you couldn't make for better optics:

you're pretty, connected to a Democratic senator, and an actual, honest-to-God elementary school librarian. Who even knew they made those anymore? You're literally wearing a cardigan. Nice girl jackpot."

I drew the cardigan tighter over my chest. Apparently, I needed to date Anita Jones. She found me more irresistible than all my exes combined.

"Enough," Logan said, leaning over the table. "Alexis isn't some prize horse at a show. You don't need to twirl her around and slap her hindquarters."

It was the first time I'd heard my real name out of Logan's mouth, and at the sound, my body betrayed me. That familiar electricity zipped through me, making me lean incrementally in his direction. *No*, I reprimanded myself. *He left you at the hotel without a backward glance. No last name, no phone number, nothing. And while that's technically the point of a one-night stand*, rude. *Plus, he never told you he was a politician—and a playboy to boot!* Okay, good, now I was properly pissed at Logan again.

I cleared my throat, and all eyes fell on me. "I understand what you all get out of this. But what do I get?"

"Other than saving face with your employer?" Nora gave me a pointed look. "How about fame, glory, and thousands of new Twitter followers?"

Cary shrugged. "Don't you have a SoundCloud to promote or something?"

It was my turn to scoff.

"Then what do you want?" Nora asked. "Because we can't offer you money. If that got out—"

"I don't want your money." But her question lingered: What *did* I want? To turn back the hands of time and never set foot in the Fleur de Lis seemed out of the realm of possibility. The truth was, I didn't know. I'd never been good at understanding how I felt or even what I thought when put on the spot. Usually, I liked to mull things over in private, preferably while reading a book. My feelings usually dawned on me hours or even days later, like watercolor paint slowly blooming on a canvas.

Every single person around the table, Logan included, watched me. "I'll have to think about it," I said, and saw them deflate. Suddenly this was the last place on earth I wanted to be: in a room full of disappointed strangers. I shoved back from the table. "I have to go."

Nora leaped to her feet. "Totally understandable. It's a big ask. Just—please don't talk to anyone about this until you talk to us. Here." She thrust a business card at me. "Take this. My cell's on the back."

"And decide fast," Anita said. "We can only stall the reporters for so long. We have to jump before Mane does."

I nodded over my shoulder, wrenching the door open. "Right. Process fast. Got it."

"The clock is ticking!" Anita called. All the people at their desks whirled to look at me. "The vultures are circling!"

I put my head down and booked it out of the office.

6

Strictly Professional

I'd almost made it across the parking lot when a deep voice called out behind me, "Alexis, wait."

I stopped, heart rate spiking. Because of course I knew that voice. I gave my silver Jetta a longing look, then took a deep breath and turned.

Logan strode out of a back door I hadn't noticed. His office was one of those quirky old renovated brick buildings that seemed to be everywhere downtown, and with its steepled roof, it looked like it could've been a church once upon a time. *Don't find a stitch of this charming*, I instructed myself. *Eyes on the man charging toward you. The clandestine political operative. The cad. The very good kisser—*

I was still shaking my head when Logan caught up to me. He looked like he was all wound up to say something, but when he clocked my face, he paused and huffed, "What?"

"I was just thinking that the last time I saw you, you were running in the opposite direction. Interesting how the tables have turned."

"Oh, good." He grinned and I thought, *Uh-oh*. His expression was the gleefully manic one of a man who loved to rumble, getting his heart's desire. "The gloves are finally coming off. Well, the last time I saw *you*, your name was—" He made sarcastic little air quotes. "Ruby Dangerfield."

It clicked: Logan wasn't just angry at the situation. He was angry at *me*. What nerve, when he was the one who'd gotten us into this mess.

"You lied about everything, all night," he said. "Your family, your friends. You're not even related to Rodney Dangerfield!"

Just like Saturday night, Logan had a strange effect on me: my brain took his unapologetic brashness as an invitation to stop worrying about everything before I said it. "Oh, come on." I snorted. "If you actually believed *Ruby Dangerfield* was a real name, that's on you."

He shoved his hands in his pockets. "I bet you never even went on an archeology trip to retrieve a stolen artifact from the mouth of the Himalayas."

I crossed my arms. "Of course I didn't, because that's the plot of a children's novel. It's disconcerting you didn't know that."

"Ha!" Logan rocked back on his heels. Okay, so we were doing this. Out here in the parking lot, with the faint tang of gasoline in the air and a beautiful robin's-egg blue sky stretched above us. "You're right. I work in politics. I should immediately suspect every person I meet is trying to pull some con on me. So what was your plan if the fire alarm hadn't gone off? Spend the night with me, then take off in the morning, secure in the knowledge that I could never track you down because I didn't have your real name?"

My cheeks were flaming. "So I told a few white lies." I spun and beelined away. Unfortunately, Logan's legs were long, so he had no trouble keeping up. "You're the one who dumped me in an ambulance and took off without another word. But I guess that's your MO, seeing as how you're a playboy and all." I finally reached my car door and started to yank it open—then thought better and turned back around. "Is that how you end it with all your women, or am I especially not worth the goodbye?"

"My *women*?" Turning around to face him had been a bad idea. Logan stepped closer, shaking his head. Despite his tone, I could feel myself drawing nearer to him, pulled by the hard planes of his chest in that fitted white dress shirt, the dark line of his jaw, shadowed with stubble, the long column of his throat, Adam's apple bobbing above the knot of his tie as he swallowed. I reversed course, backing up until my shoulders hit the car. He only leaned in closer. I was caged.

"What I don't understand," he said, in a low voice, "is why you're so bothered. Admit it. You were going to drop me at the end of the night and disappear without a trace."

"Like you *literally* did?"

"There were photographers! I was trying to avoid this exact—" He stopped and scrubbed his hands through his hair, unleashing his curls. Then he looked up at the sky. He was silent for several beats, like he was counting in his head. "Okay," he said finally, his voice tightly leashed. "For the sake of a truce, let's just say neither of us was planning to see each other again and leave it at that. I get that publicly dating me is the last thing you want to do, since you went to such elaborate lengths to ensure I knew nothing about you. But—look. Winning this race means everything to me. And my team wants it as badly as I do. I don't always agree with Nora's methods, but I trust her. And she thinks doing this is the only way to keep this story from being the meal my opponents feast on from now until November."

My car door was warm from the September sun. I leaned harder against it. Witnessing Logan prostrate himself felt unnatural. "You really don't have to..."

He sighed. "I didn't come out here to argue, or close the deal. I came to say I know we're giving you the full court press. But you don't have to do this."

This man was more confusing than an illustrated cover on a romance novel. What the hell was going on inside his head? "I don't?"

"Of course not. If you don't want to, I'll figure out a way to keep your name out of the press. I'll make sure no blowback falls on you, I promise. But—" He blew out a breath, and caught my eyes. The look on his face was intense as usual, but this time, intensely sincere, like he was gearing up to make a speech. This must be the Logan Arthur politician face. I swallowed, unable to look away. Damn, he was good.

"If you're even *considering* it," he said, "I want to assure you the last thing you need to worry about is whether I have feelings for you. I have zero interest in being in a real relationship with anyone. So if you're concerned that agreeing to date me would be awkward because we already kissed: I promise it won't be. You don't have to worry about me thinking it means anything, or, God forbid, making overtures. We both had a lot to drink Saturday, and clearly acted out of character. Probably for the best it got cut short—"

I practically tripped—standing still—in my haste to say, "*Obviously* for the best. Well done, lightning, is what I've been saying."

He gave me a quizzical look, but mercifully moved on. "The point is, if you're even considering saying yes, please know I intend for this to be entirely professional. I'll—I mean, the whole campaign—we'll treat you with the utmost respect. No funny business."

How in the world was I supposed to get a handle on *my* thoughts when Logan's were so illegible? Did he want me to say yes or did he want me to say no? I knew I should be thinking this through logically, considering all the angles, but what my brain kept returning to was *I want to assure you the last thing you need to worry about is whether I have feelings for you.* And every time it went there, it felt like poking a bruise. A tender, sore feeling.

"Thanks for the, uh...reassurance. I'll take it under advisement." I popped the car door and sank into the driver's seat. "And I'll get back to you. *Soon*," I added, at the look on his face. I shut the door, wrenched my eyes from the window, and pressed the ignition to escape.

7

A Sip of Euphoria

No one in the history of the world had ever googled anyone as furiously as I was googling Logan Arthur. I'd assembled all the essentials for a deep dive: my favorite matching pajama set and fuzzy socks, a chenille blanket, and one of those fancy chocolate bars from the grocery store I told myself I would eat slowly, one square at a time, until the next thing I knew the whole thing had mysteriously vanished. I'd already spent a full hour down the Logan rabbit hole and showed no signs of stopping. In my defense, he was everywhere: there were endless articles, Twitter threads, and YouTube videos mentioning him. (Begging the question, once again, of how I'd failed to register his existence.) That, plus my formidable librarian research skills, meant I had plenty to chew on.

The term *mixed bag* was invented to describe Logan's press coverage. No doubt, there were some great profiles, particularly among the more left-leaning outlets, with headlines like "Logan Arthur Speaks Truth to Power" and "Meet Mane's Bold Challenger, Guaranteed to Give Him a

Run for His Money." He'd even gotten a few lifestyle media hits, articles like "Rounding Up the 10 Hottest Politicians" and "Meet this Texas Political Dreamboat," which had in turn spawned some enthusiastic Twitter threads full of eggplant and peach emojis. But the vast majority of pundits didn't seem to know what to do with him. "Young, Brash and Ballsy: Is Logan Arthur a Nightmare or a Godsend?" was the most obvious, but the confusion was also plain in competing headlines like: "Out of His League: Young Arthur Can't Play the Game" followed a few days later by "Refreshing: Logan Arthur Refuses to Play Politics as Usual." Then there was the half admiring "Logan Arthur: So Young But So Angry."

YouTube was its own treasure trove. I watched "Logan Arthur Caught Yelling at Heckler," which was a thirty-second clip of Logan walking out of some restaurant at night, doggedly followed by a man in a baseball cap. The guy kept saying something the camera didn't catch, until Logan finally snapped, turning to him with a loud "Fuck off—you got nothing better to do than chase me around?" The heckler ran off, which, good call, because the way Logan had raised his shoulders reminded me of a cat hunching up to pounce. That video naturally fed into watching "Dem Candidate Caught Dropping Impressive 12 F-bombs in 10 Seconds," which was exactly what it promised. And then my attention was snagged by "Logan Arthur and NBA Rockets Cheerleader." That video was the oldest I'd found, dated over a year ago. In it, a bearded Logan—my heart skipped a beat—stumbled out of what looked like a bar or a club with his arm around a gorgeous, leggy blonde. He helped her into a waiting car and rolled his eyes at whoever was filming before running to the other side and hopping in. As the car sped off, I thought, *Well, that sheds light on those playboy rumors.*

The most recent video was from *The Watcher on the Hill*'s channel, and it was titled, "Arthur Buttons Up." The text accompanying the video read: "This latest town hall marks a clear turnaround for the once-brash candidate. Obviously, someone has started listening to his PR team. Good for his career, I suppose, but this pundit for one will miss the old Arthur. Calling out corporate sponsors. Gut-punching his own party. The memorable time he called Mendax Oil CEO Sam Slittery a cockroach who would sadly survive the destruction of the planet he helped engineer. Never a dull moment." The still image was of Logan standing behind a podium, wearing a smile that was passable—unless, like me, you'd seen the real thing. The dazzling, full-toothed grin of Logan Arthur cracking up across the table because, miraculously, you'd said something funny.

I looked up and caught my reflection in the hall mirror. If I agreed to pretend I was Logan's girlfriend, it would be *me* in those videos. As in, the girl in the mirror. My brown hair was currently hanging limply over my forehead, since I hadn't bothered to brush it before settling in, and I'd stuck on my nerdy blue-light glasses to stare at the laptop screen. Even my pajama set, originally the height of glamor (the pieces matched! Unheard of.), looked dowdy next to the sleek minidress on the leggy cheerleader. I'd gotten so caught up in the Logan of it all, I'd forgotten to consider what else saying yes would mean: namely, heaps of attention. After a lifetime of being invisible, I'd come full circle and now tried to avoid attention at all costs. Reporters, Twitter followers, all the people Logan hobnobbed with—not only would they know my name, which was bad enough, but I'd have to persuade them I was his girlfriend. Would anyone buy *me* after the women he'd been with?

I was tilting my head to check if I had any sleeker angles when a knock sounded at the door. I lived on a sleepy street in a neighborhood full of older houses split into duplexes and triplexes. It was popular with teachers, single-parent families, and grad students, basically all of us who needed peace and quiet for a steal. No one ever knocked except at Halloween.

It's Logan, my brain shouted, though that made zero sense. Still, I fluffed my hair as I ran to the door. And wrenched it open to find...Zoey Carmichael?

"Lexy!" She raised a six-pack of what I assumed was beer, though the cans were tie-dyed. "Can I call you that? It's what I call you in my head." She grinned disarmingly, which wasn't surprising, given disarming charm was her whole vibe. Even though she was my age, maybe a year older, Zoey was one of my sister's friends, engaged to Lee's grad school bestie, Annie Park. Annie's proposal to Zoey at a lovely Italian restaurant was one of the top five most romantic experiences of my life. (And yes, all of my top romantic experiences were, strictly speaking, other people's.) Zoey was a talented painter who seemed to be doing well for herself. I'd always thought she was nice, but given she hung with the art crowd and I hung with the...over fifty and under thirteen crowd, there wasn't much overlap between us.

"Hi," I said. "Um...what are you doing here?"

Zoey's smile grew wider. She was super pretty—kind of a hipster mermaid—and rotated hair colors according to her mood. Today her long, wavy hair was a faded green, like she'd spent all summer in the pool. "Your sister said it was the anniversary of when your ex-boyfriend cheated on you, and you might need emotional support. Or, technically, she told Annie, because Annie's a licensed therapist and all. She was hoping Annie would swing by and talk to you since Lee's been so swamped. But I overheard and volunteered."

Ouch, Lee. I hadn't realized we'd reached the outsourcing-sisterly-duties phase of our relationship. I understood Lee had new responsibilities now: she'd just gotten elected, and was working hard to staff up and set her policy agenda. But Lee no longer having time for me reminded me of the period a few years ago after our dad died, when she retreated and it felt like I'd lost both my father and my sister in one fell swoop. That was an achingly lonely time I hoped to never repeat.

"Can I come in?" Without waiting for an answer, Zoey nudged her foot in the doorway and peeked inside. "Oh, it's cute."

"Right. Of course." Remembering my manners, I ushered Zoey inside. "You can put your beer in the fridge."

"It's not beer." When she got to the kitchen, she dropped her six-pack on the counter and twisted a can free. "It's a euphoric beverage. Nonalcoholic. Want one?"

I accepted the can and studied it. Tie-dyed, with *Happy* written in large script...and that was it. "What's in it?"

She shrugged, opening her own can. "I don't really know. They're mood enhancers. My friend Andromeda introduced me to them when we did Lee's alcohol cleanse with her."

"Is it...drugs?"

She laughed. "Of course not." Her face grew thoughtful. "I'm like ninety percent sure."

Well, today was a day for entertaining new possibilities, apparently. I cracked the can and took a sip. "Gingery."

"Wait until the happy hits." Zoey wandered past me into the living room. I followed, trying to discreetly fluff pillows and straighten things while her back was turned. "I've always wondered what your place looked like."

"You have?"

"Of course." She ran her hand over the back of my teal couch, draped with soft blankets, then moved to study my bookcases, so stuffed with books they were stacked vertical and then horizontal. I saw my place through her eyes: the shabby old furniture and abundance of plants on the windowsill, candles, and romance DVDs stacked in a tower under the television. She nodded. "It's cool."

"Cool?"

She ran a hand over the DVDs. "Kitschy."

"You can be honest. I have the apartment of an eighty-year-old spinster. Or Cathy from the cartoon strip."

She gave me a frank look. "You don't have any cats. If you did, I'd be worried."

I nudged my laptop screen so she couldn't see my open tabs, a mixture of Logan Arthur Google searches and Austin SPCA kitten profiles. "Hadn't crossed my mind."

To my surprise, Zoey toed off her shoes, dropped onto the couch, and reached for one of my folded blankets, wrapping it like a cocoon so only her small heart-shaped face and green hair peeked out. She leaned back and sighed happily. In under five seconds, she'd made herself more at home on my couch than I'd felt anywhere.

I sat down on the other end. "I'm really happy to have you here, but why exactly *did* you volunteer to come over?"

"Because I want to be friends," she said matter-of-factly.

I blinked. "You do?"

"For sure." She wiggled an arm out of her blanket cocoon and reached for her drink. "I'm going to be a married woman soon." She waved her left hand, her gorgeous emerald engagement ring sparkling. "And I need chiller comrades. Don't get me wrong, my current friends are awesome. Some of them are artistic geniuses. But they want to go out until five a.m. every night, and that's not my lifestyle anymore."

"Five *a.m.*? Do bars even stay open that late?"

Zoey laughed like I was joking, so I took a bigger sip of my drink. Come to think of it, there was a nice little buzz of pleasure tickling the corners of my mind.

She waved a hand at my apartment. "The point is, you seem like the kind of person who enjoys a Friday movie night, if you catch my drift. That's who I'm in the market for."

"Uh...thanks?" Is this really how adults made friends? You just chose someone, invited yourself to their house, and curled on their couch? I'd been doing it all wrong.

"So." Zoey rested her chin on her hands. "His name was Chris, right? Or do we prefer The Asshole Who Shall Not Be Named?"

Oh, right. In all honesty, I hadn't thought of Chris since... well, Saturday night. "I'm really fine," I told her. "He's not even on my mind."

"Well, *something* is." She leaned closer and squinted. "Your aura's all out of whack. Fireworks everywhere. You're stressing."

Aura? I rolled with it. "I mean, there is this thing I'm dealing with. It's a bit of an...unusual situation."

"Ooh," she drawled. "My specialty. Weird, wacky, déjà vu, hauntings, existential crises. Hit me."

Maybe it was the euphoric drink shaking up my brain chemicals into a cocktail of trust. Or maybe it was Zoey's open, eager face, and the fact that she'd put herself out there first. Because even though I was normally a private person, I found myself spilling the whole Logan debacle, from the moment he'd interrupted Carter at the Fleur de Lis to his campaign team's bewildering proposal.

"So," I said, wrapping it up. "Now I have to decide whether I'm going to say yes to this bananas idea and turn my life into chaos—not to mention work closely with Logan, who's either very kind and chivalrous or very terrible and rakish, I honestly can't tell. Or I say no and the fact that we hooked up becomes a news story that could get me fired. Because I just had to try to sleep with the political playboy on the night a hotel caught fire. And because society is still so backward that an elementary school librarian caught with her boyfriend is fine, but with a stranger—oh no, a woman who likes casual sex, bust out the pitchforks!" This speech would probably be more effective if I was in fact a woman who had ever experienced casual sex, but still, the principle stood. "You see my dilemma."

"I do *not*." Zoey was buzzing, which I worried for a second was a side effect of the drink that I'd catch next. But when she dropped the blanket and scooted closer to me, I realized it was simply excitement. "I see a very clear and obvious choice."

"Say no?"

"Say *yes*! Good lord, you're lit up like a Christmas tree just talking about it. Your aura's gone haywire. And it's the most romantic thing I've ever heard."

"*Romantic?*"

"Um, this guy steps in to help get rid of some creeper at the bar—"

"Out of self-interest, he said."

"Then spends all night listening to your life story—"

"Completely made up."

"Then kisses you within an inch of your life and puts down big money for a suite—"

Okay, that part was technically true.

"Has to run off *tragically* when he sees photographers, practically Cinderella fleeing the ball—"

I snorted. "Hardly."

"And now he wants to date you—"

"*Fake* date. He made it clear he has zero real feelings for me."

Zoey rolled her eyes. "That's what I'd say if I was trying to convince a woman to fake date me without coming across as a creep or scaring her away with the intensity of my emotions." Suddenly her face scrunched up. "Wait a second. I got so wrapped up in the romance I didn't ask if you liked his politics. Lee would kill me."

Right now, Lee could suck it. Nevertheless, I groaned, because of course she'd trained me well. That had been the first thing I'd googled, and the answer was annoying. "His platform is great. Really thoughtful, super progressive, just like Lee's. In all honesty, I don't know if the state is ready for him. Lee's environmental bill gave me hope, but..."

"It's still Texas outside this Austin bubble," Zoey finished. "Or so they claim. I refuse to explore outside of Marfa."

"Right. The Texas of it all. So I admire Logan. He's really economics-focused, has all these proposals to strengthen the security net for middle-and working-class people. Which, as an elementary school librarian, obviously I'm for."

Zoey sighed. "Tell me about it. A career as a painter sadly doesn't come with things like health insurance."

"Logan was born in Odejo, this rural farming town down south," I said, warming to my subject. "He went to Harvard for undergrad and grad school—got a master's in public policy from Kennedy. Then he came back to Texas and became one of the youngest Harris County commissioners in history. Those are the people in charge of Houston, by the way. He did that for four years, built a solid reputation, then announced his run for governor. He's young and hungry, that's for sure."

Zoey whistled, which I assumed was in appreciation of Logan's résumé until she said, "What'd you do, memorize his Wiki page?"

My cheeks heated. "I can't help if I'm good at retaining information."

"Why don't you ask your sister for advice?"

I shook my head. I'd relied on Lee too many times. Besides, this one was embarrassing. When I'd decided to go to the bar alone so I didn't fall flat on my ass in front of her and her friends, I hadn't even imagined this level of blunder was possible. I loved Lee, but I didn't want her to have to rescue me yet again.

"Well, then," Zoey said. "What I'm hearing is, the

decision's up to me. So that settles it." She ticked off her fingers. "A, you like Logan's politics, which means you're actually pulling for him to be the next governor. B, he needs *you* in order to stand a chance. C, it's terribly romantic. And D, best of all, it's the adventure you've been waiting for."

"It is?"

"You just told me you went marching into the Fleur de Lis determined to shake up your life. And look what the universe dropped in your lap. You must have some very good karma, Alexis Stone."

Well—I hadn't thought of it like that. Saying yes and stepping into the spotlight, shedding my inner mouse. It would mean embracing a wild adventure. A Lee-style shenanigan. Something old Alexis wouldn't have done in a million years.

"Besides," said Zoey, draining her drink. "You're in the power position. Logan and his team need you. You could make or break him. That means you can ask for whatever you want."

Back to that infernal question.

"The truth is," I said, feeling ashamed, "I don't have the foggiest idea what I want."

To my surprise, instead of giving me a pitying look for being an undriven, wishy-washy woman with her head in the clouds, Zoey shrugged. "No problem. Just ask for a blank check to be cashed whenever you figure it out. You're holding all the cards. They won't say no."

My mouth dropped open. Was Zoey a secret political genius?

She stood up and neatly folded her blanket. "I should probably get back. Annie's making eggplant parm tonight."

She nodded at the kitchen and grinned. "You keep the drinks. Get a little drunk on happiness, ya crazy kid."

I followed her to the front door, sliding my fuzzy socks over the wood floor. "Thanks for coming over. It was really nice of you."

She stopped in the doorway and turned to give me an appraising look. "You know, I might've been wrong about you. You might just turn out to be my wildest friend yet."

Timestamp: 7:48 p.m., Monday evening. If later this whole thing blew up in my face and people were searching for answers, I'd point them here, to the exact moment I knew that, God help me, I was going to say yes.

I closed the door, found Nora's business card on the counter, and picked up my phone.

8

Lolexis

The next morning I felt slick pulling into the last available spot in the parking lot and slipping in the campaign headquarters' unmarked back door. Especially since I opened it right as Logan was passing by, and he jumped back in surprise, almost falling into the wall.

"Boo."

"Shit, you're here." He shook himself and righted his tie. "I thought you'd come in the front."

"I have been told I'm a bit wild," I said, trying it on. "Unpredictable Alexis." I'd woken up in a great mood— perhaps because I'd gone on a euphoric beverage bender after I'd called Nora to say yes and she'd asked me to come in bright and early to discuss logistics, which I'd arranged quickly with Muriel, who agreed to hold down the fort at the library. It was either the liquid courage, the idea that Zoey—an actual human woman in her twenties—wanted to be my friend, or the fact that Nora had agreed to my terms, just like Zoey predicted, that was causing this warm, fizzy feeling in the pit of my stomach. And it had positively bubbled over upon finding Logan, the exact person I'd been thinking of, delivered on a silver platter.

What was *in* those drinks? There was no way this feeling was legal.

"You were supposed to come in the front," he repeated. He looked like he was going to keep harping on it, but I leaned in and dropped my eyes to his chest, and he abruptly stopped.

"Is that the same suit you were wearing yesterday? Don't tell me you slept in your office." Two staffers in rapid-fire conversation hurtled by, giving me wide-eyed looks. Come to think of it... I peered around the corner. The whole office seemed to be in a tizzy. There were people buzzing everywhere, some of them speaking into walkie-talkies. Was this a normal day?

Logan stepped out of the way as more staffers hurried past. "It's a different suit," he said curtly. "But also the same. I don't have time to think about fashion, so Nora made me a uniform. I own five of the same suits." He looked at me like he was waiting for me to give him hell.

"Huh. You should talk to my sister's chief of staff, Ben Laderman. He's very fashionable. He could give you tips."

"I know," Logan said bitterly. "Nora used him for something called *inspo*. Made a whole posterboard about it. Exceptionally annoying." He tilted his head and gave me a suspicious once-over. "What's got you in such a good mood? Did you look outside?"

"Did Nora tell you I asked for a blank check request? Anything I want?"

"Anything within our power," he clarified, like the stickler for details I could tell, from Googling his policy proposals, he was. Logan shoved his hands deep in his pockets.

"I didn't think you'd say yes," he added in a quieter voice. "I didn't let myself... I mean, I was surprised. So, thank you."

I think it occurred to both of us at the same time, because all of a sudden I could feel my face heat, and Logan swallowed thickly and looked away. "I guess we're technically..."

He nodded, still not meeting my eyes. But his body leaned incrementally in my direction. "Dating," he finished. "I mean, as far as the world is concerned..." His eyes slid to mine. Such a warm brown. Such long lashes. The way he was looking at me was like the first night in the hotel lobby, that moment of magnetic possibility when I'd wondered if he would reach out and touch me—

"There you are!" Nora hustled through the hall at an impressive speed given her sky-high heels. Logan and I startled to attention, and he took a discreet step back. "I've been looking all over for you. I thought you were coming ten minutes ago, through the front!"

What was with this coming through the front business? "I was just talking to Logan—"

She whipped to him. "You told her?"

"Told me what?"

Nora shook her head, incredulous. "You didn't—"

"I was going to!" Logan burst. "But then she..." He waved a hand. "Distracted me."

Nora rolled her eyes. "Save the romance for the cameras."

"That wasn't a line," he protested. "I only mean whenever she starts talking, I lose my train of thought. I'm working on it."

"Good. Because I need your A game." Nora turned to me and looped an arm through mine. "Walk with me."

Apparently, I didn't have a choice, because she was already tugging me forward. "Here's the thing. I know we were supposed to talk logistics this morning. But then we got wind that Governor Mane's team is holding a press conference. Rumor is it's about you and Logan. So, change of plans."

We wound past all the desks, dodging staffers as they ran to make copies or deliver armfuls of water bottles. "We're going to have to put you and Logan on fast. As in, now."

I stopped in my tracks, causing Nora to spring back like a rubber band. "What do you mean, put us on?"

She brushed her long French braid over her shoulder. "We have to scoop Mane. Hold our own press conference before his. Whoever speaks first will own the conversation."

Oh, no. No, no, no. I'd thought this morning would be about discussing rules and conditions, all the fine details, including my blank check request. No one had said anything about being thrust into the spotlight. In an instant, the warm feeling in my stomach was replaced with wild butterflies. "You want me to talk to *reporters*?"

"Logan will do most of the talking. But—" She held out her hand. Amazingly, a staffer walked up from the copy machine and placed a piece of paper in it like clockwork. "We have your talking points right here." She side-eyed me. "Is that what you're wearing?"

My mouth dropped open. "No one *told me*—"

"Okay, okay, forget I said anything." She waved. "Come on, we're tight on time. I was hoping you'd come in through the front so the reporters could see you."

"What do I even say to them?" I'd watched some of Lee's press conferences. There was that nice controlled part at the beginning when she talked, sure, but after that it always exploded into pandemonium, reporters hurling questions like baseballs, trying to strike her out. I couldn't handle that level of confrontation—I was terrified even *thinking* about public speaking. Besides, I hadn't even been trained. There was going to be training, right? Last night before bed I'd pictured it as some sort of *Karate Kid*-style montage where I slowly improved over the course of one bitching song from the eighties.

"What did we decide on?" Nora studied the sheet. "Oh, right. You and Logan met a year ago when he started attending campaign events in support of your sister."

"He did?"

"Yup. Rallied for her hard. A total coincidence, but we've got that on record, so that'll check out nicely. He's the one who approached you after a town hall and struck up a conversation—we're painting you as the shy one."

"I think I can handle that."

She scanned farther down the sheet. "The two of you bonded over your shared passion for community engagement, improving literacy, and...children's fantasy novels. Is that last one a joke? Logan added it. Sometimes I can't tell when he's joking or not. It's the quasi-British delivery."

"More like him trolling me," I said, feeling the butterflies beat their wings.

"Right. Well, your first date was six months ago, at this Italian place called Il Tempesto. Logan says it's romantic."

That was where Annie and Zoey had gotten engaged. It was the perfect date spot. I had a sudden strange moment of wistfulness for the life Nora was describing.

"You've been dating ever since but keeping your relationship private because neither of you wanted it to distract from your work. You're coming forward now, obviously, because people have the gall to suggest you're a fling." Nora eyed me. "You're taking notes on my tone, right? The *gall*."

"Got it." Inwardly, I shook my head. I'd never pull off that kind of righteous indignation. "What do we say if someone from the bar remembers us? There was this guy, Carter—"

"Logan told me. You say the two of you have ways of keeping the spice alive, and one of them is pretending to be strangers. We figure we can get a lot of mileage out of that excuse." She turned to me. "Okay, we're here."

And somehow, we were. I'd gotten so caught up in the story of my love affair I hadn't registered we'd reached the door. Nora squinted at me, then brushed invisible lint off my dress and fluffed my hair. "Best we can do," she said, which wasn't exactly comforting.

"Wait—"

"You'll do great. Let Logan take the lead, then he'll prompt you. When in doubt, mix a little truth in with your lie. It's what the pros do. There he is. Good, you got the pin."

Logan hurried up, buffing an American flag pin on his lapel. "We ready?"

"No," I said, at the same time Nora said, "As we'll ever be. Knock 'em dead."

Two staffers swung open the double doors, and there they were, a whole crowd of reporters gathered at the bottom of the steps. Well, maybe only ten, but between the pops of light from their cameras, the yelled questions, and the scampering production assistants, it felt like a hundred. I froze, rooted to the floor.

"All good," Logan said, eyes sweeping the crowd. He slipped his hand inside mine and squeezed. "They're just nerds with microphones."

I didn't have time to wonder at the warm pressure of his hand, the way calm spread through me, because Logan was grimace-smiling and striding toward the podium at the top of the stairs, tugging me along. He stepped behind it and tilted the microphone with his free hand. Below us, the reporters fell quiet. I looked at them, heart pounding. There were a few faces I recognized—like there, in the corner, CBS 12's Trisha Smith. Actual news celebrities had turned up to hear us speak.

I was grateful for Logan's strong grip, keeping me tethered.

"Good morning." Logan's deep voice rang out, carried by the microphone. "Thanks for coming on such short notice. I'm sure you all had busy days planned chasing ambulances and trying to get the attorney general to say something about his office brothel scandal on a hot mic."

Oh, God, was he—*insulting* them? But the reporters only chuckled and shook their heads like they were used to this.

"Compared to that, this statement about my love life is going to seem pretty tame. Fewer sordid details, I can guarantee."

Open laughter. I stood straighter. He was charming them?

"I wish there was this much interest in my plan to improve public data infrastructure, but alas. Since you're all so keen to know: yes, Alexis Stone and I are dating." He paused and looked at me. In my sheer nervousness, with my heart beating like a hummingbird's, I smiled so wide there was no way I didn't look deranged. "It's been six months now. Though, to be honest, she's had my heart since the first day I saw her across the room at a town hall, wearing this ruby-red dress. I thought to myself: now that is the most beautiful, most fascinating woman I've ever seen. I would be lucky to know her. It took me a while to work up the nerve to say something, which—" his gaze shifted back to the reporters "—you jokers know is rarely an issue for me."

More appreciative laughter. It was surreal: Logan spoke the lies so effortlessly that I was half convinced myself. With his thumb rubbing a comforting circle on my hand, it was hard to distinguish fiction from reality. He was very good. I was grudgingly impressed.

"We were *trying* to keep our private life, you know, *private*. Including the evening we spent at the Fleur de Lis." This time Logan practically growled the words. "But since Governor Mane is attempting to make mountains out of molehills by going after me personally—a clear sign he knows he can't compete on policy—" More snickering. "I'm here to nip this in the bud and introduce you to Alexis. Since my girlfriend is quite capable of speaking for herself, I'll let her tell you. Alexis?"

My turn already? Logan was looking at me in a prompting sort of way, and the eyes of the gathered reporters had turned to me, their expressions anticipatory, so all signs pointed to yes. Naturally, all thoughts flew from my head.

"Uhhhh..." There was a lump in my throat. I couldn't form words around it. "Hi, I'm... Alexis...as Logan said... And we are, um...dating. Obviously." In slow motion I floated outside my body to watch the train wreck unfold from a safe distance. He'd said to tell them about me, right? But what would they want to know? What was important about me? "I'm a librarian. Lee Stone's younger sister. Senator Lee Stone, that is. I like reading and, um, children..." I like *children*? Who was I, Willy Wonka? I was bungling this so badly. I looked at Logan in desperation.

He gave my hand one quick squeeze and smiled at the reporters, who wore looks of confusion. Which was only appropriate after witnessing a grown woman struggle to string twelve words together. "It's just like Alexis to be so modest. The truth is, she serves our community in a lot of ways: as a children's librarian, an adult literacy tutor, one of Austin's yearly book drive volunteers. And as a member of Senator Stone's campaign team, where she worked to increase voter participation."

Clearly, I wasn't the only one who'd done some Googling last night. When he said it like that, I did sound rather nice.

"Most important, though, is who she is. Alexis has a warm, tender heart and a mountain of compassion." I snapped my head to him, caught by surprise. "She's the real deal, and I'm proud to be dating her. So now that you know, I hope we can get back to discussing more important issues than my dating life, like the changes Texans deserve. Thank you. Have a good day."

I didn't have time to linger over what he'd just said because, like in Lee's press conferences, the reporters took Logan's curt dismissal as an invitation to start hurling questions.

"Logan, what do you make of the governor's claim that you're too immature to govern?" a man in a baseball cap yelled.

"What do you think of Lolexis as your couple name?"

called a woman near the front, with hair so stiffly styled it looked like a blond helmet. "Loganna? Alexagan?"

We had a couple name *already*? Why did they all sound like the name of an evil witch from Arthurian lore?

"Alexis, what do you think about the rumors that your boyfriend's a playboy?" called a reporter who I swear couldn't be older than sixteen. Was it even legal for him to be here, saying the word *playboy*?

But Logan ignored them all, turning away from the podium with seasoned indifference.

"Alexis!" A familiar voice cut through the din. "What's Logan like in bed?"

The crowd quieted. Logan stiffened midstride, then turned and marched back to the podium. He dipped his head close to the mic. "That's strike two, Trisha. One more and I'm banning you from my events. You're going to be stuck covering Mane's boring-ass, two-hour-long speeches at country clubs. Do you want to drink Arnold Palmers and eat Jell-O salad, Trisha? *Do* you?"

Lights popped as the cameras flashed. The reporters were cracking up, and all heads turned to local news celebrity Trisha Smith, who merely shrugged, unapologetic. "The people want to know, Mr. Arthur. Can't blame a girl for trying."

Logan rolled his eyes in a way that made it clear he very much *could* blame her, then spun away. The reporters exploded once more, tossing questions at our backs. I flinched every time I heard my name, fighting the natural instinct to turn. But Logan strode determinedly to the office, and the double doors swung open. Staffers pulled us inside and shut the doors tight.

"Really, Logan?" Nora didn't miss a beat, waiting at the entrance with her hands on her hips. "Boring-ass speeches? You know that clip's going to play on every TV station in the state. You couldn't just leave well enough alone, could you?"

Someone thrust a water bottle at me, and I took it gratefully, chugging cold liquid down my burning throat.

"She crossed the line," Logan growled. "I think I was exceedingly nice given the circumstances."

"Oh, yes, you were a teddy bear. Such a Kennedy moment for you." Nora's eyes flicked to me. "And *you*..." I gulped the last mouthful of my water. "I can't even start on you. There's not enough time. The important thing is, the governor canceled his presser. We scooped him."

A staffer rushed up, sweat on his brow. "Logan, there's been an oil leak in the gulf. We need to get out a statement ASAP."

"Shit," he said, and the whole room exploded into motion.

"Get that environmental policy professor on the line," Nora called as Cary ran by.

"Talk soon," Logan said to me, but it was practically an afterthought. He was already moving, staffers crowding every side, on to the next disaster. It wasn't until he dropped my hand that I realized how much I'd been counting on that warm pressure to ground me. I was the lone person standing still inside a whirlwind. As I watched the back of his dark, curly head move down the hall, suddenly I felt the pressure change in my ears, like I'd jumped underwater, feet-first into the deep end.

What had I gotten myself into?

9

Hurricane Lee

The knock at the door was so forceful I jerked up from the couch. The knocking kept going, and even though this made two unannounced visitors in twenty-four hours—a personal record—my stomach curdled. I knew exactly who stood on the other side of that door. The only person in my life with the combined gall and upper body strength to take the door off the hinges.

"Alexis Rosalie Stone! You open this door right now!"

My darling sister.

The second I twisted the doorknob Lee pushed through, rocketing past me like a Tasmanian devil, rattling the pictures on my entry table and gusting up the curtains. "I cannot *believe* you're dating Logan Arthur. Of *all people*!"

It was a miracle I could parse her words, given her screech had climbed so high I was pretty sure it now registered as a dog language. I followed her. "Okay, it's actually a funny—"

"And you hid it from me. Like a *sneak*." Lee reached my living room, and in one fluid motion kicked off her heels and started pacing barefoot around the coffee table.

"Don't you know I have to endorse Mane since he backed my Green Machine bill? Are you trying to start a family war?"

"Logan backed you, too," I said, feeling like that was an important place to start. "His chief of staff says he came to your campaign events."

Lee threw up her hands. "And you forced me to find out from the *news*. When I saw you pop up on CBS 12, do you know what I did? I spit water all over my assistant Trey, and now Trey has to sign a contract agreeing he won't sue me for harassment! You know, I heard the rumor yesterday that Logan Arthur was caught half-naked in public with some woman. But I refused to gossip about it to protect the poor unwitting girl. Imagine my surprise to find out that girl was *my very own sister*!"

"I wouldn't say I was unwitting—" Lee's face darkened.

"Look, I *am* sorry about surprising you," I said, using my most mollifying tone. "I had no idea I was walking into a press conference today. Did you see my hair?"

She kicked the carpet. "It did look a little flat."

"Exactly. Not the hair of someone who knew she'd be on TV." As I looked at her, standing in my living room radiating indignation, the impulse to assuage Lee lessened. In its place, a trickle of annoyance bubbled. "Though, you know...maybe if you bothered talking to me instead of sending your friends to do it, you'd know a little more about my life."

Lee's mouth dropped open, but no sound came out. I'd actually achieved the impossible: rendered my sister speechless. "I didn't realize—" she stammered. "I've just been so busy—"

"Yeah." I gave a little laugh. "It's almost like you're perfectly fine living your life without me."

"Lex. You don't really think that, do you?"

Did I ever worry that eventually my older sister's life would get so big and full of other people and accomplishments that I'd no longer be a priority? That maybe now that we were adults, with fewer family obligations to keep us in each other's orbits, she'd realize she simply didn't like me enough as a person to stay close?

"No," I said. "Of course not."

We stood motionless in the unconvincing silence.

"It's a lie," I said, in an effort to change the subject. "Me and Logan. Our entire relationship is fake."

If I'd stumped Lee before, this time I broke her. A scarlet flush climbed her neck. "It's *what*?"

I'd sworn not to spill the secret, of course, but I'd be lying if I said there wasn't some part of me that took pleasure in being the interesting one for a change. "It's a cover-up. So Logan can ward off the governor's attack and I don't lose my job to prudish parents."

"But—how—when—" Lee's eyes danced back and forth as she tried to fit the pieces together. Finally, she settled on: "*Why?*"

As enjoyable as it was to hold all the cards, I put Lee out of her misery and told her everything. When I finished, I stood grinning, waiting for her to congratulate me on being bold and ballsy and maybe even one-upping her.

But her expression, carefully blank while I'd recounted, turned disbelieving. She shook her head. "I can't believe you're doing this again."

I blinked, caught off guard. "I know lying is wrong, but—"

"It's not about the lying. I can't believe you agreed to be Logan Arthur's trophy girlfriend. A prop to help a man win office. You shouldn't play the good wife, Alexis—you should be the damn candidate yourself!"

"I don't want to be the—" I started, but Lee rolled right over me.

"What's the plan? You're going to stand by Logan's side, silent and smiling pretty, while he tackles all the substantive policy questions with his big man brain? That's everything I fought against with that douche-canoe Hayes Adams. You remember—you were there!"

"Of course I remember." Lee had run against Hayes Adams, a high-profile billionaire, for her state senate seat. Misogyny had run rampant in everything from the different treatment they got from reporters to the public's reception of each of their strong personalities. While Lee got questions about what designers she was wearing, Hayes got policy questions. And even though Hayes was a self-proclaimed feminist, he'd let it go unchallenged. "This is totally different."

"You just met the guy days ago. Do you even agree with his ideas? Oh, God. What if he's one of those Democrats who supports charter schools or carbon taxes? That's our name attached." Lee didn't give me the opportunity to tell her I'd vetted him before she was on to the next question. "What is Logan Arthur even doing running for governor? That child is like, twenty-five years old."

"He's older than you!"

"Honestly, who does he think he is?"

"Oh my *God*," I said, sounding like a teenager. Behold the terrible time-traveling power of arguing with your sibling. "First, Logan's a progressive running against a Republican for control of the state, so you should be all over that. And *of course* I agree with his politics—so do you. In fact, he wants to build on your Green Machine law and require all private contractors to go green if they want a government contract." I felt a triumphant second wind at Lee's expression: she was impressed despite herself. Truly, Google had never let me down. "Second, you sound jealous."

"That's ridiculous. I don't ever want to be governor." Lee got a faraway look in her eyes. "Do I?" She shook her head. "No. I'm running for Congress when my term is up. The point is, you're volunteering to be an accessory for this guy and you don't even know if you *like* him."

"Ben stands next to you and he's not just an accessory. I won't be Logan's."

A speculative look crept into her eyes. "Wait a sec. You're doing that thing you do—making that face. Alexis Stone, are you *into* Logan? Is that why you're doing this?"

It was my turn to sputter. "Of course not. Did I think he was a good candidate for a one-night stand? Sure, I'll cop to that." Even the memory of Logan grinning at me from across the table had my heart rate spiking. "But in my defense, I haven't slept with anyone in months. My judgment is cloudy."

"Ew, Alexis! No wonder you're making terrible decisions. You need to sleep with someone immediately. Do you want me to make a call?"

"No!" I pulled at my hair and a disconcerting amount came off in my hands. Arguing with Lee should come with a health advisory. "I'm just saying, it never went beyond physical attraction. I *do* think Logan has great policy ideas, but personality-wise, he's a menace. Arrogant, thinks he's smarter than everyone, has zero concept of the difference between a *lie* lie and a white lie."

"Huh," Lee huffed. "He sounds like my type, not yours."

"Don't get any ideas."

"Please." She shot me an injured look. "You know I'm reformed."

We glared at each other, trapped in a deadlock, neither of us willing to admit that the conversation had veered so far off course we'd forgotten precisely where it was supposed to go.

"Aha!" She snapped her fingers. "You're a trophy wife. That's why I'm mad."

"I get something out of this, too," I protested. "They're going to give me whatever I want as soon as I figure it out. They promised."

Lee's face fell, her features shifting into an expression a million times worse than anger. Disappointment.

"Lee—" I tried to stave it off.

But she bent and scooped her heels from the floor. "You know what? It really sucks watching you wait around so hopefully for people to give you things they're never going to give you. Especially when it comes to men. You've got to stop letting other people control your life. Stop playing second fiddle."

I'd been reaching to halt her, but stopped short. *That's* what she thought of me? It was one thing to reflect on

85

my own areas for improvement, but another to have Lee—the person I admired most in the world—voice the same thoughts. But like always, the anxiety of being in an argument made my stomach tighten and throat feel thick, so I could barely speak. "I don't think that's what I'm doing," I managed.

She looked at me and sighed. "I don't want to fight, Lex. But I'm your big sister. I have to call it like I see it. I know you have a spine in there. For once, I'd like to see you use it." She walked out, squeezing my shoulder as she passed. I listened to the front door open and close quietly, but remained immobile in the living room.

Okay. That one hurt.

IO

Life Is Short, Art Is Long

"If she would've just told him about their love child and not felt she had to raise the baby in secret, the prince would've rebelled against his family and whisked her away to his castle in Italy." Muriel sighed. "Trust me, I'm all for independent women, but it's a crime to be that stubborn."

The teacher's lounge was mercifully empty today: just me, Muriel, and Gia sitting at the coveted corner table, aka the table farthest from the microwave and all its weird ambient smells. Our romance book club meetings were always lively when there was no one around to inhibit our deep dives into the steamy scenes.

"But if Sophia *didn't* have a stubborn streak, the book would be fifty pages, max," Gia countered. "It would be nothing but a meet-cute and sex scenes." She and Muriel fell silent for a moment. Then Muriel said, "I'd rather like that, come to think of it. What about you, Alexis?"

The use of my name startled me out of my head, where I'd been replaying my conversation with Lee for the hundredth time. "Sorry—what was the question?"

"You've been in another world all day." Gia tsked. She held up *The Prince's Secret* in all its baby blue–jacketed glory. The handsome prince winked at me from the cover. "What's wrong?"

"Nothing," I said, which was a bald-faced lie. Getting into arguments with anyone—especially Lee—made me physically ill. My stomach had been roiling all day, and it had been hard to concentrate on anything, even book club, which was normally my favorite part of the week.

Muriel slapped Gia's shoulder, a movement that jostled her pink and blue scarves. They matched our novel's cover because Muriel was next-level festive like that. "It's obvious, isn't it? She's daydreaming about Logan. Who needs a fictional prince when you have a real-life gorgeous governor-to-be?"

Gia's eyes went wide. Uh-oh. We were finally opening this can of worms. Ever since ambushing me with *The Watcher on the Hill* post, Muriel and Gia had respectfully skirted the topic, picking up on the fact that I was flustered by the attention. But I knew they were only biding their time, and apparently our discussion of Prince Rupert and Sophia's illicit affair was emboldening enough to make that time today. "I still can't believe you kept him a secret for so long," Gia said. "Dating six whole months."

"I love that it was a secret." Muriel sighed wistfully. "There's nothing more romantic than a clandestine relationship."

"We didn't want to distract from Logan's campaign," I said, feeling my throat dry up. How had Logan sold this story so effortlessly? He'd talked about his feelings for me in front of the reporters with startling ease. "Really, the details aren't that exciting."

Muriel snorted. "How about you spill and let me decide? Use our steam-rating system. Is Logan a three-or four-eggplant kind of guy?" At my silence, her eyes widened. "*Five* eggplants?"

"Ugh, Muriel, no eggplants."

"Logan's packing *no* eggplant?"

I huffed. "That's not what I meant—"

"You've been dating for *months*," Gia repeated. "And here I was, thinking you were still hung up on Chris." There was a hint of hurt in her voice that made me wince. First Lee, now Gia.

"I really wanted to tell you," I said gently, putting a hand on her arm. "We just knew the press would go berserk if it leaked. And you know me. That kind of attention's my nightmare." A nightmare I'd just willingly signed up for.

Gia nodded, looking slightly mollified, and I breathed a sigh of relief. My decision was feeling less like a good one with each passing day. After a restless night tossing and turning, I'd woken at an ungodly hour to find an email from Nora already waiting in my inbox. It had an intimidating NDA attached and a link to Logan's private event calendar, with dates highlighted I was "strongly encouraged" to attend. There was also a fifty-two-page media training guide, with an ominous note to expect pop quizzes. Not exactly my *Karate Kid* fantasy come to life.

"I love a good two-different-worlds story," Muriel said dreamily. "You're just like *The Prince's Secret*. A handsome ruler and his lovely peasant paramour."

I started to smile, grateful Muriel was moving the conversation along, then frowned as it dawned on me that I was the peasant.

"Just like Prince Rupert, Logan declared his love for you on television in front of the whole world, but you still stubbornly demur."

Okay, so maybe there were some parallels. But when Muriel's eyes crept down to my stomach, surreptitiously checking for a baby bump, it was a bridge too far. I folded my arms over my stomach and shot her a warning look.

"Truthfully," Gia said, "I'm glad you have such a full life outside school." She was smiling at me, but her eyes were tinged with sadness. "Since none of us know what's going to happen next..." She gestured at the empty teacher's lounge.

The weight in my chest, momentarily lifted by Muriel's silliness, dropped back with a thud. While the gossip about my relationship with Logan had been a brief but welcome distraction, the impending budget cuts had recast their pall over the teachers and staff of Barton Springs. Now that the news was out, the only thing left to do was wait and grimly speculate about who was going to get the axe. I was pretty sure that's why the teacher's lounge was empty. When we were together, it was hard not to look around and clock the people you didn't expect to return. I'm sure a lot of people were clocking me.

Muriel dropped her head in her hands. "This is why I prefer fiction to real life. When Prince Rupert discovers Sophia can't afford her medical bills, he simply makes all maternal health care in Algrovia free. Meanwhile, my daughter Carmen has been fighting to make health care affordable for years and no one will listen. This is why I read all day. To escape the blasted world."

I'd uttered the exact same sentiment on a number of occasions. Why participate in hard and disappointing reality when you could escape into a book? But then it hit me like a bolt of lightning, jarring and white-hot uncomfortable: if I was *really* honest, part of what I was doing when I curled up with my books was waiting. Waiting for someone else to swoop in and take care of the hard stuff, like Lee was so good at, or waiting to meet the right guy who would magically solve all my problems, like Prince Rupert tried to do for Sophia. No wonder Sophia ran off to take care of things on her own. Suddenly, despite Muriel's protests, Sophia's choice made a whole lot of sense to me. Sometimes you had to save yourself. Maybe I didn't have a lot of practice being the one who stepped up and took charge, but I could try. In fact, now that I thought about it, the answer to what I should ask Logan's campaign for had been staring me in the face this whole time.

God, romance novels were smart.

"Ladies," I said, raising a finger to silence their chatter. "Hold that thought." I straightened my spine, picked up my phone, and opened Logan's calendar. It was time to cash in my check.

I I

Backroom Dealing

"I'm sorry, you want what?"

If I hadn't been so nervous, I probably would've appreciated the sight of Logan's unflappable chief of staff struggling to wrap her mind around my request, blinking at me from the other side of a dingy coffee table in a back office at the Texas Antique Car Society headquarters. But since I *was* exceedingly nervous, I just gulped and forced myself to sit straighter, lest Nora interpret any slumped posture as a sign of weakness. Lee had said to show my spine, after all.

"It's really quite simple," I said. "All I'm asking is—"

The door to the room flew open. "Oi, Nora," Logan boomed. "This time you've gone too far. I don't understand why I had to show so much skin—" He rounded the corner, caught sight of me, and froze. Cary, following close behind, ran into Logan's back and bounced off.

"Hey, what the heck?" Cary glared at Logan, rubbing his jaw, then registered me. "Oh. It's you. Fake girlfriend."

"What are you doing here?" Logan hastily rebuttoned his

dress shirt, which, when open, had showed a tantalizing hint of his chest that made me recall the hotel suite, when he'd stripped while striding to me. "I wasn't expecting you."

I swept my gaze to his shoes. Safer territory. "I came to tell you what I want for my blank check request."

"And it's a doozy." Nora waved a hand at the mismatched furniture around the coffee table. "You should sit. But first, since you obviously need reminding, I told you members of the Antique Car Society are older, upper-income constituents with lots of time on their hands. *Eighty-five percent* voted in the last election. They're a uniquely engaged population and they appreciate an attractive package. You may not be an antique car, but with that second button undone, you're a package I can sell."

"Oh, don't worry. Logan revved their engines." Cary flopped onto the armchair next to mine and grinned gleefully.

Logan glowered at him. "You know, it was going pretty well. I actually got some decent questions about my retirement reforms in the Q and A. And then the meet and greet started and they mobbed me like I was '61 Ferrari. I can still feel the phantom hands patting my bum. Pretty sure the words *Aren't you a nice-looking young man, would you like to meet my granddaughter?* are going to haunt my dreams tonight." He sighed and sank next to Nora on the love seat, dropping his head back and closing his eyes. My gaze drifted down his exposed throat, Adam's apple bobbing as he swallowed, until I realized what I was doing and forced my eyes away.

It was still surreal that less than a week ago, I hadn't been able to keep my hands off this man in an elevator. The memories kept surfacing at the most inopportune moments. Like this one. The mere sight of Logan's throat cracked the veneer of my professionalism, causing a hot eruption of longing, a flashback to what it felt like to touch him. It reminded me that I knew the way he tasted, how it felt to be pressed against his chest, the sound of his breath coming shallow and fast, even if none of it would happen again.

One-night stands—even unfinished ones—were a hell of a drug.

"Is it normal for people to be all over you at events?" I asked Logan, trying to distract myself. I hadn't anticipated running for office would be so much like being a Beatle. Lee had been popular, sure—she'd won her race—but no one had ever mobbed her.

"No," Logan muttered, his eyes still closed. "Ask Cary why this time was different."

Cary crossed one leg over the other, nonplussed. "Yeah so, I'm trying to turn Logan into a sex symbol. It's my contribution to the campaign. I've made a ton of headway with people over sixty—don't ask me why, maybe it's Logan's curmudgeon factor. I figured the car society was the perfect place to test his appeal. I might have...you know, hyped the crowd a bit too much in the meet and greet line. In my defense, I forgot how handsy straight people could be."

"Remind me to fire you later," Logan sighed.

Nora shook her head. "That's the third firing this week, Mr. Berry. A new record."

Cary chuckled, then noticed me staring. "What?"

"Your name is Cary *Berry*?"

He raised an eyebrow. "You don't see me making fun of your name, Alex-but-make-it-more-complicated."

Logan opened an eye and smirked at me. "Drives him nuts when I call him by his full name out on the soccer field. The rhyme just rolls off the tongue."

Cary sighed. "I still find it outrageous that my personal assistant role has been grossly inflated to include soccer companionship."

Like the two were in a ping-pong match, I turned to Logan, but he only shrugged. "I had to drop out of my league when the campaign started. Cary said he'd play whenever I needed to blow off steam. The guy's got no one to blame but himself."

"Yes," Cary said dryly. "Don't you love it when you make ridiculous promises in a job interview and then you're forced to actually fulfill them?"

Nora tapped her watch. "And that's your two minutes allotted to nonsense. Alexis, go ahead and tell Logan what you told me."

Huh. Logan must emit some sort of hypnotic gravitational field, because whenever I was near him, it didn't matter if I was about to face down reporters or make a high-stakes sales pitch: it was too easy to get sucked into his orbit and forget about everything else, including my fear. Switching gears, I clasped my hands primly on my knees and tried to summon a sense of authority. Best to just launch into what I'd rehearsed and ignore the heat blooming everywhere Logan's dark eyes trailed.

"In the last decade," I began, "the legislature has made cuts to the education budget that have resulted in a tremendous blow to the workforce. The number of staff employed in public schools has dropped twenty-five percent in the last five years alone, which in turn has resulted in larger class sizes, less individual attention for students, lower college admissions rates, decreased access to libraries, music classes, and art trainings, and a deeply demoralized teaching body. And it has disproportionately impacted low-income communities and communities of color." I wasn't Lee by any means—I lacked her rhetorical swagger—but I had always been able to count on research. I hoped Logan and his team would find the facts and figures compelling enough. "Word is the legislature's gearing up to cut again, and if the other schools in the state are anything like mine, every teacher feels like the apocalypse is nigh."

"The budget is something legislators are responsible for," Nora said. "Not us."

"Yes, but governors endorse or reject budgets in the end. So Logan has a bully pulpit." Thank God I hadn't glazed over the last time Lee vented so I could impress them with the term *bully pulpit*.

"What exactly are you proposing?" Logan was frowning. I couldn't tell if he was deep in thought or deeply skeptical.

I took a steadying breath. "That we promise to not only stop the next budget cut, but reverse it. I want to fight for an increase in funding to hire more teachers and staff, and give everyone who works in schools a modest pay raise. At least enough so they can afford the classroom supplies they pay for out of their own pockets."

"I'm sorry, Alexis." In yet another sharp suit tonight—this time electric blue—and with her locs pulled into an immaculate French braid, Nora radiated the authority I was striving for. "It's not that I don't think it's a worthwhile cause. But putting aside the fact that doing anything to the state budget is wildly complicated, *and* that we've already chosen our policy priorities, it's a conflict of interest. Logan can't campaign for an increase in funding that would directly benefit his girlfriend."

"He's not," I said. "I'm going to campaign for it."

She blinked at me.

"Um, I'm sorry." Cary leaned closer. "What was that now?"

"I want my own platform." I sat up as straight as I could in the lumpy armchair. "I understand you'll have to crunch the numbers and figure out exactly what we can promise. And that I would be using your campaign to advocate for something that benefits me personally. But so what? Corporations hire lobbyists to fight for them all the time." I thought of Gia's sad eyes in the teacher's lounge, Muriel's fear that, even after devoting forty years, her head could be next on the chopping block. "The people making decisions about education should have expertise in it, and who has more than us? Why *shouldn't* we stick up for ourselves?"

I realized I was breathing a little too heavily, so I forced myself to relax. "If you agree to adopt this position, you'll rally educators to your side. And if you have educators on your side, I promise: the campaign will be unstoppable."

It was the closest I'd ever come to giving my own speech. My heart was beating very fast. I resisted the urge to watch their reactions from behind my hands.

"*Okay*, Rudy." Cary whistled. "Way to become everyone's favorite underdog and unexpectedly clinch the game." He turned to Logan. "Coincidentally, still the only movie to ever make my dad cry."

"We can't do it." Nora leaned forward. "We'd have to

redo our budget proposal. Talk to other constituent groups. Consult policy experts." She shook her head at me. "You were supposed to want us to make you a TikTok influencer or put in a good word with your principal. Hell, I even looked up how to get Beyoncé to come back to Texas in case you wanted to meet her. I never imagined..." She shook her head, but this time, turned to Logan. "At best, it'll look like you're grasping. At worst, it'll look like you're letting your girlfriend dictate your politics, and that'll make you look weak. Either way, you'll face the same dilettante accusations we've worked so hard to avoid."

"I'm sorry you see downsides," I said carefully, heart skipping. I never disagreed with people out loud. "But this is what I'm asking for. If you want me to be Logan's girlfriend, the campaign needs to stand up for educators. And I get to use my voice."

Silence fell around the coffee table. I tried and failed not to sweat, feeling a misty dampness creep down my back. Finally, Logan cleared his throat, and all eyes turned to him. As blunt as he could be sometimes, I was learning that when it came to making hard choices, he tended to stand back and listen before talking. It seemed like a good, though possibly unusual quality in a politician.

He met my eyes, and—oh. In this moment, there was no pretending that being looked at by Logan—*really* looked at—didn't simultaneously freeze me and make my insides soar. I could only hope the effect would fade with time.

"Fuck me," he said, scrubbing his hands over his face. "Of course we'll do it. It's the right thing to do. Should've thought of it from the beginning."

"*Logan.*" Nora's voice was sharp, but her censure was

tempered by her obvious surprise. A feeling I shared. Logan had just said yes to making a major change for me. And even though I'd asked for it, a persistent noise was now humming in the back of my mind that sounded suspiciously like the words *He's doing what? Reverse!* on loop.

He removed his hands from his face and knocked on the coffee table, one short, decisive rap. "Cary, will you call those economics guys first thing tomorrow? We need them to look at the numbers and find a way."

Cary nodded smoothly. "Sure thing, boss."

Logan turned to Nora and braced his hands on his knees. "People won't think I'm weak, Nor. I promise. They'll think I'm strong for dating someone smart and passionate, who cares enough about her work that she's willing to go to bat. It's the decision I'd make if Alexis and I were really dating, so it's what I should do now."

Nora looked like she was about to say something, a protest on the tip of her tongue, but then her eyes flitted between Logan and me and she seemed to come to a decision. "All right. If that's the way you want to play it."

"Thank you." Logan turned to me. "And of course you should own the issue. You're the expert and my partner." He rose, running his hands down his slacks. "I mean, you know, as far as the world is concerned."

I jumped to my feet and turned to include Nora and Cary. "I swear I won't let you down."

This was really happening. This year, I wasn't going to hide my head in the sand and hope someone else fought the budget cuts. I was going to do it myself.

Oh, God: I was going to do it myself. On second thought, I didn't know how to fight. And I hated the spotlight. I didn't even like meeting strangers' eyes in the grocery store. I felt an immediate gut-punch of regret.

"Have dinner with me," Logan blurted, snapping me out of my spiral. Everyone's heads whipped to him. "If we're going to merge platforms," he continued, voice softening, "I want to hear more of your thoughts."

Our eyes locked. "That makes sense." I spoke slowly, testing the words. "Like a business dinner." This was good. We'd talk shop, figure out details together. But when Logan smiled and those small commas framed his dark eyes, my mind ran footage of him ushering the svelte Rockets cheerleader into a private car, topped with a flashing neon sign that said: *Like a date*.

"Excellent idea." Nora stood and whipped out her phone. "A public outing. Something frothy so we can warm the public to Alexis before she starts campaigning. I'll get reservations for this weekend and call my guy."

"Nora," Logan growled. "This isn't a PR stunt. No photos."

"Sure thing." She put her hands up in mock surrender as she strolled to the door. "Like I said, if that's the way you want to play it. You're the boss." But as she passed me, she winked, and I had the feeling that was not, strictly speaking, the truth.

12

The Love You Earn

My mother's face popped up on my phone screen while I was up to my elbows in chopped onions. "Ugh," I groaned, but put the knife down and pressed Accept with a sticky finger. Time to clean the screen again.

"Alexis!" Mom's giant grin fell. "Oh, no, what's the matter with my baby?"

"Nothing," I said, wiping my tears on my sleeve. "I'm just cutting onions." While I'd never been able to convince my mom to call me Catherine Earnshaw or Elizabeth Wakefield growing up, I couldn't get her to stop calling me baby now that I was grown.

"Oh, good," she said—then, "Ow, Jingle Bell, no!" as a cat leaped and seized a strand of her hair.

"Cat room again?"

She wiggled her hair out of the tabby's mouth. "It's coming together so well. We're close to opening." After my parents divorced when I was thirteen, my mom started an animal welfare nonprofit. Last year they'd finally raised enough money to build their first shelter-slash-vet clinic,

Happy Homes, on a plot of farmland outside Houston. It was basically a luxury hotel for pets, entirely devoid of cages, with plenty of outdoor space for dogs to roam and elaborate rooms with trees for cats to climb. Launching Happy Homes was a dream come true for her and I was proud, but work also dominated her life, much like Lee's. Meanwhile, I spent my evenings working through five-hour Julia Child recipes and marathoning Reese Witherspoon movies. The two Stone workaholics and me. One of these things was not like the others.

"I'm really happy for you," I said. "Can't wait for the big launch."

Mom pitched forward as a tiny gray kitten scaled her back and stood, victorious, atop her head. "Thank you, but I didn't call to talk about the shelter." She extracted the kitten and pressed him to her cheek. "Gandalf and I called to squeal about your boyfriend! We saw you on TV. Logan Arthur, honey—that's fantastic. I'm so happy you're happy."

Ah. The news had reached Houston. "Sorry, Mom. I didn't mean for you to find out that way." I clutched my hands and winced when onion juice made my fingers stick together. "I was kind of ambushed by the press conference."

She waved. "If I had a nickel for every time I learned about Lee's life through the news, I'd have a hundred Happy Homes by now."

I let out a deep breath. Thank God Elise Stone wasn't easily offended.

The sound of purring grew louder in the background. "So tell me about Logan," she said, raising her voice. "You know he was a commissioner here in Houston before his campaign, right? I always thought he seemed pretty great, and then I met him at one of Lee's rallies and convinced him to join our donor list. So obviously, I was right."

"You did?" An image of Logan scowling at a troop of kittens popped unbidden to my mind. He didn't strike me as the cuddly type. Maybe Nora had arranged the donation as a PR thing. How strange that he'd intersected with my life yet again—first with Lee's campaign and now my mom's nonprofit—and still, I'd never registered him. I was starting to think I'd been living with blinders on. Maybe there were certain things—certain people and possibilities—I hadn't allowed myself to see, simply because they'd seemed so wildly outside my comfort zone.

"Tell me how you met," my mom urged. "I've got to say, honey, I'm thrilled you've put Chris behind you."

A tidal wave of guilt hit me at the thought of lying to my mom, probably the person most genuinely invested in my love life. "It's still early days," I said, fiddling with the handle of the knife and then scrambling back when I accidentally pointed the stabby end at my stomach. "It's not like we're getting engaged or moving in or anything."

"*Mischief!*" Mom shouted, throwing the phone down and startling me. "Oh, no, *bad* Mischief. Hold on a sec, Mischief got into the bag of catnip. I'm about to have a dozen stoned cats on my hands."

I went back to dicing onions, listening to the sounds of my mother shooing the kittens, then apologizing to them for using her loud voice, then sweeping catnip. Finally, she huffed back on-screen. "Crisis averted." She blew a strand of hair out of her mouth. "Speaking of moving in, I forgot to tell you Ethan asked me to move in with him a few weeks ago."

I dropped the knife with a clatter. "He *did*?" Ethan was my mom's serious boyfriend, her first in a very long time. He was so kind I'd taken to him immediately, and eventually even Lee's hackles had gone down. "That's exciting, Mom." Maybe they'd get married. I felt a complicated rush of feeling at the thought—ninety percent joy, ten percent vestigial loyalty to my father, though they'd been divorced even when he was alive.

"Oh, I told him no," she said airily. "I've finally gotten my house exactly the way I want it. Plus, Ethan's house is so big and drafty. Not for me."

"Mom." My heart beat faster. "You can't say no. What's he going to think? He's going to break up with you."

My stomach dropped like I was on a roller coaster. Suddenly I was twelve years old again, devastated by the news that my father had cheated and my parents were splitting up. Before that, our family had been happy. Just months earlier, I'd had my big birthday sleepover that, against all odds, had turned into a success. I could still remember my dad wrapping his arms around my mom while they sang me "Happy Birthday" before the girls from school arrived, both of their faces glowing in the candlelight, the picture of bliss. Fast-forward six months and everything had fallen apart: Dad was moving out and Lee was angry all the time and home was filled with icy silence.

One night when I was too upset to sleep, I'd crawled into bed with my mom and cried against her shoulder. She'd held me, rubbing my back, telling me everything would be okay. I asked her the question that burned hottest inside me: *Why* was this happening—why had dad cheated, why was he leaving? Mom had stroked my hair and said, in a bone-tired voice, "I don't know, honey. Maybe I just couldn't give him what he needed."

As I lay there, pressed to my mother's side, the fear sank in. You couldn't count on anyone to stick around, it turned out, not even your family. Before that night I'd been naive enough to assume there were some people in life you never had to worry about, that you didn't have to work to win over. Some people who would always just love you and be there. But everything was more fragile than I'd realized. No love was free: you had to constantly earn it, or else lose it. The epiphany had stuck with me, the lesson solidified a decade later when my father was killed in a car accident and I learned what it felt like to lose someone in a way more profound than divorce.

Yes, you had to work hard to keep the people you loved with you; but sometimes, no matter how hard you worked, it simply wasn't enough. That was the greatest anxiety simmering under the surface of my heart.

My mom laughed on the other end of the phone. "Ethan's not breaking up with me anytime soon, Lex. Trust me. I'm the only person who knows how to make his favorite lasagna."

I bit my tongue, resisting the urge to bark at her that it wasn't a joke. That of all people, she should know not to make this mistake again.

She must've seen the concern on my face because she said, "Ethan understands where I'm coming from, baby. We've both been on our own for a while. He gets it."

"Okay," I said, though worry tugged at me. "If you say so."

"Oh, I forgot to tell you!" Her face brightened. "Happy Homes is making our first commercial!"

I swallowed deep, willing the tendrils of anxiety to unclutch my mind. "That's great. Sounds like you'll be on TV soon, too."

She waved. "Oh, I don't want to be in front of the camera. I'm more of an ideas person. And I'm thinking, if it ain't broke, don't fix it. You know that SPCA commercial with the sad animals in cages?"

"The one with Sarah McLachlan playing in the background?"

She snapped. "Exactly. It's so popular."

I frowned. "I don't know if I'd call it popular, Mom. Emotional terrorism, maybe."

She swept a hand out, painting the scene. "Picture this: close-ups on the faces of our poor sweet pups and kitties who came from bad situations and need forever homes. You can see the longing in their eyes, hear the narrator talk about how they've been neglected and abused—"

"Ugh, Mom."

"Well, some of them have! How do you think we feel? Anyway, the camera cuts to Lee—"

"*Lee?*"

She shrugged. "She's the most famous person I know. The SPCA got Sarah, and I have Lee. So Lee walks around Happy Homes and tells viewers we're reinventing the traditional shelter model, making sure our furry friends get the best care, but we need steady adoptions, otherwise we can't keep bringing in new animals."

"So it's guilt, followed by bragging, rounded out with a threat?"

"It'll be great. But for some reason, I can't get Lee to call me back about an audition."

I snorted. No surprise there. Lee loved her two cats, but I'm sure she wasn't chomping at the bit to star in a maudlin animal shelter video. "I'm sure she's super busy," I said, schooling my face.

"And when are *you* coming down to adopt one of these kittens? You've been talking about it forever." Mom got a hopeful gleam in her eyes. "You could take Mischief."

"Oh, I don't know." I remembered how Zoey said I was one cat away from sad spinsterhood. "Maybe one day."

"You know," Mom said thoughtfully, "if Lee isn't free to do the commercial, you *were* just on TV..."

"Oh, no!" I exclaimed, turning to the stove, where I rustled a phantom saucepan. "My onions are burning. Ahh, it's a fire! Sorry Mom, gotta go, love you, byeeee!"

13

All Eyes on Us

The waiter bowed. "May I help you into your seat, sir?"

"For God's sake," Logan grumbled, tugging the seat from the man's grasp. "I'm a grown man, I can pull out my own chair." He demonstrated by pulling his chair out slowly from the table and slipping into it, watching the waiter suspiciously.

"Thank you," I said, as a second waiter finished helping me slide up to the table. He accepted something from the hostess that turned out to be an exact replica of my cream-and-gold chair, except in miniature. He picked up my purse from the floor and placed it gingerly in the tiny seat. It looked upon the room with regal haughtiness.

"Oh," I squeaked. "The purse gets a chair." Of course it did. And here my whole life I'd been resting purses on the floor like a plebe.

Across from me, Logan eyed the waiter, who was now unfolding his white napkin with great ceremony. "Don't you dare," he said, as the waiter moved to place it in his lap. Logan raised an eyebrow, and the waiter, finally seeing reason, dropped the napkin and scurried away.

Logan nodded to himself, satisfied, then caught sight of me. "What?"

I couldn't help grinning. "You hate it here."

He gestured around the gilt ballroom. "You mean this shiny, gold-plated peacock parade? Of course I hate it here. Looks like King Midas barfed it up."

"No reflection on you," I assured the new waiter, who'd stopped by to fill our water glasses. "So why come, then?"

Logan rolled his eyes. "Nora insisted. Something about this being where politicians go to see and be seen. The crème de la crème, in her words. Twatville, in mine. Oh, hi, Senator." Logan waved and grimace-smiled at an older man a few tables over. "King Twat," he muttered under his breath when the man looked away.

I eased back, resting my shoulders against the seat. I'd been nervous walking into Apex, my first Michelin-starred restaurant, especially after so many heads had turned to watch us make our way across the dining room. But Logan's disdain for the place was a tonic. "Well," I said, "I do think this might be the fanciest place I've ever been. So thanks for the experience, at least."

Apex always made Austin's best-of-fine-dining lists. It was built into a grand old mansion in a part of the city where the streets turned residential, a charming neighborhood full of shops and eateries and million-dollar homes. No steel or skyscrapers here. So even if Logan changed his mind and canceled our business date right now, I'd chalk the evening up to a success. I'd gotten to wear my emerald dress, the silk one I never had a chance to wear, a Town Car had picked me up at my front door, and when I'd walked into the restaurant, Logan had been waiting at the hostess podium in a black suit so sharp it set off his stubbled jaw and thick black hair. He'd been talking to the hostess, but stopped midsentence when he saw me. The look in his eyes before he'd swallowed and schooled his face had caused a return of that fizzy feeling in my stomach.

Now, across the table, Logan's expression softened. He cleared his throat, then took a large sip of water. "Places like this are the opposite of how I grew up. They remind me that some people have so much, while the rest of the world is struggling. That's why I don't like it."

I cocked my head and studied him. The lighting in Apex was low and moody, and the single ivory candle flickering between us cast shadows under his cheekbones as he frowned. His eyes were dark and serious. "You don't even like campaigning," I realized.

He started to say something, then stopped. When he spoke again, he did it carefully. "I want to be governor more than anything. But yes. I'll admit I don't like playing the game. Schmoozing, kissing rings. It doesn't come natural to me like it does to Mane or even that old fart Senator Abington over there. But it's the price of entry. If you want to be in a position to change things, you've got to do it."

That sounded like a line Nora had drilled into his head. I wondered if convincing Logan to play nice had been part of the turnaround *The Watcher on the Hill* had described in his blog post—the switch to more mannered behavior that had won Logan his recent spike in approval. "Was it different when you started out?"

He huffed a laugh. "Yeah. When I ran for commissioner right out of grad school, I was myself. Heckled reporters when they said something misleading. Called out other politicians when they lied through their teeth. Told my donors when they were being unreasonable. And it worked—it got me elected and saw me through all four years. But that was a small race compared to this. When I started campaigning for governor, the Dem establishment told me they'd pull their support if I didn't behave and stop calling out their old-timers. And we needed their money, so here I am." He nodded toward the senator he'd waved at. "Muzzled and making nice with dinosaurs whose voting records make me want to pull my hair out."

Huh. So, the world hadn't wanted Logan the way he came, either. He had to work at being appealing, just like me.

He frowned. "Why are you smiling?"

"It's just nice to know I'm not alone. You seemed so self-possessed at our press conference while I was having a heart attack."

"That was your heart attack face? I assumed it was your dear-God-I've-made-a-huge-mistake-tying-myself-to-this-clown face."

"And here's your wine, Mr. Arthur, compliments of our sommelier." Out of nowhere, Logan's favorite waiter materialized at his elbow.

"For fuck's sake," Logan said, as we both jumped. "Stealth of a cheetah."

"Apex thanks you for dining with us." The waiter uncorked and started pouring, unruffled.

Logan eyed the bottle, which looked old and dusty. "Okay, I'm not going to say there aren't perks to the peacock parade. But somehow, it just pisses me off more." When the waiter left, he raised his glass. "May this give us gout, as we deserve."

I gave him a look.

"Fine. Here's to you and me, playing the game so well they let us in. To tear the whole thing apart from the inside."

I clinked his glass, but inside I was thinking, *Yes, of course*. I was a chess move to Logan. Another strategic decision he had to endure because Nora said it would bring him closer to winning. Why did I keep forgetting that? It was frustrating how much being around him felt like sitting in class after pulling an all-nighter, having to constantly resist the pull of my body to relax and sink under the spell of dreaming. My instincts said to sink into Logan and forget reality. It felt so easy and natural talking to him that I had to keep jerking myself awake to the fact that it was only part of a game.

"Here's to Trojan-horsing Texas," I said softly, taking a sip, and his grin turned devilish behind his wineglass. "So." I set my wine down. "How *did* you grow up? I mean, I know you're from Odejo."

He tapped his glass. "The talking points are that I grew up on a farm as an only child. My parents were small-time farmers who moved to Texas from the UK because they had this dream of the little red American farmhouse. The reality behind the talking points is that we were alarmingly poor and constantly struggling. Neither of my parents realized how hard it would be to be a mom-and-pop farm here. No matter what they did, they couldn't compete with Big Ag, never mind how green a thumb my mum has."

"Is that what gave you your political ambitions—watching them struggle?"

"Fuck yeah it was. That and a million other things. Some of my best friends growing up, their families worked for the big corporate farms around Odejo, and they got paid pennies. Never had job security or health care, always had to move around to find the next job, which meant my friends had to keep switching schools and fell behind. Meanwhile the people they worked for raked it in."

"Have you decided on your dinner choices?" the waiter asked, materializing once again like a ghost over Logan's shoulder.

Logan squeezed the table so hard his knuckles turned white. "You," he gritted out. "Didn't even hear you... breathing. Not even a warning cough."

"I highly recommend the prime rib," said the waiter, and when I looked at the menu, I almost gagged. Ninety-five dollars. Even if I hadn't just listened to Logan talk about how he'd grown up, I never would've considered it.

"I'll have the ahi salad." At thirty-two dollars, it was one of the cheapest items on the menu.

"The vegetable lasagna for me," said Logan.

"Very well, sir." The waiter swept our menus out of our hands and melted away.

"Are you a vegetarian?" Logan presented as the kind of man who might eat a cow raw with his bare hands if it pissed him off enough.

"I've seen how the sausage gets made," he said. "Literally. And I want no part of that. Besides, it's good for my blood pressure."

Huh. Logan Arthur, full of surprises.

He took another sip of wine. "You came out of nowhere with that education pitch, by the way."

"Sorry," I said reflexively.

He shook his head. "Don't be. I liked it. Nora was convinced you were going to ask for something frivolous, no offense to Beyoncé. I'm glad you care about policy. How'd you get into education?"

"I've always wanted to be a librarian." I repressed a smile as Logan took it upon himself to pour me more wine. The earthy aroma of the liquid as it filled the glass made me wonder what it must've been like growing up on a farm. "I've been a book nerd all my life. Escaping into reading's my happy place, so libraries were always safe, whenever school and other kids—" I cleared my throat. "I had great relationships with teachers growing up. I always knew I'd major in library science—"

"At UT, like your sister. And Mane," he added with a pointed look, twisting the wine bottle away from my glass without spilling a drop. For someone who detested fancy restaurants, he sure was good at them.

"Lee and I overlapped my freshman year and her senior, and then she stuck around for grad school." I hadn't considered anywhere else for college: Lee had gone to UT, so I'd followed. Not that we'd been close back then, despite how much I'd longed to be. Those were the dark ages when Lee was still reeling from our father's betrayal and pushed everyone away, me most of all. "I always knew being a librarian wasn't going to make me rich, but it's been gutting to see the state of schools from the inside. You have all of these talented, well-meaning educators, and it's like the system is determined to bleed them dry. It's really hard to give kids your best when you're worried about getting laid off all the time. Did you know a ton of schools don't even have a library anymore, let alone a librarian?"

"Wow," he said, wide-eyed. "What can we do—"

"Alexis?" asked a familiar voice. The sound of it stopped me cold.

No. What were the odds? I looked up—and sure enough, Chris Tuttle himself was striding to our table. The sight of him was a punch to the gut. He was slimmer now than when we'd dated, and growing out his hair, which gave him a bohemian-accountant vibe. He clearly hadn't transformed into an ogre overnight, despite the many pennies I'd thrown into the school fountain wishing for it.

"Chris," I gulped. I could feel Logan's eyes on me. "What're you doing here?"

He nodded behind us. "Out to dinner with my folks. They insisted I come say hi. Sorry."

I followed the direction of his gaze and found his parents, waving at me from a corner table. I'd forgotten the Tuttles were both doctors and had fine-dining money. Dutifully, I waved back. Unlike their son, Chris's parents had always liked me.

"So what, you two used to date?" Logan asked, with his usual tact.

"Oh, sorry—Chris, this is Logan, my, um..."

"Boyfriend," Logan said, giving me a quizzical look. He stretched out his hand. "Nice to meet you, mate." Chris shook Logan's hand with a smile, though when Logan released him, he winced and discreetly flexed his fingers.

"So, how are you doing?" Chris asked. "It's been, what... over a year?"

Logan's eyebrows perked up.

I cleared my throat. "I guess it has been. Who's counting, though? Time, it flies. Can't keep track of it."

Chris rocked on his heels. "I'm still dating Kim, by the way. The woman from, uh..." His voice trailed off.

Right. Kim. The woman he'd cheated on me with (the second time around). I felt my cheeks heat. Apparently, I was supposed to congratulate Chris on his accomplishment. "That's—I guess—I'm happy for you."

I felt Logan's warm hand close over mine and looked up at him. He was leaning across the table, wearing the sappiest face I'd ever seen, practically batting his lashes. It was so un-Logan-like that I actually had to bite back a laugh.

"I was just saying to Alexis that I can't believe we only met a year ago." Logan shook his head. "And dating for six months. I feel like I've known her forever."

"Oh." Chris swallowed. "I guess you guys got together pretty soon after we..." He cleared his throat but didn't finish.

Logan turned his sappy face on Chris and lowered his voice like he was sharing a secret. "I keep trying to bring up marriage and she keeps saying not yet, we're not in any hurry, let's enjoy the honeymoon phase. You know, that rip-each-other's-clothes-off part. She's a cheeky little devil. I can barely keep up. But I'm sure I don't have to tell you."

Oh, lord. He's really going for it. I felt my face flame and dared a glance at Chris. His face was the portrait of shock.

Logan gave my hand the briefest squeeze, though his eyes stayed trained on Chris. "*I* happen to think, when you know, you know. And who could spend ten minutes with Alexis Stone and not want to keep her? I mean, you'd have to be a supreme fucking twat to let *her* get away. A colossal, gigantic, ruinous level of nitwit—"

"Okay," I said quickly, tugging his hand.

"A ne'er-do-well fuckboy," Logan finished, smiling in satisfaction. "Don't you think?"

"Uh," Chris stammered. He looked over his shoulder. "Oh, shoot, my mom's calling me back. Gotta go."

I looked over Chris's shoulder at Dr. Tuttle, who was calmly eating her soup, and felt the most absurd streak of joy.

"Great to see you," I said, sitting taller. "I'm glad we're both in better places now. Sometimes a breakup really is a blessing in disguise, don't you think?"

"Sure. I mean—yes." Chris turned to flee, then stopped and glanced between Logan and me. "Thanks for not punching me this time." He darted away.

Logan's eyes gleamed. "Well, well, well. Don't *we* have a lot to unpack?" He rubbed his hands together in anticipatory glee, then nearly shouted when a long, disembodied arm slid his lasagna in front of him.

"Your meal, sir," said the waiter.

Logan pointed his fork at the waiter as he rounded the table to place my salad in front of me. "You know what? I'm not mad this time. Your timing's impeccable. I just worked up an appetite running laps around that guy."

"You're terrible," I said. "But also, thank you." It occurred to me that Logan would probably ask for more details about Chris, all of which were humiliating, so I blurted: "I still have a lot to say about education. Don't think you're getting off the hook."

He studied me, forked poised over his pasta. In the candlelight, his eyes were rich as melted chocolate. His mouth quirked. "By all means. Change the subject."

Over dinner we fell so deep into conversation about how I'd like to see the school system change that I forgot to notice the curious stares from other diners. I forgot everything, including that Chris was in the room, until the waiter handed Logan and me dessert menus and I looked over to find Chris's table empty. At one point in the conversation, when I'd started to get on a bit of a roll, Logan had thrown up a hand to pause me, rooted in his jacket, and pulled out his phone, asking if it was okay to record what I was saying. I'd never had anyone ask to memorialize my thoughts before, and it loosened my tongue: if Logan and his team actually thought what I had to say was worth listening to, I wanted to make sure it was good.

Logan insisted on ordering chocolate cake and coffee so I could keep talking. When the waiter placed the thick slice between us, he leaned close, dipping the tines of his fork into the icing. "If you could start campaigning anywhere, where would you go? Who's the core constituency we need to rally first?"

I watched the fork as he brought it to his lips. I knew the answer to the question, but it was hard to remember at the moment. "The, uh..."

He waited patiently, fork still in his mouth. Mentally, I shook myself. "The Texas Library Council's conference is next week, right here in Austin. Thousands of librarians from all over the state come every year. It would be the perfect place to talk to a bunch of sympathetic ears. I was thinking we could put up a booth. I can look up how to do that."

His fork clattered to the plate. "Brilliant. But leave the logistics to me."

"Deal." I took a bite of cake and almost groaned. This was better than a thousand grocery store candy bars. Why had I spent my life settling for inferior imitations when something this good had been out there waiting for me this whole time?

Logan's eyes were fixed on my mouth. "Do you—" He cleared his throat. "Think we should set some ground rules?"

I finished swallowing and sat straighter. Unlike Lee, I loved rules. They existed to make you safe and comfortable. "Yes. Rules. What were you thinking?"

"I think the first has to be the obvious one: no dating other people until we're past election day so we don't blow our cover. Will that be a problem?"

Right. Because of my robust dating life. "I think I can manage." I quirked a brow. "Can you?"

"I'm assuming that's a playboy dig. In which case I'm gracefully ignoring it."

"What about touching?" I asked, and rushed to clarify when Logan's grin grew wicked. "*Guidelines* around touching. If we're out in public, people are going to expect us to act like a couple."

"Well." He dragged a finger over the tablecloth. "What are you comfortable with?"

The memory of that exact finger tracing against my lips made me wrench my eyes away. But the image haunted: Logan holding me up against the elevator rail, my legs wrapped around him, shoulders to the wall, his finger brushing my lip before he bit it softly. A mix of tender and rough, like Logan himself.

His quiet voice filled the silence. "We'll probably need to hold hands."

I nodded, trying to regain my composure. "Holding hands, putting our arms around each other, kissing on the cheek. I think those are...safe. But obviously no real kissing."

"Obviously," he said. "I can't imagine a scenario that would require..."

Our gazes locked. And we both had to be remembering the same moment, when I'd spun him around in the lobby, catching his face in my hands. We had to be, because Logan's eyes had darkened into pools of ink, his expression so intense, eyes searching. It was the look he'd given me right before he'd seized me and kissed me back.

"Maybe—" I cleared my throat. "We should just agree to run all campaign decisions by each other first. And leave it at that."

"Right," he said, voice thick. "Sounds smart."

"Your check," the waiter trilled, and without missing a beat or even moving his eyes off me, Logan held up his credit card, already at the ready. The waiter seized it, eyebrows raised, and whirled away.

"Hey," I said. "You finally saw him coming."

Logan winked. "Finally saw him coming."

There was a slight, pleasant chill to the air when we stepped out of Apex onto the sidewalk. The neighborhood lights twinkled around us.

"I think that's your car," Logan said, pulling his blazer tighter and nodding to the sleek black Town Car waiting at the curb.

"Thanks again for—"

High-speed shutter clicks cut me off. Logan and I spun to find a short man in a slubby jacket with camera, ducking in the restaurant's flowerbeds.

Logan groaned. "I told Nora *no* PR. Oi, Larry," he called. "You know you don't have to hide in the bushes like a creep, right, man?" The photographer only shrugged, and Logan turned back to face me. "Sorry."

"Hey." I slipped my hand in his, keeping my voice low. "This is why we're together, remember?"

"Right," he said slowly, as if he'd forgotten. Then his mouth cracked into a smile and he lowered his voice to match mine. "You saying you want to put on a show?"

I used my stern librarian voice. "As long as it stays within the rules."

"Come here," he growled, and in one fluid movement he'd tugged me flush against him and turned his back on the photographer. My heart beat wildly as he pushed his hands through my hair and leaned in close. When he spoke, his lips brushed my ear. "How's this?"

From where the photographer was standing, it would look like we were in the middle of a torrid embrace.

"Technically," I whispered, feeling his stubble tickle my cheek, "within bounds."

His voice was quiet. "I don't know why any pap is interested in me. Monumental waste of time."

I breathed in his spicy woodsy-berry scent—a tad stronger tonight, like he'd freshly spritzed. "Maybe it's because you're thirty-three and you could be the next governor of Texas. Or that you're a known firebrand, you've dated NBA cheerleaders, and you look the way you do."

"She googles." He pulled back an inch. "Are you saying you think I'm attractive?"

I rolled my eyes and stepped even closer to him, wrapping my arms around his neck and trying to ignore that I could feel my blood pounding through every inch of my body. "Like you haven't had your appearance dissected a million times. You know what you look like."

His hands moved slowly out of my hair and trailed down to my shoulders, where they rested for a moment. Then, as if he was hungry for more, they kept sliding down my spine.

"There was also," I said, lifting to my tiptoes to whisper in his ear, "that time I kissed you."

A breeze passed and I felt him shiver. "I seem to remember you drinking a few whiskeys that night." His voice was low. "Wasn't sure if you regretted it."

I could feel my cheeks heat. Why had I started down this road? "Well, I *am* standing here, pretending to kiss you while a middle-aged man snaps pictures, so I could see how you'd question my judgment."

He was silent for a beat. When he looked down at me, there was tender amusement in his eyes. He leaned in, tucking a strand of hair behind my ear, and whispered, "Only one."

I frowned against his cheek. "What?"

"I've only dated one NBA cheerleader."

I pulled back to find him grinning, and rolled my eyes as discreetly as possible. "Can I ask you a question?"

His reply was automatic. "If I can ask you one." Ever the negotiator.

"Why did you say those things at the press conference about me being a good person? You barely knew me, and you didn't have to. I mean, I lied to you the night we met."

The photographer moved to catch our profiles, camera lights going off rapid-fire.

Logan wrapped an arm around my waist and drew me closer, cupping my face. "I've found there can be a lot of truth in fiction." His voice came out low and gravelly, his mouth so close to mine that if I raised my chin even a millimeter, our lips would brush. Each word shivered through me. "And there are different ways to get to know someone. Sometimes it's what they tell you, but a lot of times it's what they don't. Especially in my line of work. You learn to watch the way people act. When they're alone for a moment and think no one's looking, or when they talk to strangers. Even just the way they look at you. People are constantly telling you who they are if you're willing to step back and listen."

I thought of Logan at the Fleur de Lis, listening to me go on about my life as Ruby Dangerfield. In the conference room, listening with his arms crossed as his staff discussed what to do about the photo crisis. In the Antique Car Society office, listening to me and Nora debate the education policy.

"I felt good about what I said at the presser," he said simply. "You might've made up the details that first night. But I saw you."

His words cast a spell and I couldn't look away. Just the thought of him considering who I was so seriously made my limbs feel warm and heavy. His attention was a spotlight, but one I didn't mind.

"My turn," he murmured. "You said you were out to celebrate being done with your ex, and I don't think that part was a lie. Was it?"

"No," I whispered. The photographer could've evaporated for all I knew. I couldn't be bothered to check.

"And it was Chris?"

"Yes."

His gaze moved over my shoulder to focus on something in the distance. "I meant it when I said only a deluded man wouldn't recognize what he had," he said softly. "For whatever that's worth, from the near stranger playing your boyfriend." His gaze fell back to me, and he gave me a small smile. Almost wistful.

I realized in that moment that Logan didn't, despite the length of time I'd known him, feel like a stranger. Not in the slightest.

"That's it," the photographer grunted. "Got what I needed."

Logan turned. "All right, then, Larry. Say hi to the wife and kids."

The photographer was already shuffling away, but he tossed up a hand in acknowledgment.

"Guess we don't need to, uh..." I glanced down at the small space between us.

"Right, of course." Logan released me. "Show's over and you want to go home."

It was déjà vu when he swept me into the Town Car and shut the door behind me. Just like the video with the Rockets cheerleader, except against all odds, *I* was the glamorous woman now. As the car pulled away from the curb, I watched Logan through the window, standing on the sidewalk with his hands shoved deep in his pockets, so handsome under the streetlamps. And it dawned on me in that delayed way my feelings sometimes did that I didn't want this fake date, or business meeting, or whatever it was, to end.

And that was a problem, wasn't it? Because while I was letting myself sink into dreamy fantasies, Logan had been clear from the beginning about where he stood. *I want to assure you the last thing you need to worry about is whether I have feelings for you.*

I closed my eyes and leaned my head against the leather seat, repeating the words like a mantra so they would sink in. *I want to assure you, I want to assure you, I want to assure you.*

Stay awake, Alexis. No dreaming.

14

Pretty Womaned

"Don't think of it as a makeover," Nora insisted. "Think of it as a polishing."

I eyed Logan, who sat in the hairdresser's chair next to mine, covered by a black robe, face lathered with shaving cream. One stylist trimmed his dark curls while a second shaved him. His eyes slid in my direction, though he was careful to keep still. "It's nice once you get used to it," he murmured. "World of difference from my old BargainCuts."

Nora hadn't dragged me to just any salon—we were at Acid Betty, where even Lee struggled to get an appointment. It was one of those new places Austin was famous for, both painfully hip and wildly expensive. The salon was so grunge it looked like the kind of place that would eschew money as a form of capitalist propaganda, but, as it turned out, was quite the opposite. A huge chandelier made of metal spikes hung from the vaulted ceiling, and stylists dressed in black buzzed everywhere with their hair half shaved or dyed slime green. The hypercool stylists both intrigued and intimidated me, but none more than the woman standing behind my chair, running her fingers through my hair with a scowl.

It had been four long days since my dinner with Logan, and while the photos of us leaving the restaurant had popped up on both *The Watcher on the Hill* and the *Austin American-Statesman*'s *Out on the Town* blog—which had then circulated on Twitter, accompanied by a fifty-fifty mix of single-tear and heart-eye emojis—I hadn't heard a peep from the campaign. No texts or calls from Nora or Logan. Not even a *Parks and Rec* gif from Cary, who'd been DMing them to me nonstop ever since the Antique Car Society meeting. Apparently, he thought my impassioned speech about education had "Leslie Knope overtones," which I'd decided to take as a compliment.

At first, I'd passed the time by returning to the photos, admiring what an effective sleight-of-hand Logan and I had achieved. The pictures captured him stroking my hair and leaning in to whisper, and we'd genuinely pulled off the look of two people with natural chemistry. But as the days passed without hearing anything, I'd taken to checking Logan's event calendar and reminding myself that he was a busy person. And then, of course, I had to chastise myself for even noticing how long we'd gone without talking, because *we were not actually dating*. It was sad enough to obsessively check your phone waiting for a real boyfriend to call; doing it for a fake one made me question my grip on reality.

So it was no surprise that in my emotionally fragile state Nora had been able to catfish me into meeting her on the Drag, a shopping-heavy portion of Guadalupe Street next to UT, claiming Logan had important campaign business he needed my help with. I'd driven straight over after school only to be unceremoniously yanked into Acid Betty, where Logan was in the middle of getting a haircut. Nora had announced, rather triumphantly, that it was time to "spruce me up." No amount of insistence that I didn't need a makeover had swayed her. Somehow, I'd blinked and found myself sitting in this hairdresser's chair.

"Logan, your old BargainCuts charged you seven dollars for a haircut and got shut down for health violations," Nora said.

"I didn't even know hairdressers could *receive* health violations," I said.

"Oh, trust me, they can." Nora rolled her eyes. "And he *still* grumbled when I told him we were going to a different place."

"I won't apologize for appreciating a good deal," Logan muttered. "I'm a simple man." With an air of indignation, he leaned back and settled into his stylist's head massage.

Nora cocked an eyebrow and turned to me, tugging a strand of my hair. "Is it physically possible," she asked my stylist, "to turn this into a Jackie O sort of situation?"

I yanked my hair back. "We're not cutting it." I was attached to my hair. Lee had once told me it made me look like Belle from *Beauty and the Beast*.

"Vat about a leetle trim?" It was the first my stylist had spoken since I'd arrived. I was astonished to discover that on top of her goth clothing, facial piercings, and matte black lipstick, she had an accent that could only be described as Transylvanian. "At least let me do za gloss. Your hair needs voom."

"Voom?"

She waved her hand. "Interest. Life."

Okay, *ouch*. Nora, whose picture was probably in the dictionary next to the word *voom*, gave me a pointed look in the mirror. "You're about to be in a lot of photographs, Alexis. Do you really want the internet saying you have dead hair? Because you know they will."

It was true. The internet was vicious.

"Besides, you have that library conference coming up."

I did? I spun to face Logan. "You got me a booth?"

A champagne flute had mysteriously appeared in his hand, and he tipped it in my direction. "Even better. I called the council president and made a case for you to have top billing. You're the new keynote speaker."

Speaker? My stomach dropped, but I managed to smile—I think—and force out a thanks. Because obviously I was supposed to feel grateful.

Nora leaned over the back of my chair. "Do you really want all those *librarians* saying you have dead hair?"

"Ahhh, *fine*." I had bigger things to worry about now, anyway. Like my first speech. *You're the new Alexis*, I reminded myself. *Old mouse Alexis is the one with the fear of public speaking. You'll be brave, or at least you'll die trying, thus saving you from future speeches.* I eyed my stylist. "You have my permission to trim and do a gloss treatment. But nothing else."

"And add za layers."

"Okay, fine—and add the layers. But *nothing* else, I mean it. Please." I tried to look resolute, but shied away when she made uncomfortably long eye contact.

"I'm eighty percent certain she's a vampire," Logan said when all the stylists had disappeared. With the shaving cream cleaned off, I'd expected to find him baby-faced, but the stylist had merely sculpted the edges of his facial hair into perfectly straight lines. And it was just the right length between a five-o'clock shadow and the beginnings of a beard—which, until now, I hadn't realized was The Ideal Facial Hair.

"It's his signature look," Nora said, catching me staring. I jerked my eyes away and bit the inside of my mouth. "Polled the best out of all the options." Oh, Logan had *definitely* had his appearance dissected a million ways.

"It's my preferred look," he corrected. "That's why I wear it."

"Sure." Nora turned to me. "While I've got you captive, we're going to run through some light media training."

My stylist came back with a small cauldron of hair product and a paintbrush. "This is because of the press conference, isn't it?"

Nora cocked a brow. "What do you think?"

I sighed. Well, I *had* wished for a training montage. And now with this Library Council speech, I needed all the help I could get.

"See," Nora said, "what I just gave you is a perfect example of the kind of direct and pithy answer that works well with journalists."

My stylist started painting white goo onto my hair. "Do you have to stick around for this?" I asked Logan. I was beginning to look like one of my mom's long-haired cats after a bath. Meanwhile, Logan sat there freshly groomed, at what I had to admit was peak hotness.

"Oh, definitely." He winked. "Nora says I need as many media refreshers as I can get."

"Rule number one," Nora said. "Always be respectful to reporters, but never feel indebted. Remember, they might intimidate you, but you're doing *them* the favor. No need to suck up."

"But don't tell them when they're being nitwits either," Logan said. "Hurts their feelings, what few they have."

"Come vith me to vash your hair," said my stylist, and I stumbled behind her to the washroom, dropping my head back in a large black bowl with a hose attached.

"Never, *ever* repeat a question a reporter asks you." Nora peered down at me from above the bowl. "Even if you're trying to buy time. Especially if it's a hostile question. Cause you know what they'll do? Quote you, conveniently leaving out the question mark."

Logan popped his head over the other side of the bowl. "That's how *Do you agree that you're wildly unfit to be governor?* gets turned into a viral news clip of you saying *I'm wildly unfit to be governor.*"

"Got it," I said, then winced as my stylist blasted my scalp with icy water.

"Keep things short," Nora instructed, as I walked back to the hairdresser's chair, wet head wrapped in a towel. "For God's sake, don't ramble. The less talking you do, the lower the odds you'll say something wrong."

"And it turns out no one really cares if you studied Hume in grad school and developed your own theory of skeptical progressive economics," Logan said. And he was right, because as soon as he'd started talking, my eyes glazed over.

"Lastly," Nora said, as my stylist pressed me down into the chair and started snipping, "if you're trying to avoid answering a question, never say *No comment.* It makes you look shady. Always say, *Thanks for the question. The campaign will get back to you.* We never will, but it deflects the heat. Let's practice."

"Now?" I asked, distracted as the stylist snipped a disturbingly long piece of my hair.

Nora lunged in my face. "Alexis Stone, if we searched your browser history *right now*, would we find your top-visited site is SoftRoundChonks.com, a blog devoted to pictures of chunky circular-shaped animals?"

"What?" I yelped. "How do you *know* that?"

"Wrong answer!" Nora cried, but luckily for me, the stylist turned the blow-dryer on full blast and Nora's admonishment became literal hot air.

She must've cooled down during the ten minutes it took to dry my hair, because when my stylist floofed my crown and spun me around with a loud, "Much better, yes?" Nora clapped her hands. "You're a sorceress."

I studied myself in the mirror, turning my head from side to side. I never would've asked for a cut as asymmetrical and stylish as this, but I had to admit it made my cheekbones look sharper, which in turn made my eyes pop. I looked like a woman who barked orders into her cell phone as she power-walked to her corner office.

"What do you think?" Nora asked Logan, who was milling around sniffing bottles of shampoo.

He turned and studied my reflection in the mirror. His brown eyes locked with mine. "I liked the way Alexis looked before." Before my heart could drop, he added, softly, "But this is good, too."

"Excellent." Nora was already walking out. "Now let's do something about those clothes."

★

"I don't belong here," I whispered as Nora loaded my arms with blazers. "Any second now, someone's going to come tell me they don't have anything for me and I'm obviously in the wrong place."

Logan snapped his fingers. "*Pretty Woman*."

"What?" Nora asked.

"I'm like Julia Roberts in *Pretty Woman*," I said. "Trying to buy clothes somewhere out of my league." Driftwood and Rose was only three doors down from Acid Betty, but the atelier was as refined and minimalist as Betty was grunge-chic. I'd flipped over a price tag on one of the skirts and almost gagged, dropping it before my fingerprints could do any damage.

"Isn't that the movie where she's a sex worker?" Nora rifled through the racks. "Never saw it." She shot me an interested look. "Is it a political movie? The Arthur campaign supports sex work legalization."

"It's more a lighthearted rom-com about a quirky sex worker and a billionaire with a heart of gold."

"And that's not political? Sounds like billionaire propaganda to me."

"Miraculously, they found a way to dodge politics in favor of romance."

"That's silly." Nora's eyes went back to roaming the neat rows of fabric. "Love is always political. Especially for women. Who you care for and believe in, what you do with your body, who you're dependent on, the extent of your autonomy. Strange to me that people pretend you can separate the two."

"And you don't have to worry about paying," Logan said, zeroing in on my secret fear. He flicked a price tag. "The Democratic Committee insisted on a line item in our budget for grooming, even though I told them it was a waste of money."

"Oh, yes, the long lines at your speaking events have nothing to do with what you look like and everything to do with your recycling plan." Nora gave him a look that fell somewhere between fond and exasperated. "The good news is, you use a quarter of what we budgeted. So we've got plenty to spare for Alexis."

"Does that make the Democratic Committee my Richard Gere sugar daddy?" I mused, and Logan barked a laugh just as a gaunt, impeccably dressed woman flitted over. Oh, no—this was it. The moment I got asked to leave. My heart beat like I'd stolen something.

Strangely, the woman smiled at me, her expression full of warmth. "Hello, my dear. How may I help you?"

When I didn't answer right away, taken aback, Nora rolled her eyes and said, "We'll take another one of those Paul Smith suits in navy for this guy—you have his measurements on file—and a fitting room for her. Thanks."

"My pleasure," said the woman, and scurried away.

Logan and I glanced at each other. He shook his head. "She didn't even tell you you're obviously in the wrong place. Honestly, kind of a letdown."

"You really don't have to stand there handing me things," I said to Logan through the changing room curtain. It was oatmeal-colored, nearly sheer—I could make out the outline of his broad shoulders—and short enough that I could see his polished shoes on the other side. My heart wouldn't stop hammering as I pulled clothes on and off. With only a thin barrier between us, I should have felt exposed, but instead I couldn't help picturing what would happen if he brushed the curtain aside, drank in the sight of my bare skin... I shivered, goose bumps lifting on my arms.

"It's not a problem." His outline shrugged. "You know... I'm kind of happy you don't feel comfortable here."

I froze with a green sheath dress half on. "You are?"

There was a long pause. Through the curtain, I saw him lace his fingers together. "Yeah. Makes me feel less alone." He cleared his throat. "Anyway, how's it going?"

I tugged the dress down and looked at myself in the mirror. Then I took a deep breath and opened the curtain.

I'd caught him by surprise. His wide eyes drifted down, taking me in, the look on his face more serious than I'd expected. I turned my back to him. "Zip me?"

In the mirror, I watched him hesitate before his hand came to rest on my waist, the other finding the zipper. "Green's a good color on you." He tugged the zipper slowly.

"Thank you." The world narrowed to two sensations: the warm pressure of his hand on my waist and the light skim of his fingertips up my spine as he pulled the zipper. I bit the inside of my lip, wondering if it was possible for his touch to sear my skin, leave a mark. Though he touched me lightly, it felt like it could. And I would welcome it. Then I could trace the trail of his fingertips, proof this beautiful, quiet moment between us had existed.

He brushed my hair from my neck. "All done," he said quietly. But his hands didn't move.

Slowly, I turned to face him, pulse skipping. "So. What do you think?"

His eyes rose to meet mine, full of a sentiment I couldn't parse, except that it was heavier than I'd anticipated. The space between us became charged.

"You're gorgeous," Nora called, striding over with a pair of heels.

Logan stepped back. "What Nora said," he answered gruffly.

"Try these." Nora shoved the heels at me. "At first it's going to feel like you're walking on stilts, but just roll with it. Eventually your feet will numb, and then you're in business. These suckers are so hot it's worth it."

I groaned but reached for the heels.

Thirty minutes and three shopping bags later, Logan, Nora, and I were strolling along the edge of the UT campus when she suddenly stopped to glare at her phone. "Y'all go on ahead. I need to yell at an event coordinator."

Logan nudged his Wayfarers higher on his face. "If it's that fucker from the Log Cabin Republicans who keeps insisting we buy piñatas with Grover Mane's face on them, tell him to grow up. I'm a politician, not a troll." He turned to me and crossed his arms. "Why are you laughing? Out with it."

"You would be much more intimidating right now if you didn't smell like lavender aftershave."

He sniffed himself, then glared and gestured for me to keep walking. "After you."

I fell into stride beside him. We'd reached the part of campus where you could see the UT Tower in full view, and it always gave me a jolt of nostalgia. "You're actually quite soothing. The man equivalent of an English garden."

He turned to me and laughed, face cracking into a dazzling smile, wider than I'd seen from him. He leaned over and caught my hand, lacing our fingers together. "I think that's the first time I've been accused of being soothing."

My heart took off. *We're in public*, I reminded myself, nodding at the people we passed. This part of the Drag, close to the group of dorms known as the six-pack, the heart of campus, was always the most crowded. A prime spot to be seen, which was surely why Logan was holding my hand. Playing the part. But when he squeezed my hand and tugged me closer, all reason fled. I was simply a girl having a lovely afternoon with her boyfriend.

We were closing in on a crowd standing around a guy with a microphone. I couldn't hear what he was saying or read their signs, but rallies were common here—students loved to hold them in front of the UT Tower for visual impact. Logan and I would have to skirt them.

Or not.

"Afternoon, folks," Logan boomed, and I jumped. Instead of maneuvering around the group, he was beelining toward it. A few people on the outskirts turned at the sound of his voice, and I read their burnt orange T-shirts: Longhorns for Grover Mane. This was a *rally* for Governor Mane. We were in enemy territory.

But Logan didn't seem troubled. "Hi," he said, extending his free hand to a tall man in a burnt orange Longhorn cap. "I'm Logan Arthur, running for governor against Grover Mane." The man eyed Logan skeptically, but gave his hand a polite pump. Their interaction had more people turning, and I could see the guy with the microphone eye us. I wanted to melt into the street.

Logan cocked his head. "Mind if I ask what you like so much about Mane?"

The man in the cap made a scoffing sound. "He's a *Longhorn*. You always support your fellow Horns."

"That's right," someone else boomed. Around us, people were nodding and humming their agreement.

"Where'd you go to college?" asked the man. "Lemme guess: A&M."

Logan waved a hand. "Never mind where I went." He tugged me forward. "I want you to meet my girlfriend and campaign partner, Alexis Stone. She's a librarian over at Barton Springs Elementary."

"Hi," I said, though what I wanted to say was: *Where are you going with this?*

The man tipped his cap to me.

"Hon, remind me." Logan scratched his jaw. "Where'd you go to college?"

First of all: *Hon?* Second: So *this* was why Logan had grabbed my hand. He must've known about the UT alumni rally for Mane, and thought it would be a great time to show me off. I plastered on a smile. "Right here, *hon*. UT class of 2018. Hook 'em, Horns."

It was definitely the most deflated I'd ever sounded uttering those words, but no matter—the man in the ball cap had enough enthusiasm for both of us. He whooped and made little horns with his fingers. "That's right, bay-*by*. Hook 'em!" It caught on like wildfire, as it always did, and the crowd echoed it until the man with the microphone finally resigned himself to the fact that he'd lost his audience.

"Well, there you go," said Logan, who had now successfully commandeered the attention of the crowd. "We've got a

Longhorn at the highest level in our campaign, too. And you know what, I think we have some ideas for Texas that might interest you..."

I zoned out as Logan dove into his policy platform. He was good at this—far better than he gave himself credit for. And even though he'd clearly dragged me here to bait the crowd into listening to him, I wasn't mad. The whole point of our arrangement was to help each other. And I knew how badly he wanted to win—I'd heard it in the tenor of his voice, the fire in his eyes. He was right that people told you who they were in a million different ways. And when I looked at him, I saw his longing.

I was the one who kept confusing fact and fiction. And of course I was, because that was my shtick: trying to will relationships into being more than they were capable of. I'd done it with Chris when I'd taken him back after he cheated, convinced I could will us back to normal. And though I didn't really want to think about it, I'd done the same with my dad, thinking if I just tried hard enough, I could make our family whole again. Emotionally speaking, I was stuck in a *Groundhog Day* loop.

As if he knew I was thinking about him, Logan rubbed his thumb in a gentle circle over the back of my hand while he listened to the man in the hat talk about health care costs. A woman nearby looked down at our hands and smiled wistfully. I grimace-smiled back.

"Lex, did you want talk about our education plans?" There was a momentary pause in the man's monologue, and Logan was leaping in.

"Oh," I said, caught off guard. He'd never called me Lex before. It was surely only part of the act, but a traitorous bolt of pleasure shot through my heart. "No, you go ahead."

Logan gave me a questioning look, but launched in dutifully.

It was time to break the loop. Logan had been clear our relationship was professional and he wouldn't catch feelings. So starting now, I was going to stop putting stock in ridiculous daydreams and call a spade a spade. Manage my emotions. Stop giving away my heart.

Logan squeezed my hand and gave me a small, knowing smile as the man in the ball cap started talking about how he actually *did* agree with us that teachers needed more support—his wife was a kindergarten teacher, it turned out. I smiled back, encouraging but perfunctory, the perfect politician's smile. Nothing more and nothing less.

15

Greetings, My People

One too-short week later, I stood on stage and gripped the edge of the podium, squinting past the blinding lights at the crowd. The unnaturally fast pumping of my blood made sweat gather at my temples. I was actually here, at the Texas Library Council's annual conference, otherwise known as librarian mecca, on the verge of fainting. I tried to remember the tips Logan had recited as he'd steered me backstage: *First, most people are prats, so the bar for your speech is low. Second, most people are prats, so if they don't like you, that's why. Third, most people are prats, so for the love of God, don't picture them naked.*

Okay. Deep breath. Last year I'd simply been a member of the audience, cocooned in anonymous bliss. This year I was keynoting to over two hundred people. No big deal. Maybe I did have to breathe into a paper bag if large enough crowds of schoolchildren showed up to hear me read at story hour, but no matter. I could do this.

"Good morning," I said into the microphone, voice crisp and clear.

Heads turned as audience members looked at each other in confusion. Oh, no, it was 6:00 p.m., wasn't it? Right out of the gate, I'd ruined my speech. Desperately, I searched until I found Logan in the front row. None of the librarians close to him were paying any attention to me, all of them fixated on him, whispering and elbowing each other, so at least there was that. When our eyes met, he gave me a thumbs-up and mouthed, *Prats*.

Sharp heels clacked near the back of the auditorium. I searched for the source and found Lee scurrying into one of the chairs in the back row. She waved excitedly.

Lee was here. Pride coursed through me, replacing the anxiety and freeing me to think.

"To a brand-new day in education policy," I improvised, hoping the audience would follow. "Good morning to the dawn of a new administration that doesn't just pay lip service to the importance of school employees, but actually puts their money where their mouth is."

The murmuring stopped. The two-hundred-plus people in the audience were suddenly looking at me with rapt attention. Someone in the back even let out a wolf whistle, though on second thought that was obviously Lee.

"My name is Alexis Stone, and I'm here to talk to you about what's at stake in the upcoming governor's race. More specifically, I'm here to tell you what Logan Arthur will do for school employees if he's elected. He's not offering you empty platitudes like other politicians. We wanted you to be the first to hear that Logan is officially committed to ending the school budget cuts."

The crowd burst into excited applause. Logan clapped with them, eyes shining. *He's looking at you like a supportive colleague*, I reminded myself, *and you are looking back at him respectfully*. I squared my shoulders. "Not only that, but he's committed to *increasing* funding for education. He wants to make sure you get the financial support you deserve."

This time several people whistled. "And how do you know Logan's going to do right by educators? Because he's got me on his team, and I—like all of you—am proud to be a school librarian. Let me tell you exactly what we'll do if we win."

Here's the funny thing about public speaking: surely I kept talking after that, and I had a vague sense the crowd kept applauding, but for the life of me, when I looked back, I couldn't remember. All I knew was that somehow, I arrived at the part where I said *thank you for having me* and the entire audience rose to their feet, clapping.

Which meant I'd actually done it. And it had gone okay.

"Alexis Stone for governor!" yelled Lee. Up in the front row, Logan whooped his agreement.

The conference organizers wrestled a mic into place below the stage and a queue formed for Q and A. In the back, Lee took this as her cue to scramble out of her row, waving goodbye. I wrestled back disappointment. I'm sure she had important business to get back to. At least she'd shown up for my speech. I faced the growing line at the mic and forced myself to focus. I wasn't out of the woods yet.

The first person in line was an extremely short woman with glasses. "Thank you for your remarks, Ms. Stone. My question is, could this extra funding be applied to moving my school's library out of the gymnasium?"

I blinked at her. "I'm sorry—your library is located in the gym?"

She nodded, pushing up her glasses. "My principal moved it there after last year's budget cuts. We had to lease out the old library building to a Jimmy John's for textbook money. The reason I ask is, the students keep mistaking me for a ninth grader, and I'm tired of getting pelted by dodgeballs."

And I'd thought the situation at Barton Springs was dire. "Um, yes, definitely the extra funding can go toward getting you out of the gym and back into the Jimmy John's."

The woman thanked me and returned to her seat, revealing the next questioner, a woman in a long cardigan with a headful of wiry curls. She grabbed the mic and spoke so close into it the reverb echoed through the auditorium. "I have had a rat making a mockery of my library for the last sixty-five days. He has taken over the graphic novel section and has started stealing my lunches. No matter where I hide them, he finds them. I've laid out maybe twenty-five, thirty traps, but no dice."

"Wow—" I started to say, but she wasn't done.

"He has now moved on to eating the books themselves. We're in a full-blown war, and I regret to say there have been some casualties among the student body. If I had to guess, I would say Chernobog—that's what I named him—takes up seventy-five, maybe ninety percent of my time on a day-to-day basis. Will your budget expansion help me defeat him?" She finally blinked, waiting for my response with grave anticipation.

I had so many questions. But also, an instinct not to ask them. "Sure," I said finally. "You can use the extra funding to address pest infestations."

"Great. Who will you call to help me? Specifically?"

I looked desperately at Logan. The jerk was choking on silent laughter. *FEMA*, he mouthed, and it took all my power not to roll my eyes. Some help he was.

"The, uh, Department of... Pestilence... Mitigation?"

The woman considered for a moment, then nodded in satisfaction and strode from the mic. I breathed a sigh of relief.

"Hi." The next woman's voice trembled with nerves. "My name is Gabby Bui. My middle school is located in a conservative district, and I found out we're banning a book that addresses sexuality in what I believe is a frank and helpful way. Parents have complained to the city council that teaching kids about things like masturbation and how their bodies are going to change during puberty is too graphic, but I think they're stigmatizing what's natural." She took a deep breath. "I guess my question is, could there be additional funding to strengthen the Library Council's anti-censorship committee? I'm not blaming anyone, because I know you're all as busy as I am, but it's been hard to fight back. And I can't do it on my own."

I had yet to deal with a book banning issue, for which I thanked my lucky stars. "Absolutely," I said, without thinking twice. "The campaign will see what we can do to bolster the Library Council's anti-censorship efforts. It's critical we defend First Amendment rights." From the front row, Logan gave me a discreet thumbs-up.

Relief flooded Gabby's face. "Thank you. It's been a lonely road."

"Don't worry. We're with you."

"Hi," said the man who stepped up to take Gabby's place. "Gregory Dillinger. Mine is a six-part question, but I need to preface it with a story."

"Great," I said, lifting my chin. "Hit me." Because you know what? I was kind of nailing this.

Waving goodbye to the last of the conference organizers—each of whom wanted their own selfie with him—Logan shut the door to the greenroom and leaned against it, dropping his head back against the wood. He met my eyes and a lazy grin spread over his face. "Alexis Stone. Political fucking dynamo."

"I'm just glad it's over." I flopped onto the couch, lying down and kicking off my heels, letting my bare feet dangle over the arm. As Nora had promised, a few hours in those shoes and I'd stopped feeling my toes.

Logan walked over and stood at the arm of the couch, near my feet, grinning down at me. "Remember when you wished everyone good morning?"

"Can it, jerk." Forgetting any sense of propriety—I was drunk on the sheer relief of being offstage—I kicked his thigh, hard enough to make him take a step back. Instead of swatting me away, Logan snagged my foot.

"Hey!" My momentary playfulness was replaced by a jolt of alarm. He was touching me. It was equal parts exhilarating and terrifying. I tried to kick free, but he only caught my other foot. He might've been standing while I was lying down, but the gesture felt wildly intimate.

"For real," he said. "You killed it."

I groaned, hiding my face in my hands. "I don't know how to tell you this, but...public speaking gives me hives." I peeked out from between my fingers.

He rubbed his thumbs idly over my arches and I tried not to think about how good it felt, the sudden return of sensation after the heels. "Yeah," he said. "I definitely knew that."

"What gave me away?"

He frowned. "Pretty much everything, from the beginning. Most recently, though, it was when you handed me smelling salts backstage and made me promise to use them on you when you fainted. Not if you fainted. When."

"You knew this and you said yes to me being your education spokesperson?"

His fingers slipped under the silky fabric of my slacks, circling my ankles. The slight touch crackled every nerve ending awake. "I trusted you knew what you were doing. And obviously, I was right. You're a natural."

"Hardly. My hands are still shaking." But I was so relieved at his words I felt almost buoyant.

"You know you don't have to do anything you don't want, right? We can go about this another way."

I shook my head. "It's important to me."

"You were right about how bad things have gotten. I couldn't believe some of those stories." Suddenly, he gave my ankles a firm tug, pulling me closer to him. I gasped in surprise, but it only made his mouth tug up at the corners. "Hey. I know what you need to unwind."

Dragging me even closer had caused his fingertips to slip higher up my calf, under the wide leg of my dress pants. It was only the smallest distance, but my breath caught in my throat. In an instant, I pictured Logan bending over the arm of the couch, hands sliding up my inseams until they were between my legs, the friction of his fingers sparking heat through the fabric. It was so vivid I could almost feel the pressure, the electric charge. I squeezed my legs together, hips twisting, and hoped he couldn't tell what I was thinking. Logan and the ridiculous lust he inspired—I wasn't used to my body reacting so viscerally to anyone.

He cleared his throat and gently lowered my feet, releasing me. "Come get a drink with me. I know the perfect place."

Drinks alone with Logan. *Bad idea*, whispered my voice of reason. *Too high a risk. Danger zone.*

"I'm sure you have plans," he added hurriedly. "It was just a thought. You know, figured we could celebrate your success. As colleagues."

He was just suggesting work drinks. And I *had* pulled off one of my biggest professional accomplishments to date. Maybe I deserved to let loose. After all, I knew what my night would look like if I said no: I'd go home to my apartment, curl up under a blanket, and watch the bold women in my favorite romances lead lives full of adventure. When I'd finally soothed my longing for companionship, or at least taken the edge off my loneliness, I'd click the lights and go to bed. Same as every night.

Maybe I could try something different, this once.

"You know what," I said, sitting up and smoothing my pants. "Tonight, I think I'm free."

16

The Hideaway

The instant we pulled up to the small building on the dark street, thunder boomed so loud it rattled the Town Car's windows. The sky split open, letting loose a sheet of rain.

Logan leaned over me to peer out the window. "It's a monsoon."

Our driver, an older man whose name I'd learned was Nigel, nodded. "The news reported strange weather patterns in the area." He eyed us in the rearview and spoke excitedly, giving off big dad-whose-weather-channel-watching-has-finally-paid-off energy. "They're saying the hot and cold air has been gusting up unpredictably. Opposite forces coming together. We're in for a ride tonight. Maybe the thunderstorm of the year."

I'd be drenched the minute I stepped outside. These heels were *not* made for walking, especially in a flood.

Beside me, Logan laughed.

"What's so funny?"

"First the lightning storm, now this."

"You're laughing because whoever's in charge of the universe hates us? Bold move, angering her further."

"I'm laughing because there are still people who say climate change isn't real. Take one look outside, fuckers. We've had more storms in the past few months than we usually have all year."

"What did I tell you about swearing?" Nigel asked, wagging his finger.

"I'm not putting dollars in a swear jar, Nigel. I'd be broke in a week."

I shook my head. "You and my sister are the only two people I know who laugh maniacally at bad weather."

"You want to make a break for it?" He glanced down at my feet. "Or I can carry you if you're worried about slipping." He must've read my expression, because he said, "Yeesh. Fine, too soon."

"Run on three. One, two—"

Logan burst out of the door and sprinted toward the bar, hands shielding his face.

"You didn't wait," I screeched, scrambling after him, then doubling back when I realized I forgot to shut the car door. "You monster!"

The rain was ice-cold. It took less than a second to soak through my clothes entirely, which I knew because there's no mistaking the feel of rainwater in your underwear. I stilt-walked as fast as I could to the entrance, where Logan stood under a green-and-white awning, holding the door open. He ushered me in and swung the door shut, and suddenly the pounding rain was replaced by the melancholic strings of a country song as the lights and warmth of the bar enveloped us.

The handful of bar patrons stopped talking to stare. I glanced at Logan and understood why—besides being a semifamous person, he currently looked like a six-foot-two drowned rat. I could only imagine what a sight I must be. My navy pantsuit clung to me like a second skin, and when I squeezed my hair, a small waterfall poured down. I waited for someone to recognize Logan and call him over, but all the bar patrons simply went back to their business.

"Come on," he said, nodding to the bar. I followed him, studying the place. It was tiny, no more than ten tables, and everything was made of old weathered wood. It was a dive, and not the trendy kind the hipsters had made popular on the east side. This was old-school, a dingy dartboard in one corner, a beat-up jukebox in the other, and old sepia photographs of men in cowboy hats lining the walls.

At the bar, a middle-aged guy in pearl snaps stood rinsing glasses. "Hey Jimmy, you care that we're dripping all over your floor?"

The bartender grunted and tossed Logan a single cocktail napkin. I guessed that meant no.

"It's mostly whiskey and beer here," Logan said, handing me the napkin. I took it gratefully, dabbing under my eyes. When I pulled it back, I noticed a simple logo scrawled across the center: The Hideaway. How appropriate that this was Logan's favorite bar. The man was a hideaway himself. He managed to be at once so public—literally, his opinions splashed in news coverage across the state—and yet so private, his innermost feelings closed to everyone. I especially couldn't seem to get a read on him.

As I was preparing to order, all the lights in the bar blinked out. A wave of groans echoed from the tables.

"Don't worry," Jimmy boomed. A match sparked as he lit a candle, placing it at the end of the bar. "Been open thirty years. No storm's gonna stop us now. I'm still slinging if you're still buying." He lit a second candle and placed it under Logan's face. The light danced over him like he was sitting around a campfire.

"You sure you want to stick around?" Logan asked. "I understand if you don't."

I sloshed closer to the bar. "Are you kidding? I'll take a Jack and Coke, please, Jimmy. Better make it a double."

Once we'd been served our drinks in Jimmy's finest plastic cups, Logan crooked a finger at me. "Come on. This is how you're going to unwind."

"*Darts?*" He was leading me to the board in the back corner. "You're asking me, a person with zero athletic ability, to throw needles in a blackout. I don't think you understand the concept of relaxing."

"Look, Jimmy's giving us candles." And indeed he was, placing two on a nearby table, giving our corner a warm glow. Logan set his drink down and pressed his hands together. "You're not going to make me beg, are you? Because that would be embarrassing for all of us."

"You'll never unsee it," Jimmy agreed gruffly.

I stuck out my hands. "Fine, give me the darts."

I was red—queen of hearts, Logan said—and he was black. I tossed my first dart and it narrowly skirted Logan's nose before clattering into the wall. He turned to me, amazed. "Should I be offended?"

"Told you. My lack of physical coordination is practically a party trick."

He peeled off his blazer and hung it over the back of a chair, then rolled up his wet sleeves. In the candlelight, his dress shirt was practically translucent, clinging to his chest. Oblivious to my staring, he squared up, faced the dartboard, and sailed a dart easily into the triple ring.

I narrowed my eyes. "Just how often do you play?"

"Oh, I never get to anymore." He chalked his score on the board. "Trust me, I'm rusty." As if to prove his point, he tried another and missed the ring entirely.

I squared up like I'd watched him do. Was it left foot first, or right?

"Here," he said, walking toward me. "May I?"

I took a deep breath. "Sure."

Logan's hands found my hips, tugging me toward him. "You're right-handed, so you'll want to stand like this."

I shivered against the warmth of his hands. The last time he'd held me this close was when he'd lifted me on top of the elevator handrail.

"And hold the dart like this." He put his arms around me and adjusted my fingers. "More control." He glanced down. "You're shaking."

"I'm fine," I said, unable to tell him it was ten percent rain, ninety percent his proximity.

"No, we can fix this." Ever the problem solver, Logan ran his hands up and down my arms, creating friction. "You look like some Victorian heroine come off the moor after a gale. Elizabeth Bennett or something."

I don't think he realized the enormity of the compliment. I swallowed hard as he continued to rub his hands over my arms.

"Regency," I murmured.

He stopped, hands resting on my shoulders. "What?"

"Regency heroine, not Victorian. Jane Austen published *Pride and Prejudice* in 1813... Never mind. That's the nicest thing anyone's ever said to me."

He laughed. "You're funny."

I squared up again and Logan stepped back. My muscles were loose and languid now, and when I tossed the dart, it landed in the outermost ring.

I gasped. "I got on the *board*!"

Logan tapped his glass to mine. "Cheers. Here's an idea. Why don't we make the game more interesting?"

"No way I'm letting you fleece me. I'm not that much of a sucker."

He put his hands up, the portrait of innocence. "Hear me out. No money involved. We'll play for something else. And for every dart you get on the board, you'll get double the prizes. I'll have to sink a bull's-eye to get one. You'll never get a better offer."

Hmm. I took off my own blazer and hung it carefully over the back of a chair, smoothing the wrinkles. I was acutely aware of how much this jacket had cost the Democratic Party. "It's an intriguing proposal."

He shoved his hands in his pockets. In the flickering candlelight, I could see the muscles flexing in his forearms. "What prize are we playing for?"

What did I want most from Logan? The answer came easily: I wanted to climb inside his head, know what he was thinking. But I couldn't say that, so I said the next best thing: "The truth. Whoever sinks their dart gets to ask the other a question, or two in my case. Honest answers only."

"Truth darts. A politician's nightmare."

"Oh, you're no politician." When he raised his eyebrows, I added, "I mean, not a very typical one."

"I see the honest thoughts are coming out already. Putting my ego on notice." Logan dropped the red darts into my hands. "Losers first."

Cheeky. I eyed the dartboard and made a silent plea to my arms: *We want this. We are highly incentivized. If ever there was a time for a miraculous showing of athleticism, it's now.* I pulled back and let the dart fly.

Right into the triple ring.

"No way." My hands flew to my mouth. "I didn't think that would actually work."

Logan stared at the board. "You hustled me."

"That was one hundred percent beginner's luck. Now pay up."

He dropped into a chair. "Man, Nora would kill me for agreeing to this. She says sorry for missing your speech, by the way. The campaign got invited to another event tonight. We had to tag team."

I sat down in the chair facing him. "I guess you drew the short stick?"

"Actually, I traded her to go to yours."

I blinked. He smiled, looking down at one of the candles as he cupped his hand over the flame. "It was this dental association gala. Black-tie. I hate the penguin suits."

Right. Logan trading to avoid putting on a tux made more sense than Logan trading because he was dying to watch my speech. I studied him from across the table. It was unfair, really, how beautiful he was. Moody lighting only made it more obvious, made his strong features more pronounced, showed that his lashes were so long they cast shadows. The candlelight flickering over his skin lent him a sense of motion, an outward restlessness that matched his mind inside. I could look at him forever and never grow tired of it. "Is this what your whole life is like? Double-booked on weekends, never any time for yourself?"

He shrugged, still watching the candle. "We're only two months out from election day. And I've been working on this for so long, can't let up now. Besides, I get little pockets of freedom." His eyes lifted. "Like tonight."

"It doesn't seem like anyone here recognizes you."

"I would be very surprised if Jimmy's regulars knew who the president was."

"So that's why you like it—the anonymity?"

"No. I like it because this place reminds me of home."

"The old-school cowboy vibes?"

He bent over his drink and pulled out the little black straw, sticking it in his mouth. "Simple, unpretentious. Like Odejo. Which is far from perfect, but I do miss it from time to time." He chugged the rest of his drink and dropped it on the table, ice sloshing. "Were those your two questions?"

"Oh, no." I shook my head. "You gave that away for free."

He winced. "All that media training and I'm still making rookie mistakes."

Wordlessly, Jimmy walked up and dropped two fresh drinks on the table. "Thanks, Jim," Logan said, as he returned to the bar.

"Did you order those?"

Logan shook his head. "Clairvoyance is one of many reasons Jimmy's great. Hit me with your questions."

"Okay. First one." Something that would crack Logan wide open. "What's your favorite childhood memory?"

I waited for his expression to change—a look of contempt, a groan, anything—but he stayed motionless. Finally, he said, "I can't tell you. You'll laugh."

"What? No, I won't. You can trust me."

He was quiet again, looking at me steadily across the table. Then he said, "Okay. My favorite memory is winning first place in the 4-H livestock competition when I was in eighth grade. With my pig Wilbur. Who I raised from a piglet."

My God. An image of him at thirteen flashed into my mind, clad in overalls and a red bandana—I assumed that's what farm kids wore—hugging a pig as someone handed him a blue ribbon. I squeezed my eyes shut as tight as I could. I'd promised not to laugh.

"You can ask a follow-up," he said gruffly.

"Oh, thank God." The questions flew out of me. "How often did you compete—was it like, a regular part of your childhood? What did you wear to the shows? How did you train Wilbur? Obviously, you've read *Charlotte's Web*. Was that your favorite book as a kid?" Knowing his favorite childhood book would be a Logan Information Holy Grail.

His eyes lifted to the ceiling, as if asking some higher power to lend him strength. When he spoke, he did it quickly, the verbal equivalent of ripping off a Band-Aid. "When I was young, my parents tried their hand at pig farming. I hated the idea of raising animals to kill them, so the first time one of their sows had a litter, I put my foot down. My parents were planning to raise the piglets to sell to a slaughterhouse, but I convinced them not to.

Truthfully, I was a pretty big shit about it, and I don't think they've forgiven me to this day. But I wore them down and they stopped. In exchange, I promised I'd take care of the piglets. Ended up getting close with one named Wilbur. Yes, I know naming a pig Wilbur is unoriginal, but in my defense, I was nine and I had just read *Charlotte's Web* and I was very emotionally invested. Pigs are smart and I taught Wilbur a few tricks that made him popular at fairs, and we began winning money. My parents made their expenses back, I proved I was right about not killing the pigs, and Wilbur lived a long and happy life. The end. It's not a big deal," he added brusquely.

I blinked. "Your best friend was a pig."

"You promised not to laugh."

"Your first political victory. You should tell that story to everyone, all the time. Like, every reporter."

"So they can go all moony-eyed like you?" Logan slumped in his chair. "No thanks. Let's have your next question. I want to make my bull's-eye and get out of the hot seat."

I looked at him shifting uncomfortably and grinned, deciding to go easy this time. "Favorite song."

He straightened. "They've got it here, actually."

"They've got Rage Against the Machine in the jukebox?"

"Hilarious." He took a sip of his drink and strode over to it. I watched him pull a dollar out of his wallet and slip it in. Within seconds, a song started, the melody low.

"Nice one," said Jimmy from the bar.

I could barely hear it. Was it a country song? Something old-school like George Strait? Actually, it barely mattered, because Logan was walking back to me, strumming an air guitar and looking more relaxed than I'd ever seen him.

And that was worth listening to anything, even "Amarillo by Morning."

Just as Logan reached our table, the guitars and drums came crashing in, the singer's voice soaring so I could finally hear the words: "I'd go the whole wide world, I'd go the whole wide world, just to find her."

"Your favorite song is by Wreckless Eric? That's so romantic of you."

Logan ignored me, strumming his invisible instrument. "Watch this. I'm going to make it." He grabbed a black dart as the chorus climbed. Logan threw it expertly and it landed in the triple ring, missing the bull's-eye by a centimeter. "Shit," he groaned.

"Condolences on sucking," Jimmy said, sliding a pitcher of beer onto our table like some sort of magic bar fairy.

Universe, don't fail me now. I grabbed a dart and lined up my shot. The jukebox sang "I'd go the whole wide world just to find out where they hide her," and I grinned at the image of teenage Logan belting the words in his bedroom, then threw.

"You've got to be kidding me." Logan gaped at the board. The song finally faded, and in the quiet he glanced at me. "Oh, you have a bad look in your eyes. I'm going to hate this next question, aren't I?"

I summoned my courage. "You told me you didn't want to be in a real relationship with anyone. Why?"

We were standing only a few feet apart, candlelight drawing the room closer, but still it felt like a mile. As he looked at me, his dark eyes were impossible to read.

"Because," he said finally. "I don't want to get my heart broken again."

My own heart beat too fast. For the second time tonight, our intimacy felt dangerous. A warning bell echoed in the back of my mind, but I ignored it. "Who broke it the first time?"

Logan's gaze cut away. After a beat, he said, "Tinsley Westcott."

I folded into a chair, searching my memory. I couldn't remember a Tinsley from Google. "How?"

He rubbed his jaw, looking at me doubtfully. "You really want the whole story? I don't come off well."

I nodded and he sighed, sinking back down and pouring us both beers from the pitcher. He slid one to me. "I met Tinsley in grad school."

I sipped. "At Harvard."

"Right. Most of the people who went to Kennedy grew up pretty different from me, but Tinsley was the most extreme. She was from this old Connecticut family, generations of Harvard legacies. I was the first in my family to go to college. She fascinated me, and for some reason, I fascinated her. Wrong side of the tracks allure, I guess. We were inseparable through grad school."

I tried to let go of the soreness that bubbled up. It wasn't from picturing Logan in love—though that was a little tender. It was the easy way he spoke about grad school. I'd wanted to go quite desperately, to keep following in Lee's footsteps. The plan had been to get my master of library sciences at UT, then apply for one of those higher-paying library jobs that only took people with advanced degrees. But I'd been rejected. The only person I knew who was. All of Lee's friends had gone to grad school. In fact, her friend Mac, who did something important in finance (no one knew exactly what), had what, nine degrees by now?

My mom had assured me life simply didn't go our way sometimes, but I'd always attributed the rejection to the lacking in me that I couldn't put a finger on. I felt the pang every time budget cuts rolled around and I was reminded it wasn't only Muriel's experience but her MLS degree that made her more valuable. Now, looking across the table at Logan, who'd gone to Harvard twice, all I could think was, *boy are we cut from different cloths*. He'd said this story didn't show him in a good light, but I couldn't look at him and see anything but a top-quality human. Golden-auraed, in Zoey-speak. Laurel-ringed, in Harvard. We were so different. What a comedy of errors for our paths to have crossed the way they did.

"After graduation," he continued, "Tinsley followed me back to Texas. We had all of these plans. She wanted to work politics behind the scenes, and I was going to be the person out front. She was gunning for me to run for a state position right away, but I didn't think I was ready. When I found the race for Harris County commissioner, I thought it was perfect. Tinsley cared about elections, but I was more worried about doing the job right if I won. I thought commissioner would give me good executive experience, but she was disappointed. I asked her to be part of my campaign, one of my advisors like we'd planned, but suddenly she wasn't interested. Commissioner wasn't ambitious enough, I guess."

I didn't say it, but Tinsley sounded like a real Lady Macbeth.

"I'm not proud of this, but I started to shut her out. She didn't want to be part of my campaign, so I wasn't going to give her the satisfaction of hearing about it, or invite her to events. And you know how time-consuming a campaign is: pretty soon we were living two separate lives. The week before the election, she told me she was leaving me and moving back to Connecticut. It crushed me. Thank God I was so far up in the polls, because I could hardly function the last week of the race. We barely edged it out. The night I won, after all that work, I couldn't summon a flicker of happiness. I just kept thinking, *I won, but I lost*."

"Where is she now?"

"Married to a US senator. Lives in a big house in Greenwich with two kids. She got what she wanted." He gave me a hesitant look. "That whole...playboy thing. You might remember."

"It rings a distant bell."

"The problem is, it's true. After Tinsley left, I threw myself into flings. It was...misguided, but it felt better than being sad. I had a string of meaningless hookups and got a reputation. When I started eyeing the governor's seat and hired Nora, the first thing she told me was my personal life was going to undermine my career, and I needed to get it together. I thought, wouldn't that be the kicker, if Tinsley left me and then my dumbass reaction was the reason I lost my dream. So I quit dating cold turkey. It makes sense anyway. I barely have time and it's hard to trust people. Right now, I'm focused on my career."

The message couldn't be clearer: even if I'd wanted it, Logan's heart was unavailable. Broken, then closed. But because I was a masochist, it took all of my willpower not to reach out and brush his hair off his forehead. It had curled in the rain, and he looked boyish and nervous sitting across from me, waiting for my reaction. I didn't know how else to assure him his story was safe with me other than sharing one of my own.

"You were right about the night we met. I *was* looking for someone to have a one-night stand with. That was the plan. Meet you, use you, ditch you."

Logan's eyes grew darker.

"The reason—and this is mortifying, but I'm going to say it anyway—is because when Chris and I broke up, he told me I was bad in bed. Too timid and boring."

Logan's eyebrows shot so far north they almost touched his hairline. But he didn't say anything, just waited for me to continue.

"So that...rattled me. And I started thinking he might be right. That night at the Fleur de Lis, I'd promised myself I'd be bold for once, act outside my comfort zone. It was supposed to be the start of a new chapter. And then you came along, and...the storm had other ideas."

I looked at him anxiously. After a long minute, he blinked. "Is that all?"

"Yes?"

"Good." He stood up. "Because I have to go punch a man in the face."

I tugged on his wrist. "Sit down."

"Call Nora and tell her we're going to have a crisis comms situation. And bail me out, please."

"Logan," I groaned, pulling his wrist so hard he had no choice but to fall back into his chair.

"I can't believe he said that to you. First of all, what a dick. Second, for whatever it's worth, and not to make things awkward, but he's wrong." Logan's voice grew husky. "You are—well, you're the opposite of boring. Trust me."

I could feel myself turning red. "Thank you. But I'm not mad about the way things turned out. There *are* some things I need to be more adventurous about. As for relationships, our whole—" I lowered my voice "—fake dating thing has made me realize I need to work on some of my toxic patterns. Casual relationships aren't the answer. I've got some growing to do, but once you and I are over, I'm going to look for someone real. No offense," I added, chancing a look at him.

His jaw was tight. "Yeah." He idly crushed his cup. "That makes sense."

There was a beat of silence, then he finally dropped his ruined cup. My throat thickened. *No fair*, a small voice whispered. *His whole face is simply unfair.* "Do you want to keep playing darts," he asked, "or we could just...talk. I could get you something different to drink. Whatever you want."

What I wanted was to stay here with him, in this tiny, candlelit bar in the middle of a blackout, asking questions and inching closer to him until Jimmy kicked us out. I wanted it so bad I knew it was exactly what I shouldn't do. Toxic patterns and all. "I should go."

"Really?" Logan straightened. "I mean, of course. If that's what you want. Let me text Nigel."

"You don't have to—"

"Don't be silly. He's just around the corner. I'll take an Uber."

I smiled and swallowed my protests. Good that Nigel would get me home fast, actually. Then I'd go to bed fast, and fall asleep fast, and this warm, delicious night would be over before I could spend too much time luxuriating in alone time with Logan. I could rest easy knowing I was exhibiting the wise decision-making skills of a woman maturing.

I watched him thumb a quick message to Nigel, biting his full lower lip.

This ache in my chest was simply growing pains.

17

Comfort Zones

"Tilt your chin up," Zoey instructed. "You're the Queen of the Fairies, remember? I need you to look proud and like, a *tiny* bit horny."

I winced, but tilted my chin and gave proudly horny my best shot. "Like this?"

She peeked around her canvas. "*Nailed* it. Thanks again for doing this. I can't believe my model flaked at the last minute to stay at Burning Man."

I tried to talk without moving my lips. "Wasn't Burning Man weeks ago?"

She shrugged. "Take enough drugs and apparently you never have to leave. You know you can relax, right? It won't mess up the painting. Besides, this is just a practice study. I want to test how you look in the light."

"Thanks." I massaged my stiff jaw. "I've never sat for an artist before."

Besides the art she showed in galleries, it turned out Zoey made the bulk of her living off commissioned paintings. Yesterday she'd called in a panic because the woman who'd agreed to model for a commissioned piece had bailed, and Zoey's deadline was coming up. She'd begged me to sit for her, promising the painting was a tasteful take on Edmund Spenser's poem "The Faerie Queen," a request from a UT English professor. The fact that Zoey thought I was second-string fairy material *and* she wanted to hang out again was enough to overcome my shyness.

She'd instructed me to meet her at the Tite Street Artist Collective, where she rented work space. I'd looked it up and found out Tite Street was the name of the street in London where Oscar Wilde once lived. Naively, I'd thought, *what a nice literary allusion*. Then I'd arrived and discovered it was more of a lifestyle commitment. As far as I could tell, the Tite Street Artist Collective was single-handedly keeping Austin weird. I'd popped over here after finishing school, and from the moment I'd arrived, I'd felt like a chicken accidentally let loose in a peacock coop.

"Are you sure none of this distracts you?" I waved at the courtyard, where a man covered in paint kept yelling "No!" at his canvas and shaking it, right next to a circle of people smoking a hookah, who were each taking turns nodding and puffing out ideas: "make it avant-garde but also normcore," "miniature, but like Koons, but for pets." In the fountain, a topless woman wearing a mermaid tail sunbathed and splashed while chain-smoking.

"Nope," Zoey said cheerfully. "Helps me concentrate. Careful, your leaves are slipping."

I hastily tugged the miniscule leaf top Zoey had given me in place over my chest. It had turned out Zoey's and my definitions of "tasteful" were *not* the same, which I'd realized when she revealed the costume I'd be wearing in the painting, a series of stitched-together fabric leaves and a floral tiara. Apparently, the costume had been specifically requested by the English professor, who I now suspected was less a fan of sixteenth-century poetry and more a fan of fairy porn. I patted the leaves down over my nipples and reminded myself for the millionth time I was doing this to be a good friend.

"So tell me about this library conference," Zoey said, squinting back and forth between me and the canvas. "I want to hear about your moment of triumph."

I shook out my hair like I imagined a fairy queen would. "I wouldn't go that far. But I did make it through without fainting or throwing up. And Logan seemed happy."

She arched her eyebrows. "I'm sure he did. I watched that press conference y'all did to announce you were a couple. That man was looking at you like he wanted to take you right there on the podium. Should've rated the news NC-17."

"Zoey!" I blushed and looked around, but the sunbathing mermaid didn't seem scandalized.

She put the wrong end of her paintbrush in her mouth, spit it out, turned it, and chewed. "I'm just saying, you guys put on a hell of a performance."

I groaned. "That's exactly the problem. Life cursed me with an overly romantic brain, and it's getting harder to separate what's real and what's part of our act."

Saying that out loud felt freeing. I didn't have many people to talk to—Zoey and Lee were the only two who knew Logan and I were faking it, and Lee wasn't exactly beating down the door to reopen the subject. "I'm constantly telling myself to snap out of it. Meanwhile Logan is completely unbothered. To him, all I am is a way to win. When we were out having drinks the other night—"

"Wait. Just the two of you?"

"Uh-huh."

"At a bar?"

"This hole-in-the-wall he loves."

"So no press?"

"Definitely no press. Not even any voters, apparently. Logan wanted to celebrate in private after my speech."

"Hmm."

"What?"

"Oh, nothing." But she wore a smirk that said there was definitely something. "Please continue."

"Well, he opened up and told me how his last relationship fell apart and almost cost him an election, and after that, he quit dating. Apparently he'll start again after he's achieved all his lofty goals, whatever those are."

"That sounds like a lonely life."

I couldn't help the tinge of bitterness. "Maybe after he's finally become president of America, he'll ask out another perfect heir to a Connecticut political dynasty."

"Oh, I'm loving that fire in your eyes." Zoey's paintbrush was moving a mile a minute. "You know what, this painting's going to be too good for my client. I'm getting it hung in a gallery."

I was definitely going to hang in some rich pervert's man cave, but I'd processed that and made my peace with it. Right now, all I could think about was Tinsley the Harvard-educated heiress, the leggy Rockets cheerleader, and the string of women in between. "Zo, do you think—" I swallowed past the lump in my throat. Zoey and I probably weren't close enough yet for me to ask a question like this, but my gut told me I could trust her. I took a deep breath. "Do you think people believe Logan and I are together, or do you think they're secretly laughing at the idea behind our backs?"

She set down her paintbrush. "What makes you ask that?"

I tried to shrug nonchalantly. "You know. There's the way he looks and his commanding presence and the fact that he blazes through rooms like a comet. And then there's me. I'm more of a...dwarf planet."

"If you're asking me whether I think you make the world's sexiest opposites-attract couple, then yes, I do. If you're asking if I think you're pretty or interesting enough to date him—a question I hate but forgive because I've been there—then my answer is, Alexis, you're lovely and perfect. Don't listen to the haters on Twitter."

There were haters on Twitter? Nope, not going there. "Thanks, Zo. That means a lot. But...you don't think it's weird because of...how accomplished he is? You don't think people are saying, what's that rising-star politician doing with that...non-rising-star normal person?"

"You don't think you're accomplished?"

I laughed uncomfortably. "I mean...not like him."

She frowned. "I'm suddenly a lot less concerned about you and Logan and a lot more interested in why you don't feel good enough."

This had spiraled into too-vulnerable territory. I waved a hand. "You know what? Never mind. I've just been thinking about how I'm climbing closer to thirty and it would be nice to do something that left a bigger mark on the world, like Logan and Lee. But it's not a big deal. Forget I said anything." I focused on the circle of hookah smokers, who'd moved to the lying-on-the-ground-staring-at-the-clouds phase of the creative process. They looked quite peaceful. *Be more like the stoners*, I admonished myself. *For once in your life, relax.*

Zoey was quiet for so long I figured she'd gotten lost in painting, but suddenly she said, "Back to Logan's feelings. I know I like to tease you—and I stand by the fact that he looks at you very longingly on TV—but you're the one who's living this, not me. If you think Logan's unavailable and it's important to protect your heart, then do it."

I nodded. "Thanks. I do think he's—"

"*But.*" She held up a paint-splattered finger. "I'd hate it if the way you saw *yourself* colored how you think other people see you. If that makes sense. Just—don't discount people's feelings because you're used to discounting yourself."

I couldn't help but smile. "It's almost like you're engaged to a therapist."

She winked. "Annie's upped my armchair therapy game. I'm a hot commodity here at the collective."

I comforted myself with the thought that there was no way I had weirder problems than the paint-covered man who was now quietly sobbing in front of his canvas.

"You know what I can't get out of my head?"

Zoey's tongue stuck out a bit as she concentrated. "What?"

"There was this librarian at the conference who asked for help fighting a book ban. I read the book and she's right. It's not inappropriate at all. It's really quite educational." Truthfully, the book was so open and honest about sex that I'd learned a lot. I'd spent an hour last night combing through it, murmuring, *Huh, so that's been normal this whole time* and *Oh, that's what you call that thing*. Which was a) something I would take to my grave, and b) more proof that the old methods of shame-fueled sex ed were not only ineffective but produced twenty-seven-year-old women who had to turn their whole lives upside down to reclaim their sexual power after being spurned in bed. What parent would wish that upon their child?

"I've been wracking my brain to come up with solutions for this librarian. All I can think is maybe Logan's campaign could start a petition or organize a talk with the author. But it feels too small."

"Why's the book banned?"

"Well, it's called *Sex Is Not a Dirty Word*, and it treats sex like it's nothing to be ashamed of. But Gabby's district—that's the librarian, Gabby Bui—teaches abstinence-only. They're saying it's inappropriate for kids to read about their own changing bodies. It's benign stuff, but people are going after all kinds of books these days. It's gotten so bad the Library Council's anti-censorship task force can't keep up with all the requests for help."

Zoey threw down her paintbrush so hard it clattered on the cobblestones.

"Whoa." I startled. "Everything okay?"

She shook her head, chlorine-green strands flying. "We can't let this happen. Those kids deserve shame-free sex education."

"You're totally right," I said, eyes widening. "I just had no idea you'd feel this strongly."

She ran her hands through her hair and took a deep breath. "As a bi woman, I'm sensitive to anyone being made to feel shame over their sexuality. That's not something I take lightly. And I'm sick and tired of hearing about books kids need—not just queer kids, but all kids—being banned, *especially* here in Texas."

"That makes total sense, Zo. I agree and I'm sorry I didn't think about that before bringing it up. Do you want to be involved in my petition?"

Zoey had a faraway look. Suddenly her whole face brightened and she snapped her fingers. "Forget the petition. You're right, it's way too small. We're doing a protest."

My stomach dropped. "A what?"

"A public rally." She must've read the look on my face. "Don't worry, we do it all the time. I swear, these days I go to one a week. They're always a good time and they always make the news. Half the time they even move the needle, which as you know is high ROI when it comes to protesting."

I did not know that because I'd never been to a rally before. I thought back to what Nora said, that love was political, whether you acknowledged it or not. I added to that: simply existing was political—taking up space in the world, on bookshelves.

"When you say 'we do it all the time,'" I asked cautiously, "who's this we?"

Zoey waved a hand at the courtyard. "The Austin art community. A free speech issue? They're going to be all over it, trust me. And I have a friend over at the Austin Queer Caucus who I know would get her network on board.

They're a force—always standing up for people's rights. They're amazing."

I gulped. "It sounds like this could turn into a big thing."

"No, don't worry. We have it down to a science—the permits, the participants. It's practically paint by numbers. You just worry about rounding up the librarians."

Could we actually pull this off? I was nowhere near what anyone would consider a leader. I'd spent a comfortable—if lonely—life in the background, and my resolve to be a new Alexis felt outmatched by this idea.

"Please?" Zoey pressed her hands together. "Just a tiny baby rally in front of the capitol. It'll be great."

As she stood there with her wide eyes full of hope, my heart filled with affection: for her, for Gabby and her schoolkids, for my own kids at the library. And the love made me feel brave.

"Okay," I said, and she whooped. "Just a very small, *tame* group marching down Eleventh Street. Mild chanting—no air horns. And only tasteful signs." I glanced down at my barely there leaf top. "Actually, scratch that—only *subdued* signs allowed."

"Ah," she squealed, rushing over to hug me. "Thank you! I promise, we'll be so small and subdued, you'll have zero regrets."

18

Get Your Ass Down Here, It's a Free Speech Rager

The crowd pulled me like a riptide toward Eleventh Street, only to be stopped by the sudden appearance of a full-blown marching band. They were decked out in Texas Longhorn regalia, cowboy hats and fringed shirts and all, and immediately burst into a jazzy rendition of Britney Spears's "Hit Me, Baby, One More Time." Squeals went up around me. I looked around, dazed. There had to be hundreds of people pouring through the streets of downtown Austin.

"Alexis, thank God." Quinn Xavier, the head of the Austin Queer Caucus, rushed toward me, defying the crowd. She gave me a once-over, then spoke quickly into a walkie-talkie. "Yes, I found her. She appears to be hypnotized by a Britney Spears song. Bringing her back now."

Quinn took my elbow and gently steered me back to where I'd come from. "Darling, do you want the Longhorn marching band to go before or after the First Amendment Fire Eaters? The march is about to start."

"March?" My voice was hollow. My eyes had been so wide for so long I was afraid they were going to be stuck like this. "It was supposed to be a tiny baby rally."

"Oh, this?" Quinn jerked her chin at the crowd. "This is nothing, just a little Saturday pop-up. We got who we could last minute. Now where are you on the band and fire eaters?"

"How did you get the actual college marching band? And *fire eaters*?"

"Turns out the marching band's a staunch supporter of freedom of speech, go figure, allies in unlikely places and all that. And the fire eating's some *Fahrenheit 451* reference, I don't know, do I look like the kind of person who paid attention in middle school English? No offense, darling, the work you do as a librarian is vital, obviously, that's why we're here. My two cents: the fire eaters are divas, but the news likes them since they make a good shot, so you might want to let them go first. Then if there's an accident like last time, the marching band can swoop in and distract everyone."

I turned to her, mouth agape. "Who's, uh, legally liable in case of a fire? Not the person in charge, right?" I crossed my fingers. Fire insurance aside, I couldn't shake the feeling I was missing something. Something I was supposed to do but forgot in the whirlwind of planning.

"Alexis!" The shout broke through the noise. "I was worried the crowd ate you." Quinn and I were back at the protest's central command station, aka a folding table loaded with water bottles, walkie-talkies, and clipboards. Zoey hurried over, Muriel and Gia right behind her. "Isn't this great?" Zoey squealed. "Fabulous turnout!"

The mastermind behind the mayhem. I was ready to unleash a very sternly worded reprimand—*tiny, my butt*—when I registered her outfit. "What are you wearing?"

Zoey stood next to Muriel and Gia in, as best I could tell, the erotic movie version of their outfits. Her hair was pulled back in a bun with a pencil tucked through it, and she wore a cardigan like Muriel and Gia, except hers was cropped. Instead of their sensible jeans, she wore a slitted miniskirt. All three of them blinked back at me from behind matching pairs of thick-framed glasses.

Zoey did a little twirl. "I'm a librarian, duh! Dressed in theme."

Gia cut in. "The Library Council and Texas Educators Association got a heck of a lot of people to show up. We're standing between the ACLU and the Cowboys for Intellectual Freedom. Only in Texas."

Muriel clasped her hands. "It's so exciting! I feel edgy like my daughter."

"There you are!" Lee elbowed her way through a crowd of men dressed like the Founding Fathers. "Reporting for duty."

My heart soared. *Lee was here.* That meant everything was going to be okay. "You came."

"Of course I came. This is your big day. Quinn, Muriel, Gia, nice to see you all again." Lee shook each of their hands with practiced polish, then looked around, eyebrows raised. "I'm glad so many people showed up for this. It's impressive. Now, let's talk speech lineup. I have lots of thoughts about this banning bullshit, so I'm going to need a little more time on the docket, just FYI."

It was happening exactly like I'd hoped. I was finally doing something big enough, something important, and Lee was paying attention. A swell of pride lifted my shoulders. Suddenly, the circus of people didn't seem so intimidating.

"Alexis," Zoey said, snapping me out of it. "What are you thinking for the speeches? It's almost time to walk to the stage."

I looked around and found them all staring at me. Right. I was supposed to be in charge. I took a deep breath. "In that case." I waved them forward. "Let's walk and talk. I think we open with Quinn and the head of the Library Council. They can break the ice, then we'll move to Gabby Bui, since this is her campaign, then the author. Did you know he has a PhD in sex education?"

"He's so nice he's basically the Mr. Rogers of sex ed." Lee matched me step for step despite her heels.

"Then after the author, Lee, maybe you can talk about what people can do beyond the rally? Are you okay going fourth?"

"Who am I, Mariah Carey? I'll go whenever you need me."

I felt the sudden urge to stop in my tracks and hug her, but Lee had never been a hugger. I squeezed my fists instead.

"What about you?" Quinn popped up on my other side. "Aren't you going to kick us off?"

"Yeah, Lex, you have to go first," Zoey said. "You're the face of Logan's campaign."

"Would be weird if you didn't," Lee agreed.

Ahead of us, the massive Texas State Capitol loomed in the distance, with its columns and glorious domed roof. A chill lifted the hairs on my arms. I'd stepped (fallen?) into the big leagues. Yet again, that persistent sense that I'd missed something nagged at me. But I was surrounded by a group of determined women, all of them looking at me like they expected big things, and I didn't want to let them down. I pushed the nagging feeling aside.

"Okay." I swallowed, eyes on the stage. "I'll go first."

"And that," I said into the mic, "is why it's so important to fight for students' access to books. As a school librarian, I can tell you that kids have a lot of questions, especially about loaded topics like puberty. They deserve thoughtful, shame-free books like *Sex Is Not a Dirty Word* to help them navigate."

I paused, heart pounding, waiting for the clapping to die down. It was an awe-inspiring sight, all of these people stretched before me, filling the street. Awe-inspiring and *terrifying*. My flight instincts had been screaming at me to flee from the moment I stepped on stage, which was either five minutes or ten years ago.

"Which is why I'm proud to be here on behalf of the Logan Arthur campaign," I concluded, speaking past the knot in my stomach. "So, without further ado, I'd like to introduce you to Gabby Bui, the librarian leading the charge against the book ban. She can tell you more about what she's facing in her district."

Gabby was already walking across the stage, so I waved goodbye to the audience and scurried off, squeezing Gabby's arm as I passed her. Her whole face was shining with anticipation, proving some people really were born for the spotlight. I, on the other hand, melted with relief the minute I climbed off the stage steps.

"You're a natural," Lee gushed, slinging her arm over my shoulders. "Who knew you had it in you?"

I forced a smile. "Yep, that's me. A natural."

I went to flip my phone off silent and almost dropped it. I had twelve missed calls and a laundry list of texts. It was mostly Nora, whose messages turned increasingly frantic as I scrolled, from What did I just see on my Google alerts about a book banning rally? to Why am I seeing Twitter posts tagged with #LoganArthurSupportsFreeSpeech? and finally, Alexis Rosalie Stone (yes I know your middle name and a whole lot worse!) are you SPEAKING at this rally?! There were a few texts from Cary that were mostly long strings of gravestone and skull emojis, and finally, one from Logan. It just said Call me.

My stomach dropped like a lead balloon. "Oh, no." Suddenly I realized exactly what I'd forgotten to do.

Lee peeked over my shoulder. "What's wrong?"

"On a scale of one to ten, how bad would it be if I forgot to tell the campaign I was doing this?"

The smile vanished from Lee's face. "Doing what?" she asked carefully. "Your introduction? The Logan Arthur for Free Speech T-shirt cannon?"

"Uh..." I grimaced. "Kind of..."

"No." Lee shook her head and backed up. "Don't say it."

"All of it?"

19

In the Doghouse

I hadn't expected that the first time I'd get an invitation to Logan's house, it would be for a professional-grade reaming. But here I was, forced to lie in the uncomfortable bed of my own making. I pulled up behind a Jeep I recognized as Cary's and studied Logan's home. It was small, one of those Craftsman bungalows I'd always loved, white with blue trim and a wide front porch that would be perfect for a swinging chair. Logan probably wasn't open to home improvement suggestions at this particular moment, so I'd have to suggest it later. His street was lovely and full of trees. What a shame to see it for the first time with this black cloud hanging over me. I took a deep breath, then exhaled. Time to face the music.

I'd barely finished knocking before the door swung open to reveal Cary. He slouched, one hand braced against the door frame, and shook his head. "Oooh, Rudy, you really did it this time."

"I know." I tried to push past him, but he kept blocking me. "Are you going to let me in?"

"Cary, let the girl in," came a deep, throaty voice I recognized as Anita's. Oh, boy. They'd brought in the big guns.

Cary reluctantly let me pass, and suddenly I was in Logan's living room. It was warm and homey, glowing with lamplight and filled with a hodgepodge of furniture that looked like he'd collected it over the years from family castoffs, much like I'd collected mine. But the coziness of the overstuffed couch and throw rug was drastically undercut by the gauntlet of icy stares. Nora and Anita sat stone-faced on the couch, and Logan sat in a nearby armchair, frowning. His eyes flicked to mine as I walked in and I felt a surge of adrenaline. When he looked away, I was left alone with a racing heart.

Cary shut the front door and darted around me to sit on the couch, where he resumed shaking his head. He was enjoying not being the one in trouble far too much.

"Now that we're all here," Nora said. "Alexis, would you mind reading this press release?"

Not the most promising start, but... "Sure." I took her phone and read from her screen. The release carried Governor Mane's seal. "Governor in Negotiations with Collinsburg City Council to Reverse Controversial Book Ban," the headline announced, followed by a subhead: "Governor leading the fight to defend constituents' First Amendment rights."

I frowned as I scanned the rest. It was time stamped only thirty minutes ago. Not only was the rally still going on, but this move seemed out of character for the governor. "I thought Mane would defend the book ban, not try to get it reversed. That's *our* position. How did this happen?"

"I'm so glad you asked," Nora said coolly, and my mind yelled *trap!* "This happened because one of the members of the Logan Arthur campaign, a young upstart by the name of Alexis Rosalie Stone—"

I winced. Hearing my full name never meant good things.

"Decided to take it upon herself to organize an entire rally in defense of an issue she'd barely talked to the rest of the campaign about. Instead of asking our strategists to come up with the best approach to score a political victory, she just slapdashed things and handed our opponent the perfect opportunity to look like a hero. And how has that changed favorability numbers, Anita?"

Anita glanced up from her iPad. "We're up four percent positive from the rally. Governor's up fourteen percent positive from actually solving the problem."

"The rally could've solved the problem if we'd given it time to work," I squeaked.

Nora's eyebrows rose. I gulped.

"Nora," Logan warned, and she sighed.

"I know you're new at this, Alexis." This time, her voice came out gentler. "But this is why you bring ideas to us first and don't go rushing out into the field all idealistic and Pollyanna. We have to be strategic. Grover Mane is savvy. He'll snake our own ideas out from under us."

I lifted my chin higher. Lee had given me a pep talk before I drove over. She'd told me to apologize for genuine missteps, but otherwise hold my ground. "I understand the way I went about this was wrong, and I'm very sorry. I mean, I can't say I'm sorry the governor swooped in and solved the problem, because I'm glad he did, for Gabby and her kids. If you think about it, in a way you could say our rally *did* work, it just didn't benefit our campaign."

Cary coughed, but I plunged forward. "And I know I should have confirmed that everyone knew what I was planning, but in my defense, I did send Cary a Twitter DM."

"You sent me a gif of Leslie Knope yelling 'boot and rally,' with a caption that said, 'I have no idea what I'm doing with this government stuff but I hope to see you there,'" he said.

"See? I don't know how I could've been clearer. It says 'rally' right in the gif. That's how gifs work, right? Layered meanings."

Cary tsked. "A gif isn't a proper message."

"Then why do you send me so many?" I glared at him. "You sent me gifs, so I sent you gifs." I pointed back and forth between us. "Gif, gif—"

"As fascinating as this insight into Gen Z communication styles is..." Nora drawled.

I threw up my hands. "I'm sorry. I know I messed up. I guess I got excited about actually being able to do something for Gabby and the book, you know, having this new platform. I got carried away." I chanced a look at Logan, who was quietly hunched in his chair, elbows braced on his thighs, listening.

He must've felt my gaze, because he looked up and met my eyes. The adrenaline came back full force. I wished I would hurry up and become immune to the sight of him so I could finally have some peace.

He swallowed. "Look, I'm glad the ban's getting reversed." He spoke in a low voice that was no less powerful for being quiet. "But you and I promised we'd run campaign decisions by each other, remember? It was one of our three rules. That way we're on the same page and no one gets left behind. I could've helped."

I couldn't stop looking at the tight way he held his jaw. It was like he was forcing himself to look at me, like the very act cost him. But Logan never had trouble dealing with work problems. He was always cut and dry. Then it hit me: he wasn't disappointed in me like a colleague, the way Nora was. He was hurt the way a person was when someone they trusted betrayed them. I remembered what he'd told me about Tinsley, how they hadn't been on the same page, and how much it had hurt him when she'd left him behind.

I'd hurt Logan personally, not professionally. I knew it should make me feel terrible, but as I searched his face, this man who was holding my eyes even though his were telegraphing feelings he clearly wanted to keep hidden, I felt a sense of wonder. Logan cared about me.

"I think we're probably done here," Nora sighed. "Alexis knows to keep us in the loop in the future. Right, Alexis?"

I turned to her. For the first time, my normal urge to do anything to smooth over a thorny situation was gone. In its place, I felt a tiny flame of rebellion. "Once again," I said carefully. "I'm sorry for not double-checking with you and letting the governor steal a win..." I took a deep breath. "But I'm not sorry I did it. It was the right thing to do."

As Nora sighed and Anita cackled, "So much for our nice librarian," I straightened my spine. "I appreciate your time," I added, because that seemed polite. As I turned to leave, I chanced one last look at Logan—and found, to my surprise, that while his dark eyes were still fixed on the floor, he wore the tiniest hint of a smile.

20

Escalation

There was one word for the audience of Barton Springs teachers who sat around me in the teachers' lounge, watching me with shining faces, lobbing questions about the book ban and Logan's budget expansion so fast I could barely keep up, and that word was *entourage*. It was a dreaded Monday, and yet the atmosphere inside the lounge was buzzing. It was standing room only, and new people kept squeezing in like they were inching past velvet ropes into a club. The book ban rally seemed to have turned me into the educators' version of Harry Styles overnight.

"Did you hear your book ban reversal is one of the fastest reversals on record?" asked Jon Reeves, a third grade language arts teacher. "That's going to make other districts think twice."

"I didn't know that," I said, trying to warm to the attention. "But honestly, all credit goes to Gabby Bui and the Austin Queer—"

"Do you really think Logan can get the legislators to give us more money?" interrupted Principal Zimmerman's assistant, Megan Kwan. She leaned over Jon, tapping her long, vivid pink nails against the table.

"If he gets elected, it's going to be one of his top priorities. He had a team of economists do projections to figure out how to increase the budget." Spouting research, at least, I felt safe. "Did you know Texas gives tax cuts to athletic teams and businesses to get them to relocate here? If you make those tax cuts even a *little* less generous, you're already looking at a surplus—" On the table in front of me, my phone started buzzing. "Uh." I frowned. "Excuse me for a minute."

Conversation continued while I turned to my phone. It looked like I was getting tagged dozens of times on Twitter and Instagram. With a sinking feeling, I opened Twitter. The tags were on a news clip. In the still image, Logan stood in front of Trisha Smith from CBS 12. That alone made me nervous. I clicked Play.

"Now Mr. Arthur," Trisha said, in that assertive voice I'd always admired. "Coming off this morning's town hall on the importance of free speech—kudos on the record number of attendees, by the way—"

Logan, who'd been leaning in and nodding as she spoke, gave her a quick, "Thank you."

"I have to ask: How did it feel when Governor Mane recently swept in to get the ban on *Sex Is Not a Dirty Word* reversed? That was obviously a free speech issue spearheaded by your girlfriend. Do you worry the governor's action makes you look weak by comparison? All bark, no bite?"

Ouch.

Logan's face remained untroubled. "Thanks for the question, Trisha, and for being so consistently charming."

Surprisingly, he turned and looked directly into the camera. "I applaud Governor Mane for taking swift and decisive action to support educators and students in Collinsburg. I'm not worried about what voters will think for two reasons. One, I've always made my campaign about action instead of hot air, and I believe voters can see the difference between doing the work consistently and jumping in to take advantage of a splashy media moment. The second reason is, as you mentioned, I have Alexis Stone by my side."

My heart somersaulted in my chest.

"Alexis is an educator herself—so, unlike Governor Mane, the issue isn't one-and-done for my campaign. In fact—" He grinned into the camera. "I'm happy to announce Alexis will be back out at the capitol this weekend, marching with the teachers union for increased salaries."

Excuse me—I was doing *what*?

Trisha, who clearly didn't like how Logan was hogging the camera, not-so-subtly shouldered him out of the way. "Wow, there you have it, folks. Breaking news here at CBS 12. Teachers, it sounds like you have a new champion in Alexis Stone. We'll see you at the capitol."

The clip ended, and my jaw dropped. Logan had just volunteered me to lead a march in a few days' time *on television*. A march people were now rabidly discussing on Twitter. "Oh, no," I murmured. "Oh, no, no, no." I leaped out of my chair and ducked into the empty hallway. I couldn't scroll through my contacts fast enough, jabbing Call and tapping my foot as the phone rang.

Logan's voice was the smuggest I'd ever heard it. "If it isn't the teachers' champion. I've been expecting you."

The *nerve*. "Where are you?"

"My house—"

"Stay there." I hung up. Logan and the campaign wanted more direct communication? I would show them direct communication.

I pounded on the door of Logan's annoyingly adorable bungalow. He better not have left. He better not make me wait—

The door swung open, and Logan stood in front of me in joggers and a T-shirt, eating a sandwich with a serene smile. "Alexis!" His voice was cheery. "Come on in."

I froze, caught off guard. Then I narrowed my eyes and strode past him. "You get on my case for not giving you enough of a heads-up about the book rally, then you commit me to a protest on *live TV*. Without even telling me."

"Oh, good, you saw the news. Hey, aren't you supposed to be at school right now?"

I waved. "I have a half day. It's a cost-cutting measure so the school district can keep our hours down. Don't try to distract me. What do you have to say for yourself?"

Logan looked up at the ceiling thoughtfully. "I guess I'd say..." He sounded way too happy. "I'm sorry for not telling you, but I'm not sorry I did it. It was the right thing to do." He grinned at me.

Using my own words against me. "So is this what we're doing now? Tit for tat?" I folded my arms over my chest, emboldened as always by his shamelessness. "Okay, then. Game on." I frowned. "Wait, what are *you* doing home? I just saw you in a suit on the news."

Logan sauntered into the kitchen, but his voice carried. "I had an early town hall—pancake breakfast, though of course I didn't get to eat. Now I'm taking a reading day. Prepping for my first debate with Mane."

I shivered at the idea of having to debate someone on TV. That ranked high on my list of personal nightmares. Now that I took stock of his living room, I noticed his armchair and coffee table were buried in stacks of paper, notebooks, and highlighters. Serious debate research.

He returned sans sandwich and stopped a few feet in front of me, sticking his hands in his pockets. Now that my indignation was fading, I realized this was the first time I'd seen Logan out of a suit. His gray T-shirt was stretched taut over his biceps. His joggers hugged his athletic thighs, ending right above his bare feet, which were surprisingly... elegant. In casual clothes, it was easy to tell he played soccer. He had a body built for power.

I twisted my hands together, face heating. Seeing Logan like this felt as intimate as watching him undress in the hotel. "I'll get out of your hair. Though consider this my formal complaint about the march. I'll go, but I'll hate every minute of it. Or probably not, because it's a good cause. But I will be highly annoyed for at least the first third." I turned to leave.

"Wait," he said. "Stay."

I looked at him, standing there all casual and beautiful, and my heart pounded traitorously.

"I was just about to make tea. Do you have any work you need to do? We could keep each other company. I promise I'm a quiet reader. I won't bother you."

The same warning bells that had gone off at the Hideaway went off now. I should probably leave. At the very least, put some distance between me and the sight of Logan's chest in that shirt. But it would be nice to have company instead of working alone in my apartment. And I'd been doing a good job keeping my instinct to romanticize in check.

"I do have some book catalogues to read." I lifted my tote bag, where they were stuffed.

His face brightened. "Really? Great." He suddenly looked at a loss for what to do next. "Uh. You want Earl Grey?"

"Sure," I said, and he sprinted for the kitchen.

I put my bag down and sank into Logan's couch. Worn, but comfy. I could work with this. There was even a cream blanket draped over the back, an unexpected touch of cozy. In fact, Logan's entire house—as much as I could see—was unexpected. Given the amount of time he spent working, I'd assumed his place would be barely furnished, or dominated by the campaign: whiteboard, posters, three-ring binders, you name it. But this was different—lived-in and nice.

I am sitting in Logan's house. Each new thing—the blanket, the stack of vinyl records in the corner, the fact that he seemed to like warm colors—was a piece of Logan trivia I memorized to dissect later.

I was still cataloguing when he rushed back, holding two steaming mugs. "I remembered your coffee order from that day Cary got us Starbucks. Splash of milk and spoonful of sugar. Hope that works for tea." He set the mug on the coffee table and I blinked at it.

"That's perfect, actually." It was hard to forget the day Cary had been sent to get us coffee because he'd complained so loudly about being an errand boy. But I hadn't thought Logan was paying attention to me.

He settled in his armchair, kicking one leg over the other. "I'm going to dive in on some economic impact studies. You good?"

I nodded, bending over and pulling out my children's literature catalogue. Muriel had turned over most of the book buying to me because she said I had a better sense of trends. I studied the catalogue. "Looks like it's a lot of tiny witches solving crimes in my future." I looked at him. "I'm feeling very smug about my career choices relative to yours at the moment."

His smile was instant and warm. "Little do you know bemoaning your career choices is the first step of all debate prep, so I'm right on target. Come talk to me when you need to know the economic impacts of tiny witches solving crimes. Obviously, the decreased crime rates will improve living conditions, but on the other hand, the magical security industry takes a hit."

I shook my head and uttered the word I'd recently learned was a grievous insult in the political world. "Wonk."

Logan clutched his chest like I'd shot him in the heart. I smiled and we got busy reading. There really were a lot of upcoming children's books about young witches solving crimes. Funny how these things always seemed to come in waves. Absently, I tugged the cream blanket off the back of the couch and unfolded it, wrapping myself in the soft, fuzzy layers. Then I froze. It smelled so powerfully like Logan, so richly of that peculiar mix of woods and berries, it was like being folded in his arms. I reached for the other pillows on the couch and pulled them closer.

"Are you cold?" he asked. "I can turn down the AC."

I shook my head. "I just like being cozy." His look of concern relaxed into a small smile, and I pulled the blanket higher under my chin. A Logan-scented cocoon was almost as good as a Logan-scented embrace, and far less complicated.

"Have you ever thought about writing books?" he asked abruptly.

I lowered the catalogue. "What?"

"It's just, you love them." He leaned forward. "You're so well-read. And you're a really good writer. All your speeches have been great. And you seemed so happy that night at the bar, inventing those stories."

I felt a hot flush creep up my neck. Logan was describing how I'd lied to him, no matter how generously he framed it. "Back in the day, I guess." In high school and college, I used to dream of being a writer. The flush crept further north. "I used to write these long lists of ideas for kids' books. I even took a few writing classes in college." I had at least a dozen beginnings of stories stored in an old laptop somewhere in my closet. At one point, with my family splintered and Lee off doing her thing, writing had made me feel less alone, the way reading had when I was younger. "It was a pipe dream. I know how hard it is to get published. It feels kind of arrogant to think I'd beat the odds." I'd stopped writing around the time I'd gotten rejected for grad school and had to devote my time to searching for an entry-level librarian job. Dreams, meet reality.

"I get it," he said. "I don't like failing, either. But I'm a big believer in taking risks."

"You haven't really failed before, Harvard. Talk to me after you do."

"Fair enough." He picked up his mug and smiled into it. "If you ever need to borrow some arrogance, I guess I've got it in spades."

I laughed in surprise, and after that a comfortable silence fell between us. I studied the book catalogue, trying to focus on purchases for the library, but the thought of those old stories abandoned on my laptop dogged me. *If I ever wrote again, what stories would I tell?* Maybe a story about a girl who didn't feel comfortable in the world, who felt alone and overlooked, but slowly, over time, built friendships and courage and love. Something kids like Mildred could see themselves in...

I got lost in thought as time passed. Then, out of the blue, Logan made a noise of pure disgust.

I looked up from the catalogue. "What?"

He shot me a guilty look. "Sorry. I know I promised to be quiet. It's just, I need to hammer Mane about his coziness with big corporations. I want to say companies shouldn't have lobbying access to the governor or legislature, but my team thinks it's too radical and will piss off everyone. Including the Dems and companies we need to support us."

From listening to Lee explain the way things worked, it would be a pretty big change if corporations weren't allowed to hire lobbyists who could march right into politicians' offices. "So your team wants you to hammer the governor but they don't want you to hammer too hard?"

He nodded, scooting to the edge of his seat. "They want me to say something tepid like, we should limit corporate influence on state politics. And I want to say we should ban corporate lobbying and hike corporate taxes. Big businesses have dominated politics for so long the idea of a free republic is practically a farce."

I raised my eyebrows. "I can see how that would be controversial."

"Yeah, but—" Logan stood up and seized his notebook, walking over to the couch. "Can I?"

My heartbeat skipped as I looked up at him. "Of course."

He paused. "Did you gather every blanket and pillow in the living room?"

I glanced at the Logan-scented fortress surrounding me. "Uh... I guess I did."

"You're like a soft-thing magnet." He sat down next to me, closer than I'd expected, and leaned in, showing me his notebook. It was covered in his jaunty, spiky handwriting, each letter written like it was bursting with energy. Our bodies brushed at the shoulders, elbows, knees—a sudden sensory overload. How was his skin so warm? How was it possible he could send so much electricity racing through me at the lightest touch? In all the years I'd devoured romance novels, I'd read description after description of the way it could feel when someone touched you: *a charge like lightning* or *the whole world stilling at the brush of his fingertips*. I'd always skimmed those parts, thinking they were an exaggeration, since I'd never felt that way with anyone in real life. But it *could* happen. It wasn't fiction. My whole body was rigid, attuned to Logan's every movement. It was exquisite torture.

"What would you say about corporate influence if you were me?" he asked.

I blinked at him. "You should probably ask someone on your team. I'm no expert."

"I want to know what I could say to win you." Logan gripped his notebook. And there it was again, in his furrowed brow, his serious eyes, the earnest expression. *Care.*

"Well," I said, taking a deep breath. It was hard to think straight with him so close. "I'd want you to be genuine. Yourself, but the polite version. There *is* that version," I insisted, off the look on his face. "Maybe something like, 'The reason I want to be governor is because I've experienced firsthand how choosing corporations over people harms Texans. Like many voters, I've been disappointed by how often Grover Mane privileges big business. That's why life doesn't feel much different even though he made big promises. We need more substantive change. That's why I'm proposing we ask corporations to pay at least as much in taxes as the average Texan, and we hold a referendum on their ability to lobby."

Logan was scribbling furiously. "I knew you would be good at this. Straightforward but nonconfrontational."

"Well." I cocked my head. "I guess I am an expert at nonconfrontational."

"Much better than me." He grinned and inched closer. Our thighs touched. An almost overwhelming desire to cup his face and kiss him left me clutching my fists to keep them still.

"Would you mind running through a few more questions with me? I can return the favor if there's anything you need to talk through. And I can make us a snack later if you're hungry."

I pictured Logan in an apron and immediately brightened. "This is hard work, isn't it? Debates aren't just politicians vamping for the camera."

"It's not answering the questions that's hard. I could talk about this stuff until I was blue in the face. It's the damn tiptoeing the team wants me to do. I can't look angry or call Mane out because voters might find it too aggressive. Basically, I can't be myself."

I bumped his shoulder. "Don't worry. We'll figure out a middle ground."

"Thank you," he said. "Really."

"Of course." I deserved an Oscar for keeping my face this neutral while my nerves exploded like the Fourth of July. "We're a team. Besides, it's nice you want my opinion."

He flipped to a blank page. "It's pretty much all I ever think about." He looked over quickly. "I mean, for the debate. You know, because I trust you." He cleared his throat and tugged on the blanket. "Do you mind if I get some of this?"

"Of course." I lifted the blanket and Logan draped it over his lap. Then he leaned back against the couch and rested his head in his hand, facing me.

"This next question's about health care."

I started to face him, then hesitated. Was this wise? I studied his face as he frowned at his notebook, chewing his pen, and it hit me with a sudden fierceness: I liked this man so much. My inconvenient physical attraction and his annoying habit of surprising me on live TV aside, I cared about him. And in small ways, he was showing me he cared, too. Maybe it was safe to allow myself a small increase in affection, a slight upgrade from coworkers to friends. That couldn't hurt, right?

I felt a warm glow in my chest as I turned. He shook his head and crossed something out. "Definitely need your take on this. The statistics alone, I mean, the whole debate could be about this issue. I need to find a way to center advocates' voices, especially women's. Between me and Mane, this debate's already a total bro-fest. Big dick energy, and not in the good way."

I suppressed a smile. Yeah, I could get used to being Logan Arthur's friend.

21

If I'm Going Down, You're Coming with Me

If I had my way, I would simply crawl into a cave and never give a speech again. But since Logan had signed me up to speak at the teachers union march, here I was, sweating on yet another stage. Thank God for Muriel Lopez, the one-woman hype machine. She'd brought her whole family to the march—husband, kids, cousins, even her tiny dog, clutched to her husband's chest. A whole army of Lopez supporters in the audience. While Gia and her husband had arrived dressed sensibly in blue-and-white TEA sweaters, Muriel and her family had gone for drama: makeup, glitter, a banner, the whole nine yards. Buried under about twelve feet of scarves, Muriel wore an official licensed Logan Arthur for Governor T-shirt, and the rest of her family wore unofficial, unlicensed Muriel Lopez for President T-shirts. Every time I hit a pause in my speech, they cheered me like I was Oprah giving away free cars. It was thanks to them that I was getting through this.

"Let's acknowledge the truth," I said, eyes tracking over the crowd. People filled Eleventh Street, stretching as far as the eye could see under the cloudless late-September sky, holding signs that said *Put Your Money Where Your Mouth Is, Texas* and *Teachers Deserve a Living Wage*. The campaign and the TEA had done a hell of a job organizing. The campaign had set up what Nora called a "publicity gauntlet" the week before the march to hype it. I had to ask Principal Zimmerman for permission to miss school so Logan and I could do back-to-back interviews about our education plan. In the mornings, we hit radio shows, drinking coffee with velvet-voiced emcees; in the afternoons, we sat down with newspaper journalists, who paused their fervent Twitter scrolling to ask us questions; and in the evenings, we smiled for the cameras with preening TV anchors.

It was a whirlwind that would have dizzied me if not for my own anchors: Logan, who was a grounding presence next to me in every interview; Nora and Cary, who dutifully hung in the wings, clutching phones and Starbucks cups; and Nigel, who drove us around town while reciting the day's forecast. By gauntlet day five, when Nora checked to see how I was doing, I told her the five of us had started to feel like an eccentric little family. She'd nodded knowingly and told me what I was describing was called proximity bonding, commonly experienced by kidnapping victims. Then she'd laughed at the look on my face and assured me that we were, in fact, a family.

Now here I was, delivering the speech I'd spent all week hyping. (No pressure.) "Politicians have ignored educators for years," I told the crowd. "They've taken away retirement benefits, cut workforce numbers, and let salaries flatline." The crowd roared its agreement, and I silently thanked the speechwriter on Logan's team who'd convinced me to go with flatline. Drama seemed to be a winner.

"Most politicians talk a good game about supporting teachers and students, but what do we actually have to show for it?" I looked into the front row where Logan stood, tall and dark and dashing in a navy blazer. He grinned up at me, shielding his eyes against the sun. Truth be told, he came in a close second to Muriel as an ideal audience member.

I glanced at my notes. "That's why I'm honored to introduce someone who will change teachers' and students' lives for the better." This was off-script, and Logan was already being shepherded to the stage by his security team, but I added, "He's a man who wants nothing more than to make life better for his fellow Texans. I believe in him, and I hope you do, too."

On my right, Logan stepped onto the stage.

"Logan Arthur, everyone!"

The crowd cheered and Logan waved. I clutched my notes, thrilled to be done, and beelined in his direction. When we met, he folded me into a giant hug like the campaign team had instructed. Performance or not, I breathed a deep sigh of relief as his arms closed around me. He hugged me tight.

"I would follow you anywhere," he whispered, his lips brushing my cheek, and then he was striding forward and waving at the crowd.

The words rooted me for a moment before I shook myself and scurried as gracefully as possible off stage. Security guards hovered, guiding me down the stairs and around the back where the rest of the speakers stood. As I thanked them and settled in to watch Logan on one of the monitors, my phone lit with a text from my mom.

I'm spending my day prepping for my commercial (still no word from Lee) and watching you on TV! You were amazing. I'm so proud. And you and Logan looked so romantic on stage. I'm dying to know what he whispered in your ear!

I smiled to myself. He said he would follow me anywhere.

Immediately, the little dots started bouncing. Oh, my, she wrote. That's even better than I imagined.

I looked up at Logan's face on the monitor. He was, wasn't he?

"Hey-o, Alexis Stone, nice to meet ya."

I turned to find two men my mother's age walking over. They were both on the short side, but while one was balding, the other had long hair that made him look like a hippie. In a flash, I placed them from those TEA pamphlets that got mailed to my apartment every month: It was Sonny Yarrow, president of the teachers union, and Kai West, secretary-treasurer.

"Oh my gosh." I stuck out my hand. "Sonny and Kai. It's an honor to meet you." My students might worship Taylor Swift and Ariana Grande, but I was looking at my celebrities. These were the two men in charge of sticking up for Texas teachers, which basically made them heroes, in my opinion.

Sonny, the one without the hair, gave my hand a brief pump. Long-haired Kai said, "I don't shake at these things. Too many germs."

"Oh." I yanked my hand back. "Of course." After a beat where they looked at me expectantly, I added, "Thank you for agreeing to hold this march with us. I'm a huge fan of the work you do."

"That's great," Kai said. "Listen. What do you think the odds are Arthur actually follows through on these promises?"

I searched his face, waiting for the punchline. When it didn't come, I swallowed my surprise. "I think the odds are a hundred percent." I nodded at the screen. "He wouldn't be up there if he wasn't invested."

"Ha," Sonny laughed. "You're cute, doll. Now give it to me straight. When your guy says he's going to expand salaries, that's going to be on a weighted basis, right?"

I frowned. "What do you mean, weighted?"

"Obviously the people at the top of the ecosystem have been working on this issue the longest," Kai said smoothly. "It's only fair they get a bigger cut of any new money."

Did Kai mean him and Sonny? "Um..."

"Let's make a deal," Sonny said, reaching in his pocket and producing a business card. "My cell's on the back. You're one of us. A union gal. Why don't you keep us in the loop about Arthur's thinking, huh? Can you do that for us? We can make it worth your while."

I could practically feel the oil dripping from my hand as I took Sonny's business card. "I'll think about it."

Thunderous applause came from the crowd. On the monitor, Logan smiled and waved as he turned and walked off stage.

"Looks like we're up," Kai said, straightening his TEA polo.

Sonny pointed at me. "Think about it." Thankfully, the security team descended to usher them on stage. As they passed Logan, they shook hands quickly, clapping each other on the back, and then Logan strode toward me, face lit up.

"Did you hear that shout out I gave Muriel at the end?" He practically bounced with excitement, looking over his shoulder as if he could see Muriel from here. "Her whole family went nuts."

"I was a little busy talking to Sonny and Kai." Whoever said *don't meet your heroes* was right.

"What's wrong? You've got that look you get when something's eating you."

"Are Sonny and Kai terrible?" I burst.

Logan frowned at the monitor, where the two of them took turns addressing the crowd. "I wondered if it was just me. Sometimes people are slimy when they think I can do something for them."

"They were so...transactional." That was the kindest way I could think to frame the two men who were supposedly our biggest allies.

Logan nodded, brow furrowing. "Most union leaders I've met are great. Really selfless. These two...let's keep an eye on them."

"Mr. Arthur!" someone shouted. "Hey, Mr. Arthur, it's Caleb Gruber, ABC 24. Do you have a minute?"

We turned to find the young reporter from our first press conference—the one who didn't look a day older than sixteen—standing on the other side of the barricades next to a TV crew. He waved rather desperately. Immediately, the security guards hustled over.

"I just want a quick interview with you and Alexis!" shouted Caleb. He was hidden behind a guard's chest. "My boss said not to bother coming back unless I got you for the five o'clock."

Logan looked at me and sighed. "Want to save a reporter's day?"

I hit him on the shoulder. "Of course I do. Where's that famous empathy for the working class?"

"Eh." He shrugged. "Reporters don't count." But he was already walking up to the guards. "Kyle, Steve, it's okay. We'll give him five minutes." The security guards backed off and Logan crouched under the barricade, then lifted it so all I had to do was duck.

"Thank you so much," gushed Caleb the baby-faced reporter. He turned to his camera crew. "Ready to rock?"

"Ready to roll," confirmed the giant, grizzled man behind the video camera. I stifled a laugh. It might've been all the middle grade fiction I read, but I'd always found motley crews endearing.

"Should I put my arm around you for the camera?" Logan whispered.

"Probably."

He drew me against his side, arm circling my waist. I slipped my arm around him, too, feeling his solidness. We inched nearer until we were as close as humanly possible, touching from head to foot. His hand found mine and we laced our fingers together. There. Good. It was convenient how perfectly we fit. *As friends*, I reminded myself. You never knew when having a friend who fit you so comfortably you could melt against him would come in handy. Music festivals, definitely. Sporting events. Long lines at airports.

"I'm Caleb Gruber," Caleb said into the camera, and *right*, we were rolling. "Here at the capitol with gubernatorial candidate Logan Arthur and his girlfriend and campaign partner, Alexis Stone, who—" Caleb winked. "He's holding on to pretty tightly."

"You have to soak up the opportunities you're given," Logan said.

"Speaking of the two of you." Caleb's voice turned brusque. "Logan, you've really jumped into the issue of education reform. Is it fair to say credit goes to Alexis for getting you to pay teachers some attention?"

Okay, fresh-faced Caleb had come to play.

Logan grinned and hugged me tighter. I squashed the urge to tell Caleb the grin meant he should run. "Since you covered my benefit for teachers a year ago, Caleb, I'd say you probably know this issue has been important to me for some time."

Caleb's eyes widened. Logan winked. "I remember you were enjoying the open bar that night. And did I hear something about you and the NBC 17 anchors doing karaoke after? Something about a video?"

"Uh—" Caleb did not like Logan's receipts.

"With that said—" Logan waved a hand "—all credit does go to Alexis. She's the reason education has become so central. In fact..." This time, he directed his smile down at me. I looked up in time to catch the mischievous glint in his eyes. "You could say she's the entire reason we're here today."

All right. Logan thought he was very smart. It was obvious from the delighted look on his face. But two could play this game.

"Logan's being modest," I said, and Caleb jerked the microphone in my direction. Beside me, Logan tensed. "He's constantly expanding his platform to include important new issues." I pulled back to grin up at him. His returning smile was forced. "In fact, because of his lifelong commitment to protecting animals, Logan just agreed to appear in a commercial to promote a new no-kill animal rescue called Happy Homes. He told me he felt it was only right to put his name and face on the line."

I'd finally stumped him. Logan's face was so frozen that when this clip went online, people would check their buffering.

"He's so excited he barely has the words," I told Caleb, whose eyes darted back and forth between us.

Logan finally unpaused, giving the camera one of his patented grimace-smiles. "I'm always happy to support a worthy cause." Each word sounded like it cost him.

"Well, viewers, you heard it here first!" As weird as we were being, Caleb at least seemed happy to get a scoop for the five o'clock news. "Logan Arthur adds animal rights to his long list of causes. We'll watch out for what's sure to be a star-making turn in his Happy Homes commercial. Back to you in the studio, Roger!"

The lights in the camera went off and the grizzled cameraman spun away. I could tell Logan wanted to have some choice words with me, but he was hampered by the fact that Caleb had pounced, begging him to reveal the location of that karaoke video.

"Got to go," I called, and Logan's eyes widened. "Caleb, thanks for the time. Logan, see you later!"

"No, Alexis—" Logan bit off what he was going to say with a quick glance at Caleb. I winked, spun, and started pushing my way through the crowd. Ante upped, Logan.

Just as I spotted Muriel and her family in the madness, my phone flashed with a new text. It was my mom in all caps, followed by a string of heart-eyes.

LOGAN'S GOING TO STAR IN MY COMMERCIAL?!!!

22

Ask Not What Your Boyfriend Can Do for You

"Flirting with each other via live interviews is a brilliant idea," Cary said, tilting back in his conference chair. He gave me an appraising look. "Kudos, Rudy. I love the drama. Really spices up the local news."

"We weren't flirting," I said, jiggling my own conference chair. It seemed to be broken. I couldn't get the seat to rise, so I was stuck with my chin only slightly higher than the conference table, like a child wheeled in to sit with the adults. I suspected Cary was behind it. It was making it hard for the other members of the campaign to take me seriously—I could see it in their eyes. Luckily, Nora had gathered a small crew this evening: just me, Logan, Cary, and a nervous woman who'd been introduced as Anita's research assistant, Gail. Poor Gail, to have Anita as a boss. I kept shooting her sympathetic looks, despite the fact that I was the one who'd been called in to get my wrist slapped for throwing Logan under the bus on live TV. With all my transgressions, it was starting to feel like I was a rebel instead of the rule-abiding nerd I'd always been. I was surprised to find I liked it.

"Even if we were flirting," Logan said from the head of the table, "that's the point of our arrangement, right? Alexis and I are putting on a show. Not to be confused with real flirting, even if..." He shook his head and cleared his throat. He had an ink stain on his oxford shirt, his dark hair was fluffier and messier than normal, and he had dark circles under his eyes. The man looked frazzled. Granted, we were only six weeks out from election day, a period of time known as "The Final Countdown," aka "Welcome to Hell," aka "This Campaign Owns You Now," according to the messages scrawled across the whiteboard. Yes, his stress had to be due to that, and not the fact that I'd volunteered him to star in a last-minute commercial.

Though Logan had directed his remarks at Cary and Nora, his eyes drifted to me. When he caught me studying him, he dropped his gaze quickly and clasped his hands together on the table. Under the table, I could hear his foot tapping the floor.

Yeah, on second thought, the source of his stress might be me.

"Cary may call it flirting, but I call it playing chicken with my campaign." Nora pointed a long nail, today a stylish gray, between me and Logan. "You better be glad the two of you one-upping each other on TV is aligned with my action plan. Just take your performances down a notch, okay?"

I nodded contritely. Logan crossed his arms and kicked back in his seat. "Of course, Nora dear. Anything you say."

"Don't 'Nora dear' me in your little accent. I'm not saving you from doing the commercial. I think it's brilliant."

I snapped to attention. "You do?"

Logan frowned. "You do?"

"Watch." Nora got up and sauntered like a fashion model to the whiteboard. She uncapped a marker and wrote *Grew up on a farm, loves animals*. Then she drew a plus sign, scribbling *Donates shitload of personal money to rescues*.

Huh. I'd assumed any donations Logan made to rescues like my mom's were tied to the campaign. But it sounded like he gave to shelters quietly, not for the publicity.

Nora was still going, scribbling, *Fifty-eight percent of Texans own pets*, then a plus sign, *Star in animal shelter video*, then a big fat equal sign, ending with *Huge-ass optics win*. She circled that last part twice and spun to face us. "Do you follow?"

"Thanks for spelling it out," Logan said dryly.

"Great thinking, Nora." I tried to lean back as suavely as I could in my child's chair. "I agree that it makes sense for Logan to help out Happy Homes. And my mom is thrilled. A win-win."

Nora sat down at the table. "Don't get too cocky. Logan's not the only one with a task. You have one, too."

"I do?"

Logan perked up.

"Yep." Nora tapped her nails on the table. "It's time for you to deliver Lee Stone."

I blinked at the suddenly serious faces around the table. "Uh...dead or alive?"

"I swear." Nora shook her head. "The fact that all of you graduated high school says all we need to know about the Texas education system."

"Hey," Cary complained. "All I said was I liked the flirting drama."

"An *endorsement*, Alexis. We need your sister to give Logan her endorsement. It's time. Tell her, Gail."

Gail looked down at her iPad. "All the state reps are lining up behind candidates. If Senator Stone gives her endorsement to Governor Mane—or if she abstains from endorsing anyone—it'll be a huge blow to us. Projections show drops in voter trust if Logan's girlfriend's sister won't give him her blessing."

"It'll be a PR disaster," Nora said.

"That's going to be...difficult," I said carefully. All four of them frowned at me. "Lee has history with Governor Mane and she's not exactly the biggest fan of our... relationship."

Logan tensed over the table. "She doesn't like me?"

"I'm sorry, Logan, I promise it's nothing personal."

"Should I invite her over? Do a dinner with your family? Is there a cause she wants me to promote?" He frowned. "Does she like flowers?"

"Whatever you need to do, Alexis." Nora's face was the gravest I'd seen it. "If you care about Logan and his chances of winning, I need you to get that endorsement."

I pulled up in front of Lee's adorable peach-and-cream house, which was an authentic Craftsman like Logan's. I'd always loved this house. It was beautiful and girly, a house you could show off, throw parties in—the opposite of my spinster hole. I'd fled here after Chris and I broke up and Lee had nursed me back to good spirits, then I'd lived here with her until Ben moved in. The house was a delight and a refuge.

I was terrified to knock on the front door.

But since I held Logan's future in my hands, I pounded dutifully. No one answered. Lee's and Ben's cars were in the driveway, so I knew they were home. I knocked again and put my ear to the door. I heard shuffling, quick footsteps, and suddenly the door wrenched open and Lee stood in front of me, her hair falling out of an updo and lipstick smudged, wearing an honest-to-God Belle costume from *Beauty and the Beast*. Over Lee's shoulder, a shirtless Ben darted out of the living room toward the bedroom, wearing a teal wig and an outfit that was vaguely familiar. "Hi, Lex!" he called, then, "Sorry!"

"Lee Stone!" I gaped at her. "Are you wearing a *sex* costume?"

She leaned against the door frame. "Maybe."

"You can't just answer your door like this. And Ben all half-naked and blue and...why is Ben blue, Lee?"

She smiled fondly. "Bet you can't guess what Ben is."

"On second thought, I don't want to know."

"He's—"

"No." I covered my ears.

"Captain Planet." The words snaked in anyway.

"Ugh, Lee! You're a state senator."

"I'm off duty," she said. "Besides, you're the one playing roulette, showing up unannounced."

I bit back my next retort, reminding myself I was here to beg for Lee's help. Probably not the best time to lecture her about her fondness for role play. I tried a different tack. "Thank you for answering even though you're busy."

"You're my little sister. No matter who or what I'm doing, I'm always going to answer. Come in. Don't mind the living room."

Of course, I couldn't help but look. Was that a candlestick on the coffee table, and ladder propped against the bookshelf? What did you even do with a ladder and a candlestick... No. I shielded my eyes.

"Kitchen?" Lee asked.

"Definitely let's go to the kitchen."

By the time I'd settled at her kitchen table Ben was back, changed into gym shorts and a T-shirt. "Proper greeting this time," he said, leaning over to hug me. I loved Ben hugs. I loved Ben everything, really. If he and my sister hadn't figured out they were perfect for each other, I would've found a way to make him my honorary big brother.

He pulled back, grinning. "It's good to see you, Lex. Been a while."

I tapped my cheek. "You've got a little...blue."

"Oh, sorry." Ben rubbed the spot furiously. Unlike Lee, he had the good grace to flush with embarrassment.

"So what's up?" Lee stood behind her breakfast counter, biting into an apple from her fruit bowl. "Good for stamina," she explained, which I very much did not need to know.

"Um, okay. Where to start. Well, first, thank you for meeting me here." Nope, I'd come to them. Ugh, the two of them standing there scrutinizing me was making me nervous. I felt a sympathy for their political opponents.

"I need you to endorse Logan," I blurted. Apparently, approaching this strategically was outside my wheelhouse.

"Oh, really?" Lee cocked an eyebrow.

"Yes. Please, please, *please* endorse him. The campaign says if you don't, he has no shot at voters trusting him. Because now you're more than just another politician. You're his girlfriend's sister. It carries weight."

"His fake girlfriend's sister."

"Well, obviously no one should know that."

Ben leaned back against the counter and crossed his muscular arms. "I've been following your TV appearances. You're putting on a hell of a performance, Lex. Really selling the couple thing."

"Mmm-hmm," Lee agreed. "It's almost *too* convincing. But I do have to thank you for getting Logan to do Mom's commercial. The thought of doing it was giving me hives. She'd already emailed me a fifty-six-page screenplay. *Fifty-six pages*, Alexis. Apparently, she took Martin Scorsese's Master Class and she's convinced the whole commercial should be filmed in one long continuous shot like that scene from *Goodfellas*. Have fun with that."

"You're welcome," I said smoothly, though inside I was thinking, *Oh, lord, what have I gotten Logan into?* "See how nice it can be when we scratch each other's backs?" Who was I, a gangster from *Goodfellas*? I backed up and tried another approach. "Anita Jones's assistant says—"

Both Ben and Lee cracked up. "Oh, God," Ben said, turning to Lee. "Remember Anita?"

"I forgot she went over to the Arthur campaign." Lee shook her head. "Mane's HR department must've thrown a party the day she quit. Remember the things she used to say to you?"

Ben smiled fondly. "She used to tell me she was giving me the female-in-a-male-dominated-field experience."

Lee rolled her eyes. "Oh, yes, Anita is performing one long

act of community service on behalf of women everywhere. What a brave activist."

"*Anyway,*" I said, "Anita's assistant says it'll be a deathblow if you don't endorse him. So I'm here to beg you. Please."

Lee and Ben eyed each other and shared a small, secret smile. Oh, I did not like that.

"You know Ben used to work for Governor Mane," Lee said. "And Mane's the one who helped us pass the bill that launched my political career. *And* he endorsed me for state senator."

"I know," I said, swallowing. "But you also said you didn't like the way he treated your boss Dakota after their affair leaked. I mean, Ben quit over it! And Logan's politics are so in line with yours—"

"You also know I'm not a fan of this elaborate farce you two have going on. I don't like people using my sister to further their careers."

"He's not using me. If anything, I'm using *him* to fight the education cuts. We've become friends—"

"You'll have to owe me," she interrupted.

"What?"

She leaned against the counter and crunched on the apple. "If I agree to betray Mane and endorse Logan, you'll have to owe me one massive favor in return. Anything I want, whenever I want it."

The last person on earth you ever wanted to make a promise like that to was Lee Stone. Honestly, I would've preferred a deal with the devil. There was a solid chance whatever Lee would ask me to do would be miles outside my comfort zone and possibly illegal.

But then I thought of Logan. His beautiful, tired face on the other side of the conference table. The way he'd chewed his pen and written out debate notes for hours under our shared blanket. How his eyes lit with longing whenever he talked to me. He'd been working toward this goal his whole life. Year after year of laser focus, putting aside everything—love, a personal life, even his ability to be himself in public—just for a shot.

The tenderness that flooded me left no other option. I'd do whatever Lee asked.

"Okay," I said, taking a deep breath. "You have a deal."

23

Projecting

"Release the kittens!" shouted my mother.

Two Happy Homes volunteers pulled away the safety gates and a horde of mewling kittens rushed forward into the giant Happy Homes playroom, where Logan sat in the middle of the floor, wearing a Happy Homes–branded polo that was dusted, like the rest of him, with high-grade catnip. As I watched the wave of cats overtake him—bouncing into his lap and climbing his back like a mountain—it occurred to me that between my mom and me, the Stone women were uniquely skilled at finding inventive ways to torture Logan.

"Welcome to Happy Homes!" he recited nonetheless, spitting cat hair out of his mouth. His face was stretched in a grin as the kittens used him as a human climbing wall. He was doing his best to convey he was having the time of his life, bless his heart.

"Cut!" my mom yelled. Thankfully, between me and the professional camera crew she'd hired, we'd convinced her one long continuous shot was both impractical and a painstaking craft detail no one who watched the commercial would notice or care about. The downside was, my mother had insisted we try out a few variations on the opening. This particular one involved Logan covered in cats.

"Quick break. Logan, I love what you're doing, you're a divine leading man. But I'm not getting the right energy from the cats." Mom narrowed her eyes. "Alexis, will you jump in and play with them a little? Get them in the mood. We want the right kind of playful—sweet, not rabid."

"I'm sorry." I crossed my arms. "Are you asking me to be a kitten fluffer?"

"Just get in there." She waved in Logan's direction. "Get them to deliver."

"Ugh. Fine." I left my comfortable perch and walked to Logan. "But has anyone mentioned you're taking this a little too seriously?" Mom was dressed in head-to-toe black like some sort of auteur filmmaker. I was honestly surprised she wasn't sporting a beret. Behind her, the team of Happy Homes volunteers widened their eyes and shook their heads at me in silent warning. Touchy subject, apparently.

"There's no such thing as taking it too seriously," Mom said sweetly. Lee liked to say she took after our dad and I took after Mom, but sometimes it couldn't be more obvious that Lee was Elise Stone's daughter. They were two peas in a very demanding pod.

"No filming me," I warned. "I'm just fluffing, then I'm out." I crept through the kittens, then knelt next to Logan. "You doing okay?" It had already been a whirlwind day. After meeting my mom, the crew, and the "creative team" here at the Houston Happy Homes headquarters at the unhealthy hour of 7:00 a.m., Logan had borne a solid half hour of my mom's effusive thanks, and then he'd been ushered into a closed-door storyboarding meeting I wasn't allowed to attend. He'd walked into the meeting wearing a suit and a determined expression. He'd walked out wearing a Happy Homes polo, looking dazed.

"Of course I'm doing okay," Logan growled, clutching a wriggling cat. "I'm covered in kittens. This is the best fucking day of my life."

"Language!" chirped my mother, and Logan called back, "Sorry, Elise!"

I frowned. "Then why do you look so angry?"

"Because this camera is going to capture me eating my heart out with these adorable fucking monsters—*sorry, Elise*—and the whole state is going to see me being soft. Mane's going to seize on my weakness like a shark smelling blood in the water. I know because it's what I would do."

"This commercial is *meant* to show your softer side." I lunged, removing a kitten who was about to spring into Logan's face. "It could win over new voters."

Logan's eyebrows drew together. "If you say so." He eyed me. "Will you get down here already?"

I crouched slowly, checking I wasn't going to squash any cats. As soon as I was on the floor, I was bombarded by wet noses and tiny claws. I scooped a midnight-black kitten who was climbing a little too deep into my lap. "Getting fresh, Count Dracula." Around us, the room buzzed with Happy Homes staff and the camera crew, but no one from the campaign. "Why didn't you bring anyone with you? Did Cary and Nora not want to make the drive?" It was only two hours from Austin to Houston.

Logan shrugged, dangling a string. A tiny calico gave it everything she had, launching her body all of three inches in the air and still missing. "I didn't want to meet your mom as a candidate. You know, with security and entourage. I wanted to meet her as myself. Besides, they're all freaking out about the first debate. T-minus two days now."

"Well, I think my mom likes you, for whatever that's worth."

His eyes lit up. "Really?"

"Oh, sure. Almost as much as Ben, I bet."

"Almost? Hey, your mom thinks we're actually dating." He watched the leaping calico and frowned. "*Almost as much*."

"Welcome to my life. Second-place trophies as far as the eye can see." I leaned over and tried fluffing a few kittens so their fur stood taller. I honestly had no idea what my mom expected. When I looked up, Logan was studying me. "What?"

"Nothing," he said, though the way he was looking at me suggested otherwise. "Will you look at this guy?" He pointed to gray-and-white Mischief, who chose that moment to spring up and bite the collar of Logan's polo, hanging on for dear life. Logan turned to me with an amazed expression. "He's trying to eat me."

"Mischief tries to eat everything. In your case, I think it's because you let my mom rub you down with catnip. Which was ridiculous, by the way. You could've said no."

"To Elise? Ha." Logan scooped up Mischief and cradled him. "Seriously, look at this face. As soon as I'm done campaigning, I'm adopting as many animals as I can fit in my house."

"Your post-election dream is to become an animal hoarder?"

He smiled wistfully. "I have a lot of post-election dreams."

"Well, you might not want to mention that one to Nora. You can fit a lot of cats in the governor's mansion." I looked at Mischief, who was now curled into a ball in Logan's hands. "I've wanted a cat for a long time."

"I know my excuse. Zero time. Why are you waiting?"

Normally, I told my mom I didn't have enough space in my apartment or a million other practical excuses. But with Logan, the truth came out. "I guess I'm scared to be the most important person in something's life. I'm scared to have it all come down to me. What if I'm not good enough? What if there are better options for parents?"

Logan was opening his mouth to respond when two kittens launched what could only have been a coordinated attack. They both sailed past Mischief to land on Logan's head, where they clung to his hair like mountain rappelers. "Oh, shit," Logan yelped, then, "sorry, Elise!" He jerked backward and Mischief leaped away.

"Alexis!" my mother called, but I was already on it.

"Hold still, let me help." I crawled into the empty space between Logan's long legs and reached for his head—then slipped on the linoleum. I fell hard against his chest, knocking him backward on the floor and collapsing on top of him. Logan's entire body went rigid.

Oops. Carefully, I extracted the cats, then studied him. No tiny claw marks on his face. He looked normal, except for the fact that he was staring at me.

"Hi." His soft voice didn't match the intensity of his eyes. "Did I crush any cats?"

"If you did, they deserved it."

We grinned at each other. His body was warm and solid beneath mine, the firmness of his muscles easy to feel under his thin polo. All those hours playing soccer were evident in the hard planes of his body. I'd collapsed between his thighs, where I fit snugly, and our faces were close enough that if he tilted his head, he'd brush my lips.

"Good idea," my mom called. "We'll get B-roll."

"Oh, shoot, my mom." I'd honestly forgotten about her. I started to jerk up.

"No, stay there," my mom insisted. "For the B-roll. You're hearing me say B-roll, right, honey? Like Scorsese."

Logan shrugged, a small, pleased smile curving his mouth. "Director's orders. You're going to have to stay." He lowered his voice. "Don't forget—she thinks we're dating."

"Right." I couldn't leap away from Logan in embarrassment. I had to act like I was his girlfriend, used to touching him. What would that look like?

I started by relaxing my shoulders. In response, he put an arm around me, drawing me even tighter against his chest. The sensation of my body rubbing against his—against his soft polo, the starchy denim pulled tight over his thighs—made me look away so he couldn't catch my expression. This is what it would feel like to lie in bed with him on Sunday mornings, stretch out on the couch watching movies. To be his real girlfriend. Logan—strong, tall, chiseled-jawed, and gruffly beautiful—would hold me just like this, look down at me just like this. Smile just like this. The sense of certainty was so vivid it felt like getting a glimpse into an alternate universe.

I met his eyes cautiously, hoping he couldn't read what I was thinking.

He stroked my hair away from my face, lightly skimming my temple. "Have I told you I like that you're an animal person?"

I smiled. "I like that you're tall. Makes you an excellent floor cushion."

His grin grew wider. "You know, when you *really* smile, you do it with your whole face. I can see your smile in your eyes. It's the best thing."

The same tender feeling that made me agree to Lee's deal washed back now, somehow warmer.

"Great shots," my mom yelled. "Now let's get going on a new scene."

The sound of her voice had me scrambling up like a teenager caught with my bedroom door closed.

"Easy," Logan warned, hands covering his crotch.

As I tried to roll both safely and elegantly away, I spotted something in the corner of the room under the cat tree. It was a full-grown cat, a tabby. I picked myself up and edged nearer. It was obvious the cat had been through an ordeal. Its fur was ragged, missing in places, and the tip of one ear was gone. It was curled up under the cat tree, quietly watching the kittens with large, wistful green eyes that flicked back and forth as the kittens played.

"Mom," I called. "Who's this?"

She looked up from where she'd been pointing at something in the cameraman's notebook. "Oh—that's Patches. She's our oldest cat. Been with us for close to a year, I think. We took her from a shelter that was going to put her down."

I walked slowly to Patches so I didn't scare her and crouched down, sticking out my hand. She sniffed it experimentally.

"I don't understand why no one wants her," Mom said. "She's a little rough-looking, sure—we think she got attacked by another animal. But she's the sweetest girl. I hate that she's spending so much of her life in the shelter."

Now that I was close up, I could see that the spots where Patches' fur was missing looked scarred, like she'd been bitten and the fur refused to grow back. To my surprise, she leaned into my touch and rubbed her face against my fingers. I scratched her head and ears and heard the sound of the world's tiniest, quietest motor. She was purring.

"We let her hang out with the kittens because she gets lonely," Mom said. "She's perfectly happy to sit and watch."

I stroked Patches' face. She'd been overlooked. That wasn't fair. Patches had love to give. She deserved better.

"I'll take her," I said.

The sounds of the camera crew moving behind me stopped. "What was that, Lex?"

I turned around. Everyone was watching me. I took a deep breath and said, in a louder voice, "I want Patches. I'll take her home."

My mom almost dropped her clapboard. "Really? Oh, Alexis, that's fabulous! Two of my favorite girls, coming together!" She turned to the cameraman. "Please tell me you got that."

The intensity of her enthusiasm made my face heat. As did the look on Logan's face as he walked over and scooped Patches up.

"Hey, Patches," he crooned, letting her settle into the crook of his arm. "You coming back with us to Austin? Going to help me campaign?" He gave me a knowing look. "I can tell she's a Democrat."

Patches was looking at him and purring, so it was safe to say she was at least a Logan Arthur fan. And I was starting to see why Logan had been reluctant to go on camera. It turned out *l'enfant terrible* of Texas politics, the man who sent paparazzi running, the politician with the most f-bombs on record, got really, *really* soft around small, four-legged creatures. I scratched behind Patches' ears, brushing Logan's forearm with my own. "I'll allow you to recruit her if you agree Cary still does the coffee runs. He hates it too much to take it away from him."

"Deal," Logan said. Then, just as lightly, "Big decision you just made. Feeling good about it? None of those worries creeping in?"

It was a big decision. Taking Patches home meant my whole life would change. I took a deep breath. "No, I'm terrified. But look at her. Even if I'm not the best, fanciest cat mom, I can at least make sure she's not alone. Always coming in last while the other cats get all the attention. I know what you're thinking," I added quickly, watching Logan's mouth quirk. "And before you say it, I am *not* projecting."

"Smile for the camera," Mom called, and we turned to find one of her Happy Homes staffers snapping pictures of us on her phone. "This one's for the adoption wall." My mother's eyes shone as she looked between me and Logan. "Look at the three of you. What an adorable family."

To my surprise, Logan wrapped his arm around me and tugged me closer.

"So sweet," Mom sighed. "Logan, hats off. I've been trying to get Alexis to adopt for years and the first time you're here, she's sold." She tapped her chin. "This bodes well for our commercial. Speaking of!" She whipped around to the camera crew. "Next scene is in the dog wing, and after that the reptiles." She spun on her heels. "Location change!" As she strode out of the room, everyone scrambled to break down equipment and follow.

Logan's face had turned pale at the mention of reptiles. I elbowed him. "I think my mom might like you as much as Ben now."

That raised his spirits. He kissed Patches' head and thrust her at me, then started jogging backward, careful to avoid the kittens. "Watch this. I'm about to climb into the lead. Oi, Elise!" he called, cupping his hands around his mouth. "Where were we on Scorsese? I think we got up to hour two of that Master Class. I'm dying to hear about hour three." He winked at me, holding up a finger for number one, then hurried out of the room.

"He's very competitive," I whispered to Patches. She made a half exasperated, half amused sound, which were my thoughts exactly.

24

The Favor

When I got home from work on Monday, I found my apartment door unlocked. Immediately, my heart jumped into my throat. I took out my phone and dialed nine, then twisted the door and crept inside, calling, "Hello? Anyone in here?" Bracing myself, I turned the corner to the living room and shrieked.

"Hello, Alexis," said Lee, from her perch on my couch. She sat there with Patches in her lap. "Welcome home."

"Jesus, Lee!" I pressed a hand to my chest. "How did you get in?"

She shrugged. "I used my key."

"That key is for emergencies. You scared the daylights out of me."

She nodded at the living room. "I'm pretty sure you'd hear a robber coming from a mile away. Your place is booby-trapped better than Macaulay Culkin's in *Home Alone*."

I winced. My apartment was slightly chaotic. Strewn around the living room was every kind of cat toy—string, ball, feather, light-up—plus cat brushes, a cat tree, scratch pads, and catnip.

"What'd you do," Lee asked, "buy the entire cat aisle at PetSmart?"

I sank onto the couch. "I hope so. How else am I supposed to know what Patches likes?" I was determined to be a good cat mom, even if I had to sell my soul to PetSmart to do it.

Lee raised her eyebrows. "You know cats are fine playing with a cardboard box, right?" She leaned over and hugged Patches tighter. "Though this little angel does deserve the world." Lee cradled Patches on her back like an infant, rocking her back and forth.

"Is that how you're supposed to hold cats?" I practiced, making my arms into a bassinet.

"Oh, oops." Lee halted her rocking. "I've been holding too many babies lately. You'd be shocked at how people just hand their babies over to politicians. Like what am I going to do, bless it? I'm not the Pope. Anyway, glad you bit the bullet and got Patches. How's motherhood?"

I was trying not to be jealous of how blissful Patches looked in Lee's arms. Patches had been glued to my side since I brought her home, but if she was willing to cozy up to strangers at the first invitation, I guess that was fine. "Going well. We're getting to know each other." I threw up a hand. "Wait, stop doing your Lee-distracting-thing. Why did I find you sitting in my living room like a movie villain?"

Her eyes darted away, which was suspicious. "You know, I got quite an earful from Mom about what a foul-mouthed, softhearted sweetheart Logan is. You realize you're going to break her heart when the two of you fake breakup, right?"

I gulped. "It's a good thing she's gotten used to my

heartbreaks. Par for the course." I flung my hand at my living room. "And look, now I have a cat. The last missing ingredient for peak spinsterhood. I accept my fate. Mom will, too."

"So nothing's changed on the Logan front? You two are just business partners who will go your separate ways once the voters are properly hoodwinked? No romantic feelings?"

I straightened, holding my head high. "For your information, I've finally broken my toxic pattern. Logan and I are just friends, and I'm good with that. No pining. No trying to make us into anything we're not."

"Excellent." Lee clapped her hands so suddenly Patches startled and leaped away. "Then you're ready to hear my favor."

"You're calling it in already?" I'd expected Lee to hold on to her leverage for a while, if for no other reason than to torture me.

"I am. In exchange for endorsing Logan, I want you to go on a date with Will Laderman."

I had to be hearing things. "As in Ben's *brother*?"

"Exactly." Lee brightened, giving me a very Vanna-White-presenting-a-car-smile. "As you know, Will moved back to Austin to do his residency at Dell Medical Center. He's a *surgeon*, Alexis. A handsome, funny, nice surgeon, and Ben and I think the two of you would really hit it off. I'd actually describe Ben as downright giddy about it."

I shook my head. I'd met Will a few times, but he always seemed to witness me when I was at my lowest. For example: he'd been at Lee's house when Chris Tuttle and I broke up for the final time. Will had heard Chris call me a timid mouse who was bad in bed. "What makes you so sure Will even wants to go out with me?" That last scene hadn't exactly been a ringing endorsement of my skills in the girlfriend department.

"He said yes immediately," Lee said. "Between you and me, I think Will's had a crush on you for a while."

He had? I let this strange—and strangely flattering—news sink in.

"And the thing is," she added, "Will's lonely. It's hard for him to meet people since he works such long hours at the hospital. The head of his cardiology department invited him to his wedding in two weeks and he really needs a date. Ben and I figured, Will's lonely, you're lonely—"

"I'm not lonely," I said quickly. The idea of Lee thinking that was mortifying. Besides, even if that *had* been true a month ago, ever since I'd met Logan at the Fleur de Lis, my life had been a whirlwind of people and projects and—come to think of it, I hadn't felt alone once. "Besides, I'm not allowed to date anyone while I'm fake dating Logan. That's rule number one. It would be a PR nightmare if I got caught."

"Will knows about your deal with Logan—"

"You *told* him?"

"He says he's not bothered by it! He'll cook you dinner at his place, where no one will see you. Completely private. You can test the waters. If you like each other, maybe you can be his date to the wedding. He makes a mean chicken cacciatore, according to Ben."

"I really can't. It's too risky."

She narrowed her eyes and leaned back, folding her arms

over her chest. She was wearing the same look on her face Mom had when we'd pushed into hour sixteen of filming. Dangerously stubborn. "If you want this endorsement, all it takes is one date. Maybe two, if you're willing to go to the wedding. Don't worry about being exposed there—Will says most of the surgeons are too busy to track politics. It's a really big deal for him, Lex. All of his colleagues are bringing dates."

I hated the idea of letting someone down. And Lee was just talking about one date, *maybe* two. Private events, with a person who was guaranteed, since he shared so much of Ben's DNA, to be a pretty good egg. I recalled Nora's warning: *Whatever it takes to get that endorsement.*

"Fine," I snapped. "I'll test the waters with Will. But this is the last time you matchmake for me. Promise. You're a real-life Emma Woodhouse, and that's not a compliment."

Lee sprang off the couch. "Easy promise. Because you and Will are going to fall in love and I'll never need to matchmake again." Her voice turned softer as she walked over and put a hand on my shoulder. "In all seriousness, Lex. You deserve more than a fake relationship. You deserve someone who worships you."

I remembered the way Logan had looked at me when we were sprawled out on the floor of Happy Homes—the way his eyes had shone when he told me I smiled with my whole face. "I do want that," I said softly. Maybe I wouldn't have believed I was worth it a few months ago, but now that I'd had a taste of what it could feel like— even if it was only for show—I wanted it. Finding truth in fiction, like Logan said.

She squeezed my shoulder and headed for the door.

"Then you're going to love Will. Oh, and hey." Lee turned back. "Tell Logan to break a leg at the debate tomorrow. I don't usually get nervous, but if I were him, going up against Mane, I'd be quaking in my boots."

25

The First Debate

If the general seating area of the Lady Bird Johnson Auditorium was chaotic—ushers directing audience members, staffers running to fill last-minute requests, crews adjusting cameras on fifteen-foot mounts, top brass from the DNC and RNC settling into opposite sides of the auditorium—backstage managed to be busier. It was tight quarters back here, and production assistants rushed everywhere on holy missions with zero concern for boundaries, which is why I'd almost been mowed over three separate times. What's more, a solid half of the people backstage seemed to belong to the governor. I hadn't realized how big his team was until I was standing in the hallway outside Logan's dressing room and Grover Mane himself strode by, followed by a sea of staff.

Mane gave me the same impression he always did: he was an enormous man, undoubtedly a former linebacker, a well-coiffed bear stuffed into an expensive suit. He didn't give me the time of day, but his staff eyed me and whispered as they passed. If anyone on the internet was spreading rumors about me, I felt certain I was looking at them. When the parade finally passed, all I could think was: *Holy hell*. Logan wasn't just challenging some image on a poster or a floating head on TV. He was battling a man who was essentially an institution, with an army at his beck and call. Logan versus Mane suddenly felt like David versus Goliath.

These were thoughts I kept to myself as I helped Logan prep in his dressing room. "Mr. Arthur," I said, using my best no-nonsense reporter voice. "What would you say to voters worried about the cost of their prescription drugs?"

He paced in front of me. "I would say, first and foremost, that I hear you. What good is an innovative pharmaceutical industry if people can't afford drugs that are supposed to save their lives? If elected, I would enact my ten-point health care plan, the center of which is getting Medicaid expanded in the state, going to battle with pharma companies blocking sales of cheaper generics, and increasing health care support for the elderly, who are our most needs-intensive citizens."

"Rebuttal: Mane says your plan costs too much and is unrealistic."

Logan hit the wall with his palm and spun back. "I would tell him to shove his head up his ass for valuing corporations over people's lives."

"Now what you'll really say."

He grimaced. "I would agree with the governor that keeping a balanced budget is important, which is why my plan has been vetted by a team of economists who've found ways to cut down on insurance company profiteering to account for any increased costs."

"Great," I said, flipping to the next postcard. "Next up—"

The door to the dressing room burst open and Nora strode in, wearing a headset. She was looking slick in a royal blue sheath dress and movie star red lips. "Logan, you're up in two."

Butterflies whirled in my stomach. Even though it wasn't me in the hot seat, just being close to someone under this much pressure was enough to crack me. But Logan nodded smoothly. "All right. I think we've prepped all we can."

Cary, Anita, Gail, and a throng of other staffers crowded the doorway.

"Remember," Nora said, "be strong but not combative. No cursing. The voter is always right. And what are Mane's weaknesses?"

"Economy. Poor follow-through. Disingenuous."

"Exactly. Hit 'em all."

"Excellent suit choice," Cary said. "You look like you mean business, like Matt Bomer in *White Collar*." Logan was in a formal midnight blue suit tonight. It was all about downplaying his youth, making him seem as qualified and capable as Mane. His hair was carefully brushed back— no soft curls this evening—and his beard was precisely trimmed, a darker version of a five-o'clock shadow. He looked razor-sharp.

"He's ready," Nora said. "Team, clear out. Alexis."

I snapped to attention, hopping out of my chair.

"Fix his pin, straighten his tie, then send him out."

I nodded as the rest of the campaign filtered out, honored to have a job.

"Not combative, not combative," Logan murmured. His eyes were fixed on the middle distance. Mentally, he was already on the debate stage.

I righted his flag pin. "You've got this. You're a million times the politician Mane is."

He rocked on his heels and shook his arms out, tilting his head from left to right like a boxer prepping for a match. "I've got this."

I straightened his tie and brushed his arms free of wrinkles. "You're going to get out there and crush it."

He nodded, still rocking. "Going to crush it."

"Good. Now go. Good luck."

"Thank you," he said quickly, then twisted his watch into place, cupped my face, and kissed me. His warm lips pressed to mine for the briefest moment, then he spun for the door.

And froze.

I stood shell-shocked against the high table.

Slowly, Logan turned, face as white as a ghost's, eyes wide as saucers. "Fuck. I'm so sorry. It was a reflex."

We stared at each other for a long moment. My heart pounded. "It's okay. Don't worry about it."

"Logan, get out here!" Nora's head popped in. "*Now!*"

"Right," he said dazedly, and walked out the door, eyes still unblinking. Immediately, his staffers caught him by the shoulders and marched him toward the stage.

I watched the back of his head until he disappeared, my fingers tracing my lips. Mistake or not, I needed a minute to remember how to breathe.

The entire row of Logan's staffers winced as Governor Mane cut in yet again, interrupting Logan's carefully worded point about immigration. We were seated close to the stage in the large, moodily lit auditorium, but it was still easier to look up at the giant TV monitors hanging on either side of the curtains, which showed Logan's face closeup. In high-definition, he frowned and gripped the sides of his podium until his knuckles went white. The governor droned on, but he didn't jump in. Didn't berate him, call Mane a phony or indulge in a single one of what I knew were his natural instincts. Mane finished making his point and the crowd burst into applause, loudest from the RNC camp in the corner.

Thirty minutes in, and the debate was not going well.

"Why is he being so *weak*?" Cary hissed. I'd ended up sandwiched between him and Nora, which at least meant that every time I recoiled or cringed watching the governor trample Logan, they'd been right there with me. Shared suffering.

"I don't know." Nora shook her head, eyes searching Logan's image on the screen. "He knows this stuff cold, and Mane isn't saying anything unexpected. But Logan's pulling all his punches."

"I think he's overcorrecting," I said quietly, and both Cary and Nora turned.

"What do you mean?" Nora asked.

"I think he's so worried about coming across as combative that he's checking himself too much."

"Maybe," she murmured, and we all looked back at the stage. One of the moderators was asking Logan the next question.

"Mr. Arthur, rising health care costs are one of Texans' greatest sources of anxiety, according to a new *Texas Tribune* poll. What would you say to those worried about the costs of their prescription drugs?"

"He *knows* this one," I whispered excitedly. "We practiced."

Nora shot me a hopeful look—and, to my surprise, grabbed my hand. We gripped each other while we waited for Logan to answer.

"I would say, first and foremost, that I hear them." Logan's voice was strong and sure. "It's unacceptable for medicine to be priced so astronomically that the very people it's meant to help can't afford it. No one should have to choose between their rent and their cancer treatment."

Nora squeezed my hand.

"That's why one of the first things I'll do if elected..." Logan's gaze cast out into the audience. A strange look came over his face, as if he'd just gone somewhere else. He looked down at his podium. A collective pall fell over our row. In front of us, the DNC guys started whispering furiously.

"What is *happening* right now?" Cary's face was horrified.

"Where are you, Logan?" Nora whispered. "Get your head back in the game."

"Is..." Logan's attention returned to the moderator. "Enact my ten-point health care reform plan, which will expand Medicaid..." Logan wrapped up his answer succinctly and the question was tossed over to Mane, who leaped in immediately and started hammering out his plans. It was hard not to compare their energy.

"He's *distracted*," Nora said. She had an *aha* light in her eyes. "Something's throwing him."

I felt the ghostly pressure of his lips on mine. Then the look of horror on his face that followed. Guilt stabbed through me.

"Logan is *never* distracted," Cary whispered. "Not when he's arguing, not when he's talking to voters, hell, not even playing soccer. Whatever this is, it has to be big."

I remembered what Logan told me about his breakup with Tinsley, how it had been so bad he'd all but checked out the last week. Relationships got in his head, which is why he'd stopped dating in the first place. Somehow, our fake relationship was having the same effect.

"Did he tell you anything in the dressing room?" Nora asked me, snapping me out of my thoughts. "Do you have any clue what's distracting him?"

With Nora's and Cary's eyes on me, I dipped in my seat. "No." My cheeks flamed. "Nothing I can think of."

I peeked up at Logan's face on-screen. His mouth was set in a frustrated line as the moderator asked Governor Mane the next question, but his eyes...once again, they cast out into the audience, as if he couldn't help searching for someone. What if he was looking for me, driven by the compulsion to make sure I knew the kiss was a mistake?

The guilt sank me lower in my seat.

26

A Real-Life Prince Charming

I looked at the glowing headline on my phone, this one from The *Watcher on the Hill*: "Where Did Logan Arthur Go?" Underneath, the subhead read: "Arthur turned in a mystifyingly meek performance against Mane in last night's debate. Has the famously feisty Democrat finally been neutered?" I sighed and clicked the phone dark.

The news coverage of the debate, while not as colorful as Daniel Watcher's commentary, had all been in the same vein. Which was yet another reason I was here. Not only did Logan need Lee's endorsement more than ever, he and I needed space. When security rushed him past me into Nigel's waiting car after the debate, he hadn't even glanced my way, but I didn't blame him. I took a deep breath, straightened my spine, and knocked on the front door of Will Laderman's townhouse.

After a moment, the door swung open to reveal Will. It had been a while, so seeing him standing there framed in the doorway was a little like seeing him for the first time. You could tell he and Ben were brothers. They were both tall with coal black hair, blue eyes, and the same defined jawlines. But while Lee liked to say Ben looked like Clark Kent, Will was like if Clark Kent had a leaner, longer-haired cousin who worked in IT. Clark Kent meets Timothée Chalamet. He was so handsome my heart gave an unexpected lurch.

Will grinned at me. He wore a navy Oxford with the sleeves rolled up and below his jeans, he was barefoot. "It's so nice to see you again."

I was unprepared for the smoky quality of his voice. "Hi, it's, uh, nice to see you, too."

"Come in," Will said, opening the door wider. "I just started cooking. Lee said you were good with chicken cacciatore, so I hope that's still okay."

I followed him in, unabashedly scoping as we moved through the living room into the kitchen. This is what I'd expected Logan's house to look like. Will's townhouse was new and sleekly modern, but it looked barely lived-in: some perfunctory furniture and a few lamps, but little else. There were even a few posters sitting in shrink-wrap against the living room wall.

He caught me looking and rubbed the back of his neck sheepishly. "Yeah, it's a ghost town. I'm barely here because of residency, and when I am, I'm sleeping. Not that I don't know how to have fun," he added quickly. "I'm not making myself sound very appealing, am I?"

"You're very appealing," I said reassuringly, then blushed and hurried into the kitchen. Unlike the rest of the townhouse, it was lived-in, strewn with pots, pans, and a knife block that looked lovingly cared for. There were leafy vegetables sitting freshly washed in a colander and a bottle of red wine next to two glasses.

"Can I pour you a glass? Your sister said you liked wine. I had the guy at the store help me pick it out."

Oh, Will was *nervous*. I recognized the signs, even if the idea of someone being nervous around me was laughable. I smiled gently, a little high on the power. "A big one, please."

"Yes, ma'am." He grinned and poured. "I'm going to cook, and I thought maybe you could sit at the counter and keep me company? Or you could go to the living room. Or—anywhere you want, honestly."

"Here's good." I settled on one of his barstools and took a big sip of wine, which was excellent. I checked the bottle. Bloody Good Wine, a vineyard out in Fredericksburg. That was Texas wine country, only an hour and a half outside Austin. I'd have to tell Zoey about it. We were going to Fredericksburg next weekend for her and Annie's joint bachelorette. I was extremely honored to have scored an invite.

"So, is it weird our siblings set us up?" Will diced an onion expertly, in a way I'd never been able to master. Maybe it was his surgeon skills. "I mean, it's not for me. Ben's constantly meddling in my life. He appointed himself my stand-in dad after ours left." When Will glanced up, his eyes were misty.

"Oh, Will." I reached over the counter and put my hand on his arm. "I'm so sorry." He froze, looking down at my hand and then meeting my eyes. "*Ohhh*," I said. "The tears are from the onion, aren't they?"

He laughed, a warm sound that curled pleasantly inside me. "They are, but thank you. I've actually never been particularly torn up by my dad leaving. I was young, so I never got to know him. It hit Ben way harder. Sometimes

I think he worked so hard to be a father to me as a way of coping with his own grief. But I do appreciate the gesture."

I retreated back to my barstool, taking a large gulp of wine. *Good job, Alexis. Treat a grown man like you would your first grade students.* "For what it's worth, I'm used to Lee meddling, too. She did the opposite of Ben when our family broke up—she kind of retreated. For a long time I was the one trying to insert myself into her life. But the last couple of years we've grown closer, and she's jumped headfirst into that annoying older sibling thing of thinking they know what's best for you."

Will walked to his cast iron pan and slid the chopped onions off the cutting board into the pan. They sizzled, filling the air with a delicious grilled aroma. "It has to get exhausting for them, don't you think? All that plotting on our behalf, on top of managing their own lives." He turned to me and grinned. "Think Lee and Ben stay up at night, scheming about us?"

I pictured Lee in her Belle costume and Ben in his blue Captain Planet wig and blanched. "I'm going to suggest we don't talk about what Lee and Ben get up to at night." Despite the joke, my mind wandered to more serious territory. Will and I had a lot in common. Unlike me and Logan, who couldn't be more opposite. As soon as I thought it, I reprimanded myself: *No Logan thoughts.*

Will snorted. "Fair." He picked up his knife, then set it back down, seeming to come to a decision. He brushed a dark curl behind his ear and looked at me. When I met his eyes, all the hairs on my arms rose. His eyes were distractingly blue, so vivid they kept taking me by surprise.

They were the opposite of Logan's warm brown eyes, with their thousand shades of amber. *Stop, you addict.*

"In the interest of transparency," Will said haltingly. "I think Ben and Lee set us up because they knew I've liked you since the first time we met. Way back when they dated the first time, and you were just a freshman at UT, I came to visit Ben and met you and...well, I never stopped thinking about you."

My face flamed at his admission. I didn't know what to do with my eyes or my hands—or, frankly, my mouth. I directed my words to Will's cutting board. "I feel like I should say thank you for noticing me, but that sounds kind of uncool, so...uh..."

He laughed, sparing me. "No need to say anything. Sorry if that's too many cards on the table. I just believe in being honest. No games, you know?"

I nodded slowly, willing myself not to compare him to Logan. "That sounds...refreshing."

Over the next two hours, Will finished cooking and we ate his delicious chicken cacciatore and salad—followed by homemade tiramisu, because when the man did take a break from his surgical residency, apparently he moonlighted as a professional chef. We sat at his homey little dining table and our conversation flowed easily, helped in no small part by the fact that we downed the entire bottle of Bloody Good Wine, causing Will to open a second he'd bought "in case the night went as well as he'd hoped." The man was charming, funny, and had very little interest in Texas politics, which made the whole night feel like an escape.

When I checked my phone and saw it was well past eleven, I gasped. "I didn't realize how late it was. You probably have to work tomorrow. I mean, I have to work tomorrow, too, but I'm not cutting anyone open."

Will laughed. "I'm working the late shift tomorrow, so I'll be fine. I could probably sit here all night if you let me. You're easy to talk to."

Once again, that annoying flush, the one that would always keep me from appearing cool and unaffected, crept up my neck. "I had a really good time. Thank you for everything."

"Let me walk you out." We both rose and made our way through his house. When we got to his front door, Will stopped and I turned to face him, suddenly lit with nerves. "I'd love to see you again," he said softly. "Maybe take you to a wedding?"

It had to be the wine making me bold. "Lee said she told you about Logan Arthur. Does it really not bother you that I'm publicly seeing someone?"

An affectionate smile crept over Will's mouth, making his eyes twinkle. "You know, I'm pretty used to Stone family shenanigans by now. I'm sure you're doing it for a good reason, and Lee said you and Logan are just friends behind the scenes. So if you're open to seeing me, I'll take what I can get."

I was torn between pride at being part of the Stone family tradition, a tender soreness at the reminder that Logan and I weren't real, and exhilaration over Will's sweetness. It was a confusing emotional maelstrom, and Will must've sensed it, because he leaned in and kissed me quickly on the cheek.

"Take whatever time you need," he said, pulling back. "I'm not going anywhere."

His words set off a riot of thoughts. Will was wrong—*Logan* was the one not going anywhere, and I needed to remember that. He and I were a business arrangement morphed into a friendship, and for all I knew, he was going to call any minute to end our fake relationship since it was starting to distract him. I needed to stop acting like on some level, I was taken. I wasn't—I was free as a bird. And come election day on November 7th, it would be official for the world to see.

I placed my hand on Will's soft shirt. "You know what? I don't need time. I'm happy to be your date to the wedding."

His face broke into a dazzling smile. Yes, this was a good choice. A wise one. For once I would move *toward* the nice, available man—truly, Prince Charming in scrubs—and *away* from the beautiful, sarcastic, unavailable one.

This was the choice that would protect my heart. Besides, Logan never had to know.

27

Texas Wine Country

Not only did Zoey and Annie take my Bloody Good Wine recommendation, they ran with it, making it the first stop on "Zoey and Annie's Bacchic Bachelorette Weekend," which was the title of the itinerary my sister's friend Claire handed me the minute I pulled up to the enormous Airbnb we were renting for the weekend. The itinerary was laminated and attached to a lanyard because, as Claire curtly explained, this was not their first rodeo. It came with an NDA I had to sign before entering the house, and no amount of protesting that I was Lee's sister and would obviously not leak drunk pictures of her at a bachelorette party got me out of having to slash my name across all three pages. Reminder to hire Claire if I ever needed a lawyer, because she was ruthless.

When she invited me to her bachelorette, Zoey had explained that since she and Annie shared so many of the same friends, they'd decided to hold a joint party and turn it into a couples' weekend. Claire and Simon, Mac and Ted, Lee and Ben, and a few of Zoey's artist friends—Duke and

Jeremy, who were both sculptors, and Layla and Helen, an actress and a glassblower—were all here. I was the lone single person, so I was relieved to find they hadn't stiffed me on my bedroom—as a Frequent Single, I was used to being shoved in closets or given bunk beds on group trips, but this time my assignment was a cozy second-floor bedroom with a king-sized bed and claw-foot tub. After freshening up, I'd joined the whole merry crew in a shuttle bus that chugged us outside the postcard-cute town of Fredericksburg to the long stretch of vineyards that surrounded it. Forget Napa. It was gorgeous out here in Texas wine country, with an added dash of quaint and homey.

Now, climbing out of the shuttle and facing the Bloody Good Wine vineyard, I nearly swooned. The tasting room was a charming, modestly sized wooden building surrounded by large oak trees, wooden swings and a fire pit. Behind that stretched rows and rows of carefully cosseted grapevines. "This place is adorable."

Zoey seized my arm and bounced, knocking her tiara askew. It was her one concession to our group's demand that she and Annie parade their status as bachelorettes. They had absolutely refused Mac's glitter sashes and "Kiss Me, I'm Going to Be a Bride" pins, so we considered the tiaras a win. "I'm so excited I can't stand it," Zoey squealed.

I righted her crown. "I'm glad you liked my suggestion so much."

Her responding smile was suspiciously satisfied. "I have a surprise for you inside." She tugged me ahead of the group.

"It's your weekend," I protested. "We should be surprising *you*." But I fell quiet when we burst into the tasting room. It was just as charming as the outside, all cozy and wood-paneled, with a few British flags and pieces of soccer memorabilia. In the faintest way, it reminded me of Logan's house. It was nicely busy, too, even at three in the afternoon, and the hum of chatter from couples glugging wine formed an inviting ambiance. One of the staff led us through the crowd to the best table, a round one in the corner with a great view of the vineyard. As we all fit ourselves around it—Zoey insisted on sitting next to me—I searched the tasting room, trying to suss out my surprise. I found zero clues.

"The owners will be right with you," the staff member promised, and whisked away.

"Owners?" Lee's eyebrows raised. "I'm glad Ann and Zo are getting the VIP treatment they deserve."

I thought Zoey would keel over from delight. She and Annie both beamed at me. "We have a little surprise for Alexis. When she recommended this place and we looked it up, we thought, *surely*, she has to know. But she clearly doesn't."

"Know what?" What had I recommended without realizing it? Oh, God, did this place turn into a burlesque club or something? I would never hear the end of it.

Lee looked just as confused as I was. She glanced at Ben, who shrugged. "No idea."

"Eeee," Zoey squealed, and I turned.

The double doors to the back of the tasting room burst open and Logan, of all people, emerged, flanked by a man and woman who bore a remarkable resemblance to him. He grinned at me from across the room, dressed down in jeans and a black T-shirt, looking happier and more relaxed than I'd seen him in a long time. He shook his head when he got closer, giving me a wide, toothy smile. "Of all the wine joints in all the towns in all the world, she walks into mine." His deep, familiar voice sent shivers down my spine.

I blinked, mouth open. "What are you doing here?"

Logan and company reached our table and he smiled down at us. "Hi everyone. I'd like to introduce you to my parents, Kit and Petra. They own the place."

You could've knocked me over with a feather. "Your *parents* own Bloody Good Wine? I thought you were farmers."

Behind me, Duke whispered, "Is that Logan Arthur the politician?" followed by the familiar tapping sounds of a rapid Google search.

Petra's dark eyes sparkled. She was short—Logan had gotten his height from his dad—and lovely, with the wide face and high cheekbones I associated with eastern Europeans, and curly dark hair like Logan's. "We had this right annoying son who kept pestering us to stop farming livestock and get in on the wine boom, so we made the leap from Odejo to Fredericksburg about—" She looked at her husband for confirmation. "Six years ago?"

Kit nodded. "Sounds about right. The timeline *and* the cheeky son." Both his and Petra's British accents were so strong I was now amazed Logan's wasn't stronger. Kit grinned at me. "Though I suppose I don't have to tell you about the cheekiness, do I?" He stuck out his hand. "It's a pleasure to finally meet you, my dear."

Oh. *Of course.* Logan would've told his parents we were dating, just like I'd told my mom. Zoey elbowed me, and I hurriedly shook Mr. Arthur's hand. "It's very nice to meet you." I glanced at Logan and he arched his eyebrows at me.

I had so many things I wanted to ask him, but couldn't in public. I hadn't seen him all week since the debate fiasco. He'd texted me once to apologize for being MIA, telling me the campaign was in hyperdrive trying to do damage control, and he'd call as soon as he wasn't in meetings twenty-three hours a day. I'd been so unsure how to respond—did I ask if he was okay? Did I ask if it was my fault he'd been distracted? Did I tell him I was here if he needed to vent?—that it had taken me an hour of pacing, typing, and deleting before I'd settled on a safe *Sounds good*. And now he was here, out of my daydreams and in the flesh. It was surreal.

"I understand we have some brides here on their hen weekend," Petra crooned, clasping her hands.

"Right here," Mac said, pointing at Annie and Zoey, who beamed.

"Pretty sure the crowns gave it away," Claire quipped, which earned her a glare from Mac.

"Well, Kit and I wanted to say congratulations, and as our gift, your wine is on the house."

The table exploded into polite protests.

"You really don't have to do that," Annie said. "We're happy to support you."

Arthur waved her away. "We insist. We're big fans of love in the Arthur household." He squeezed Petra. "Been happily married thirty years ourselves."

Happily married parents. Could Logan and I be any different?

"And we want to make a good impression on Alexis." Petra winked at me. "Logan's so besotted we're hoping to woo her into sticking around—"

"Okay, Mom," he interrupted, shooting her a death glare. "Why don't we bring the nice hen party the wine they came for?"

"Ah, right," said Petra, and Logan hustled his parents in the direction of the bar.

As soon as their backs were turned, everyone started whispering.

"Do you like your surprise?" Zoey clutched my arm. "Logan's spending the weekend with us!"

My eyebrows were going to be permanently stuck in my hairline. "He is?" Now I understood why I'd been given a king bed. Oh, God, Logan and I only had that one bed. I'd read too many romance novels not to understand what kind of trouble I was setting myself up for.

"He *is*?" Lee echoed, even louder than me. She shot Ben a furtive look. They must be thinking of Will.

"Props, Alexis." Mac reached across the table and lifted her hand for a high five. "Your governor's hot on TV with that whole dark, angry British thing, but in real life he's *smoking*. Sorry Ted, I call 'em like I see 'em." Her face brightened. "I bet he says *governor* all British. *Gov'na*."

Her boyfriend, Ted, eyed her. "My Midwest accent really isn't doing it for you, huh?"

"He's a gubernatorial *candidate*," Claire corrected. "He hasn't won yet. And right now it's not looking so hot. If he's staying the weekend, no one's allowed to mention that shit show of a debate. That means no drunk politics, Stoner."

Lee rolled her eyes. "When have I ever—"

"All the time," everyone said in unison.

"That debate was painful." Claire's husband, Simon, cringed. "Best not bring it up."

"You dummies," I hissed. "He's only a few feet away. He'll *hear* you."

To my horror, Logan turned from the bar with a bottle of rosé and a tight-lipped smile. "Don't worry. No one has to tiptoe. I know I bloody well choked."

I'd never witnessed Claire look so mortified. "Logan, I'm sorry—"

"No need to apologize." He shook his head and tipped her wineglass over, filling it with rosé, the pour coming out in one smooth arc. I hadn't realized watching someone expertly pour wine was a kink a person could have until now. "I had a bad night. I'll do better next time. There's still hope I'll be gov'na yet." He winked at Mac, then his eyes shifted to me. "Bombing puts things in perspective, at least. Shows you what you need to do differently."

I don't know why that struck a painful chord in my chest, but it did. God help me, I'd gotten used to being Logan's friend. What if one of the things he needed to do differently was get rid of me?

"Lex," he said lightly, filling each glass remarkably quickly. "Will you come to the back office with me and my parents? They're begging to talk to you." He turned to the rest of the table. "Courtney will be over in a second to tell you about what you're drinking."

I felt everyone's eyes on me as I left the table and followed Logan through the double doors. He glanced down at me and extended his hand. "Do you mind if we..."

"Of course not." I slid my fingers through his, feeling the familiar comfort of our hands locking together. If he was holding my hand, he couldn't regret me, could he? Though, of course, we were turning the corner to a big kitchen, where his parents crouched over an island. The handholding was for show. *This is why you're taking a chance with Will*, I told myself. *With him, you don't have to guess.*

"Ah, Alexis!" Logan's dad beamed. "Thank you for ducking away to see us."

"Are you a hugger?" asked Petra. She barely waited for me to nod before flinging her arms around me. I dropped Logan's hand and hugged her back.

"Okay, Mom," Logan said gently, tugging her away. "Let Alexis breathe."

Petra rubbed my back before releasing me. "We're just so excited to meet you. Logan's been gushing for weeks, and of course we've seen you on TV. Kit and I were kicking ourselves we hadn't met you yet."

"Mostly you were kicking me," Logan corrected.

"Six months of dating without telling us!" Kit turned to me. "He's always been private, but hiding you was beyond the pale."

I stepped up to the island next to Petra. "In Logan's defense, we both thought it would be best to keep things quiet. We didn't want anything distracting from his election. Or my sister's before that," I added, in an inspired moment.

"That's right, your sister's a state senator." Kit nodded as if that settled something. "You're used to the political life. That's important. Logan needs someone who understands what it's like."

"How about we talk about Logan like he's standing right here," Logan said, though he was smiling fondly at his father. Away from the campaign, he was remarkably at ease.

"How's the wine-making business? Do you like it better than the farming you did before?"

Petra nodded. "Oh, much." She reached up on her tiptoes and ruffled Logan's hair. "This one kept telling us the Texas wine scene was going to blow up and we should get in on it. I'm so glad we listened. He was right. Business is booming. And we love working with the grapes."

"Nice not to be on the verge of bankruptcy, too," Kit said with a wink.

"At least I got one thing right," Logan said. "Rare these days."

I shot him a sympathetic look. He was clearly talking about the debate.

"We're just two old hippies, really." Kit smiled warmly across the counter at Petra. "We'll go wherever the wind takes us, try our hand at anything. All you need is love, and the rest follows. Isn't that right, dear?"

They *did* give off a mellow hippie vibe. I blurted the first thing that came to mind: "How in the world did you two make Logan?"

Petra and Kit burst out laughing. "You know, sometimes I think he fashioned himself in opposition to us," Petra admitted.

"Someone had to be the bloody responsible one," Logan muttered.

"Oi, we were responsible," Kit said. "Taught you all the essentials. Love, laughter, and Tottenham supremacy."

The opportunity to get to know Logan better was too good not to press. "Was he always a serious child?"

"I have to show you pictures," Petra said. "I know I have them here somewhere. I was going to scrapbook in my down time." She started fluttering around the kitchen drawers, opening and closing. "Where did they go?"

"Mum," Logan groaned. "There's no need—"

"Here they are!" She waved a fistful of photos. "Look at him," she said, pointing to the first. "Isn't he the most handsome little boy? He got all our best features."

In the photo stood a miniature Logan, glowering at the camera, wearing—I almost gasped—a pair of jean overalls. Just as I'd hoped. He stood in front of a large tree with his arms spread possessively around the trunk.

"He was guarding that tree," Kit explained. "It was an old oak right in the center of town, had been there for hundreds of years. When Tex-Ag bought the land and was planning to tear it down, Logan chained himself to it and refused to leave for days. Petra and I had to bring him food and water and camp out with him at night. He was only ten."

I looked at Logan, amazed. A faint redness tinged his cheeks. "You were a literal tree hugger. You can never let the RNC see this. What happened to the tree?"

"Those fuckers threatened legal action, then tore it down," he said. "I'll never forgive them."

Petra spread the other photos out on the island. I pored over them. "Logan's not smiling in a single one."

"Smiling's for people who save trees," he said.

"He was our little crusader," Petra said fondly. "Never met an animal he didn't take care of or a hurting person he didn't want to help. And mind you, Odejo was full of people like us, struggling to make ends meet on farms that didn't stand a chance against the Tex-Ags of the world. He had a lot of causes. I think that's where he grew his heart for justice." She winked at me. "Still can't believe the two of us made a kid like him."

"Oh my goodness." I snatched a picture out of the pile. In it, Logan crouched next to a large, fat pig with brown spots. "Is this Wilbur?"

Logan's eye twitched. After a moment of grudging silence, he growled, "That's him."

I looked at young Logan's face, unsmiling but still shining with pride. "It's even better than I imagined."

"He was the one to beat in the 4-H shows," Kit said proudly. "For a while we thought he'd go into agriculture, but we should've known it would be politics for him. Logan's always had a single-minded drive."

"So while the rest of his friends from high school went off to A&M like proper country boys, he went off to Cambridge," his mother said. "And came back to us all *Harvard*."

Logan rolled his eyes and I grinned. His parents teased, but the love was obvious.

"I know you're busy this weekend with your hen party," Kit said to me. "But you can come back anytime. We'd love to put you up and show you the whole place from top to bottom. Cook you a big dinner with wine pairings."

"That sounds amazing," I said. "Count me in." *Stop making promises you can't keep*, a little voice warned.

Petra leaned close to me and spoke softly. "I could tell by the way Logan talked about you that you were someone special." She glanced at Logan, who was describing something to his dad. "Now, seeing him around you, the way he looks at you, how much he smiles... I've never seen him so happy. Thank you for being so good to him."

I smiled at Petra, hoping my deep well of guilt didn't shine through. Logan's parents were lovely and I hated lying to them. "I just want him to be happy," I said quietly. At least that was the truth. I wanted more than anything for Logan to get his victory, the goal he'd been working toward since he was ten years old, guarding that tree. "I should probably get back to my friends," I added, and Logan looked over.

"Of course." Petra rubbed my arm.

"I'll be out in a minute with some reserve bottles," Logan promised. "And hey, Lex." He tugged me away from the island and I saw his parents smile at each other, charmed at the thought that he couldn't keep his hands off me. He lowered his voice. "Later tonight, can we talk?"

My stomach dropped. "Is everything okay?"

He nodded, but his gaze shifted to his hands. "Yeah. I've just been doing a lot of thinking—" He stopped, then laughed at himself. "Actually, I've been doing a lot of torturing myself. There's something I want to talk to you about."

The pit in my stomach deepened. He'd said bombing at the debate had given him clarity. He was going to end our fake relationship, wasn't he? Tonight, despite introducing me to his parents, Logan would sit me down and explain it was more prudent to call it off. Or maybe he'd ask to scale us back to a single appearance a week. Something to keep up the ruse but insert some distance.

This is why you're giving Will a shot, I reminded myself. Even though it wasn't the most charitable thought, it comforted me enough to take a deep breath and say, weakly, "Great. Can't wait."

28

Everything Gets Twisted

"**Z**oey, off the top of your head: five celebrities you would let step on your neck. If you don't answer, you drink."

"Lee!" Annie squealed. "You weirdo."

"Sandra Oh," Zoey said, holding up a finger. "And for that matter, Jodie Comer. Oh, hell, the entire *Killing Eve* cast."

Claire swirled her wine dramatically. "Does anyone remember when being a politician used to mean something? Like when it came with gravitas?"

"That's what *I* said." I shot Lee a look lest she forget the Belle sex costume incident.

"It's a bachelorette party!" Lee threw up her hands. "This is my time to shine."

"What happened to politicians exhibiting decorum?" Claire asked Logan.

He grinned. "Hell if I know." Then his attention caught on something over Claire's shoulder. "Oi, wait a second. What's that in the corner?"

The entire bachelorette party stopped talking and turned to look. And, despite the fact that I'd been avoiding Logan all day—through the gauntlet of wineries and dinner here at the Airbnb (quite a feat, considering he was seated next to me and kept trying to catch my eye every time he passed the butter)—I looked, too.

And immediately felt my face flame. *Oh, no.* I recognized the dark-haired sprite staring back from a canvas half buried under half a dozen others. The paintings were piled next to the rest of Zoey's art supplies, stuffed into a corner of the living room. I don't know how I'd overlooked it during dinner—probably because I was so focused on ignoring the small private smiles Logan kept shooting my way anytime someone said something funny. Now his eyes were fixed on the painting and I wanted to spontaneously combust.

"It's my study of Alexis!" Zoey's lips were stained berry-red from a full day of drinking. To my horror, she ran over and dug the canvas out from behind the others, putting it on full display. "She's been sitting for me for a big commission. I brought it in case I have time to work in the mornings when Annie gets up for yoga. Isn't the closeup beautiful? I think I'm going to try to sell it separately." Zoey beamed innocently around the dining table, unaware of the bomb she'd dropped.

The entire table was silent for a beat in which I could actually *feel* sweat forming at my temples—then finally, Ben regained the ability to speak. "You got *Alexis Stone* to dress up as a *fairy* for a *painting*? Like, all of those things happened in a row?"

"Hey," I said hotly. "I'm not *that* shy."

"Are those leaves on her boobs?" Mac asked.

"It's tasteful," Zoey insisted.

Lee pointed at Zoey with her wineglass. "I will give you three hundred dollars right now. You don't even have to finish it."

"No." I turned so quickly to Zoey I almost gave myself whiplash. "You can sell it to anyone in the world but Lee. Or Ben," I added, seeing the devious light in his eyes.

"I knew this painting was a winner," she said happily. "What do you think of it, Logan?"

"Oh," Logan said hoarsely. His eyes were fixed on the canvas. "It's very, uh—"

I shoved back from the table. "How about I volunteer to do the dishes and in exchange, everyone agrees to wipe the painting from their memories." I started noisily collecting silverware.

"I'll help." Logan rose quickly from his seat.

"How lovely." Annie beamed at us from the head of the table. Her lips were every bit as berry stained as Zoey's, which probably accounted for the dreamy look on her face. "It's so nice when couples share responsibilities. That's a sign of a healthy relationship."

Claire raised her glass to me. "I agree with drunk Dr. Park. He's a keeper, Alexis."

Apparently even Logan Arthur had limits on public humiliation, because he ducked his head. "Better get these into the dishwasher as fast as possible. Excuse me, then." He beelined in the direction of the kitchen, balancing a stack of plates.

"And he's so cute," Mac gushed. "Not to harp on the point, but does anyone else find him too handsome to be a real politician? I mean, they don't usually look like that."

"Rude," Lee said. "I get plenty of emails from people propositioning me."

Ben raised his eyebrows. "You *do*?"

"Yes. Foot fetishists, mostly. I have very alluring feet."

Logan nearly broke into a run. While his back was turned, I took the opportunity to slice my finger across my throat and hiss, "*Stop embarrassing me*" at the entire table. The problem with hanging out with your older sister's friends was that they inevitably appointed themselves your honorary big sisters, thereby granting themselves unlimited license to mortify you.

When we'd arrived back at the Airbnb to find two chefs working on an extravagant three-course dinner, I'd panicked about the fact that Logan didn't know anyone, and if I was in his shoes, I'd be climbing the walls. But it turned out I had nothing to worry about. He was a natural at getting to know people. Dinner had gone very well—especially, to my surprise, between Logan and Lee. They'd bonded over their shared vegetarianism, the only two people to request grilled mushrooms instead of steaks. And if I wasn't imagining things, I could've sworn Logan's salty dissection of the attorney general's recent brothel scandal had won my sister over despite herself. I could tell he was trying hard to impress Lee. It had done a pretty solid job of distracting me from thinking about whatever Logan wanted to say. But now that we were alone in the kitchen, I had to face the music.

He stood at the sink, scrubbing plates, a towel folded over his shoulder. He turned to me. "I wash, you dry?"

I nodded and slipped the towel from his shoulder, getting to work as he handed me wet dishes. "Sorry about them," I said. "They're a lot."

Logan glanced down at me and grinned. "I love them."

"Even Lee? Even *Claire*?"

He laughed while he scrubbed, sending soap bubbles flying. "All of them. They seem like good people. And I like how protective they are of you."

"Well, none of them went toe-to-toe with Carter at the Fleur de Lis for me, so I'd say you still come in first place."

He flicked soap bubbles and they landed on my nose. "Thank you for knowing winning's important to me."

I wiped my nose and splashed him back—and to my delight, the bubbles got caught in his stubble, giving him a bubble beard.

Instead of shaking them off, Logan stilled, his gaze intensifying. My heart raced at the sudden charge in the air. "Lex, that thing I wanted to talk to you about—"

Behind us, heavy knocking sounded at the door, making me jump. Lee flew to it, followed by Ben, who threw open the door.

It was *Will*. Standing in the entrance, wearing jeans and a Dell Medical T-shirt, his dark hair mussed and floating away from his face, a duffel bag over his shoulder.

"William!" my sister shouted. "You're here."

"You made good time, buddy." Ben leaned over and gave his brother a brief hug, followed by a clap on the back. Side by side, their shared Laderman beauty was even more pronounced. "Welcome to the world outside the hospital."

"Is this what it looks like?" Will joked. "Barely recognize it." When he pulled back from Ben, Will's eyes searched the house, stopping when they landed on me. He smiled a little shyly. "Hi, Alexis."

It occurred to me that my mouth had dropped open. "Uh—hi. What are you doing here?"

"Surprise!" Lee threw out her arms. "Will had a rare weekend off, so we invited him. With Annie's permission, of course." She gave me a show smile, willing me to play along. "That was obviously before we knew the full guest list. But isn't this great?"

Will moved into the kitchen and gave me a quick hug. "I hope this is okay," he whispered.

"Of course," I said, and gulped. Because Will was now looking at Logan, who stood by the sink, staring back. How had I gotten myself into this situation? The obvious answer was Lee, but I meant more existentially. Maybe Zoey was wrong about my good karma.

"You're Logan Arthur," Will said, lurching forward with his hand outstretched. "I recognize you from the news. I'm Will, Ben's brother. It's nice to meet you. I didn't realize you'd be here."

Logan shook his hand. "Cheers. It's a couples thing and I'm Alexis's boyfriend, so...you know."

"Right." Will dropped Logan's hand and gave him a conspiratorial wink. "Boyfriend."

Logan shot me a confused look. *Oh, great lightning in the sky, strike me now.*

"Come on, Will." Lee waved him in the direction of the living room. "Throw your stuff in the corner. You came right in time for drinking games."

"Uh-oh." Will shook his head good-naturedly. "I drove here right after my shift, so I'm going to need to catch up with the rest of you."

"I'll pour you some wine," Logan offered, dropping the

dish towel. He was studying Will like he was a puzzle, one I very much didn't want him to solve.

While Logan and Will headed for the wine on the dining table, I grabbed Lee and hissed, "What were you *thinking*?"

"I swear I didn't realize Logan was coming. When you told us you were into Will, Ben and I got so excited, we thought you guys could have a weekend together out of the spotlight. And then Will was so happy to be invited I couldn't bear the thought of uninviting him after Logan showed up. He would've been sitting around alone in Austin."

"Ugh," I groaned. I wanted to be angry at her, but her reasons were frustratingly charitable. I covered my face with my hands, watching from between my fingers as Logan showed Will a bottle of Bloody Good Wine. "What am I supposed to do now?"

Lee gave the two men a thoughtful look. "Remember that episode of *Sabrina, the Teenage Witch* when Sabrina accidentally brings two dates to the school dance?" I'd been obsessed with *Sabrina* when we were younger and used to make Lee watch it with me, obviously unaware she was gathering material for future evil plots. "It'll be like that. Just keep them apart as much as possible. Easy."

"Lee! Sabrina had magical powers and she *still* got caught."

Lee rested her hands on my shoulders. "I think we should take a moment to appreciate the fact that a few months ago, you had zero boyfriends. And now, look!" She waved at the living room. "You have two. Honestly, you're welcome."

I took back everything I'd ever said about wanting to be part of a Lee Stone shenanigan. I was pretty sure I was going to kill her.

★

Nope. Forty-five minutes later, contorted like a pretzel between Will's legs and Logan's arms, barely holding on in the world's highest-stakes game of drunk Twister, it turned out I wished death upon no one but myself. I'd tried to bow out when Zoey suggested the adult-themed version of the game—it was undoubtedly the opposite of the *Sabrina, the Teenage Witch*–approach to keeping one's dates apart— but I was censored with loud boos from everyone. So I'd folded to peer pressure and here I was, dying slowly of handsome-man-proximity-overload. Logan, Will, and I were the last three contestants left on the mat: Will was the least drunk, Logan the most competitive, and I seemed to have been granted near superhuman strength through sheer adrenaline. The entire bachelorette party ringed us, watching as Will placed his right hand on a yellow dot underneath me, bringing his face closer. "Hey," he whispered. "I think this might be my new favorite game."

Logan was inches away in the other direction. I could actually *feel* the heat emanating from his skin. I glanced over and sure enough, he was watching Will and me intently, frowning. If only I could tell Will to stop being so obvious without being so...obvious.

"Alexis, right hand red," called Ted, our referee. I searched the mat, hoping against hope to find a red circle far away from both Will and Logan. But no. Of course the only one I could feasibly touch had me shifting my weight away from Will to press my body against Logan's. We were chest to chest now, his muscled arms on either side of me, flexing as he held himself still. Inch by inch, I let my gaze climb higher until I met his eyes. He was so close, his eyes dark and burning with unspoken questions. His gaze dropped to my lips and stayed there. Suddenly it didn't matter that we were surrounded by people. A tremor ran through me that had nothing to do with the strain of holding myself up.

The corners of Logan's mouth tugged up. "I think this might be my new favorite game," he breathed, so quiet only I could hear. All I could do was stare at his mouth, wondering why he was echoing Will, what that ghost of a smile meant.

"Logan, left hand blue," Ted said, cutting my torture short as Logan shifted away from me in search of a blue circle. With the next spin, Will apologetically placed his hand right under my butt.

"Logan, someone's getting fresh with your girl," Mac warned.

Will raised his eyebrows at me and smiled knowingly. It was the intimate look of two people sharing a secret. I cut my gaze over his shoulder, hoping Logan hadn't seen—but sure enough, he was staring at Will, his eyebrows knitting together. And then I watched the truth hit. Comprehension dawned in Logan's eyes and he slipped, falling to his elbows.

"Logan's out!" Claire yelled. "Anyone want to put money on Alexis versus Will?"

Logan shoved himself off the mat and jumped to his feet, keeping his back to me. He slipped out of the circle and fled in the direction of the stairs.

"No need for a bet," I said, dropping to my side. "I'm out, too."

"Laderman *dominance*," Ben crowed, pulling Will off the

mat. "Never met a middle school party game we couldn't crush."

"No fair, Alexis threw the game," Claire protested, but I ignored her and everyone else and hurried after Logan up the stairs. *He knew.* The second-floor hall was empty, which meant he was in "our" room. I cracked the door and found him pacing in front of the large windows, against the backdrop of a starry sky. He made it from one end of the rug to the other, then turned and started again, hands flexing like he was struggling to keep something inside. The sight of his suitcase lined up neatly next to mine in the corner of the room made my throat thick.

I slipped in and closed the door behind me. "Logan."

He stopped moving, but didn't meet my eyes. "How does Will know we're not really dating?" His voice was low and contained. "Do they all know?"

"No." I shook my head. "I promise."

Logan's chin lifted, and finally he looked at me, waiting for me to explain.

"I..." My mind scrambled for something, but of course I couldn't lie. "I went on a date with Will. In secret," I added quickly. "No one saw us. Trust me, our cover isn't blown. But first he had to know that you and I—" I gestured weakly between Logan and me "—weren't real."

Logan was completely stone-faced, standing stock-still against the stars. I couldn't read him beyond the tension in the way he clenched his jaw. Faced with his silence, I babbled. "It was Lee's condition to endorse you. She wanted me to go on a date with Will to see if there was something there. I know it's against our rules and if anyone had spotted us or taken a picture, it could've undermined your campaign, and I'm so sorry." I was talking a mile a minute, desperate to change the hard lines on Logan's face. "For some reason Lee got it into her head that Will and I would hit it off and he has this wedding coming up he needs a date for and I—I'm sorry for keeping it a secret and for ambushing you. I had no idea Will was coming this weekend."

It sounded like the most pathetic excuse in the world—*I'm sorry the secret I was keeping from you got so inconveniently blown*. I flinched, waiting for Logan's explosion, or maybe the barrage of barbed quips like I would've gotten from previous boyfriends. But Logan didn't speak. He didn't even move. His eyes were fixed on the large four-poster bed between us. I watched as a thousand emotions played over his face, each one flickering, then quashed, like he was wrestling them under control. He was working to keep himself in check, but I wished—I wished he would just open up. Yell if he wanted to. I needed to decode him.

"Please tell me what you're thinking." I moved around the bed to get closer. "I know I violated the terms of our agreement and you're angry and Nora's probably going to sue me—"

"Was your sister right?" His eyes were still fixed on the bed. His voice was quiet. While I couldn't quite parse his emotions, he didn't sound angry.

I froze at the unexpected question. "What?"

Each word sounded like it cost him. "Did you hit it off with Will? Is he someone you could see yourself with?"

There—I could read that. Logan was steeling himself. He wanted to know if I was going to make this relationship with Will an ongoing problem for him.

"Don't worry," I said. "I won't see him anymore."

"But do you want to?" He looked at me finally, his eyes searching, voice urgent. "Would you, if it wasn't for me?"

I blinked, unable to track the permutations of his thoughts. "Well—yes. I guess if you and I didn't have this... arrangement... I could see myself with him."

Why did this feel so painful? Logan had grown into my friend, and besides, I'd been waiting all day for his hammer to drop, for him to tell me we should end our fake relationship. "What were you going to tell me?" I was desperate to segue. "That thing, in private. You were going to say our thing has gotten too complicated, right?"

Logan laughed—a curt sound that burst from him. He closed his eyes. "No, I...you know what, it doesn't matter anymore." When he opened his eyes, my breath caught at the torrent of feelings he couldn't hide. "Can you excuse me?" he asked. "I just need a minute."

I didn't even get a chance to respond before he'd barreled past me out the door. It shut behind him and I stood alone in the empty room, blinking at where he'd stood, my surprise thick enough to hold off the disappointment, but I knew it was only a matter of time. Soon there would be tears in my eyes—I could never help it. I lowered myself gingerly on the corner of the bed, feeling a hot, pricking sensation in my face.

Then the door flew back open and Logan strode in, his hair sticking on end like he'd touched an electrical wire. I startled and gripped the comforter. He stopped in front of me. How he'd managed to come back after a minute looking like he'd aged a year was beyond me.

"That night at the Hideaway," he said, voice thick. "You said you were looking for something real. That once we were done, you were going to try for it. Well, if you found it, I'm not going to be selfish and stand in your way."

"What are you saying?" My throat felt like it was closing.

He held my eyes. "You should date him."

"But what if—"

He shook his head. "If you get caught and our cover is blown, I'll deal with the consequences. You deserve something real." He smiled bitterly. "That's what I was going to say to you tonight."

Ice spread through my chest.

He swallowed. "I'm glad you have someone." He twisted to the side, then paused, looking back at me. "I'll sleep on the couch tonight so you and Will can...if you want..."

"No," I said quickly. "We just started seeing each other. And—I still don't want to blow our cover."

Logan nodded. Then, as if he'd come to a decision, he took a deep breath. At his sides, his hands flexed against his jeans. "I want you to be happy," he said. And before I could react, he swept out of the room.

I sat for a long time on the bed, still gripping the comforter, wondering why those kind words had me spinning.

29

This is Happiness, Right?

Three sleepless nights later, I ran to my front door at the sound of knocking, flinging it open to find Will on my doorstep, holding a bouquet of pink roses. He grinned and thrust the flowers at me. "These are for you."

I took them gingerly, taking care with the petals. "They're beautiful. Thank you." I kicked the door open wider. "Come in."

Will bent and grabbed a brown bag full of groceries. "Is it weird I'm nervous to meet Patches? Ben and I didn't have pets growing up. I hope she likes me."

When Will asked me out on a second date near the end of Zoey and Annie's bachelorette—which had turned into a long, torturous weekend—he'd promised to cook again. Since our options for privacy were limited and we'd already been to his place, I'd invited him to mine. That was before I'd remembered that having company—of the sexy variety, not pop-ins from Zoey or Lee—meant deep cleaning. Leading Will to the kitchen, I looked around and admired my handiwork. At least I'd been able to channel my anxiety into a sparkling apartment.

"Patches loves everyone," I assured him. "It's part of her charm." I flung out my arms, presenting my kitchen. "Ta-da. It's tiny. Sorry."

Will slung his bag of groceries on the counter. "Are you kidding? My kitchen in med school was like a single hot plate on an inch of counter. An actual refrigerator? Pure luxury." He dug in his bag and pulled out a black apron, then tied it behind him. "See? I'm a pro."

I bit my lip as I looked at him. Will was so handsome, all dark hair and sharp cheekbones.

"Why are you giving me that look?" His mouth quirked. "Do I look silly in this apron?"

I shook my head. "You're just...really great."

He leaned down and kissed me on the cheek, lingering for a beat. "You're great, too," he said. "For the record."

Something warm and soft brushed my legs. I bent down and seized Patches. "Will, meet the lady of the house. Patches, meet Will, the..."

"Suitor," he supplied. Will took Patches from me carefully and held her against his chest, rubbing her ears. "Hey, kitty. That's what you say, right?"

"You're a natural." I stepped back and cleared my throat. "Do you need any help?"

"Nah." He put Patches down and waved me in the direction of the living room. "You're the one who actually went in to work today. I'm not due back to the hospital until tomorrow for a double shift. So you relax. I'll cook. Want to cue up a movie? I'll hear it from the kitchen."

I narrowed my eyes at him.

"What?" he asked, pulling out a handful of parsley from his grocery bag.

I slunk in the direction of the living room and sat on the couch, testing the concept of relaxing. "Suspiciously nice, is all."

As Will got busy washing his hands again, I picked up the remote. I was the last twenty-something in America still paying for cable, but I liked to see my sister on the news. I flipped through the channels: *Price is Right* rerun, old Western, infomercial, Lee, supermarket gameshow—wait, *what*? I flipped back and turned up the volume.

Lee stood outside her office with a handful of other women I recognized as fellow state legislators Lee was close to. Next to her stood Logan.

"I'm delighted to endorse Logan Arthur for governor," Lee said. "As are my colleagues in the women's caucus. While I have respect for Governor Mane and the ways we've worked together, I believe Logan represents the future of Texas. For any voters still on the fence, here's my pitch: you may not have expected the perfect fit to come in the shape of a sharp-tongued thirty-three-year-old policy wonk who's as at home in the halls of Cambridge as he is on a farm in Odejo, but that's the beauty of life, isn't it? Sometimes the unexpected thing is the right thing. And that's Logan Arthur in a nutshell."

"Is that Lee endorsing Logan?" Will called. "Guess her relationship with Governor Mane is over."

I couldn't speak because it felt like a boulder was sitting on my heart. "I couldn't be more grateful for Senator Stone's endorsement," Logan said, "or the endorsements from her fellow senators in the women's caucus." He'd smiled politely through Lee's words, and now he offered the camera that same congenial look. But I could see through the performance. There was no light in his eyes. His words were rote and hollow.

"Pasta's cooking for a few minutes," Will said, flopping down next to me. "Good for Logan for getting this endorsement. Underneath the short fuse, addiction to swearing, and competitive drive that at one point made me suspect he legitimately wanted to kill me, he seemed like a pretty nice guy."

I forced my eyes away from the screen, taking in Will, Patches, and the steam plumes from the pasta in the kitchen. This cozy scene was unfolding right here, right now, for real. It wasn't a fiction. I had everything I wanted: a handsome date, a cat, friends, a thing I was doing with my life I could be proud of. So why didn't it feel enough? Why did the mere sight of Logan on-screen make me feel like my heart was too large for my chest to contain it?

"Want to start that movie?" Will asked. "Host's choice."

Maybe I'd gotten so used to aching—so used to wanting, to longing—that now I couldn't turn it off. Maybe unhappiness had become like a worn-out armchair, a place I'd grown comfortable and familiar with. Maybe the last bad habit I needed to break was my inability to feel satisfied.

"Lucky for you," I said, "host's choice means *The Princess Bride*." And with the feeling that I was making progress, I pressed the button and turned Logan off.

30

All the World's a Stage

"**R**emember those perks I promised you?" Nora, resplendent in a bright red ball gown, slipped a gloved arm through mine. "Well, welcome to heaven. Otherwise known as the thirty-fifth annual Friends of Texas black-tie gala."

"Wow," I whispered, canting my head to take in the enormity of the mansion. The white stone turrets practically glowed in the evening air, and orchestra music swelled from inside as men in tuxedos and women in gowns strode up the staircase. "It's beautiful."

"Some of the most important people in the state are here," Nora said. "It's a tradition before every election. All the bigwigs meet to size up the candidates. Our poll numbers are climbing back, so everyone's going to want to kiss Logan's ring in case he becomes the next governor. They'll want leverage for future favors."

"Sounds high pressure." I couldn't stop looking at the sprawling manor, the closest thing to a castle I'd seen in real life. "What do I need to know? What's my angle? Prep me."

"Actually." Her vivid red lips spread into a smile. "Tonight, you're just going to sit back and enjoy the sucking up."

We picked up the skirts of our gowns and ascended the stairs toward the glowing entrance. "You realize this is Logan's nightmare, don't you?" I smiled at a passing man who nodded so deeply he practically bowed. "Getting complimented for hours is going to send him through the roof."

Nora rolled her eyes as the ushers at the front doors checked our names and swept us inside. "Figures mine is the one politician in the country without a praise kink."

I patted her arm sympathetically and turned to take it all in. Inside was even more beautiful than outside. We stood at the top of a tall staircase, upholstered in red carpet, which led to an enormous ballroom. Ornate chandeliers hung from the high ceilings, and people were spread thick, filling every corner of the room, interspersed with waiters carrying trays of champagne and hors d'ouevres. Massive oil paintings, the kind that belonged in museums, covered the walls.

"Excuse me?" asked a woman who was dripping with diamonds. "Are you Alexis Stone?"

I looked at Nora as if I needed her to confirm. "Um, yes?"

"Oh my God," the woman gushed. "You and Logan make the sweetest couple. And the way you're standing up for public schoolteachers—my children go to private school but their au pair wanted to be a teacher until she heard how little they make. She had to become an Instagram model instead. It was tragic. What you're doing is *so* important."

"Thank you?" No idea why everything was coming out a question.

Nora smiled stiffly at the woman. "Thanks for your support. I'm sure Alexis and Logan will be happy to speak more to you later once they're settled." Then she tugged me down the stairs.

"You weren't kidding about the sucking up," I whispered. "I think I could get used to..." I trailed off. Logan stood in the center of the thickest crowd, wearing a classic black-and-white tuxedo that fit him so well it looked like he'd been born wearing it. He nodded to someone and took a sip of his drink—a tumbler, so it was whiskey. His hair was carefully styled, his ten-o'clock shadow perfectly shaped to accentuate the cut of his jaw. His smile was polite, but above it, his dark eyes danced, sizing up the people around him, making quick calculations. This was Logan the achiever, formal and formidable. He was devastating. I'd never been able to picture him at Harvard so clearly, occupying those ornate, storied spaces where presidents and justices once walked. He belonged here in a tuxedo as much as he belonged on a farm or at a rally. I felt it in my bones: his complexity, the layers of him. Why he was so endlessly fascinating. He might protest or demur, but I saw the truth of him.

He took another sip and his eyes drifted to the staircase, finding my face as if drawn by a magnet. My heart skipped. He gave me the smallest smile—not flashy or toothy but warm and intimate, a look that was only for me.

Heat rushed through me. It felt like a thousand pounds lifted off my chest. If he was smiling at me, then we were okay, despite how we'd left things in Fredericksburg. I squeezed Nora's arm without thinking.

"He cleans up well," she said, tracing my stare. "I'll give him that. Come on, it's almost time for dinner. Some of these people paid more than ten thousand dollars for the honor of sitting at your table."

All thoughts of Logan in a tux fled as Nora trailed away. "They did *what*?" I screeched, and scampered after her.

"And here's the man of the hour," boomed the tall financier sitting opposite me. Everyone at the table turned to look as Logan strode toward us across the dining room, which was smaller than the ballroom but just as ornate, the ceilings high and painted with Renaissance-style frescoes. To my surprise, every guest rose to their feet—the financier and his wife, the wind farm owner and her wife, and the elderly heiress and her husband, who I'd actually thought was asleep over his soup bowl. I followed Nora's lead and scrambled up, shoving my chair back.

"Oh, Jesus, sit down," Logan growled. "I'm not the bloody king of England." Nevertheless, he seized the financier's hand and worked his way around the table, greeting everyone with enthusiasm. The elderly heiress wouldn't let go of his hand, giving Logan moon eyes her husband seemed either unaware of or unbothered by.

Logan finally extracted himself and found his seat beside me. He cupped a warm hand to my face in greeting and drew me close. "This okay?" he breathed, and when I nodded, he kissed me on the cheek. "You look beautiful," he whispered.

I'd balked at the idea of the campaign buying me a gown, so I'd borrowed a dress from Lee. It happened to be forest green, my favorite color. "Thank you."

"I never realized how much I loved the color green until I met you," he said quietly, and my heart raced. *We're in public*, I reminded myself. *Performing.*

"Well, as much as you hate black tie, you pull it off." I swallowed. "Well."

"I feel like a penguin," he whispered, brown eyes shining.

"You two are the most *delicious* couple," crowed the heiress. "I follow all the gossip blogs and I could just eat you up. Can I? Just a little taste?" She burst into raucous laughter.

Logan gave her a tight smile and grasped my chair, waiting for me to sit. "I'm afraid we're off-menu, Mrs. Vandergriff."

That only made her laugh more wickedly. *Clocking Vandergriff,* I noted. *Loud. Interest bordering on prurient.*

Once we were settled and waiters appeared at our elbows offering not only red wine, but white wine and champagne—I stifled a squeal that the exact same scene had occurred in *The Prince's Secret*—talk at the table turned to the economy and I gave myself permission to check out. I let my eyes wander over the salad course, taking in the beauty of the towering floral arrangements. This place would make a wonderful setting for a children's book—maybe about a group of spunky orphans growing up in a castle together. They would be given a mission to save the world from a brawny evil villain who, in my imagination, looked remarkably like Governor Mane.

Logan gently brushed my elbow when our entrees arrived: a beautiful roast chicken for me, mushroom risotto for him. "So," he murmured. "How's Dr. Laderman?"

I studied his face, looking for a hint of anger, but he only wore a smile. Behind his eyes was that emotion I could sense but not name.

"Fine," I said cautiously. "We're being careful about staying private."

Logan nodded, eyes dropping to my hands in my lap. I realized I was fidgeting and stilled.

"I love watching you two together," Mrs. Vandergriff burst, interrupting a point the financier had been making about the market. "You remind me of these little dolls I had when I was a child. Mummy had them shipped in for me from Austria. I used to make them kiss and have little weddings."

Yikes. Upgrading Mrs. Vandergriff from prurient to off her rocker. Maybe growing up so wealthy you could have dolls flown in from Austria did that to a person.

"Thanks," Logan grunted, looking anything but thankful.

"I want to see you kiss," Mrs. Vandergriff pouted.

"Oh, no," I said. "We don't—no PDA."

The financier cleared his throat and launched back into his subject. Nora leaned over to Logan and me. "Be nice," she hissed. "That woman is a mega-donor."

Logan gritted his teeth, but I gulped. The last thing I needed to do was put Logan's campaign in any more jeopardy. "Roger that," I whispered to Nora, and she backed off.

"How've you been since the bachelorette?" Logan whispered. "We missed you at the last strategy meeting."

"Oh, please, just one kiss, I'm begging," Mrs. Vandergriff called, but I pretended not to hear.

"Nora said I could skip it. I had...plans." I swallowed guiltily. That had been the night of my second date with Will.

It seemed Logan could read the truth in my eyes. "Right. Of course."

"One measly kiss for an old woman," said Mrs. Vandergriff, lifting her empty champagne glass for a refill.

Logan gave her another forced smile, shaking his head. "I'm not a marionette, Mrs. Vandergriff. I don't dance for coins."

"Logan," Nora warned.

"This roast chicken is delicious," I said, forcing cheeriness. "Anyone else loving it?"

Logan turned back to me. "You don't want to take a step back, do you?" He studied my face. "I mean, from the campaign."

"The signature Arthur gruffness," Mrs. Vandergriff swooned, so loud she startled everyone except her husband, whose upper lip trembled as he softly snored. "What I wouldn't give to be fifty years younger—"

"Oh, for God's sake," Logan snapped. The whole table stilled and Nora's eyes flew open in horror. "One more—"

I seized his face and kissed him.

I could feel my own surprise at what I'd done mirrored back at me through Logan. For an agonizing second, he was frozen. I started to pull back until I heard the faintest growl, the sound coming from low in his throat, frustration or desire, I couldn't tell. And then Logan cupped my face and pulled me closer. He kissed me like he was a starved man, twining his fingers in my hair, tugging me toward him with such urgency I practically tipped out of my chair. In a moment of recklessness, I returned his kiss just as fiercely, wanting nothing more than for this bubble of time to last. *Fiction*, I told myself. *Only a convincing fiction.*

Logan wrenched away from me, breathing heavy, his eyes searching mine and then flicking around the table. Only then did I look at our audience. Our quiet, stunned audience.

"There's your damn kiss, Mrs. Vandergriff." Logan shoved away from the table. "Now please excuse me."

The whole table watched him stalk through the dining room.

"Oh, my," drawled Mrs. Vandergriff, putting a hand to her chest. "That's definitely the man I want to watch for four years in the governor's office."

"Sorry," I whispered to Nora, who was looking at me like she'd never seen me before. "I'll be right back." I gathered my ball gown and moved as quickly as I could in the direction Logan had fled.

Racing out of the dining room, I caught him cutting across the empty ballroom. "Logan, wait!"

He stiffened, then turned.

"What's wrong?" I closed the remaining distance, skirt still clutched in my hands. "I was just trying to get Mrs. Vandergriff off our backs."

His voice was low and dark. "I try not to kiss women who are in relationships."

"Oh, please. Will and I have been on two dates. I'd hardly call that a relationship."

"I thought kissing each other was against the rules. Am I the only person who can ever remember the damn rules?"

"You hate rules," I said hotly, feeling a flush creep up my neck. "Everyone knows that."

"But I *follow* them," he burst. "You're right, I do hate them. They hurt. Holding myself back makes me feel like I'm dying inside. But I do it, Alexis. I keep myself in check. And if I do fuck up, I try to make it right." The heat drained from his voice. "I don't want to make mistakes. Not with you. This is too important."

The way he was looking at me was charged, and suddenly I didn't know what he was talking about. Me and his campaign? The two of us appealing to voters? The two of us...?

"Mr. Arthur, sir," came a voice. "We were just about to find you for your dance."

We turned to the man wearing a discrete headset, eyeing us expectantly.

"Ughhh." Logan closed his eyes and canted his face to the ceiling. "Why are you torturing me?" He opened his eyes and gave the man a forced smile. "Of course. When does it start? Oh, now? Perfect." He turned to me. "I'm guessing Nora didn't tell you we're supposed to open the ballroom dancing portion of the evening?"

"She said there were no expectations!" I could feel my cheeks heating. "I would've prepared. I'm fine," I reassured the man in the headset, who was watching me with alarm. "I'm going to die," I whispered to Logan, once the man scampered away.

"Don't worry. Just follow my lead."

"You know how to dance?"

"Of course I know how to dance. I'm a poor kid from a farming town. I wasn't going to give people another thing to sneer at."

The orchestra settled on the mezzanine, the perfect distance so guests could hear them without being overwhelmed by the music. They'd be able to see us through the wide-open French doors separating the ballroom from the dining room. Near the orchestra, the man in the headset motioned at Logan and me to come together.

Logan took a deep breath and held out his hand. There was a question in his eyes, and for a wild moment, it felt like he was asking for something bigger than a dance. I laid my hand in his and he placed his other on my waist. "Put your hand on my arm," he said quietly. "Mirror what I do. Take the steps I take—"

"Don't cross any lines you don't cross," I quipped.

The ghost of a smile. "Not unless you want to fall apart in front of everyone."

That time I knew he meant something bigger than dancing. I gripped his arm and the orchestra started, violin strings quivering, sending stirring, hopeful notes into the air. Logan launched into motion, pulling me with him across the floor, and I heard the shifting sounds of the diners turning in their seats to watch. For a while, it took all my focus to concentrate on Logan's gliding feet and mirror his movements, though with his hand firm around my waist, and the strength and sureness of his steps, I felt certain he wouldn't let me falter. After a while I caught on to the rhythm and relaxed, straightening my shoulders and actually listening to the music. It had moved from hopeful to swelling and dramatic.

Logan noticed my relaxing and frowned. "I'm sorry," he said quietly.

I raised my eyebrows as he swept me in a circle.

"I know none of this has been easy on you. Everything the campaign has asked you to do—it's been a lot. But we're nearing the finish line. The election's only a few weeks away." He steeled himself. "If I win, I told my team to jump into Phase Two immediately."

"Phase Two?"

He dropped his head lower, and pulled me in closer. "Seeding the ground for our public breakup. Of course, if I lose the election, no one will care about me anymore, so our breakup won't even be news." He looked down. "In that case, feel free to dump me immediately. People will probably cheer you for moving on to the good doctor."

There—a note of bitterness, right at the end. Before I could say anything, Logan charged on. "Either way, the silver lining is that you've built capital, notoriety. You can use it however you want. Keep rallying for teachers. Run for a union position. Start a nonprofit. The sky's the limit for you."

That infernal question again: *What did I want?* I heard Lee's voice in my head, telling me to stop sitting on the sidelines and do something gutsy. That's what everyone had always wanted from me. The orchestra music swelled, tragic and beautiful, and the notes pulled back memories. I ducked my head, pressing my temple to Logan's shoulder. I could see myself at thirteen, shy and gawky and heartbroken by my parents' divorce, but trying to hide it. Because Lee— seventeen-year-old Lee—was so angry, and there wasn't room for two of us.

For years she'd refused to see or talk to our father, and that scared me. I couldn't forget what my mother told me that night alone in her bedroom, that my father left because she'd stopped being what he needed. The realization that family was as fragile as glass made me heartsick that Lee's behavior would push my father even further away, that she'd lose him for all of us. I did everything in my power to balance her out, spending time with our dad when Lee shunned him, reassuring him I loved him when her anger was at its sharpest. I felt the pressure of holding my family together like a weight on my shoulders every day.

As the years passed, I buried my own feelings of anger and disappointment so I could keep my father's love. I went to his house every holiday and made nice with his new wife, Michelle. I said yes to every invitation, called him, texted him, hung his Christmas cards on the corkboard in my room. From thirteen to twenty-three, I tried so hard to be accommodating, to be the glue.

I could remember settling into a chair next to Dad's at Lee's college graduation, an orchestra playing sweeping, swelling music, just like the music tonight. Lee had refused to acknowledge our father's presence yet again, and I knew that unless I sat with him, he would be alone. I wanted so much for none of us to hurt.

When Lee's name was called and she strode across the stage, the way he *looked* at her. The pain in his eyes. I could feel him slipping away—not just from her but from me—and there was nothing I could do to stop it, no matter how affectionate I was, no matter how I contorted myself to be what he needed. When the ceremony was over, he disappeared with a few gruff words, and for weeks it was strained between us. Things eventually got more normal, but I couldn't help but feel a new distance between us, one I wasn't ever able to mend. Because the year after *I* graduated from college, he left in the most permanent way a person could, his life stolen by a car accident. Despite how hard I'd worked to keep him, to keep some semblance of our family together, in the end I failed.

The violins trembled their final quiet notes, mournful and resigned, and applause sounded from the dining room.

Logan's steps slowed, but I shook my head and pressed my face into his jacket. Tears spilled down my cheeks. I couldn't let anyone see me like this. "I'm sorry. I don't know why..." My voice broke. "My father..."

His hand moved from my waist to the back of my head, clutching me tighter. As the orchestra began their next song, Logan pressed his lips into my hair and whispered, "As many songs as you need."

31

Forces of Nature

When I woke Monday morning to an NPR report of a severe thunderstorm warning for Travis County, I lay in bed and smiled, thinking of Lee and Logan in their houses, laughing at the weather. It remained wild and windy all day, tree branches beating against the library windows, driving the students inside at lunchtime. They mostly holed up in the cafeteria, but a few trickled in and out of the library. The thunderstorm made me contemplative—rain was the perfect background for reading, and as I reshelved books, my mind roamed. I wondered what it would feel like to see a book with my name on it on a library shelf. I hadn't been able to stop replaying my conversation with Logan about writing a children's book. It seemed like a nearly impossible thing to turn a dream like that into something real, but I'd been doing some impossible things lately, so... what if?

I was idly imagining a plot when an alarm pierced the air, high-pitched and urgent, a sound that came from the walls. I jolted from the bookshelf and looked up at them, as if expecting the walls to explain themselves. Strangely, they did.

"This is a tornado warning," a tinny voice said through the loudspeaker. "Staff, please gather students and shelter in place until further notice."

A tornado? We'd prepped for the possibility, but tornadoes were rare, especially in the fall. Suddenly Lee's and Logan's warnings about climate change didn't seem like something to laugh about.

My training kicked in as the alarm kept firing. I rushed out of the aisle and took stock of my library. I was alone today, Muriel off for a dentist appointment, but the room looked fairly empty. "Students," I called, trying to keep my voice calm and authoritative. "I need everyone in the library to please come find me."

I swept through bookshelves and came upon the Beanbag Cranny—there was Sable, curled in the squishiest chair, looking stricken. "Come on, Sable. We need to find a safe place."

She jerked her head no.

"I have to insist," I called, voice raised over the alarm, my hands on my hips.

"Ms. Stone, I'm here." Mildred appeared, clutching a copy of *Oona Battles the Monsters of the Rainbow Ravine.* "Where should we go?"

"Stay right there," I said, and crouched to meet Sable's eyes. "Hey," I said gently. "Everything is going to be okay. Look." I pointed back to Mildred. "It'll just be you, me, and Mildred. We're going to be fine."

Sable looked at Mildred, who waited patiently. "She isn't scared?"

"She might be, but she knows the best thing to do is shelter in place. So she's being brave. You can be, too."

"Okay," Sable whispered. I helped her up and we scurried back to Mildred. I led them to a tiny closet tucked away in the corner of the library, far from any windows. Leaving them, I did one more sweep of the library, satisfying myself that it was empty, then dashed back to the closet, creaking the door closed. The minute I sat down next to the girls, a great wailing noise sounded, farther away but more monstrous than the tornado alarm. It sounded like the very walls were groaning.

"What do we do?" Sable was shaking.

"I have a book," Mildred said quietly. "We could read it. But it's...about..."

"It's an Oona the unicorn book," I said, when it became clear Mildred was too embarrassed to finish. "It's an award-winning series, you know. That's very nice of you to share, Mildred."

Sable and Mildred eyed each other in the dimly lit space.

"Okay," Sable whispered. Fear seemed to have stolen her bluster.

I got out my phone and turned the flashlight on so Mildred could read the story aloud to Sable. Minutes passed, then half an hour, with Mildred's soft voice battling against the sounds of a freight train coming from outside. At one point, something wrenched and crashed, and all three of us jumped, gripping each other. But as Mildred came to the end of chapter three, the noise from outside faded and died, leaving an eerie quiet. No wind, no alarms.

"Chapter four," Mildred intoned, and then Principal Zimmerman's voice cut her off.

"Attention staff and students. The tornado has passed and we're clear to move again. I'm asking all staff to bring students to the cafeteria for a headcount. Students will remain there until our ground crew assesses damages." The loudspeaker clicked off.

I rose to my feet and helped the girls up. "Look at that, we're all okay." I patted them on the back. "I'm proud of you both for being so brave. Come on, I bet they're serving snacks in the cafeteria."

"Will you keep reading *Oona*?" Sable asked Mildred. It was the first time I'd heard the queen of sixth grade sound shy.

"Here," Mildred said, offering the book. "You can borrow it." She looked up at me. "Is that against the rules, Ms. Stone? I've got it checked out for another week."

"It's perfectly fine," I said, unable to hide my smile.

After I dropped the girls off with their homeroom leaders in the cafeteria, I was just settling in to the teachers' table, ready to speculate about what the giant crash had been, when I realized I'd left my phone back in the library closet.

"Shit," I muttered, leaping from the table. "Oh, sorry," I said, at the row of surprised faces. "Bad habit." *Logan and his swearing.*

I dashed back down the hall to the library and ducked inside the closet, grabbing my phone and stuffing it in my pocket. Since I was here, it would be useful to do an inventory of damage. I was about to sweep the bookshelves when I sensed quick motion.

I turned to face the library's double doors just as they flew open. Logan streaked through. He looked like he'd run across the entire city. His navy suit was disheveled, his tie askew, his face sweaty and stricken. Worry radiated from him.

He saw me and his face crumpled in relief. To my astonishment, he seized me, wrapping his arms around me and clutching me to him. I blinked into his shoulder, cheek pressed against the smooth wool of his suit, feeling the rapid thump of his heart. I pulled back. "Logan—what in the world?"

He gripped my face like he needed to make sure I was real. "I was in a meeting with the wind farm people when Cary came in and said a tornado had ripped through the city and hit your school, and no one knew the extent of the damage."

"Wait—you left your donor meeting?"

"All I could think was, what if something happened to you? What if you were hurt? I ran every stop sign." He was still breathing heavy, his chest rising and falling. I stepped back from him, half out of surprise, half out of an instinct to give him room to breathe.

He pressed a hand to his mouth. "But you're fine. I overreacted." He yanked his hand away, warm brown eyes searching. "You're fine, right?"

I nodded mutely. I felt like I'd stepped into an alternate reality. Was Logan really here in my library, undone by the thought that I was in danger?

"Okay." He mirrored my nodding. "All right." He was trying to compose himself, repeating words like a self-soothing mantra, but there was still a wildness about him. He looked like a man on the edge, and that made it hard to do anything but stare. Logan Arthur was always in control, even when he was pushing boundaries.

"The tornado passed right by us," I said. "It sounded like it roughed up some of the buildings, but everyone is fine. I promise." I gestured down at myself. "Look. All in one piece."

"Yes. Good." He nodded again and then shook his head, laughing a little. "I'm an idiot. I'll let you get back to your day."

I felt a sudden pang at the thought of him leaving. "It's okay. It's sweet."

He waved me off, still shaking his head, and before I could say anything more, he turned and paced away, shoving open the doors to the library and disappearing. It became very quiet. The doors still swinging gently in his wake were the only proof he'd blown through here and it wasn't a fever dream.

I remained rooted to the floor, mind racing. Logan had been so worried about me he'd walked out in the middle of a donor meeting. He'd burst into the library looking like a man about to lose his mind. It seemed too extreme a reaction for colleagues or even friends—

The double doors flew open again. "I can't take this anymore." Logan strode through. He was still shaking his head, but this time he looked determined, not ashamed. "Fuck the rules." His sudden presence, the single-minded focus in his eyes—it was so strong I took a step back. He came within reaching distance and stopped, hands gripped by his sides, as if he was restraining himself. His pulse beat visibly in his throat as his eyes searched my face. "Please." His voice was rough. The voice of a man at the end of his rope. "Please let me kiss you."

The flame of attraction I'd held at bay since the night at the Fleur de Lis—the lust so intense it was unprecedented, the ache I carried everywhere, trying so hard to ignore—unleashed, flaring white-hot. All I could do was nod, overwhelmed by how much and how quickly I *wanted*, the well of it so deep and obvious the moment I looked for it.

It was all the answer he needed. He closed the distance and caught my face, kissing me so fiercely I lifted to my toes to meet him. Like they always did around him, my inhibitions disappeared. His lips were so warm and soft. I almost laughed marveling that a man as gruff as him could kiss like this, so tenderly, making me feel like I was the only person on earth who mattered. I met each stroke of his hands and his tongue with the fervor of a person who'd wanted this a thousand times, across a thousand moments. When he finally wrenched away and looked at me in wonder, I whispered his name, in awe that we'd kissed for us—not for show. What did it mean? What did I *want* it to mean?

He misunderstood me, thinking I was admonishing him. "I know," he said huskily. He kissed me on the forehead. "We can't cross lines. I'm sorry. It won't happen again." He pressed a hand over his mouth and turned to leave. The final dam broke inside me and I grabbed his arm, twisting him back to me. "No. Stay."

He looked at my hand. Then at my face, through downcast lashes. I saw the exact moment he understood what I wanted. He had me up against the stacks quickly, catching my mouth with his, hands cupping my jaw. He kissed me feverishly, nearly growling when I tilted my head for a better angle.

I knew how he felt. All reason fled: I wanted as much of him as I could get, as he would give me. I pulled at his tie, at the buttons of his shirt, turning into a version of myself

I didn't recognize, my desire so powerful I was nearly feral. I was desperate to take the edge off the ache between my legs, and Logan seemed to know. He lifted me against the bookshelf and I wrapped my legs around him until there was only the silk of my panties and the wool of his suit separating me from the rock-hard evidence of his desire. I rolled my hips, gasping at the hot-wire sensation, feeling the bookshelf wobble. Logan groaned in my ear and ground against me, following my lead, matching my rhythm.

All I could think about was getting closer to him, sinking deeper into the feeling building inside me. I had never been so turned on in my life.

Then a voice sounded from the hallway and we froze. In the drugged haze of kissing, I'd completely forgotten where we were.

Logan pressed his forehead to mine and shut his eyes, taking a deep breath. "Talk about this later?"

I nodded, and he released me, setting me gently on my feet. Then he turned and strode out of the library, clearing his throat and readjusting his suit as he walked. I could hear him call a terse hello to someone and then his footsteps faded, leaving me alone with my heart and my thoughts, both racing.

32

Full Hearts

Not even thirty minutes after I got home from school, I heard the now-familiar sound of my front door swinging open. "SOS received!" Rapid footsteps echoed from the hall and then Zoey stood peering down at me. "Why are you strewn on the couch like some Victorian aristocrat who caught the vapors?"

I removed the arm I'd flung over my face. "Because I'm dy—wait. Why is your hair and makeup so fancy?" Zoey's mermaid hair fell over her shoulders in movie star ringlets, her lips were a lovely mauve, and when she blinked, the tips of her faux lashes hit her brow bone. She looked like a magazine cover star.

She winked at her reflection in the hall mirror. "I came straight from my hair and makeup trial."

I sat up, sending Patches leaping from my chest. "Oh, Zo, you look *gorgeous*. Do you need any help with wedding stuff? It's right around the corner—"

"Stop it right there." She shook her head. "Don't do that thing where you bury your problems and focus on other people. You're the main character today. Now tell me what's up?"

I wilted against the couch and threw my arm back over my face. "Logan kissed me."

"Ahh!" She sank down next to my feet. "Wait—a performance kiss or a real kiss?"

"Real. Maybe the realest of my life. I didn't even know it could feel like that." Before this afternoon in the library, the first night I met Logan would've gone down as my hottest experience. But...well, I knew him better now. The electric attraction was still there, whatever it was about him and his pheromones that called my body to attention, but now it was magnified tenfold. Every action had weight. Because it wasn't just some attractive stranger kissing me—it was *Logan. Logan* sliding his hands into my hair like he couldn't get me close enough. Maybe I was different from Lee and her friends, who were able to enjoy a one-night-stand with a hot stranger. Maybe it took an emotional connection to really turn me on.

The moment the thought entered my head, so many things clicked into place: why sex with Chris Tuttle had never been great, *especially* after he cheated and our connection was thin and fragile; why my attempts at the kinds of casual hookups other people were capable of always fizzled. Maybe it wasn't a matter of shyness, a roadblock I needed to overcome: maybe it was just a part of what made me me.

Zoey swooned over my legs. "I've been waiting for this moment since day one. I *told you* he loves you! I love being right."

"Oh my God, Zoey, he doesn't *love* me. I don't know how he feels, actually." I stared up at the ceiling. "He's a mess of contradictions. I think it's safe to say he's attracted to me. I mean, between the hotel and the library..."

"Of course he's attracted to you."

"But," I countered, raising my eyebrows at her. "One of those situations involved alcohol and the other involved stress. And Logan told me outright he's not looking for a relationship. I mean, he practically pushed me toward Will. Oh, God." I sat up again, jostling Zoey. "What do I do about Will? Do I come clean? Apologize?"

"How many dates have you gone on with Will?"

"Two."

"Just two? Did you guys agree to be exclusive?"

"No. We haven't even kissed."

"Ugh." Zoey gently slapped my leg. "Lex, I love you, but you do realize you're allowed to be a modern woman who dates multiple people, right? You don't owe anyone your immediate undying devotion. Even if they're really nice."

I took a deep breath. "It's important to me not to be a cheater."

Her eyes filled with knowing. "I get that. But unless you and Will agreed to be exclusive, you're not doing anything wrong. Try putting your needs first for once."

I squeezed her hand. "Thank *you* for being such a good friend."

She squeezed back. "Here's what you do with Logan. It's simple. You need to know how he feels, so you're going to... ask him."

"Just like that?"

"Just like that. The next time you see him, you're going to have an honest conversation about how you both feel. If he's busy, stand up for yourself and tell him to make time for you. And if he *still* brushes you off, then you have your answer anyway. Either way, you'll leave knowing."

Even the thought of getting clarity from Logan was a relief. And this sounded like the way Lee would approach the situation. She would take charge, insist on being taken seriously. "What if he regrets kissing me? Or it meant nothing more to him than a momentary attraction?"

Zoey lay back on the couch. "You know, sometimes I *still* worry I'm not good enough for Annie."

"Really?"

"Yeah. I worry she's going to wake up one morning and realize she's making a huge mistake marrying me."

"But Annie loves you so much."

Zoey looked at me. "I know. I really do. But the fear is natural. All this stuff is terrifying, you know? Caring about someone is such a risk. We shove our hearts in their hands and all we can do is hope they don't crush us. I'm an artist. I make things. I like control. Love is the opposite."

It was actually stunning that Zoey—beautiful, talented, confident Zoey—shared my insecurities. "You are one of the most magnetic people I've ever met," I said. "One in a million. You're worth lifetimes of loving."

She squeezed my legs. "See, this is why I volunteered to come talk to you that day Lee needed someone to fill in. I always had a feeling you and I could be good friends if we gave it a shot."

My throat grew thick. "Thanks for believing in me."

"You're worth lifetimes of loving, too," she said. "Talk to Logan."

33

The Rug Pulled Out

I didn't have to wait long to see Logan. The next day after school, as I dug in my closet for my old laptop full of story ideas, my phone dinged with a text from Nora. I scrambled to open it.

Please come to the office. We have a situation.

My stomach sank. That sounded dire. I thumbed back, On my way and immediately googled *The Watcher on the Hill*. If news had broken, Daniel Watcher would have it.

It was the top story. In big black letters, the headline screamed "TEA Flips: Teachers Union Recants Arthur Endorsement in Favor of Mane." In the picture, Governor Mane stood between a beaming Sonny and Kai, hands clasping their shoulders.

It made no sense. The teachers union was one of Logan's biggest allies—they should've been unequivocally on our side, given what Logan was prepared to do with the budget. And they were the people *I'd* brought in. Why had they betrayed us? I squinted at Sonny's and Kai's faces and remembered how oily they'd been at the rally, how they'd angled for preferential treatment. That had something to do with this, I knew it.

I grabbed my bag and raced out the door.

"I won't lie to you," Anita said. "This is bad. We were counting on teacher support. Even worse, we've positioned Logan as the working-class champion. The fact that a massive labor union switched its allegiance to Mane is, in technical terms, a disaster. Our polling shows a sizeable dip in Logan's credibility rating."

Nearly the entire campaign team was stuffed into the large conference room at headquarters, most of us standing in rows against the walls. Nora had offered me a seat at the table, but I'd declined. A real staff member could have it. Instead, I pressed into a corner of the room. Logan had swept in at the last minute, his face grave, and the second our eyes met, my adrenaline spiked, remembering kissing him up against the stacks. But he'd only given me a small, grim smile before sitting at the head of the table, and then it was time for business. The mood in the room was funereal.

"Okay," Nora said. "That's hard to swallow, but our job now is to counter the blow with new wins."

"I'm sorry to interrupt," said Cary, not sounding sorry at all. "But do we know what happened? How Mane was able to snake the TEA away from us? In the words of our fearless leader, what the fuck?"

The room broke into murmurs.

"I don't know if we should dwell—" Nora started, but Logan held up a hand and the room fell silent.

"I just got off the phone with friends who are close to Mane's campaign. The rumor is Sonny Yarrow and Kai West cut some sort of deal with the governor. He's not going to change the education budget, but in exchange for the endorsement, they get some sort of personal kickback. No one knows what yet."

Protests broke out.

"But that means they betrayed every educator in the state," I burst, and all eyes turned to me, Logan's included.

He nodded. "We knew they were trouble, remember? Our instincts were right. It's my fault for taking my eyes off them." He looked down at his hands, which were clutched on the conference table.

"We should tell people," I said. "The rest of the union will be livid."

He shook his head. "We would need proof, and that's hard to get. I think Nora's right. There's no time to dwell on things we can't change. Election day is in three weeks. Right now, we have to focus all our attention on new wins."

"Logan's going to reach out to the head of every major association that hasn't already chosen a side," Nora said. "For the next few days, he's going to be physically attached to the phone, so if you need him for something, don't. Everyone else, I want you knocking on doors, making personal connections with voters. Don't let Mane signs in front yards stop you." She shot a look at Logan and he nodded. "All right, people. Let's bring this home."

She and Logan rose and hurried out, and the rest of us filed after them. Once I'd made it out of the conference room, I stood in the middle of the bullpen and bit my lip, eyeing Logan's closed door. He was obviously busy. I probably shouldn't bother him. But Zoey had told me to insist I was important, too, worth prioritizing. Besides, there would always be one reason or another not to have this conversation with Logan. I just had to go for it.

Resolved, I marched to his office and knocked on the door. "Make it quick," he barked.

I opened the door and his face changed the instant he saw me. "Sorry. I didn't realize it was you."

Logan had looked grave but composed in the conference room. Now, in private, it was like he'd taken off a mask. He sat behind a desk piled with stacks of paper and sticky notes, anxiety radiating from him, etching exhausted lines into his handsome face. He scrubbed his hands through his hair. "If you want to talk about leaking the deal Sonny and Kai made, trust me, I wish we could, but I just don't have time to work out a strategy."

"That's not why I'm here." My God, my heart was pounding so fast you'd think I was lining up in front of a firing squad. *You're worth it*, I reminded myself, and planted myself directly in front of his desk. "I wanted to talk about yesterday. In the library."

He swallowed. "Lex, I'm sorry, but I *really* don't have time right now."

I tried not to flinch. "I know you're busy, but it's important we talk about what happened. Sooner, rather than later."

The phone on his desk started ringing and he glanced at it, then back at me. "Can we just wait until this dies down? Every minute I'm not on the phone with someone is a minute closer this campaign comes to crashing and burning."

I could feel disappointment crashing against the gates of my heart. "Just five minutes," I whispered, nearly wincing at how pathetic it sounded. But part of me refused to believe this moment was unfolding this way.

The phone rang one last time and Logan lunged for it. He pressed a hand to the receiver. "I'm sorry, Lex, I have to take this." Then his voice brightened. "Senator Wortham, thanks for getting back to me on such short notice."

I stood there blinking at him. Logan wasn't even looking at me anymore. He was nodding and trying to reach a stack of papers at the farthest edge of his desk, like I didn't exist.

I knew this feeling. I was twelve years old and small again. A second-tier priority. You would've thought I'd be used to it by now, but the riot of feelings in my chest was as fierce and fresh as the first time. Zoey's voice floated back: *If he brushes you off, you have your answer*. Message received, Logan Arthur.

I pushed the papers closer so he could reach them, then fled as fast as I could.

34

Three's a Crowd

"Wow, what a...healthy amount of champagne." Will's eyes widened as I snagged not one but two flutes off the server's tray. "You really love weddings, huh?"

I felt my cheeks heat under the extra layers of blush I'd swiped on to be as glamorous as possible for Will. Tonight was his boss's wedding, and we were at the Four Seasons Hotel downtown, a dark wood-paneled, marble-floored venue right on Lady Bird Lake that was a little too rich for my blood, though Will and his fellow doctor colleagues seemed at home. From the moment I'd arrived, I'd heard Logan's voice in my ear, whispering about the peacock parade, and I'd been trying to drown him out all night with champagne and cake and dancing. But it was a wedding, which meant love was on display everywhere I turned, and though Will was right that I *did* normally love them, on the heels of Logan's more-or-less rejection, attending this wedding felt like death by a thousand paper cuts. I'd cried during the vows, which was typical of me—I just hadn't corrected Will when he'd handed me his pocket square and whispered, "I love how happy you are for them." That *should* have been the reason I'd teared up.

I looked at Will, good-natured teasing shining in his eyes, and resolved to put Logan out of my mind once and for all. "Actually," I said, holding up one of my flutes, "I'm celebrating. Here's to picking yourself up after a fall. To having good instincts about danger and learning to listen to them. And to getting closure."

"Cheers," Will said, and clinked my glass. I took a long, fortifying sip of champagne, letting the bubbles tickle my throat. It had been a little more than twenty-four hours since Logan had dismissed me in his office. And though my instincts begged me to stay home and wallow, there was no way I'd miss Will's big event. So through sheer will, I put on the mantle of new Alexis, who did not crumple after rejection, but instead had a steel spine and a sense of purpose and, most importantly, a fancy yellow dress from Rent the Runway that demanded to be worn.

"About your toast," Will said. "I'm really sorry about the teachers union switching to endorse Mane. I heard it on NPR this morning. Sounds like the betrayal's hitting you hard."

"Let's not talk about the campaign." I downed the rest of the first glass and suppressed the urge to hiccup at the bubbles. "How's the hospital lately?" This was Will's night, after all. I gestured with my empty flute at the sharply dressed people in the ballroom around us. "They seem like a pretty fun crew to work with." Will's colleagues had been kind to me all night, even if Will didn't seem particularly close to anyone, lending evidence to Lee's claim that he hadn't found his people yet. No wonder he'd really wanted a date.

"It's actually been hard lately." Will's face softened. "One of my favorite patients isn't doing so well. Her surgery didn't have the impact we'd hoped."

The worry in his voice was sobering. Here Will was dealing with a real problem, one that put my small troubles into perspective. I took his hand and squeezed it. "I'm so sorry to hear that. I hope she improves."

He squeezed back. "Thanks." Then he shook his head and smiled. "Enough of that. Sorry. We're here to have fun."

"Dr. Laderman!" called a crisp voice, one I recognized from the ceremony.

Will and I turned to find the two grooms striding toward us. Dr. Samuel Kelis, chair of the cardiology department and Will's boss, was a tall, distinguished Black man with graying temples. His new husband, Morgan, was only a little taller than me, with bright red hair and freckles, and from what I'd gathered was an independent filmmaker in Austin's burgeoning film scene. They walked up to us with their fingers laced together, beaming.

"Having fun, Will?" Dr. Kelis held himself rather formally, each word spoken with sharp elocution.

"Yes, sir," Will answered. "A great time."

"Congratulations," I gushed, unable to help myself. "Your wedding was gorgeous and you make a beautiful pair."

"Dr. Kelis, Morgan, this is Alexis Stone." Will beamed at me as I dropped my empty champagne glass on a nearby table and shook the two men's hands.

"Double-fisting." Morgan's eyes gleamed. "I like the way your protégé's date rolls."

Even though Will's whole face brightened at the word *protégé*, I flushed and thrust the second glass of champagne at Morgan. "No, this one's for you." God forbid Will's boss think he was dating a lush.

"Even better," Morgan said, and whether or not he believed me, he happily accepted the champagne.

"You too make a charming couple," said Dr. Kelis. He nodded stiffly. "Well done."

I felt like I'd just been blessed by the Pope. I shot a glance at Will and saw everything Dr. Kelis did: how handsome Will was in his suit, his genuine smile. Being Will's girlfriend would be easy and uncomplicated and happy. I could practically see it.

"We're going to continue making the rounds," Dr. Kelis said. "Enjoy yourself, Will. But not too much, since you're on call tomorrow."

"That's my husband." Morgan winked. "It's his wedding night and he's still thinking about the hospital." The tease sounded like an old joke between them.

"Will do," Will said nervously. "I mean, won't do."

When the grooms walked away to greet another couple, Will bent his head down and whispered, "A little intense, right?"

"A lot intense."

He looked at our empty hands, then around at the ballroom. "So...we've checked all our boxes... Do you want to leave? I'll get an Uber."

"Lead the way, Dr. Laderman."

As we waited outside the hotel for our car, a cool breeze blew past, rustling the trees that shrouded the valet circle and making me shiver. "Good old Texas. Fall is finally coming in."

Will slipped his arm around me. "A good excuse to hold you."

I glanced up at him and caught my breath. His smile was so warm. Before I could think, he bent down and kissed me, gently at first, and then when I leaned in, he deepened it. It took me a long, protracted second before I realized what we were doing.

"Oh, no." I wrenched back. "We're in public."

"Shit. I totally forgot." We both spun, searching the street in front of the hotel with the obviousness of the world's worst secret agents. We were downtown, which wasn't great, but as I scanned, I saw no camera flashes or telltale signs of paparazzi. Just a bunch of regular people going about their business.

"I think we're safe," Will said. "I'm really sorry again. I think it's all the hospital shifts. My brain is melted."

"No big deal." I was being paranoid. It's not like I was famous or anything. People weren't following my every move.

Our Uber pulled up. Automatically, Will reached for my hand, then caught himself and shook his head. "See? This is why I'm a surgeon and not a spy. Can't pretend for anything."

"Come on." I laughed, opening the car door. "Let's get you out of public view."

He caught the door. "Hey, Lex... Do you want to make this a one-stop ride?"

Oh—so *that* was how you propositioned someone. I swallowed thickly. *You are not sad about Logan,* I reminded myself. *So what if he didn't feel the same way? You have Will, and Will is great. Going home with him after a beautiful wedding is great. Everything is great.* "Yes. I'm great—I mean, that sounds good."

Twenty minutes later, Will and I were walking up the tree-lined path to my front door when he froze and patted his suit jacket. "Oh, no. I think I left my phone in the Uber."

"He's at the end of the street—run!"

Will spun and took off to hail the departing car. I continued up the sidewalk, clutching my yellow gown, talking myself up—*having Will over was no big deal, this is exactly what you wanted*—when I turned the corner and came face-to-face with Logan, sitting hunched over on my front stoop. He jerked up, a tired smile breaking across his face. "You're home." He blinked. "And you're all dressed up."

I stared at him, heart pounding. "What are you doing here?" Logan looked like he hadn't slept for a week. His navy suit was rumpled and there were dark circles under his eyes. "Are you wearing the same clothes as yesterday?"

He rubbed his face, laughing bitterly. "Yeah, well, I haven't left the office since I saw you." He pulled something out of his pocket. "I did stop to get this on the way, though."

It was a pack of red-tipped darts, topped with a red bow. *Queen of hearts*, he'd said. Numbly, I accepted it.

"Figured you might want to use me for target practice after how we left things." He gave me a tight smile. When I didn't smile back, still caught in shock, he cleared his throat. "Right. Look, I came as soon as I could. I know we need to talk, in person and probably at length, so I'm not going back to the office until—"

"I got it!" Will crowed, rounding the corner and brandishing his recovered cell phone. He did a double-take when he saw Logan. "Oh. Hey, man. What are you doing here?"

For all my powers of imagination, I couldn't have dreamed up a more uncomfortable scene. My heart stopped its frenetic pounding and simply sank at Logan's face—because for once, I could read his expressions clearly. Surprise, then a recoil, as if he'd been hit. Then his politician's training took over and he masked it, producing a thin smile. Somehow, that smile was the most painful of all to witness.

"I—" Logan's voice came out too thick. He cleared his throat. "I didn't realize the two of you had plans tonight."

"It was my boss's wedding," Will offered. I still couldn't speak.

Logan's eyes darted to me, then quickly away. "I think I misunderstood something. I'm sorry. I'll let you two get back to your night." He pushed away from the stoop and cut into the lawn to avoid walking past Will and me.

I watched Logan retreat for a single desperate moment before turning to Will. "Can you give me a minute?"

He frowned. "Everything okay? He seems...tense."

"I'll explain later. Just—stay right here, okay?" I took off as soon as Will nodded.

Logan was making great time, booking it down my street. I rushed after him as fast as I could in my dress and heels. "Stop!" I called. "Logan. Please."

He came to a halt near a lamppost. When he swung to face me, I expected to see anger or frustration, but he was stone-faced.

"I'm sorry." The words flew out, knee-jerk, as I made it to his bubble of light on the dark street.

"You have nothing to apologize for." Logan scrubbed both hands over his face and then...left them there. I resisted the urge to pull them back. Finally, he did it himself. And this time, all I saw was weariness. "I'm the one who owes you an apology. I shouldn't have shown up like this. I thought you wanted to talk because...well, I thought after the library, you wouldn't..." His gaze jerked back to my apartment, where Will was waiting. "You know what, never mind." He shook his head. "All I seem to do lately is make the wrong calls. Mess things up, one thing after the other. I honestly think I lose my mind a little when I'm around you."

"You didn't mess anything up."

He laughed and looked around. "I kissed you, Alexis. I promised you when we started that you'd never have to worry about me crossing lines. And I've worked so hard—" His voice caught. "I've worked so hard not to. Then I made a mistake."

A mistake. There, in black-and-white, was the verdict I'd spent so much time wondering about: Logan thought our kiss was wrong. That's why he'd come tonight. To tell me he was sorry and it wouldn't happen again. "I kissed you back," I said, my pride forcing me to say it. "If it was a mistake, we both made it."

He blew out a breath. "Like I said, you have nothing to apologize for. I'm the one who crossed a line, then I was rude to you, then I spent thirty-six hours in the middle of a crisis with half my head in the game and the other half wishing everything would disappear so I could find you and fix it." He glanced in the direction of my apartment. "At least I clearly didn't mess up you and Will. Since you were on a date..."

"Yes." Why did I feel a pit in my stomach confirming it? Yes, we'd kissed, but Logan didn't have feelings for me. He'd made that clear a few times now. So I didn't owe him an explanation.

He nodded, his Adam's apple bobbing, like he was trying to swallow my *yes* fast.

"I'm not mad at you," I said quickly. "Everything's okay." It was my oldest instinct, the lesson I'd learned from my father: repair the relationship. Swallow the fact that he'd hurt me so I didn't lose him. Whether he was just a friend or something more, Logan was too important. Jesus, when had this man become so important to me?

He laughed. The bitterness was back. "Okay, Lex. If you say so. Well, whether you're angry or not, I'm still sorry." His eyes fell to my lips and lingered. With effort, he finally pulled them away. "I should go. I really need to sleep."

"Don't," I said, but I couldn't think of what to say next, a reason to keep him. The thing that always happened when I got overwhelmed was happening now: I couldn't parse my thoughts. All I knew was I didn't want him to leave.

Logan put his hands up, walking backward. "Trust me, I need to go before I say something else that messes everything up." With one last look, he turned, and I watched him walk away in his wrinkled suit until he melted into the night.

When I made it back to my apartment, Will was leaning against my front door. "Alexis." His voice was wary. "What's going on with you and Logan?"

Of course Will had seen us talking. And of course we'd looked anything but professional. As soon as Will asked, the fog in my brain cleared and I knew what to do. As Nora had said, even romantic love was about your values, about putting your beliefs about the way the world should work into practice. And I believed in honesty and fairness.

"I'm sorry, Will." I wanted to slump against the wall, but I forced myself to deliver this straight-backed, with the dignity Will deserved. "It's gotten...complicated with Logan. And you deserve better."

"I don't know about that."

"I do. You're an incredible guy. In another lifetime, I think we could've been perfect."

Will gave me a small, wistful smile. "But this is the lifetime where you met him?"

The answer was clear in my face. He leaned in and kissed me on the cheek. "Then I'll see you around."

"See you at Lee and Ben's wedding," I said, then wished for a sinkhole to swallow me. I'd never been on this side of a breakup before. It turned out I was bad at it.

Thank God Will was kind. He just smiled again and said, "Take care of yourself, Lex." Then he became the second man of the night to walk away from me.

Alexis Stone: honest, fair, and alone.

35

The Buck Stops Here

"What drives me bananas," Muriel said, swishing her scarves, "is that every teacher I've talked to thinks Sonny and Kai endorsed Governor Mane because he promised better reform than Logan."

"And they're not going to know the truth until after they help Mane get elected." I sighed, not bothering to pick my head up off the table. Now that my status as the Teacher's Champion was revoked—Governor Mane, not Logan, was in vogue at Barton Springs—Muriel, Gia, and I had been relegated back to the grossest table in the teacher's lounge, the one closest to the microwave. Someone had reheated eggs for lunch, but I was too despondent to do anything but waste away in microwaved-egg air. New Alexis might be a strong, independent person who didn't wallow, but exceptions had to be made for certified romantic disasters, such as enduring the emotional equivalent of two breakups in one night. Luckily, I had enough professional disasters to distract Muriel and Gia from asking me about the romantic ones.

"I just think if we told people the truth, they'd want to fight back," Gia said. "The union's supposed to represent all of us. And look at them, going about their lives. They're clueless."

Dutifully, Muriel and I looked around the lounge at the other teachers. They did look rather blissfully obtuse, eating their antibiotic yogurts and doing crossword puzzles, unaware they were about to get betrayed by Sonny and Kai and run over by a speeding train of budget cuts.

"Even if we did manage to spread the word," I said, "what makes you think people would believe me over the president and secretary of the TEA?"

"Honey." Muriel rested a warm hand on my shoulder. "You've been showing up nonstop for educators. I think you should trust they would show up for you."

In my experience, you couldn't trust other people to reciprocate your feelings: not your devotion, your care, or even your loyalty. But I sat up in my chair, the wheels in my mind turning. "Let's say we did manage to spread the word and people actually believed me that Sonny and Kai made a shady deal. How do we...change anything?" We couldn't hold another rally because I didn't have the expertise to plan one— you needed permits and manpower and all sorts of things real activists knew that I didn't. Besides, time was running out.

"Hmm," said Gia. Silence fell as we thought. What had I learned in my time with the campaign? I had to have picked up some useful lessons. I tried to remember things I'd heard Nora say. "You have to hit them where it hurts." I tapped my foot, thinking harder. "You get people's attention by dialing up the pressure. You should always look for leverage."

"What kind of leverage do we have?" Muriel mused.

I looked around the lounge at the other teachers. Eating their brown bag lunches because no one could afford to go out. Dutifully making crafts for their classrooms during their lunch hour. And it hit me. "*We're* the leverage. No matter how hard we get dicked over by lawmakers—"

Half a dozen heads turned to give me censorious looks.

"Sorry. No matter how hard we get *jerked over* by lawmakers, we keep showing up. The day after they told us they were cutting our retirement savings, what did we do?"

"We came to work like always," Muriel said.

Gia's eyes lit up. "You want to stage a walkout."

"Think about it." My mind was whirring a mile a minute. "No one has to get event permits or T-shirt cannons. All we have to do is...stay home. And we make a statement reporters can't ignore."

"It's genius," Muriel said. She thumbed through her phone. "I'll start calling my contacts from the Library Council."

"I'll call my friends from the TEA who won't leak it to Sonny and Kai," Gia said. "The TEA has a massive contact list. We can use Sonny and Kai's own resources against them."

"Perfect," I said. "And call your families, too. We'll need to get a phone bank running if we're going to reach a ton of people fast." I picked up my own phone and thought, for a fleeting moment, of calling Logan. Then I remembered his disappointed face in the lamplight. No matter what, though, I wanted to do this. Not just for my fellow educators, but for him. Even if he never talked to me again, I wanted to help Logan win more than anything.

So I'd call Nora to inform the campaign. But first, I would call my secret weapon. The queen of making a scene, my own one-woman political tornado, the lady whose antics never failed to go viral: my dear sister, Lee. It was time to put both the Stone sisters into action.

36

A Moment of Vision

"Get ready," Nora said, beaming. I barely had time to take a breath before she swung open the conference room door and the entire campaign team leaped to their feet and clapped. "Say hello," Nora called, "to the woman who saved our asses."

They cheered even louder. Cary wolf whistled and led a chant of "*Rudy, Rudy, Rudy*." I covered my face with my hands, completely overwhelmed. Thanks to the walkout, I'd barely gotten any sleep for the last four days, and now I was bone-tired, which meant I was wearing my heart on my sleeve. Nora only laughed and pushed me into the room.

"Thank you," I said, as staffers hugged me and clapped me on the back. "Thank you so much."

"Shh," someone hissed. "It's about to start."

Everyone's eyes turned to the giant TV that had been wheeled into the corner. Cary grabbed the remote and dialed the volume up as Trisha Smith's face filled the screen. With everyone's attention off me, I did a quick scan for Logan. My heart lurched.

"He's hammering out the details with union reps," Nora whispered. "Otherwise, he would've been here."

I nodded, forcing my spine to straighten. I'd accomplished the single greatest feat of my career, and nothing would diminish that.

"Trisha Smith here, reporting breaking news from the capitol." A strong breeze managed to blow some of Trisha's stiffly styled hair across her face, but she didn't flinch. "After a statewide teacher walkout led the *Texas Tribune* to uncover explosive evidence of quid pro quo dealings between Governor Mane and top officials at the Texas Educators Association, the state's largest teachers union has reversed its endorsement for the second time. By popular demand, the TEA once again endorses Logan Arthur for governor."

Cheers broke out so loudly it was almost impossible to hear what Trisha said next. "...making history with this reversal. In a stunning move, TEA members protested the actions of their own leadership, staging what ended up being a three-day walkout to protest unfair dealings between Governor Mane and their president and secretary-treasurer. Here to say more is one of the leaders of the walkout, Mrs. Muriel Lopez."

I nearly clapped when the camera turned to Muriel. She stood in front of her beaming daughter Carmen, who kept trying to pop her head around her mom and get in the shot. Muriel, who dressed for the spotlight every day of her life, was finally getting it. Good for her.

She blinked into the camera with a deer-in-the-headlights expression.

"My mom's a hero!" Carmen shouted, bouncing behind her.

Thankfully, it jolted Muriel out of her stage fright. "Yes, uh...thank you, Trisha. We were disappointed in the decision Sonny Yarrow and Kai Harris made to endorse Governor Mane, given Logan Arthur is the candidate with a plan to support teachers. We knew we had to make our voices heard. So while it pained us not to go in to work, we needed people to take us seriously."

"And that they did," said Trisha. The camera moved smoothly back to her. "Insiders report pressure from the walkout already had the governor's office scrambling, and the final nail in the coffin came on day three, when the *Tribune* published leaked emails between TEA President Sonny Yarrow and his golfing buddies, in which Yarrow claimed he'd held Mane over a barrel and, quote, 'spanked him real good until he gave me and Kai what we wanted.'"

"Tragic," Cary whispered. "Never trust your secrets to men who golf."

"Once that story broke," Trisha continued, "TEA leadership held a virtual town hall and agreed to their members' terms: a reversal of the endorsement and an ousting of Yarrow and Harris. As for who will replace Yarrow as union president, one key front-runner has emerged: Alexis Stone, who Arthur campaign insiders credit with getting the campaign to make education a top priority."

"That was me." Nora winked. "I'm insiders."

"While Alexis Stone's reps declined an interview, citing a need for rest, we're here with her sister, Senator Lee Stone."

Nerves fizzled in my stomach as the camera turned to Lee. The chyron under her face read *Sen. Lee Stone, aka #SadCrawler*.

Lee flipped her hair. "Thanks, Trisha. And may I also

thank you for including that footage of me crawling to the marathon finish line in CBS 12's *Best News Clips of the Decade documentary, ensuring it will live forever*. Please know I can't wait to return the favor one day." Trisha blanched, but Lee barreled on. "Alexis has shown real leadership over the last few months. Not just in the walkout, but in consistently amplifying the voices of teachers and school staff. I think she'd make a fine union president if that's what she wants. In fact, I think she'd make a fine politician."

"Following in your footsteps," Trisha prompted.

Lee grinned. "What's important is that the world is seeing the Alexis Stone I've always known. She's a powerhouse."

All the hairs on my arms rose.

Trisha squared off with the camera. "Will Alexis Stone be the next TEA president or state senator? More on this story as it develops. Now, back to the studio for a timely Halloween topic: razor blades in your kids' candy—myth or modern scourge? The answer may surprise you."

Cary turned off the TV and the volume in the room rose back to a dizzying level.

"Cary, crack open that champagne," Nora called. "One hour of celebrating, and then I want everyone back to work."

Cary saluted. "Aye-aye, captain!" He lunged for the minifridge.

"Come on." Nora tugged me toward the door. "If I know anything about my people, things are about to get weird."

I followed her out, grateful to escape. I was thrilled we'd pulled off the walkout. And later, I was going to find that news clip of Lee saying I was a powerhouse and play it on repeat. But right now, I was so tired I could barely think.

"Now that I've got you alone," Nora said, hopping up to sit on a cubicle desk. "And we have a brief window of sanity before the next crisis hits, I want to hear what you're thinking."

"This might be my exhaustion talking, but *what*?"

She kicked her legs. "Well, do you want that union job?"

That, at least, was easy. "Not in the slightest."

Her mouth quirked. "Then where do you see yourself after the campaign? You've built all this capital with us. What are you going do with it? Your sister is clearly seeding the ground for you to move into politics. Does that interest you?"

Like every other time I tried to picture what I wanted, there was nothing but white noise. I groaned and pressed my hands to my face. "I don't know, Nora. I just don't."

"You want my advice?"

I peeked through my fingers. "Sure."

She gave me an appraising look. "I know you're an introvert, but so are a lot of people in the public eye. I think you have something. I think you could be exactly like your sister. A leader with a bright future."

I could be like Lee. *There* was a desire I finally recognized, because it was my oldest one. Just hearing Nora say it out loud brought an embarrassing prickling heat to my eyes. I hastily wiped the moisture away.

Her voice grew softer. "I could help, you know. Taking on campaign challenges is what I live for. We could do it together."

I'd never been this close. All I had to do was reach out and take what Nora was offering, and I could be a person my father would've been proud of. A go-getter, a front-runner, no more second fiddle. All I had to do was say yes, and I could have Lee's life.

I didn't want it.

It hit me with sudden clarity: I didn't want to be a leader, or live a public life, or be in the spotlight. Hell, I was tired of orchestrating shenanigans, and I couldn't sail through life with the cool, confident nonchalance that always made Lee so enviable. Right or wrong, it wasn't my way. I didn't fit into her mold.

And that was okay.

It was more than okay. Dear God, I'd overlaid Lee's desires, and what I thought my father valued, and what I figured the world wanted from me on top of my own wishes for so long that it had become nearly impossible to know how *I* really felt. What *I* wanted. No wonder all I got was white noise when I thought about it. My own hopes and preferences had been buried under other people's for so long.

Standing in front of Nora in the middle of the empty cubicles, I experimented with lifting their expectations off my shoulders, ignoring the voices that said *Lee this* or *You should really* or *People will be disappointed*. Without the voices, there was nothing left but me. Was it really meant to be this easy? Was I really supposed to think about what would make me happy, and simply listen to the answer?

"I've loved this experience," I said to Nora, feeling it out. "It's helped me grow, and it's been amazing to feel like I'm fighting for something. But the truth is...politics isn't where my heart belongs. I love stories. I always have. And strangely, all this pretending has made me realize that I want to do more of it. Storytelling, I mean." I thought back to that night at the Fleur de Lis when Logan listened to me embody Ruby Dangerfield, that day in his living room when he asked me if I'd ever thought about writing. He was always so good at seeing me. Maybe better than I'd been at seeing myself. "I think I want to try to write a book."

I could tell what I was saying was right because it felt like settling into myself. No more fitting into uncomfortable molds.

Nora, who'd been listening stoically, finally smiled. "A writer. I can see that." A new wave of popping sounds came from the conference room and she shook her head. "They're on to round two. You better get out of here before they charge out, lift you on their shoulders, and carry you around the room. I've seen it happen."

I blanched and moved to leave.

"Wait—Alexis..."

I stilled.

"My family still doesn't understand my career. They think I'm nuts for living and breathing politics. But it's what makes me happy. So I better see you do what makes you happy, and fuck what anyone else says. Otherwise, you're back in my doghouse."

I smiled at her. "Nora, you know I wouldn't dream of disappointing you."

37

The Bomb Drops

"And that's why I'm requesting a promotion to full librarian," I said, plowing to the end of my speech. I glanced up to meet Principal Zimmerman's eyes and gulped. "I know the future of the budget is precarious, but I hope you'll still consider this based on the strength of my record."

Zimmerman sat on the other side of his massive desk, which he kept neat as a pin and in a very particular arrangement, a fact his assistant, Megan, liked to complain about. He was an older man, with wiry salt-and-pepper hair and a thick Sam Elliott–style mustache. The mustache twitched as he smiled. "I would say—"

A quick burst of knocking sounded before the door swung open, and Megan ducked her head in. "Alexis, I'm getting calls for you up front. Journalists."

"Megan." Principal Zimmerman's voice was exasperated. "What did we agree about barging in?"

"I know, I know. Privacy is a virtue." She started to close the door, then added, rapid-fire, "But I think you might want to check the news!"

When the door shut, Zimmerman looked at me expectantly. "Do you need to go?"

I shook my head and sat taller. "I'm sure it's just reporters wanting to follow up on the walkout. Whatever it is can wait. I do want to add, though, that if you're worried about how to pay for my promotion, I have an idea. In addition to becoming a full librarian, I'd like to work four days a week so I can use Fridays for a personal writing project. That way, you don't have to pay me as much."

There. I hadn't held anything back. I'd put everything I wanted on the table. No matter what happened, at least I'd been true to myself.

To my surprise, Principal Zimmerman laughed. "It's fitting you offered me a solution to an anticipated problem. Problem-solving seems to be among your strengths." He leaned forward, folding his arms on his desk. "Alexis, you're an asset to this school. Not only do you have a strong rapport with your students, but lately you've proven yourself as a leader." He shook his silvery head. "The truth is, I should've given you a promotion a long time ago. I appreciate your patience."

Was I hearing right? I resisted the urge to rub my ears.

"And you can have Fridays off without the reduced pay. As for the matter of funding, I'm sure I'll find a way. These last few years of budget cuts have at least taught me how to stretch pennies. Let's just cross our fingers Mr. Arthur wins the election, shall we?"

He stood up and I followed suit, slinging my bag over my shoulder. "Congratulations, Alexis." He held out his hand and I shook it. "You've earned it." His eyes twinkled. "I got a lot of knitting done during those three days of the walkout. Not a bad way to spend one's time."

The fact that Zimmerman had joined us in the walkout would never cease to amaze me. Muriel was right: sometimes you could trust people to show up. "Thank you—for everything."

I was going to be a full librarian. And I'd get the time and space to write my book. It was more than a dream come true. I felt like I was walking on clouds leaving Zimmerman's office—until I glided past Megan's desk. "You checked your phone yet?" she asked, deep in a game of Minesweeper.

I wanted to linger more in this lovely bubble of triumph, but I supposed I owed it to the campaign to respond to reporters in a timely fashion. I couldn't wait to tell Nora the news about my new job. I dug around in my bag, yanked out my phone, and—

I had twenty-two missed calls, fifty-four texts, and *three hundred* Twitter notifications. My heart dropped into my stomach. I opened Twitter first, because I was a masochist.

And there, flooding my mentions, were the pictures. Not of me and Logan, but of me and Will. The photos were dark and grainy, taken at night from a cell phone, but you could see we were standing outside the Four Seasons Hotel, dressed for a wedding. Will was kissing me, hands cupping my face.

I thought we'd gone unnoticed, dodged a bullet. But here we were, blasted for the whole world to see. I caught only the first headline—"Logan Arthur's Girlfriend Caught Cheating"—and the first response—"How dare that dumb whore??!!"—before I pressed the screen dark, hands shaking. Then the phone slipped and clattered to the floor.

38

Never Met a Sword I Didn't Fall On

I watched campaign staff argue with each other across Cary's living room with the blurry, muted distance of a person a thousand leagues underwater. I sat at one end of the room, Logan at the other, our gazes fixed on our hands. Between us, Nora, Cary, Anita, and a small cadre of crisis comms consultants yelled back and forth, debating what to do.

We'd gathered here at Cary's house because Nora said the campaign office was a zoo, and reporters would likely camp out at the houses of anyone high-profile. That comment had been a blow to Cary, who'd insisted he was a very famous member of the campaign. But since it turned out that, high-profile or not, Cary was a trust fund baby whose parents had purchased him a house bigger than Lee's and Logan's combined, I couldn't find it in myself to feel sorry for him. The one thing that had broken through my misery was seeing evidence of Cary's last-minute attempt at concealing his true personality before we arrived. Things had been awkwardly shoved in about a dozen hiding places. The best: a life-sized cutout of Matt Bomer from *Magic*

Mike peeked its handsome head out from behind Cary's pantry door.

I had to turn off my phone because of the sheer influx of notifications, but before I did, my neighbor called to confirm there were reporters outside my apartment. Nora had put a gag order on everyone gathered here, asking them not to mention the latest coverage. It was a mercy all the more remarkable because she could barely bring herself to look at me.

How quickly I'd fallen from cloud nine to twenty-thousand leagues under the sea.

Anita's voice broke through. "What were you thinking, cookie?"

I looked up to find the entire living room watching me.

"I understand wanting to go for seconds in a hot man buffet," she said. "Logan plus Will, yum. But why do it in public?"

"Because she *wasn't* thinking," Nora said coolly. When we locked eyes, her icy mask faltered. "She made a move without considering the consequences. *Again.*"

"It's a rookie mistake," said one of the consultants, adjusting his glasses. "We see it with clients all the time, thinking they can outsmart the public—"

"Enough," Logan cracked, and everyone fell silent. His steel gaze swept the room. "Back off Alexis. I'm the one who told her to date Will if she wanted to. If you have shit to say, say it to me."

"You did *what*?" Nora screeched. "How could you?"

He looked at me and the anger in his eyes melted away. "Because she shouldn't have had to put her life on hold just to help me." He cleared his throat. "Will is the real deal for her."

His kindness was so unexpected a lump formed in my throat. Here I was drowning in guilt over what my mistake had done to his campaign, and Logan was defending my ability to date Will. He didn't even know Will and I were over. It was enough to make me take a deep breath and say the thing I'd been working out while they yelled.

"I'm the one who messed up." I used my firm speech voice. "As far as the world is concerned, I'm the villain. If I own it, make a public apology, Logan can dump me and that will be the end of it for him. This doesn't have to be Logan's burden."

"It *would* make him sympathetic," Cary said, scratching his chin. "It could actually help the campaign."

Nora jerked to Anita. "Can your team look into how this would play?"

"Of course—"

"Absolutely *not*." This time, Logan surprised everyone by pushing to his feet. He looked around the room with an incredulous expression. "Jesus Christ, we're not throwing Alexis under the bus. Have you seen what people are saying about her? It's disgusting. Not in a million years."

Nora threw her hands up. "Then what's our move? I know you like to process, but time's up, Logan. We've got reporters beating down our doors. We have to do something."

"I know," he said, and took a deep breath, like he was steeling himself. "Call your press contacts. I'm making a statement."

The suits buzzed. "What kind of statement?" Nora asked.

I recognized that look on his face. It was the same he'd worn when he stood up from the bar and told Carter the creep to come fight him. Too defiant for his own good.

"I'm telling everyone the truth," Logan said. "The whole story. That I asked Alexis to pretend to date me to save me from press scrutiny. Which means she was free to see Will. She did nothing wrong."

"You can't." Disbelief turned my voice hollow.

"Over my dead body," agreed Nora, and she and everyone in the room launched into arguments about why Logan couldn't, their protests tangling together.

He threw his hands up. "It's not a debate. I appreciate your advice, but I've made up my mind."

"Logan," Nora whispered, and her quietness was the scariest thing of all. "If you do this, it's career suicide."

"Maybe," he said, just as softly. His eyes tracked to mine and I held my breath. "But I'm not winning at the cost of Alexis."

"The two of you." Nora pointed between us. "First you're competing to throw each other under the bus, and now you're trying to out-sacrifice each other. Both games are equally infuriating, for the record."

"Tell the reporters I'll meet them at the office." Logan nodded at me. "I'm going to fix this, I promise." Then he took off.

Once the front door shut behind him, the whole room deflated. Cary fell onto his couch. "We're fucked. I have to start sending my résumé out. And I was already choosing drapes for my new capitol office."

Nora smacked his arm. "Don't be a quitter."

"Excuse me," I said, fumbling out of my seat. I had to catch Logan before he made a life-altering mistake.

Luckily, the driveway to Cary's mini-mansion was long, and Logan was just nearing the end. "Wait!" I called, suppressing the memory of the last time I'd chased after him and how poorly that had turned out.

He stopped so I could catch up, but he was already shaking his head. "There's no use trying to convince me."

Now that we were alone, panic leaked into my voice. "You don't have to do this."

"Of course I do. It's the bloody right thing. We both knew this arrangement had the potential to blow up, and I promised you if it did, I'd deal with it. So here I am. Let me."

"Will and I aren't seeing each other anymore." The words flew out before I could think.

He grew unnaturally still. "But you liked him."

"I did. I do. Just—as a friend, it turns out."

I could practically see the wheels turning as Logan studied me, trying to see inside my head.

"I'm sorry," I said. *Fix it, mend it,* the familiar voice whispered. *You're going to lose him.* "I'm sorry for going out in public with Will after our argument, and kissing him, and bringing him home. It was thoughtless, like Nora said, and I'm so—"

"No, you're not," Logan interrupted.

"Excuse me?"

He shook his head. "You're not sorry, Alexis. You were *mad*. Admit you were mad at me for blowing you off when the union crisis hit."

I felt a surge of panic. "No, I wasn't—"

"You were *justifiably* mad. Own it." He watched me, waiting.

It was getting hard to breathe. I wasn't allowed to make demands of other people. I was the one who accommodated.

Logan raised a hand as if to touch me, then clenched his jaw and pulled it back. "Lex. You're allowed to be angry. You're allowed to be *furious*, and vengeful, and whatever else you're actually feeling. Fuck, you're allowed to be a downright shitty person every once in a while, no one's perfect. You could've told me I pissed you off, and I would've tried to make up for it. That's all that would have happened. We would've argued, then made up." When he laughed, the sound was so sad it made me sink my teeth into my tongue. "I wouldn't have gone anywhere."

"You made me feel *small*," I burst, surprising even myself. But *why* was I surprised? My filter had always been weakest around Logan. From the first night on, his brashness had been a magnet, pulling me out of my hiding place. "*Yes*, I was angry, okay? I was furious at you for dismissing me and making me feel less important than your campaign, even though I know that's ridiculous. Of course I'm less important than your campaign! Your campaign is everything you've been working toward since you were ten years old, chaining yourself to that tree." My chest heaved. "There. That's how I felt. Are you happy?"

This time Logan did touch me, brushing his fingers down the side of my face. "Yes. Very." As my heart hammered, he leaned in and kissed my forehead. I closed my eyes. "You're not less important than the campaign," he whispered. "I'm trying to show you."

His phone pinged and my eyes opened. Reluctantly, Logan looked down at the screen. "I'm sorry." He gave me a weary look. "I have to go now."

"Please," I choked. "Don't throw your campaign away for me."

Logan looked back over his shoulder, his smile small and sad. "Sorry, Lex. I've got to piss you off one last time."

We lined the sofa, staring at Cary's giant flat-screen. In the center of it, Logan stood in front of the campaign headquarters, flanked by reporters. The campaign's comms director was visible in the background, biting her nails. Underneath, the chyron scrolled the headline *Arthur Breaks Silence About Cheating Rumors.*

"I'm going to make this brief." Logan's face was the sternest I'd seen it. Goose bumps rose on my arms. "I asked Alexis Stone to pretend to date me after compromising pictures of us surfaced that I deemed a risk to my political career. The entire deception was my idea and carried out at my request."

Beside me, Nora winced, but Cary looked at the screen with shining eyes.

"Because of the nature of our arrangement, Alexis had every right to date other people." His sternness slipped into anger. "So I'm asking—*demanding*—that the media leave her alone. As for me, I want to offer my apologies for misleading you. I let the pressure of the race warp my judgment. Rest assured I'm done pretending to be someone I'm not to appease people. From now on, you'll get only the real Logan Arthur. I hope it's enough. Thank you."

He turned his back on the cameras. Predictably, the reporters exploded into questions, but he kept walking to the campaign office, where the comms director put an arm over his shoulders, shielding him, and they disappeared through the double doors. The cameras returned to the anchors in the studio, whose mouths were almost comically agape.

"What a fall," said one of the comms consultants, shaking his head. "I wouldn't be surprised if Logan ends up on a syllabus at the Kennedy School."

"Epic Fuck-Ups of the Twenty-First Century," agreed another consultant.

I tuned them out. All I could think about was what Logan had said: that he was going to stop pretending to be someone he wasn't to appease people. All this time I'd thought he and I were complete opposites, but where it mattered, we were the same.

I was pulled out of my thoughts by Nora, squeezing my hand. When I saw her face, I knew what she was going to say. "I should leave now, shouldn't I?"

At least her voice was regretful. "I'm sorry. But I need you to keep your distance from Logan from this moment forward."

I could feel everyone's eyes on me and swallowed hard, willing myself not to cry.

"You're part of a scandal now," Nora said. "Which means you're toxic to him. All people will see when they look at you is his lie. If he's going to have a shot at coming back from this—"

Cary scoffed.

"We can't have you anywhere near him," Nora finished. "Do you understand what I'm asking?"

It was only logical. *Still*, how it stung. "Yes," I said quietly. "You want me to disappear."

39

My Favorite Person in the World

Silver lining of being asked to disappear after a terrible scandal: as an introvert, I'd been training for this all my life. Two days after Logan had taken all the blame, public interest in me finally waned, judging by the way my social media notifications dried up. Still, I wasn't taking any chances, so indoors I remained. I finally had the apartment sorted, anyway: I'd closed the blinds until the whole place was dark and forlorn—at first to block photographers and now simply for the ambiance—my pantry was stocked with chocolate bars, I'd hunted down every chenille blanket and draped them over me until I was shielded by a mountain of softness, and now I was curled on the couch with Patches, whose steady purring kept my serotonin levels high, all things considered.

I rubbed her ears until she closed her eyes. "It's going to be you and me from now on. Just two golden girls living out the sunset of their lives." True, I was only twenty-seven, but after these last few months in politics, I felt whatever age Patches was in cat years. Forget giving in to my inner sex goddess; it was time to cede the floor to my inner sexagenarian.

"This is your daily reminder that I love you." I booped Patches on the nose, then lifted the remote. "Time to torture ourselves."

I still couldn't bring myself to sit through the news, what with the constant danger of Logan's face cropping up. Instead of the real world, Patches and I had chosen to live in a sunnier one, burning through about two decades' worth of romantic comedies during my two days of exile. But what we were about to watch had arrived in the mail from my mother: the final cut of the Happy Homes commercial. She'd attached a note that said, cryptically: *Went in a different direction*.

The opening credits flashed, white words against a black background: *Directed by Elise Stone (in spirit)*. Then: *Directed by Roger Akins and the Bayou City Film Crew (in terms of actual direction)*.

I shook my head. I never should've taught her how to use Adobe Premiere.

Logan appeared on-screen with a toothpaste commercial smile, walking through the main hall of Happy Homes. "Welcome to the happiest animal rescue in Texas." He spanned his arms wide like Vanna White. I let out a sound halfway between a laugh and a sob.

The commercial cut to him kneeling down to pet two dogs side by side. "Where every animal is precious, and gets the care, attention and love they deserve. Whether they're dogs—" The screen shifted to Logan wearing muck boots, out in the horse stables. "Farm animals—" It cut to him giving a thumbs-up next to a gerbil racing in a wheel.

"Gerbils, hamsters, and rabbits—" Then it cut to him wide-eyed, trying to smile through terror as a thick snake was draped over his shoulders. "Friendly reptiles," he quivered. The shot changed to Logan sitting cross-legged in the kitten room. "Or all the cats you could ever want." On cue, the army of kittens barreled on-screen, running him over.

My jaw dropped as I entered the frame, crouching next to Logan. *Elise Stone, you monster!* She'd promised she wouldn't get me on camera.

"You should adopt from Happy Homes because they're all about love," said Logan's voiceover. On-screen, he and I grinned at each other. I sat up straighter on the couch.

"Come find your soul mate," he said, voice rich and warm. "The next member of your family." The shot shifted to him standing next to me, holding Patches, which made Patches perk up in my lap. On-screen, Logan and I smiled at each other over her head, eyes shining.

"You have no idea the love that's waiting for you." The commercial started to dissolve into a black screen with the Happy Homes address but I rewound it, freezing on the frame of Logan and me.

I'd never seen myself so happy.

Without warning, I burst into tears. I'd worked so hard to care only the appropriate amount. I'd pulled myself back in every situation, held my heart so carefully at bay, and it was all for nothing. Because there I was on-screen for everyone to see, adoration plain on my face. It had been there all along, hadn't it? Even though he was supposed to be a one-night stand, I'd liked Logan so much—*too* much—that first night at the Fleur de Lis, and it only intensified with every day I got to know him better. There was no use telling myself to stop, because I loved him beyond logic and reason.

I *loved* him.

Banging sounded at my door, making Patches and me jump. I wiped my tears hurriedly, feeling like I'd been caught.

"Alexis!" Lee called. "It's me."

I stalked to the door and wrenched it open. "Why don't you ever call first?"

Lee was in full politician mode, her business suit sharp, sunglasses dark and mirrored, lips crimson. "Because then you'd tell me not to come." She breezed past me. "You look like you haven't gone outside in days, by the way. Real bunker hole vibe."

I followed her to my living room, tugging my blankets over my shoulders. "Yeah, well...you look like a villain from *House of Cards*."

She sat on my couch and beamed. "Aw, thank you. I had back-to-back interviews today. Everyone's asking if I knew you and Logan were fake when I endorsed him. Our phones have been ringing off the hook."

"Oh, no." I sank next to her. "I'm so sorry. I didn't even think about that."

She waved me off. "Please. I love going toe-to-toe with anyone who thinks they can badmouth *you* to *me*. Those clowns. Wait." She leaned closer. "Have you been crying? The last time I texted, you seemed fine."

I scrubbed my eyes and let out a tremulous "No."

Lee inched closer. "Look, you were right about Logan, okay? He turned out to be a really good guy. The way he threw himself under the bus for you is all anyone can talk about."

I ducked my head so she couldn't see my eyes.

"Hey, Lex. Talk to me. We're going to get through this, I promise. You can still be an activist or a union leader, even a politician. It'll be the new family business and it'll be great."

My emotions balanced on a knife's edge. The old habits were tugging at me, urging me to keep things bottled up, not rock the boat. Then, on the other side, was my burning desire to have a truthful moment with my sister *finally*.

I caught sight of the TV over Lee's shoulder. On-screen, I glowed at a man I'd never been honest with, and now my chance was gone. There were too many shots I hadn't taken. No more.

"You're my role model," I said.

Lee's eyes widened in surprise. I didn't try to hide the shakiness in my voice. "You're the person I look up to most in the world. I've spent my whole life trying to be like you. And every time I fall short, it hurts."

"What?" Her voice was faint.

"I've always known you were who I should strive to be. It was so obvious after mom and dad split. Dad admired you no matter what, and next to you, I think he barely saw me." My voice broke. "But no matter what I do, Lee, I just can't make myself be like you. I'm a different person, and I have to admit that. I don't want a big, zany life. I'm happy with a small, quiet one. And after the last few months, and especially the last week, I think I'm learning to be okay with that, but—" I took a deep breath, summoning my courage "—I need you to be okay with it, too. I need you to stop pushing me to be someone I'm not. I want you to be proud of me for who I am."

342

In the silence that followed I was too scared to look. Finally, I forced my eyes up—and when I did, I saw that Lee was crying.

"I'm *so* proud of you," she managed to say. "Alexis, you're my favorite person in the world."

Before I could process, she leaned over and did the thing I'd been craving for so long: she hugged me. "I'm sorry I didn't know you felt that way about Dad—I *should've* known. But instead of checking in on you, I pushed you away. I was just so hurt he betrayed us and then it felt like you were siding with him, and then we lost him before I could fix it, and I couldn't ever... It was so painful. There was this physical block whenever I tried to talk about it. I had so many regrets. But because of that, I let you drift away from me."

I pressed my face into her shoulder. "I never drifted. I followed you everywhere."

"I can't tell you how many times I wanted to...to hug you or just be close to you...but I held myself back." She gripped me tighter. "Please forgive me. I promise I'll do better."

I squeezed her, unable to speak.

"And everything you said about me pushing you is true. But it wasn't because I wanted you to be like me, Alexis—I wanted you to have it better. Telling you to use your backbone and everything with Chris and Logan and Will, I just didn't want you to make the same mistakes I did. I didn't want you to wait so long to find what fulfilled you, or settle for anything less than *real* love, healthy love. It took me so long to figure myself out. I wanted you to learn from my mistakes." She laughed a little and pulled back to wipe her eyes. "I should've remembered you were always naturally smarter at these things."

I dragged my shirt against my eyes. Even though they stung, and my head was cloudy from crying, I felt indescribably lighter. "I think," I said carefully, "because we never really talked about the heavy stuff, some part of me worried that if I tried, I'd push you away. And I couldn't lose you again. Our relationship felt fragile, and that hurt more than anything."

She squeezed my hands. "Hear this: you cannot lose me. There's no one in this world I love more. You're my little sister, Alexis. You're the greatest gift life ever gave me."

When I pressed my hands to my face, she got up and ran to the bathroom, returning with a box of tissues. I took them gratefully, and while I dabbed my eyes, she glanced at my TV.

"Hey, that's mom's commercial." Lee stared, then turned to me with a questioning look. "You and Logan..."

"I love him," I said, unable to keep it inside.

Her eyebrows flew up. "You say this *now*?"

"Lee!"

"Sorry, sorry."

I looked at the screen, where past Logan gave past me a tender look. "I think he had feelings for me, too. But I was so convinced it wasn't possible, I wouldn't let myself see it."

She flopped back on the couch. "He certainly *looks* like a man with feelings." She whistled. "Damn. What a time to fall in love, right in the middle of the biggest race of your life. I guess that explains why he blew up his career for you."

We sat side by side, heads back, looking at the screen.

"He always put me first," I said. "From the beginning. All I had to do was tell him education was important to me, and he let me co-own his campaign. He told me to date Will because he thought me being happy was more important than him staying safe. And then he took the blame for those photographs even though letting people think I cheated would've saved him."

"Oof." Lee winced. "That stacks up."

"I was so convinced I wasn't enough for him that anytime I thought *maybe there's something here*, I told myself I was doing my normal thing of wanting too much from people."

Lee shrugged. "It *is* a bad habit to keep expecting things from people who always let you down. You used to do that a lot."

"Like with Chris."

"Exactly. But it's not a bad thing to put your heart on the line with someone who has a track record of showing up. That's when you can be vulnerable without being a doormat."

I groaned. "Why do I have to learn every lesson too late? Now if Logan wins the election by some miracle, I won't be allowed to talk to him because I'm toxic. And if he loses, I'll always be the person who cost him his dream. It's lose-lose. I'm in love with someone I can never have."

Lee reached over and squeezed my hand. "I may be new to doling out wisdom, but if there's one thing I've learned, it's that people have to come to things in their own time. You had to change your relationship with yourself before you ever would've been happy with someone else, even Logan. And really, when people love each other, things have a way of working out. You can trust me. I'm your big sister."

40

The Second Debate

Yes, technically I'd promised to stay far away from Logan. But if my brief foray into politics had taught me anything, it was that there was always a loophole. I figured as long as no one ever *knew* I'd attended his second and final debate, that was as good as not going. Which is why I'd come to the Palmer Event Center in full disguise.

"Name?" asked the matronly woman behind the registration desk.

"Ruby Dangerfield."

She rifled through the lanyards until she found it. "Here you go, Ruby." She smiled. "I love seeing young people participate in our country's grand democratic tradition."

Feeling buoyed by her approval—I was a simple creature, alas—I put on the lanyard and let myself get caught up in the crowd. The Palmer Center was much bigger than where they'd held the first debate. Lee had told me the audience demand was so high this time around that the debate organizers had decided to switch to a larger venue. Not only were there tons of people, but the atmosphere felt buzzy and electric, almost like a concert. Clearly, people loved drama, and if nothing else, the gubernatorial race had served that up on a silver platter. At least Logan could take heart knowing his public implosion had enticed more people to engage with politics.

The crowd was perfect for hiding in. I'd borrowed a blond wig from Lee—refusing to let her tell me why she owned it— and wore my blue-light glasses and one of my old cardigan sets, cosplaying as a blonde me before the campaign makeover. I kept my head ducked as I found a seat in the back, sinking lower when I spotted Nora and Cary slide into the front row right before the curtains lifted. From that moment on, my heart was a runaway train. This was the final debate. If Logan repeated his last performance, he was done for.

The lights flashed and the announcer introduced Logan and Governor Mane, who strode out to applause and a swelling rendition of "America the Beautiful." When the crowd settled, one of the moderators, a UT professor, directed the first question to the governor.

"Governor Mane, what do you plan to do about the state's rising unemployment rate?"

The governor grinned and adjusted his signature bolo tie. "You know, professor, I'm proud of my tax incentive plan that makes Texas attractive to big businesses. We've had a lot of success getting corporations to relocate their plants to Texas, and I'm going to build on that. More plants means more jobs. And also—"

"But what kind of jobs?" Logan interrupted. "Low-paying jobs with terrible benefits that burn people out, or good quality jobs people can turn into careers?"

I sat straighter as murmurs rippled through the audience.

Logan's face was large on the jumbo screen, and I knew that dogged look: This was the old Logan. The *real* Logan, the man who loved to fight and didn't care about things like decorum or deference.

"Excuse me?" Mane asked.

"It's not Mr. Arthur's—" the moderator started, but Logan barreled on.

"You think bringing more factories to Texas is the solution to helping the economy, but your last four years disprove that approach. That's why unemployment's still as high as it is."

Loud grumbling sounded from the RNC side, but Logan wasn't done.

"You can't toss shitty jobs at people, jobs without health care, *back*-breaking jobs with sky-high attrition rates, and call that a win. These factory jobs you're bragging about? The only people truly helped by those are the billionaire CEOs who get to dodge taxes thanks to your incentive plan."

"Mr. Logan, swearing is *not* allowed," exclaimed the moderator, who was visibly sweating. I caught Nora clutching her hair.

"They're good jobs," argued the governor, who'd grown a little red in the face. "Honest, hardworking people are just asking for a shot—"

"They should be asking for more than a shot," Logan countered. "They *want* more, and you'd know if you ever stepped outside those swanky country clubs you like to hole up in with your old football pals."

Oh, God—Logan was going for it, full throttle. No more noncombative. He was ignoring his advisers' instructions. I didn't know whether to cheer or wring my hands.

"At the same time you're bringing these so-called great jobs to the state, you're gutting unions or making shady deals with union leaders—" The audience erupted into whispers at the reference to Sonny and Kai. "Thereby destroying protections for workers. People need health care, governor. They need to be paid more than minimum wage. They need to be able to afford their rent. You can't brag about bringing jobs to the state unless you're talking about the kinds of jobs you'd be willing to work yourself. Until then, your 'unemployment plan—'" of course he was making air quotes "—is just a corporate tax break by another name."

The entire left side of the auditorium broke into applause, drowning the governor's response. His face had gone from red-tinged to full-blown tomato.

"If we could pivot to thoughts on nuclear power," a second moderator tried, but Governor Mane was eyeing the audience, several of whom had climbed to their feet to cheer Logan.

"Bold talk from a man who just publicly admitted he's a liar," burst the governor, and the applause died in a sudden arctic gust. "How are voters supposed to have faith in a man who concocted a harebrained scheme to fake date a woman to hide his sexual indiscretions?"

My heart leaped into my throat. Of course the governor was bringing up Logan's worst mistake—he'd be a fool not to. But knowing it was inevitable didn't lessen the pain when I saw panic flash over Logan's face.

But then the most unexpected thing happened. Maybe it was because he was so close to the end and there was nothing left to lose. Maybe he figured he was a goner anyway. Or maybe Logan Arthur was just that much of a stubborn jackass. Whatever it was, the panic melted from his expression and he smiled. "You know what, governor? I don't regret it."

You could've heard a pin drop.

Governor Mane blinked, wheels turning in his head, before it occurred to him that Logan had just handed him a gift. His eyes gleamed. "You don't regret *lying* to your future constituents?" He swept a hand at the audience. "These fine people?"

"No, I do regret lying. I knew it was a bad idea and I did it anyway. I didn't think I could be fully honest about who I was and stand a chance of winning. So I regret not having more faith in myself, or the people of Texas. But what I don't regret is making Alexis Stone my partner."

My hands flew to my mouth. On-screen, the camera zoomed in on Logan's face. He lifted his chin, eyes blazing. "I believe in the campaign Alexis and I built together, and I admire the hell out of her brain, her heart, and her spine. She was endlessly brave, leaping out of her comfort zone, and watching her do that made me better. You can't be around someone like that without the example soaking in."

He was describing me like I was some sort of hero. All around me, audience members were glancing at each other in disbelief. But I only had eyes for him.

"So I'm going to leap out of my comfort zone right now and do something my campaign is going to kill me for. But what the hell—I've already tangled my personal and professional lives. My relationship with Alexis might've been a lie, but it was real for me. *She* was real for me, the entire time. And she woke me up to what I really wanted. What I care about the most."

Someone on the RNC side wolf whistled, and the rest of the audience laughed. My cheeks were on fire. On stage—on screen—Logan smiled, blush tinging his cheeks for the first time since I'd known him.

To me he'd felt like a dream I wanted desperately to sink into, and to him I'd been real from the start. I pressed my hands to my chest, feeling my heart pound through my ribcage, my fingers, my throat. I couldn't believe this was happening.

"So no, Governor, I don't regret it," Logan said. "And personally, I'd rather elect a candidate who made a mistake and owned it than one who's made false promises for years but never shows remorse. I hope voters will agree."

Mane started sputtering a counterpoint, but for a long moment the cameras stayed on Logan, drawn by the shining look he was giving the audience, the whole of his face radiating confidence. *Here* was the man I'd met at the Fleur de Lis, the man who'd helped teach me about sticking to my guns, the firebrand from every practice session.

Here was the man I loved, prevailing against the odds. I clapped with the rest of the audience, pushing away tendrils of sadness that I was stuck here, watching with pride from the shadows.

41

Macoween

So much had changed since the night I sat in the Italian restaurant Il Tempesto, bawling my eyes out as Annie proposed to Zoey—both for the good and the bad. But the changes I was most grateful for were the twists of fate that had brought me to this moment, standing on Zoey's side of the aisle in my black bridesmaid's dress. All of Zoey and Annie's bridesmaids were lined up, awaiting the change in music that would signal the brides' big entrance. Across from me, on Annie's side, Lee stood proud in her own black dress, which was grander and fluffier than the rest of ours to denote her status as Annie's maid of honor (a difference she'd insisted on). Behind Lee stood Claire, Mac, and Annie's older sister, Karen. On Zoey's side, I was squished between Layla and Helen, the actress and glassblower from the bachelorette, as well as Zoey's beaming mother, who was Zoey's matron of honor. Apparently, traditions were to Zoey what they were to Logan: things to be nodded at, then ignored. How funny that I'd given my heart to so many rule breakers.

On the other side of the wedding arch, Lee swished her ball gown to get my attention. "This venue is gorgeous, isn't it?" She glanced back at Mac, who stood behind her. "Sorry Mac, but this is the best Macoween yet."

Halloween fell on Mac's birthday, so Lee and her friends had called it Macoween ever since college. According to them, it was a magical night, bringing good luck to all. Lee used to swear she couldn't get hungover after Macoween, though recently she'd conceded that she may have confused the power of Macoween with the power of her twenties.

"I'm okay with that," Mac said. "It's Annie and Zoey's year to get the lion's share of the Macoween magic."

We stood in an old renovated church, surrounded by brick walls and exposed wooden beams. The walls were lit golden by flickering candles and hung with art from the Tite Street Artist Collective, none of which was technically appropriate for a wedding—a few of the older guests couldn't stop staring at a painting of a bare-chested mermaid, for example. White flowers trailed from the chairs guests slid into, and a string quartet sat in the corner playing dreamy music. It was a mash-up of elegant and playful, perfectly Annie and Zoey.

The music started to swell. I straightened to attention with the rest of the bridesmaids, eyes keyed on the place the brides would make their entrance, then caught movement out of the corner of my eye. A last-minute guest dashed to their seat. I turned to glare, then gasped.

It was Logan, in a tuxedo, ducking into a chair.

Our eyes locked and a warm grin spread over his face. *Hi*, he mouthed, then, *Wait, you know them?* He pointed at where Annie and Zoey would arrive, feigning shock.

"Is that *Logan*?" Lee hissed.

"Shh," Claire reprimanded.

He was *here*. But we weren't supposed to be anywhere near each other. What was he doing?

"I think someone else might've gotten the Macoween magic this year," Lee whispered.

I couldn't drag my eyes from Logan. He was looking at me like I was the one walking down the aisle toward him, and I was everything he'd ever wanted... My whole body tingled, almost painfully alive.

Then the quartet started the bridal procession and Logan rose with the other guests, breaking our stare. Zoey appeared, radiant in a white dress, arm in arm with her father, and everything except my pounding heart, filled to the brim with love and pride, faded away.

Once Annie and Zoey kissed to an explosion of cheering and the bridesmaids swept after them down the aisle, and *then* we posed for twelve million pictures, we were finally let loose for cocktail hour. I practically ran into the white tent in the garden, scanning the tables, the dance floor, the people at the bar. No Logan. My heart dropped. Had I hallucinated him? I wouldn't put it past me.

"Alexis." A deep voice came from behind me. *The* voice.

I let my eyes flutter closed for a second before I turned. When I did, I drank him in. Sharp suit, sharp jaw, sharp eyes. I took a deep breath. "What are you doing here?"

He held out a champagne flute. "Zoey invited me. I hope that's okay."

Just like her bachelorette party, Zoey had invited Logan

without telling me. That beautiful, wonderful traitor. I took the glass from him, downed it, and set it aside, ignoring his raised eyebrows. "But we're not allowed near each other. What about the election?"

His eyes grew dark and serious. "I came to ask if, for tonight, we could pretend there was no election. Just be ourselves—be normal. I'll be a hot-headed Tottenham fan with a swearing problem, and you can be a brilliant, softhearted storyteller." The corners of his mouth tugged up. "Who looks really good in a cardigan, as I was reminded of recently."

I felt my cheeks heat. *Caught.* "The debate was free and open to the public—wait, that's not the point." The urge to protect him was too strong. "If someone catches us... Logan, the election's only days away."

He shook his head. "The campaign has taken enough. I just want one night." He held out his hand. "Please—dance with me?"

I looked at the dance floor. Never one for tradition, Zoey and Annie had opened it early, but only Zoey's grandparents swayed to the soft music. "Everyone will stare."

He gave me a crooked grin. "That's never stopped us before."

Logan Arthur looked like a prince in a midnight-black tuxedo, his hand extended. Behind him, the quartet ran their bows slowly across slender strings, and the light from the candles made the tent glow, giving him a soft, diffused halo. This was a scene from a dream if there ever was one. For the first time, I allowed myself to sink into it, sliding my fingertips across his palm. He curled his hand around mine and led me to the dance floor.

We drew close, his other arm circling my waist. The

heat of his body relaxed me, and I rested my head on his shoulder. I could feel people's eyes, but suddenly I didn't care. This was my dream, after all.

"You know." Logan spoke softly into my ear, making me shiver. "I only went to the Fleur de Lis that night to blow off steam after a bad day."

I took a deep inhale of his woodsy-berry scent and pictured him the night we met, sleeves rolled up and expression weary, but with that spark in his eyes. The stranger-turned-surprise-defender. The beautiful troublemaker.

"The bar was close to the office, and I thought, hey, why not stop in and have one drink, then go home. That's what I had every intention of doing. Until I met you."

I looked up at him, unable to stop myself from teasing. "And what, you figured a night with me would unwind you better?"

"No." He shook his head. "You weren't part of the plan. None of what's happened since that night was part of the plan."

I cast my eyes down, but he cupped my jaw and lifted it until our eyes met. I drew a sharp breath. Because Logan was no longer a book I couldn't read. His whole heart was in his eyes. "You're so much better than the plan."

The lightness that filled my chest lifted us both off the floor until we floated on a cloud, the candlelight twinkling like stars, or at least that's how it felt, how I pictured it. And sometimes, as Logan had tried so hard to tell me, fictions could be the truest parts of life.

"I've missed you," he whispered. "So much."

I closed my eyes. "I have a hundred things to tell you and I don't know how to choose."

"Then tell me everything." He brushed his cheek against mine, his stubble tickling. "Will you give me tonight?"

In response, because this was my dream, I took his face in my hands and I kissed him. I kissed him until he groaned softly and pushed his hands through my hair, until his lips parted to let me in, until my heart beat its way out of my chest, and took off soaring. I kissed Logan for all I was worth—which was so much, as he had tried so many times to tell me.

42

Alexis Stone's One-Night Stand

"Cheers!" Inside the tent, everyone raised glittering glasses of champagne as Annie's father ended his speech, impressively delivered first in Korean, then in English. As the party buzzed back to high volume, I slid my chair closer to Logan's. He turned to me, his face lit with the pure pleasure of seeing two families dizzy in love, and from the simple happiness of watching someone else give a speech for once. I squeezed his hand and he looked down at where our fingers intertwined on his thigh. His thumb tapped an impatient rhythm, the staccato beat of restraint. He raised our hands and pressed a kiss to my knuckles. As I looked at him, the full weight of how much I wanted him hit me. After holding it in for so long, I nearly trembled with it. Goose bumps raced up my arms.

"Cold?" he asked, reaching to take off his jacket.

This time, I didn't have to lie. "No. Put your hands on me. Please."

His eyes grew instantly darker. "Here?"

"Everywhere." It turned out it wasn't hard to be bold when

you wanted so badly you couldn't think straight. All this time, I hadn't been deficient: I'd simply been missing Logan. I uncrossed my legs under the table and slid his hand under the chiffon layers of my dress. His palm was rough where the dress had been silky, and I shivered at the difference. He looked at me a moment, the lines of his face traced by candlelight and shadows, and then with one strong tug he pulled my chair closer. I was practically in his lap now, but the people around us were drunk and getting up to dance.

"Don't move." His mouth crooked into a smile. "Act like everything's normal."

"Good thing I'm practiced."

His hand traced a path of heat up my thigh. I tilted my hip in his direction, but he didn't obey, skimming close to the seam of my panties, then dipping away.

I made a soft strangled sound and closed my eyes. When I opened them, Logan looked at me like he wanted to devour me.

"You close your eyes whenever I touch you. Why?"

His long finger traced the lace at the seam and I quivered. "Because being with you feels like a dream, and I want to stay inside it."

He swallowed hard. Under the table, his fingers slipped up and stroked me, his touch growing more insistent. I checked that no one was watching and rolled my hips, moving against his hand. It was enough to make me catch fire. He answered by moving his fingers in slow, teasing circles. I caught his free hand and bit his thumb.

"Come on," he said, rescinding his hands and standing. I groaned at the loss of contact, but he reached down and smoothed my dress, then tugged me up.

I had to skip to keep pace with him as he strode out of the tent, hand wrapped firmly around mine. We entered a dark garden, a maze of cypress trees tall and thin as matchsticks, peachy-pink roses, and perfectly trimmed hedges, the dreamy music and twinkling stars forming a fairy-tale setting. I looked around in wonder. "Where are we going?"

He pulled out his phone. "I have a surprise."

It felt like I'd spent twenty-seven years waiting for him, and I didn't want to wait anymore. I pushed Logan against a cypress tree and heard the satisfying crunch of the branches giving, then holding his weight. He blinked and threw his phone into the grass, sinking his hands into my hair. For a single moment the thought blazed that Lee would be very proud of me right now, and then I put away all thoughts of my sister.

I stepped between Logan's legs and his hands slipped down, sliding over my curves, cupping my ass. He ground me against his hips. My voice came out breathless. "I've wanted to do this every day of the campaign."

His feverish eyes dropped to my lips. I pressed a hand to his forehead and he trembled. "You should have. I could never tell what you wanted."

I tipped my head back and laughed. Logan took advantage and kissed a column down my throat. "What's so funny?"

"You were the one who was impossible to read."

He rested his forehead against mine. "I was trying to stick to our rules. That's what I thought you wanted. But inside I was drowning."

"You and those damn rules," I whispered, brushing my lips against his.

He spoke between kisses. "I wanted to do it right. Be the kind of person you deserve."

I stood on my tiptoes to deepen the kiss, but his gaze fell over my shoulder to his phone, lit in the grass. "Uber's here."

I groaned.

He lunged for the phone. "Trust me. It'll be worth the wait."

The Uber swept to a stop in front of the Fleur de Lis, its tall spire rebuilt, gleaming against the night sky. When I turned to Logan, I knew my heart was in my eyes.

He squeezed my knee. "I owe you a night here."

I swallowed past the lump in my throat and managed a smile. "If a freak thunderstorm hits tonight, I'm quitting the library to become a climate activist."

He roared a laugh and pushed open the door. "Come on, Ruby. I've been waiting a long time to kiss you in the Governor's suite."

Unlike the first night, this time we didn't stumble down the hall to our room. We might only have this one night together, but it wasn't casual. When we stepped inside the suite and the lights glowed, illuminating Logan's serious face, my heart began to race.

"What?" He stepped closer. The perfect picture, standing where he'd stood months before.

I shook my head. "You're too beautiful. Too much."

He stared at me for a long, charged moment. And then slowly, he sank to his knees.

"Logan—"

"Ever since the night we met, I've been trying to figure out what your eyes reminded me of. I finally decided they're honey-brown with green flecks. A constellation trapped in amber. The gold is brightest when you're happy." He looked up at me like a knight pledging allegiance. "They're so beautiful I had to train myself not to look at you too long when I spoke. Otherwise, I would've been lost every time I tried to give a speech." Gently, he pulled up the layers of my dress. "The way you smell drives me wild. Flowers, but so light it disappears when you try to chase it. Every time it hit me in the conference room it took all my willpower not to climb across the table and kiss you. My couch smelled like you for a full day after you came over and I curled in those blankets when I got home from work and tried to tell myself I was just in the mood to watch movies all night."

I stood stock-still, drowning in his litany. Logan hooked his fingers under the lace of my panties and tugged them down. My legs felt boneless as I leaned against the wall, shoulder blades first. When he looked up, his eyes were smoldering, his voice hypnotic. "I've memorized the way you look when you're happy, the way you sound when you laugh, how you press your eyes closed when I touch you." His voice thickened. "Like now."

My eyes fluttered open.

"All I've thought about since the last time we were in this suite is how much I wanted to rewind time and come back. Do everything different." He touched me between my legs; long, unhurried strokes. My head fell back against the wall. "I told you I think I lose my mind around you. The truth is, I feel like a teenager again, the way I can't stop thinking about you, the things I have to do just to get relief. You think *I'm* too much for *you*?" He shook his head. "*You're* the one who's too much. Do you know what it's like to work for something your whole life and then have someone walk in and become the most important thing to you in an instant? Everything changed at the drop of a hat. It's fucking disorienting, Alexis. You turned me upside down."

"Please," I whispered. My knees bent at his touch, his words. My shoulders sank down the wall.

"And now all I can think is..." He moved closer still, sliding on his knees across the floor. "Fuck leading anyone. I want to follow you on my hands and knees across the desert."

I was already so turned on that when his fingers slid inside me, even so carefully, I arched off the wall. He followed his fingers with his mouth, licking and curling his tongue until I made a sound close to a sob. Each stroke made my body crackle to life, a landscape of small fireworks. The sensations built and built until I felt like I might scream.

I twisted my fingers in his thick hair and he hummed into me, making me rise to my tiptoes. He released my dress and his hands slid to the small of my back, pulling me nearer, fingers digging into my spine like he couldn't get me close enough. The pressure of his tongue intensified and I realized he was showing me how hungry he was, how desperate I made him, in a way that was stronger than words, strong enough to erase what any other man had ever told me. The knowledge that he craved me this intensely—had craved me for months—made me feel so powerful. Powerful, and safe. I sank against the wall, muscles relaxing that final crucial inch. So when he circled his thumb, tongue urging me on, building a pulsing pleasure inside me, I cried out. He squeezed my hips, licking me softly as I came down.

I dragged in mouthfuls of air as Logan staggered to his feet, pupils blown, looking half-drugged. "Your mouth,"

I rasped. "Of course you can do that with your mouth." Logan Arthur's mouth was trouble in so many ways.

He grinned and seized me, kissing me fiercely in a way that told me he was just getting started. For a minute I simply drowned in him. Kissing him, touching him, was the best feeling on earth. When I finally pulled back for air, I was no longer embarrassed by what I wanted. "More," I whispered.

He bit my bottom lip. "Turn around."

I obeyed. Logan's hand spanned my waist, keeping me steady, while he slowly unzipped my dress. The straps fell away like petals off a rose. He traced a finger down my spine. "So beautiful it hurts," he whispered, kissing my neck. Goose bumps lifted over my whole body.

I was naked and he was still in his tux, but for once I didn't mind being the center of attention. I tilted my head to give him better access to my neck. My nipples peaked as Logan's hands slipped around me to cup my breasts, drawing me closer until my back was pressed firmly against his chest. For a moment we just stood there, lost in how perfectly our bodies fit together.

I could feel the evidence of how much he wanted me pressed against my back, and pushed past my shyness. "When I imagined this, I pictured..."

He sank his teeth gently into my neck. "Tell me."

"Upstairs."

He stilled. And then in one fluid movement, Logan picked me up, an echo of the way he'd carried me that very first night. Except this time, he carried me up the spiral staircase to the second floor of the suite. To the bedroom.

Dimmed lamps bookended a soft white bed. Logan bent and set me gently on it.

Before he could retreat, I caught his face in my hands. "You weren't the only one who was tortured these last months, you know."

He drew a deep breath. His eyes burned. "Good."

I pulled his mouth to mine and he dropped to his knees in front of the bed. This kiss was decadent, slow and unhurried. Each time I tilted my head he chased me, seeking more, and it became a dance. Retreat, pursue, capture. Desire spilled through my body like warm honey. *This* was what I wanted: slow and luxurious. I wanted someone to burn for me so white-hot his handprints branded my skin. I wanted someone to tongue his name into me, to carve his feelings into my skin with his teeth. I wanted passion and love and security—all three at the same time, no compromise. It turned out *that* was what unleashed me.

With new urgency I slid my hands under Logan's suit jacket until he wrestled it off. He tugged at the knot of his bow tie as I fumbled to unbutton his shirt. When it fell open, I drank in the sight of him, the slashes of his collarbones meeting the hard swell of his shoulders, his firm biceps, his golden skin. The hint of abs sketching over his stomach.

"Stand up," I said. I needed to confirm a suspicion.

Logan obeyed, standing, his eyes trained on me, so dark with desire they were almost black. I ran my fingers over the ridges of his hip bones, the black hair trailing lightly from his belly button. I swallowed hard and his cock twitched. This time Logan closed his eyes.

I unzipped his pants slowly, tugging them and his boxers down until he stepped out of both. Then Logan Arthur was naked in front of me: All six feet, two inches, firm, muscular ass, thick soccer player's thighs, his hard length rising against his stomach. I stared in wonder. My suspicion was right. He was bigger than any man I'd ever been with, his size something I'd felt through his clothes and wondered at. I resisted the sudden urge to joke that while he may not talk soft, Logan did carry a big stick.

He opened one eye and looked down at me. "Fuck, Alexis. Say something."

I told him the truth. "Everything about you makes me very nervous and very happy at the same time."

He loomed over me, all height and bulk, and smiled, small and soft. Briefly, I felt the fear that comes with wanting someone so deeply you know nothing in your life will ever be the same. Then Logan said, "I know exactly what you mean." And the fear melted away.

I reached out, taking his hard length in my hand, stroking him softly at first and then more insistently, getting used to his size. I built a rhythm that had Logan groaning until he suddenly arched up on the balls of his feet and stilled me. "Stop—you have to stop."

He bent to pick up his wallet and pulled a condom out of it. I slid back on the bed, watching as he rolled it on deftly. Then, without warning, Logan grinned and seized my ankles, dragging me back to him while I yelped.

"Tell me more about what you imagined," he said, a wicked glint in his eyes.

I willed courage. "You inside me, over and over. All night. Until neither of us can walk."

His eyes shut briefly. "Yeah," he rasped. He sat next to me on the bed and pulled me on top of him. "Well. You know I live to serve."

He cupped my jaw, kissing me feverishly. Slowly, I sank

onto him, gasping into his mouth when he filled me so deep I had to still for a moment. This was going to be it for me, wasn't it? I was going to become addicted to this man, to this feeling, and there would be no going back.

Logan gripped my waist and rolled his hips, pushing deeper. I sucked in a breath, fingernails digging into his shoulders. And then, as soon as my body adjusted, the switch flipped. All I wanted was more. I ground against him.

Logan's lips skimmed my ear. "Trust me," he whispered. Then he swept his hands to my back and dipped me lower, changing the angle.

I almost cried out. Every movement sent him so deep. That feeling started to build again, except this time it was almost unrecognizable in its depth, as if I was drawing from a deep untapped well of sensation. When I moaned, it was a ragged sound.

"Good," he coaxed, gripping my hips.

I stopped thinking and let go, riding him until we were both sweating and gasping, until my fingernails left half-moon marks in his biceps, until I was nothing more than the steady pulse between my thighs. He re-angled me and thrust deeper, clutching at my hair, sucking my lip, and I shattered, coming so hard it hit me in waves, refusing to be done with me. I crumpled and he pulled me into his chest.

"Shh." He spoke into my damp hair. "Catch your breath so we can go again."

I looked up at him, my chest heaving, gasping for breath, and he grinned. "You gave me orders. All night. Every position. There's no way I'm letting you down. So buckle up."

Good God. Alexis Stone: not a mouse. A sex genius.

*

Hours later we lay tangled, bodies spent. I suspected I'd come apart more in one night with Logan than I had in all my past relationships combined. His eyes were closed, his face so close our noses touched. I stroked his hair. It was wrecked, sticking up in every angle. Logan Arthur, fierce brash man, was now tender and vulnerable.

His long lashes stirred against the pillow and he opened his eyes, smiling drowsily. "Hey, you. What's that look for?"

"This feels like the part where I wake up and realize it was all in my head."

Logan's eyes turned worried, but I smiled. "It's okay. We said one night. I know your life's up in the air until the election. But you're going to win, and then everything will be..." *Then there will be no chance for us.* I swallowed. "Great. You'll finally have your dream."

He studied me. "Right now, the only thing I want is to fall asleep holding you."

I moved closer and he wrapped his arms around me. I took deep lungfuls of his scent, pressing my cheek to where his pulse moved in his throat, listening to the steady beat of his heart.

When I was very nearly asleep and the world was warm and hazy, I felt him kiss my temple softly. Then he whispered, so faint it was barely more than a breath, "Whatever it takes, let me keep her."

43

Election Night

"You really didn't have to come," I told my mom, opening my arms to hug her. I stood outside Lee's house at dusk, stars shining weakly above us in the deepening sky.

"Nonsense." She shut the passenger door and squeezed me. "I was planning to come the minute the news broke about you and Logan breaking up, but Lee said to give you time."

"We're always happy to make the drive." Mom's boyfriend, Ethan, climbed out of the driver's side. "Nothing makes your mom happier than seeing you girls."

I pulled back. "I'm sorry for lying to you about being in a relationship with Logan. For what it's worth, I also wasn't lying. It's complicated."

She kissed my forehead. "Alexis, honey, I'm your mother *and* your director. And I hate to break it to you, but you're not that good of an actor. I knew you were really in love."

Before I could feel too chastened, Ethan interrupted, pulling an aluminum-wrapped casserole dish out of the back seat. "Where do you want the seven-layer dip?" The man was a wizard in the kitchen. Lee liked to say he'd wormed his way into our hearts through our stomachs. He also always dressed like a professor, which was not only endearing but a one-eighty from my father, who I remembered in business suits more often than not. I squeezed my mom's hand. Sometimes the people who ended up being right for us were not the ones we expected.

"You can put it out in the living room," I told Ethan. "The gang's already here. Votes should start rolling in any minute."

As Ethan hurried to deliver his dip, Mom turned to me. "How nervous are you, on a scale of one to ten?"

"Fifteen." I swallowed the lump in my throat. All of Logan's hard work and sacrifice came down to tonight. I'd never wanted anything so badly for another person.

"I'm feeling hopeful," she said, tugging me toward the house. "He's been doing great since the second debate. And since the commercial aired, not to toot my own horn."

I laughed. "Toot away. I'm sure any gains he's made this last week all come down to the commercial."

Everyone had come to Lee and Ben's election party: Claire and Simon, Mac and Ted, Muriel and Carmen, Gia and her husband. Even Will, that class act. Only Zoey and Annie were missing, off in the Maldives on their honeymoon.

Part of me was glad I wasn't invited to the official campaign party. I didn't think I could've handled this level of pressure while putting on a smile. It was hard enough wearing a brave face now. When my mom and I walked into the living room, every pair of eyes swung to me like I was the one whose fate would be decided tonight. Which, in a way, I guess I was.

As expected, Logan had been gone by the time I woke up in the hotel room, escaping in the early morning hours to minimize the chance someone would spot him. He'd left a note on the hotel stationary that said *One last push*.

"Pundits are saying Logan is polling really high." Lee pointed her wine at the talking head on TV. "This last week since the debate has been huge for him."

Ben nodded. "People liked his honesty at the debate. I think he could pull off an upset."

They both sounded like they were trying hard to be optimistic.

"Why don't you help me find serving dishes," said my mom, steering me into the kitchen.

For a few minutes we combed through Lee's cabinets in companionable silence. "I guess you were right about Ethan not taking it hard that you didn't want to move in with him," I said. "He seems cheerful as ever."

Mom was silent for a moment, pushing past some of Ben's protein mixers. But when she spoke, her tone stilled me. "Honey. What makes you think love is such a precarious thing?"

I drew up, letting go of the cabinet door. Wasn't it obvious? "You and Dad. When he cheated, then left."

She gripped the counter as she stood. "Your dad and I divorced, true. But none of the love our family had for each other went away."

"But..." How did she not understand? "He stopped loving you. And you said it was because you stopped giving him what he needed."

"I said that?"

"Yes. One night when I was crying and came to sleep in your bed."

My mother shook her head. "I don't remember that. The truth is, I was so afraid your relationship with your father would be damaged after what he did—Lee was already so angry—that I tried to find ways to talk about it without blaming him. I'm sorry if I made you think your dad left because I'd stopped... I don't know, appeasing him."

"You never blamed yourself?"

She actually laughed. "Not for a minute. The dissolution of my marriage, as much as you can ever say these things are anyone's fault, certainly wasn't mine. It wasn't due to some failing on my part. It was about Richard falling in love with another person and making a choice. I could no less have stopped that from happening than I could've stopped that drunk driver from running the red light."

The grief that lurked ever present in my heart rose to the surface. "But I was like you. I couldn't get Dad to love me either, not as much as he loved Lee. No matter what I did."

"Alexis." My mother was so surprised it sounded like an admonishment. "Your father loved you just as much as Lee. So much. If there's one thing I admired about Richard, it's that you girls were always his first priority. When things got heated with our lawyers over custody, Richard put a stop to it immediately. He said he'd do whatever it took to share custody of you two. He was willing to give me anything I wanted. Even not move in with Michelle if that's what it would take."

"Are you serious?" I remembered the cold feeling of my father drifting away, not fighting to keep me.

"I wanted you to have good relationships with him," Mom said. "The only time I put my foot down was when he came to ask if you could live full-time with him. He really begged."

I blinked at her. "*Me?* Dad wanted me to live with him?"

She smiled wistfully. "He said getting you half the time wasn't enough. He missed you when you weren't together. He used to say he didn't know what he'd do without you, that you were the light of his life, his anchor. Little Lex, his most constant source of love and joy. But I had to tell him no, because you were mine, too."

I stood stock-still as my mother's words filled the whole kitchen. As they sank under my skin. The truth had been so different than I'd realized.

When I started to cry, it was for not knowing how much he loved me while he was still alive. For the version of me who'd tried so hard when what she wanted was there all along. It was almost painful, feeling long-broken pieces of my heart finally mend back together. My mother swept me in her arms and held me.

"Alexis!" Lee yelled. "The votes are coming in!"

"Go on," my mom said. "We'll talk more later."

I pulled back and wiped my eyes, then joined the party huddled around the TV screen, still feeling shaky.

"The first few counties came back fifty-fifty," Mac said, chewing her nails.

Together, we watched the results leak in, cheering when a county went blue, throwing popcorn at the screen went it went red. My stomach roiled. The race was maddeningly close.

"No matter what, it's amazing Logan put up this kind of a fight against an incumbent Republican in Texas," Ben said. I narrowed my eyes at him.

Another county came in for the governor. Then another.

Finally, a blue county. "Ha!" I yelled, pointing triumphantly. Lee's answering smile was halfhearted.

"An astonishingly close gubernatorial race this evening," said the news anchor. "No one could've predicted even a week and a half ago that the race would be this tight. We're coming down to the last two counties."

"I think I'm going to faint," Ted said. "Stoner, where are your cats? I need emotional support animals."

"Shh," Mac said, because now the anchor was saying, "And here they are, folks. The tallies are in. It looks like it's fifty-one, forty-nine Mane in Williamson County, fifty-two, forty-eight Mane in Tarrant. NBC 17 is officially calling the Texas governor's race for incumbent Grover Mane. Wow, what a close one, folks."

Lee scrambled for the remote and shut off the TV. Painful silence filled the room.

Logan lost. Dear God, after everything he'd given. I couldn't imagine what he was feeling. My heart dropped into my stomach.

"Alexis?" Ben's voice was gentle. "Are you okay?"

I staggered to my feet. "I have to go."

The official campaign party was at the Hotel Saint Cecilia on the other side of the river. I drove as quickly as I could. By the time I got to the hotel's famous courtyard, all lit up with celebratory twinkle lights, banners, and balloons, the crowd was sad and thin except for around the bar, where the campaign staff had flocked to drown their sorrows. A lone figure dressed in a three-piece suit floated on his back in the pool: Cary, staring morosely at the night sky. I kicked stray silver tinsel out of my way as I crouched near the edge. "Hi, Cary. You look how I feel."

"Rudy," he said miserably. "We failed him."

"Where is he?"

Cary sighed. "He had to give a concession speech. That man shouldn't have to concede a damn thing in his life. He's the real deal, you know? A genuinely good person. Not Matt Bomer on the outside, but on the inside, where it counts."

"I know." I spotted someone out of the corner of my eye and rose. "Nora!"

She was in the farthest corner, idly pulling streamers up from the ground, though there was no way cleanup was on her list of responsibilities. I ran to her and she dropped them. "I'm so sorry," I said, and rushed into her arms.

"Me too." Her voice was thick. "But we put up a hell of a fight. We can be proud of that."

"If it was my fault—"

She shook her head. "Stop. It wasn't."

"Where is he?"

She pulled back and gave me a sad smile. "He gave it everything, you know? It was too hard. After the speech, he left."

44

I'll Find You in the Dark

I pounded on Logan's door. Please open. The shades were drawn so I couldn't see inside. I paced away from the door, then raced back, lifting my hand to knock again.

The door swung open. Logan stood there in his joggers and a gray T-shirt. His black curls were in chaos, cheeks red under his stubble, eyes glassy. The minute our eyes met, I felt like I'd been punched, and staggered forward just in time to catch him as he bent, hands pressed to his mouth, his heart breaking open.

I held him as he wept. "It's okay, it's okay." I repeated it like a mantra.

"I failed everyone who was counting on me." He choked on the words.

"No, you didn't. Everyone's so proud of you."

He shook his head, eyes wild with grief. "I let everyone down. You, Nora, my staff, my family. Everyone who voted for me."

"Come on." We needed to get out of the doorway in case of reporters. I pulled Logan to his couch, where he sank with his head in his hands. Then I shoved the front door closed and locked it. When I came back, I sat next to him and drew him to my chest. He pressed his face into my shoulder and shook.

"I know this hurts," I said softly. "I know it's gutting. But you didn't fail. You did something remarkable."

His arms circled me, holding on like I was a buoy in a storm. "If I was better, I would've won."

I stroked his back. "You were so good you almost beat a Republican in *Texas*. You almost won a race you were never supposed to win."

"I wanted it so much." His voice was ragged. In it I heard his raw and ravaged heart. "My whole life. I gave everything. And I still failed."

I smoothed his hair from his forehead. "You know what? So what if you did fail? I've failed before. Countless times. This is only one terrible day. Your worth and your value aren't tied to this one thing, no matter how much you gave it. There's so much more out there for you."

I could feel him shaking his head against my chest, unwilling or unable to believe it. So I reached deep inside myself. "No one's disappointed in you, Logan. No one's going anywhere. You are enough all on your own, with or without that title, whether you ever run another race or not. Just you. Logan Arthur. You are worth a thousand lifetimes of devotion." It was everything I'd always needed to hear, and I'd finally healed myself so well I was able to give it to him.

Lee had been right: everything in its time.

"You are so important to me," I whispered, and he tensed.

Logan pulled his tear-stained face from my chest. His eyes were dark with pain and desire. Before I could say anything, he cupped my face and caught my lips, kissing me hungrily. He tasted like salt and heat. A small groan sounded in the back of my throat and he dragged me on top of him, lunging for his wallet on the table and pulling out a condom.

I was no stranger to grief. I knew what he needed.

I ran my fingers down his wet cheeks, rubbing my thumb across his swollen bottom lip, and he bit it. With my finger in his mouth I ground against him, and he tore at his sweatpants, pushing them down, rolling the condom on. We moved quickly, the only sounds our heavy breathing. Logan reached under my skirt to yank my panties aside, and pulled me down by my hips, filling me in one swift movement. It was so much I rocked back and cried out.

He was merciless. I mirrored him, and together we moved faster, harder, not letting up. The way his fingers dug into my hips would leave bruises, but I didn't care. My climax was already building, and when my orgasm hit and I started to still, he didn't stop. He flipped me over on my hands and knees on the couch and pushed inside me deeper, pounding harder. My fingers curled into the couch cushions. I thought I would dissolve under his force, and it surprised me how much I wanted it. When he found that place, the deep well of sensation, I pressed my forehead to the couch. He bent lower, his fingers finding me and stroking like he was determined to wring every last feeling out of me. I was sweating, my breathing ragged, muscles liquid. There was still no sound except our rough exhales. The feeling inside me spiked and spilled over, and as I gasped his hand gripped my mouth, fingers splayed. I sank my teeth into him as he kept pounding, until he shuddered and stilled.

For a long moment we simply stayed there, panting, Logan's forehead pressed into my spine. Then slowly he retreated and we sank into his couch.

"I'm sorry," he said hoarsely. "I needed—"

"I know." I smoothed his damp hair. "Let me get you some water."

When I came back from the kitchen he was already back from the bathroom, pulling on his joggers and T-shirt. I sat next to him and watched him drink the water greedily. When he looked at me again, his red-rimmed eyes were full of tentative hope.

"Do have somewhere you need to be?" he whispered.

"Only wherever you are." I pulled him against my chest and he curled around me, breathing deeply, until he finally closed his eyes.

45

The First New Day

I woke to soft sunshine streaming through curtains I didn't recognize. I blinked at the butter yellow light, the peek of blue sky through the sheer fabric, and realized I was lying in bed, enveloped in soft sheets. This was Logan's bedroom. He must've woken at some point in the night and carried me here.

I rolled over to find him on his side, his beautiful face peaceful in sleep. When I shifted, his eyes cracked open.

"Hi," I said shyly. Waking up next to him was so intimate. My heart beat faster.

"Hi," he echoed. He studied my face, seriousness and tenderness in his eyes. A small voice inside me whispered, *You know this look*. It was pulled straight from my dreams.

A lump formed in my throat. To distract myself, I flitted my eyes around his room, cataloguing his framed Tottenham jersey, his tall bookshelf crammed with books— an organizational method I knew well—his closet full of identical pressed navy suits. And then my eyes landed on the most remarkable thing: it was my painted face, captured on a canvas propped carefully against the wall.

I turned to Logan, my mouth dropping open. "What's that doing here?"

His voice was quiet but deep. "I asked Zoey for it."

"Why?"

His gaze was steady, pinning me. "Alexis. I think you know I've loved you from the beginning."

He loved me. And I did know—of course I knew. Now that I was seeing clearly, with the weight of self-doubt lifted, my heart free, I could see his love had been in all of his decisions, in every action, from the very first night.

I reached for him and smoothed his hair. "I love you, too. So much."

Logan's eyes shone. "I know." He caught my hand and kissed my palm, then kept it there, pressing it against his face.

We lay in the soft sunshine, drinking each other in, until the reason I'd come over last night hit me like a freight train. "I'm so sorry about the election," I whispered. "For how it all turned out."

He didn't flinch. Instead, he slowly shook his head, his stubble tickling my palm. "You know what? I'm not. I may have lost, but I still won."

My heart cracked open. I closed the distance between us and kissed him. Logan's arms slid around me as he deepened the kiss. "What happens next?" I whispered.

He kissed my forehead softly, then pulled back to study me. "What do you want to happen?"

He was always letting me lead. Luckily, it was easy to say

what I wanted these days. "To hold onto you for as long as you'll let me."

His voice was gravelly. "That's what I want, too. To hold onto you, and start again."

I looked at him—my dream man—and slowly smiled. I'd been waiting so long for a love I could keep, a love that felt secure and exhilarating in equal measures. And now that I had it, I could say: the reality was far better than I'd ever imagined.

Epilogue

Six Months Later

"Thanks for making the time, Mr. Arthur, Ms. Igwe." Kiki Arturo from *Texas Monthly* adjusted in her seat across the living room, flashing us a smile. "You too, Ms. Stone. It's an honor to get you all for this feature, and in the Stone-Arthur household, no less."

"Well, this is basically our office these days." Next to me on the couch, Logan crossed his legs and returned Kiki's smile with an easy one of his own—a genuine smile, not a half grimace. The sight of it never got old.

"And don't forget Cary Berry," I added, nodding to Cary, who hurried back from the kitchen with a cup of coffee and settled into an armchair. "As the COO, he's a very high-profile member of the new organization."

"Of course," Kiki said. "Nice to meet you, Mr. Berry."

Cary shot me a grateful look and mouthed, *Thanks, Rudy.*

"Okay, let's get started." Kiki glanced at her notebook. "We're thrilled you're giving *Texas Monthly* the exclusive on your announcement. I want to hear everything about your new venture. Ungoverned Advocates—where does that name come from?"

A loud crash sounded from the kitchen, and Lee popped around the corner. "Sorry! I was just trying to eavesdrop, and then I tripped over Patches' water bowl, and it was a whole...you know what, never mind. I'm just a fan. Carry on."

The sound of Ben softly snickering filled the room as we turned our attention back to Kiki and her photography crew from the magazine, who were angling light reflectors at our faces.

"Truthfully," Logan said, "I wanted to name us the Hotspurs." He reached for my hand and I laced my fingers through his. Even after six months of dating, sometimes I still couldn't believe I could hold his hand whenever I wanted. "But Nora vetoed me. And since she's the president, she wins."

"We decided after Logan's gubernatorial race that running for office isn't how we're best positioned to make a difference," Nora said. She was dressed to the nines as always in a black suit and crisp white shirt. "The name Ungoverned Advocates reflects that."

"Tell me more about that decision," Kiki urged. "Logan got so close to winning. Why not run him for something else? senator, House rep?"

"I realized campaigning wasn't the right fit for me." Logan squeezed my hand, and I knew he was thinking of all the conversations he and I had had on this very couch, late into the night, weighing that decision. "It requires me to button up and play by a set of rules I don't believe in." He gestured at Nora and Cary. "We realized that if we really wanted to speak truth to power and stand up for people, we needed to be freer."

"Now Logan can be himself," Cary added. "As angry and inflammatory as he wants. And instead of a liability, his personality's a strength. Nora and I will direct his firepower at politicians. We're going to keep them accountable."

Kiki arched an eyebrow. "And you chose Ms. Igwe as president?"

"Nora's always been the mastermind," Logan said. "It fits. And I get to be the bulldog." He looked inordinately pleased at that.

Nora nodded. "We'll give you a peek at our plans when we head into the Ungoverned office."

"Also known as Logan and Alexis's spare bedroom." Cary glared at me. "Which Alexis refuses to let me decorate."

I bit back the urge to say our house wasn't in need of any life-sized Matt Bomer cutouts. Patches and I had moved in with Logan only a month ago, and the truth was, we'd barely finished melding our things together. For example, Logan had an entire closet of Tottenham player bobbleheads we were in negotiations over (him: keep, possibly display; me: lose, possibly burn).

Kiki turned her attention to me. "Ms. Stone. Can the public expect to see you out leading rallies with the Ungoverned team?"

I laughed and crossed my legs, grateful Lee had convinced me to splurge on the fancy green suit I was wearing. Not only did I look as sharp as Nora, but green was Logan's favorite color, a fact he'd reminded me of over and over again this morning...which was how we'd almost been late to an event in our very own house. "Not anytime soon. I've realized there are a lot of ways to contribute to a cause you believe in, and I'm happiest behind the scenes."

"She's one of our best education advisors," Logan said.

"What *are* you up to, then?" Kiki tapped her pen. "I know a lot of people were disappointed you didn't run for TEA president."

One of the photographers started snapping shots of me, but I managed to ignore it. "I'm comanaging the Barton Springs Elementary library and writing my first middle grade novel. It's about a girl who's so shy she prefers to disappear into books, until one day her favorite stories spring to life. Then she has to navigate a world with blurry boundaries between fact and fiction."

"It's genius," said Logan, who didn't even know he'd inspired it. "It's going to sell like hotcakes."

I patted his leg, but couldn't help blushing. "No matter what happens, I'm fulfilled just writing it. This is what I was meant to do."

Kiki leaned in. "Speaking of meant to be. Logan and Alexis, a lot of people fell for your unusual love story. From a one-night stand to a public scandal to a power couple. Would you say the two of you have finally found yourselves where you belong?"

Logan and I glanced at each other, surprised. That phrase—*I've finally found myself where I belong*—was something Lee used to say at her campaign rallies, so often it became a bit of a Lee Stone catchphrase. I squeezed Logan's hand and smiled gently at Kiki. "With all due respect, Kiki, I'd like to put it in my own words. Logan and I fell in love while we were also learning to love ourselves. So for us, it was more a discovery that we were where we belonged all along. We didn't have to change. We just had to open our eyes to see it."

He took my hand and kissed it.

"A fitting end to your story," Kiki said, motioning to the photographers to move to the spare bedroom.

"Wait," I said, and the whole room stilled in a way that once would have made me nervous. "It's not the end." I looked around, buoyed by the people smiling back, including the ones peeking from the kitchen. These were the people I loved, who believed in me and made me feel safe being myself. "Trust me. Our story's just beginning."

Acknowledgments

This acknowledgments section is going to look a little different than my usual—but then again, everything is different now that life has split so irrevocably into two timelines: Life With Dad and This Miserable and Bewildering Existence Without Him.

On August 10, 2022, right before this book came back from copyedits, I lost my beloved father Ron Winstead. I always add that word in—*beloved*—because I'm so anxious for you to know up-front how much I loved him. I'm anxious that *he* knew how much I loved him, and will probably spend the rest of my life haunted by the fact that I can never really know. The reason I'm writing about the loss of my father in my acknowledgments is not only because it's the single most important thing that's ever happened to me. It's also because my father is directly responsible for my reading and writing life, and thus this book. He loved books—all stories, actually, in whatever forms. I learned how to love things passionately from my father; like, truly fall down rabbit holes. Books, movies, TV, music—he liked it all rock 'n' roll loud, emotionally charged, and with the heroes coming out on top in the end. So I did, too.

I was a hero to my dad. I know that sounds strange, but I mean my father was otherworldly proud of me. I knew it as a kid in school, as a teenager competing for college scholarships, when he used to drive me thousands of miles across the country to compete in various merit scholarship weekends, certain I'd be the first in our family to go to college, and I knew it as an adult with a book career. The first time I ever really believed I could publish a book was when I presented him, years ago, with my first MS—a YA fantasy, way out of his usual taste—and he devoured it, chronicling how he couldn't put it down through a series of excited texts and phone calls. Every book since, we've had a ritual: he and my mom would get early drafts, and I eagerly awaited their thoughts. Boy, did my dad make me feel like I was something special every time. For a relatively quiet man, he loved so fiercely and loudly. My heart, my mind, and my books are all a product of that love.

This is the first book he never got to read. If life was fair, I would've sent it to him right after copyediting was done. Instead, I'm copyediting while helping to plan his celebration of life. But the wondrous thing about returning to this book is that even though it's principally a romance, it's also a story about a woman finding peace after the loss of her father. Why did I write a story about grief—this particular grief—while I still had my precious father with me? It's hard to say, but maybe some part of me knew how difficult it would be to lose him one day and was trying to prepare. Whatever the reason, coming back to Alexis's story—reading her journey to heal her broken heart and find joy and love again, a journey I wrote, as if composing instructions to myself—made me cry, made me laugh, and ultimately brought me a small measure of peace. I hope my dad would've loved this story, but I know with certainty he would have been proud. I can never thank you enough, Dad.

Enormous gratitude to my wonderful editor, Cat Clyne, and agent, Melissa Edwards, not only for everything they did to shape this book but for their extraordinary support and kindness, above and beyond. All my thanks to the whole Graydon House team who worked on getting this book out into the world: Susan Swinwood, Amy Jones, Diane Lavoie, and Erin Craig.

Huge thanks to my wonderful family: my incredible, resilient mother; my brother Ryan, sister Amanda, niece Celeste, and nephew Ezra; my brother Taylor and sister Catherine; and my little sister Mallory. Mallory, you know this book is yours, too, and it is so like you to gracefully share it. You are all lights in the dark.

And as always, Alex, thank you for being my rock, the one who pushes me, the person by my side through thick and thin. You went from the boy I couldn't get out of my head to the man holding my hand through every challenge. I love you.

About the Author

ASHLEY WINSTEAD is an academic turned novelist with a Ph.D. in contemporary American literature. She lives in Houston with her husband, two cats, and beloved wine fridge. You can find her at www.ashleywinstead.com.